I0648015

superlative
speculative
erotica

superlative speculative erotica

THE BEST OF CIRCLET PRESS 2012-2017

EDITED BY
CECILIA TAN AND BETHANY ZAIATZ

Circlet Press, Inc.
Cambridge, MA

Contents

Introduction

Welcome to Superlative Speculative Erotica, the finest stories published by Circlet Press over the past five years. Circlet has now been publishing for 25 years (well, 26 by the time you read this) and every five years we've marked the occasion with an anthology of our "best."

The staff told me that this year I was absolutely not allowed to use either the words "best" or "fantastic" in the title of the book. People are already confused enough between Fantastic Erotica, Best Fantastic Erotica, Erotic Fantastic, and Best Erotic Fantasy and Science Fiction. Point taken! Hence our tack toward the multisyllabic, Superlative Speculative Erotica.

This book, like the cohort of authors and staff of Circlet Press itself, features characters who identify as lesbian, gay, genderqueer, bisexual, trans, and heterosexual. The erotic activities expressed within the stories cover a similar variety, though it's not an identical match: a gay male author can write a lesbian witch who has sex with a gender-changing demon. What label do you put on that? We call it... superlative speculative erotica.

This book also reflects many of the genres we've published at Circlet Press: a little cyberpunk, a little high fantasy, a touch of horror, some superheroes, a bit of space opera, some paranormal... you get the gist. What unites these stories is their quality.

This book was funded through a Kickstarter campaign run in 2017, the year of Circlet's 25th anniversary. Contributors to the campaign—and to our Patreon—were given access to about 60 stories (out of the hundreds we published since 2012) chosen by our staff. Their votes winnowed the list down to about 25, and then the staff had to make the hard choices to get it down to the 20 stories included here. You might be interested to know, though, that Annabeth Leong not only had the most stories in the top ten, she was the overall top vote-getter. As such we picked her story, "Bête Noire," to open the volume.

One of the other top vote-getters was a parody that appeared in an anthology of meta-fiction called *Like a Circlet Editor*, in which various authors imagined what it "must" be like to work at an erotic science fiction publishing house. "I Am the Very Model of a Modern Circlet Editor" is included here last as the cherry on the sundae, by popular demand.

And in between, there is... everything in between. Enjoy.

Cecilia Tan and Bethany Zaiatz, editors
Cambridge, MA

Bête Noire
Annabeth Leong

I. *Beautiful, Beastly Revenge*

Before we shoot out a window and start killing all the guards in sight, Beauty leans in to kiss me.

I stop her. "You're making me feel pretty, darling." I hold up one matted, woolly hand, protract the obsidian claws still dripping blood from what we had to do to get this close to Orlagh's fancy house. "We can't risk breaking the curse here."

"I just thought... This might be our last chance, Bête. If she kills us...."

"She won't."

Neither of us is sure of that, but there's no choice besides pretending. True love and its urges aside, Beauty knows there couldn't be a worse time for me to return to my former, softer self. She pulls back her face and reaches for my hand instead. Even the brush of her fingers—oily from her gun—makes my heart shiver with sweet visions of who I could become for her. I take my hand away and shove it into my pocket, ignoring her quiet, hurt sigh. We'll have time to talk this over after we deal with Orlagh.

I force myself to stop contemplating the subtle scent of roses that manages to linger around Beauty even after three saddle-sore days of bloodshed, dust, and magic so cut-rate and ragged it could give a person tetanus.

The sound of a footstep makes me press myself flat against the stucco wall in front of us, though we're well hidden for the moment. Orlagh is the sort of rich asshole who grows a lush formal garden around her desert mansion—whether she has the water shipped or conjured, it's disgustingly ostentatious—but I do admit some gratitude for the thick blue-and-pink endless-summer hydrangeas currently concealing our position. Still, assuming we got an accurate map of the grounds from the former servant we bribed back in town, we're kneeling right outside Orlagh's bedroom window. Her habit of tossing around curses when she's drunk and horny have made her a lot of enemies, and by all accounts she compensates by hiring vigilant guards.

Beauty and I exchange a glance. Her chest doesn't move until the footsteps fade away. Then she offers a tentative smile. "I guess we should...." She nods upward.

"No point killing time when we could be killing the enemy," I agree.

I can feel her wanting more from me, some acknowledgement of all the ways she embodies my private version of perfection. She ought to know, I think. I'm up against my own revulsion, too. Back when I was all bosoms and ribbons and gently curling raven hair, I heard more than my fair share of romantic flattery, and it made my stomach twist every time. Those words still leave a sour taste in my mouth, and that doesn't change when they're true, or intended for my Beauty.

So I say nothing and jump lightly onto the wall, using claws to hold myself in place. I climb easily to the window and peek in. Orlagh is making the beast with two backs, though her lover's face is hidden under darkness and bedclothes. A lump forms in my throat, forcing me away from the view. I can't help imagining myself in the spaces Orlagh's body leaves. It's not that I'm jealous—refusing her earned me this form, and I'm not sorry. It's that Orlagh has a way of making herself seem inescapable. Even here, now, looking like this, even when I'm sure she wouldn't want me anymore.

The point of this is to get free, I remind myself, and signal down to Beauty, so she knows this is the correct window, and Orlagh is on the other side of it.

My girl stands smoothly. She's shadow and sinew and dark eyes that see everything. Her gun rises.

A moment later the glass falls out of the window in pieces like the loudest, most aggressive rain you've ever heard. Orlagh's lover screams—sounds like she's with a man tonight—though Orlagh doesn't. More than a dozen feet crunch on gravel paths, converging on our position.

As we planned, I scramble down for Beauty and guide her through the window, because glass shards won't pierce my curse-hardened skin. Then, like a flame consuming a pile of paper scraps, I fall into the midst of Orlagh's guards and display the full horror of what their mistress turned me into.

II. My Claws, Her Roses

Beauty and I were introduced by my contact Whisky Ginny, who described her as "someone you probably oughta know." By trading the work of my teeth and claws for information, I'd tracked Orlagh to a magic rush town called Adamana, only to find the mine tapped and all the fine houses abandoned. Wasn't much left there besides Whisky Ginny's establishment, which sold booze, women, and vague leads to supposedly better places.

I did my best to hide my frustration and let Whisky Ginny lead me over to a woman dressed in men's clothes, who clearly knew how to use the weapon holstered at her hip. She had more freckles than skin with the sun-weathered squint to match, smelled of leather and, somehow, roses, and didn't flinch or look pitying when I walked over.

Over many rounds of booze so strong it could have made a barstool tear up, we explained to each other why we were both after Orlagh.

"I loved my Beast very much, but as a friend," Beauty said. "I didn't want to marry him, and he didn't want to force me. He let me go back to my family, and I was glad he did. I promised I'd visit, but it took me longer to get back than I'd intended. When I did return, I found a dead man I didn't recognize in his bed. The diary beside him revealed the truth of the whole thing—the way

Orlagh transformed and cursed him when he didn't cotton to her advances—"

That part, too familiar to me, made me growl. Beauty paused, giving me a chance to speak if I wanted, but I wasn't ready to tell my story yet, and nodded for her to go on.

"Anyhow, that book told me the part I'd been supposed to play. True love and all that. For a while, I was devastated because he died pining for me. I failed my friend, I thought. I caused his death. It made me feel so meek and ashamed, like the beauty on the outside of me was just a cover for this ugly selfishness inside."

Indeed, though her current attire didn't emphasize it, I could see her beauty quite clearly. She had curves as thrilling as a switch-back trail through the Rockies, a smile that could change your whole opinion of yourself, and eyes that sparked in a way that made me wonder what it would be like to see them catch fire entirely.

"You'll forgive me for saying you don't seem meek and ashamed anymore," I observed.

Pleasure flashed through her expression, which warmed me more than the liquor. "You got that right," Beauty said, slamming down the rest of her drink. I noticed her hands, scarred, and her lips, dangerously full. She leaned in close, hundred-proof breath tickling the fur around my nostrils, eyes not quite seeing mine. "I came this close to marrying the next man who asked, just out of guilt. Came to my senses before I walked down the aisle, though. One night, courting, he said, 'You're so beautiful it ought to be a crime.' I threw him out on the spot, and then I stared in the mirror for a long time."

She took my paw and guided it to her face.

"It's just flesh," Beauty said. "Lips, eyes, nose, chin. That's all it is, and I didn't make it. I didn't declare how people ought to feel about it. I thought about my Beast. He loved me, yes, but he took me in the first place because I was a beautiful, sweet-looking woman and he thought that meant I'd love him back and break his curse. And you know what? I'm not going to take the fucking

blame for any of this. I'm not the one going around cursing people. And my face? My body? Nothing more than flesh."

My heart pounded with sympathy and inspiration. These were
things I'd never been able to say while I still looked lovely. The ferocity it took to repudiate beauty while wearing it struck me as
wilder and more beastly than anything I'd managed in the ugliness
I'd been learning to treasure. I let her feel my claws, lightly. "If you
don't think you're to blame, why'd you come out here? You could
have washed your hands of Orlagh. She's not your problem."

"You see many other people looking out for justice?"

I followed her gaze around the saloon. Inside, it was just us. It
felt like it was only us in the whole goddamn world right then.
My body pulsed. The excitement had gotten me hungry for blood
or sex or both, and I pulled away from Beauty.

"Where you going?" She looked at me like she knew.

I cleared my throat. "Whisky Ginny's got women...."

"I'm a woman."

"All due respect, I wouldn't ask that of you."

Her eyes narrowed. "And if you weren't the one asking?"

I stopped. "What do you mean?"

She cocked her head and put a hand on her hip, as if flirting
with drawing her gun. "I know a few things about going to bed
with a beast. It's an experience I'd recommend, and I'd be jealous
if someone else got paid for it while I'm offering to do it free."

She said beast matter-of-factly, the way I said it to myself, and
as a result it didn't sting. It did make me curious, though. "I
thought you said you loved him as a friend."

"Precisely. And we had good times together, until he needed it
to be something more."

"I'm a girl-beast, not a boy-beast," I clarified, because I wasn't
sure how well that showed. "Does that bother you?"

"Doesn't seem to bother you."

I ducked out and paid Whisky Ginny for a key to an upstairs
room. With Beauty waiting for me, it was easy to ignore her obvious relief at not having to put a price on my ugliness. In other

company, I might have slunk upstairs, but Beauty marched, and I followed suit.

The room boasted a bed one sigh short of collapse, a window that looked out on a road that wasn't trafficked anymore, and the scents of dust, dried bodily fluids, and, now that she had entered, roses.

Beauty turned to me with a grin. "We're going to tear this motherfucker apart," she said.

I blinked. I'd gotten used to holding back. "I don't want to hurt you."

"Don't do anything permanent to my face." She winked. "But don't skimp on the claws, either. Or the teeth."

"You're serious."

"Deadly, darling."

She began unfastening things. The freckles stopped where she didn't get as much sun. Her curves, unbound, occupied more space. She smoothed her hands over her bare body as she peeled clothes away, as if checking that everything was as it should be.

From where I stood, every part of her was so much better than should be.

Beauty smirked slightly, watching me watch her, as if she knew how the sight of her usually hidden skin made my teeth ache at the roots. The blood inside my body seemed to dance the polka—it spun from paws to heart to clit and back again, settling nowhere, getting dizzier with each revolution. I stumbled toward her and saw more scars. Pale and well-healed, they were subtle against her skin until I got in close.

I made so bold as to touch one with the very point of a protracted claw, pressing Beauty's skin into a dimple, but far from piercing it. "He did this to you?"

She pulled a face and peered down at the top of her breast. "Probably not. He was gentler than I've been with myself, in the time since. To be honest, I wish more of the marks he made had stayed."

"You did this to yourself?"

"Trying to reproduce an experience that doesn't lend itself to imitation," she said, grinning again.

Disbelief froze me in place. I'd gotten used to settling for one or the other, the blood or the sex, though I always bore the urges twinned. Try as I might to negotiate with people of Whisky Ginny's ilk, I could only occasionally afford the exorbitant sums they wanted to charge, and could even more rarely assure them of my good and non-lethal intentions with the elusive balance of vigor and sobriety that won their trust. I had only truly sated myself a few times, and always with the queasy sense that my partner of the moment saw our liaison as something to be endured.

"Are all beasts such cowards?" Beauty asked with a sigh. She reached for her discarded boot and unsheathed a knife, and then stroked its blade casually over her breast before I had a chance to speak or stop her. She glared into my stunned silence, but soon the rust-red scent of blood budding from the fresh wound drew both our attention. Her fingers twined with mine as we dipped our chins to watch it spread. "Go on," Beauty urged.

I cupped her ass uncertainly, but that slight encouragement was all she needed to climb me like a vine, to bring her blooming breast straight up to my lips. It was only a matter of not resisting then. We slammed into the bed, awkwardly, as my knees gave out from the shock of fulfilled desire and my tongue began to learn the shape of her nipple.

She grabbed handfuls of my fur. "Take off the clothes," she demanded. "I want to see you."

No one had said anything remotely similar to me since that fateful evening with Orlagh. I'd been relieved about that, so I was completely unprepared for the exquisite thrill that passed through me in the wake of her words.

I released Beauty long enough to stand, and revealed myself, fully beast, to a woman who looked at me all the while with a lover's hunger.

Coyly, she slid a finger through her blood, then brought it up to paint her lips. I whimpered, and bent to lick it away. Her hands urged me all the way onto the bed, until my full weight pinned her in place. Her legs wrapped my waist, and her hips jerked against me so vigorously that I thought she'd make the bed give way.

"Please," Beauty whispered. "Use your claws."

I pulled back far enough to stare into her eyes, perhaps because I needed yet more assurance that she truly wanted this. She guided my paw to her inner thigh, close to the sex. Her heat radiated through my fur, and her arousal soaked it.

"Here?" My heart pounded as if I were the one about to be raked.

"Lick me while you do it." When I still hesitated, she shoved my head downward and rocked her hips. "Please."

I couldn't break her gaze, so it was her gasp and the hot, heady scent that told me when I'd parted skin. It felt like a dream, air thicker than usual, woman willing in a way I didn't fathom, her body tense but unresisting as I dragged my claw slowly toward her knee.

"Your tongue!" she cried.

I'd forgotten. When I used it to part her folds, she flinched as if that was the touch that wounded her.

Her legs trembled where they lay against me. I could feel her wanting me to be quick, rough, forceful, but she had me too dazed for any of that. I let the taste of her sex soak into me, then shifted to her inner thigh, where my tongue crept along the path my claw had traveled.

"Oh, you fucking beautiful, horrible...." Her words made me smile. They made me feel we might be more alike than I would ever have guessed. They made me believe she understood the tangle beauty and ugliness made with each other, the way these supposed opposites turned out to be so deadly close together.

I found the courage to really fuck her then. I showed her the maw Orlagh had made from what was once a mouth, spread it wide, and settled it over her sex. Beauty shivered as I engulfed her, and begged for more. I reached up and pressed claws into each of her arms, trapping her with them, and let her feel my teeth at the top of her mons veneris. She screamed as I settled myself and sank in, then sobbed when I put my tongue to work as well. Her shuddering orgasms filled my mouth with the mingled flavors of sex, blood, fear, and desire, and nothing before or after my transformation had ever been as sweet or as unbearable.

When I released her, I wished I could still cry. I was shaken, and she, though spent, was knowing and triumphant and faintly smug. She held me for a long time before we spoke again, and I licked away all traces of blood that remained on her body with a gentleness I hadn't realized I was still capable of. I was half in love with her already, and so I told her what Orlagh had done to me, and how I'd realized I liked the gifts the curse had given me and hoped never to see it broken.

"Well, you're safe with me," Beauty said. "I've already failed to break one beast's curse, and I did try." She punctuated her sentence with a hollow laugh.

I shifted out of her embrace and studied her face, the old pain around her eyes like the tracks of ancient rivers dried into the walls of an arroyo. "How exactly does it break? It seemed lucky I didn't want it to, and unlikely anyhow, so I never sought out the specifics."

"Orlagh told him 'true love.' My beast thought at first that meant the act of love, as we just shared, would do it, but we tried often and that never took. Then he thought it was the feeling— but I'm not sure I know what the feeling is or how Orlagh's magic would recognize it. What is love? The ache when the beloved is absent? The leap in the chest at their presence? I felt those things."

"As a friend, you said." I tried to conceal the thin, dry jealousy that threatened to catch in my chest.

She shrugged. "I was pleased to see him each evening. I was— I am—deeply sorry he is gone. I shared his bed gladly. It was love, I'm sure of it. It brought me here. It changed who I am."

I pulled away and stood, worrying a patch of fur matted with Beauty's blood. "Orlagh changed who I am. It wasn't with love."

"I'm sure it wasn't." She shook her head. "There was a reason I didn't want to marry him, though. I felt like there could be something more, or different. I never wanted to write him poetry. Do you understand?"

I sighed, working my jaw and flexing my fingers as if it was possible to shake off the taint I always felt in the wake of a mention of Orlagh. I wanted to move on. I managed to convince myself that night that, if what Beauty said was true, the curse might not be possible to break after all. What if Orlagh only let people believe they could go back to their former selves? Hope would be its own torment, and the woman I'd met liked to make people suffer in every form she could think up.

I forced a grin, knowing after what we'd shared that Beauty wouldn't find the expression frightening. "So I'm safely a beast unless you write me a sonnet?"

She looked away. "That's if we stick together."

"Do you want to?" I was already dizzy at the thought of losing her, and too naive to be frightened by that.

The corner of her mouth quirked up. "Your fur would keep me warm at night."

III. *A Curse in Disguise*

Beauty's gun presses into the side of Orlagh's head. Blood-spattered and still panting from my exertions, I hold Orlagh's lover against my chest, paw over his mouth, grip as gentle as I can make it. I don't want to hurt him, but we can't afford to trust him.

I've imagined this moment many times, but never guessed how frightened I would feel. I can't look at Orlagh's body, though I can feel her looking at mine.

"I really did make you ugly," Orlagh says. She laughs. "The first time I saw you, you dabbed the corners of your mouth with a napkin after every bite you took, wiping away things that weren't even there. You're certainly no lady now."

Beauty grabs a fistful of Orlagh's hair. The woman's glamour is such that even in the darkness, even in the violence of the moment, all three of us notice how thick and shining and supple those blonde tresses are. They seem as full of possibility as so many hand-fuls of gold, and for an awful moment I fantasize about falling to my knees and burying my face in them.

The scents of blood and roses bring me back to myself. I meet Beauty's eyes above Orlagh's head. I may look like a monster, but I'm quivering. All I want to do is find Orlagh's lover his clothes, to carry him out of the building, to ask if he truly chose to be here with her, or if she threatened him.

I spot discarded cloth on the floor beside Orlagh's jewel-en-crusted vanity. I mark the solidity of the pine door and the latch across it. I smell the activity that twisted the sheets, smell the musk of Orlagh all over the man I'm holding. There are things I want from Orlagh, questions I want to ask, but they're not coming out of my mouth, and I'm not sure they're going to. Helpless, I look back at my girl.

The line of Beauty's jaw hardens. "I should kill her, no?"

We've endlessly debated what we ought to do with Orlagh once we find and finish with her. The promises of death are the only ones Beauty trusts. I've always worried that Orlagh's evil is more essential than Orlagh, that the end of one embodiment will only mean I won't know it for what it is the next time I see it.

"She must not love you like you think she does, if you still look like that," Orlagh comments.

"You don't understand a goddamn thing," I say.

"Kill her, yes?" Beauty pulls Orlagh's hair until her chin tips up. I look away from the flash of her pale throat.

In some depth of my heart, yes, I want Orlagh to cease existing, but that isn't why I've chased her from one tapped-out town to the next. More than anything I wish I could choose not to see or think about her again, but Orlagh's curse has never allowed me that luxury.

I square my shoulders, brace Orlagh's trembling lover against my hip. "No, not yet."

"You want to be beautiful again," Orlagh croons, in exactly the tone she used years ago to declare what she believed I wanted her to do to me.

I shove Orlagh's lover away because I can't keep my claws in. "Shut up," I growl.

"Oh, you want to tear me limb from limb," Orlagh says, as if delighted.

"You don't know anything about what I want." My paw is on her throat, but my stomach lurches because I'm touching her and that's not something I can bear.

"Bête," Beauty says, her voice full of authority. "We can fall apart later."

I'm on my knees looking up at her, and for a moment Orlagh disappears. Every part of me aches for Beauty, as if I'm nothing but the tender skin of a healing wound. Is her love going to turn me into a person she doesn't want anymore? Will it rip away the lessons I've learned as predator, strip me of my teeth and claws and restore me to the life of prey?

"What happens to your magic if you die?" I growl the words in Orlagh's general direction, still unable to meet her eyes. "What happens to me?"

Orlagh's laugh is as light as the steps of a person who's never wanted for anything. "I've never wasted time wondering. If I'm dead, I won't care, will I?"

"We can find out," Beauty says through gritted teeth.

"No!" I take a deep breath, forcing down the lump that rises into my throat as I take in the civet secretions Orlagh has smeared at every pulse point. "Can you make your curse unconditional? Can you make sure I stay this way?"

I dare a glance at her. I get an impression of eyes as cold as water thrown over a drunk come morning, of fine wrinkles that don't seem able to catch hold of the face they're spreading over. She is smiling, but her lips are thin. Her chin and cheekbones are sharp.

She strokes the fur of my upper arm, chuckling when I stiffen, unruffled by the click of Beauty cocking her gun. "It makes you feel safe to be a beast."

It took her three guesses to get me right, but the moment doesn't feel scattershot. It feels like she's invading me, and that she'll never leave now she's gotten in. I shudder, but can't pull away from Orlagh's grip on my fur.

"You trust her to do more magic on you?" I can hear Beauty's frown.

"There's no other choice," Orlagh says, before I can. "But you know very well that magic always has a price."

The temperature in the room is wrong. The air isn't really breathable. My joints aren't on at the right angles. I can't think about Orlagh or her price or her hand in my fur. Beauty is saying something, but I can't hear it. My jaw works, but only animal sounds come out.

I am going to agree to Orlagh's terms, and I am going to hate myself for agreeing.

Then a crimson floret appears in the center of Orlagh's chest. It grows rapidly. I know it's blood and gore, but Beauty's gun hasn't gone off and my claws are retracted.

It takes a moment for me to get my head to the right angle, to see Orlagh's lover standing wide-eyed, knife in hand, mouth open but wordless.

I see the person I used to be in the beauty of his face, in the soft, shadowed hollow at the base of his throat.

Orlagh shrieks one last laugh. "Now you'll know," she says, eerie, smiling, "what happens when I die."

But I can already feel it, starting in the marrow of my bones and twisting outward from there. The curve of my spine is changing, as are the angles of my face. Black fur falls in clumps to the floor all around me. Without my sharp teeth, there is too much room in my mouth. I hold up a hand. So small—how did I ever do anything with it?

I look at Beauty in despair.

IV.The Softness of Love

For a while, Beauty and I made each other invincible. She relished every beastly part of me, and so I found myself trusting her with anything and everything—even secrets I hid while I was still a lady. I saw subtle changes in her as well. Her swagger lost its self-conscious embellishments and more closely resembled the walk of a veteran. We shared long stretches of comfortable silence. While I loved the bravado of her grin, sometimes I caught her smiling, softly, to herself.

The taste of her blood or cunt always seemed to be in my mouth back then, the scent of my fur on her fingers.

We chased rumors of Orlagh, but at times the effort felt like an excuse to camp together each night, to lie down under open skies, to greet the dawn with arching gasps and unabashed screams.

One morning when we hadn't slept, she turned in my arms and rubbed her cheek against the fur over my breastbone. "I want you," Beauty murmured.

I chuckled, too satisfied to consider her meaning. My physical limits were hard to exceed, but I'd crossed them, and my body ached for it. "You've had me."

"No," Beauty said. "You've had me." Her fingers, teasing down my belly, made her meaning clear.

I stiffened, and Beauty froze. She sat up, the gently glowing clouds above us seeming to tangle around her head as if trying to replace the hair she'd chopped short. "Is that not something you enjoy?"

I coughed. "You're the first to express interest since Orlagh transformed me."

"And before?"

I struck a pose, knowing how ridiculous my solid, hairy limbs would make it look. "Before? I was a proper lady, darling. I would never have dreamed of letting anyone put fingers—or anything else—into me."

Beauty's wicked grin spread over her face, and I had to wonder where the woman found the energy. "I'm starting to understand the fuss people make over undiscovered territory," she observed, leaning over me to press our foreheads together. "Are you curious? Interested? Excited? Or does a growling beast prefer a lady keep her fingers to herself?"

Her tone was teasing, but I recognized the space she was giving me, the choices. I rested a paw on the small of her back as I considered, and let my other paw cup her breast. Her body fit itself into my grip, and I realized I'd do anything for this woman. "Maybe curious," I said, "but also nervous."

"We'll go slow," Beauty promised.

I didn't know how to hold myself as she began to explore me. I knew she craved the sensation of my teeth and claws, but it was hard to believe she'd simply want to look at me. As her fingers found my folds and parted them, I protracted my claws, feeling obligated to immediately return any pleasure she gave me.

For the first time, Beauty pulled my clawed paw away. "No," she murmured. "Not now. I can't have you distracting me when I need to focus on you."

"What am I supposed to do?"

She laughed, but her eyes gleamed with sympathy that made me uncomfortable. "Feel it," Beauty said. "Stop me from doing things you don't like. Encourage me to do things you do."

I sighed and tried not to imagine how I looked with legs spread—ugliness, I had learned, did not confine itself to the face, and Orlagh had been thorough. Was Beauty staring into a monstrous sex? I could not even have begun to resolve the question, and so I had no choice but to trust that she had chosen me.

Because of my anxiety, it took some time to register the way her fingers felt. She was stroking me very lightly, her hot breath nearly as present as her touch. My limbs began to shake. Beauty rested one palm on my trembling thigh. "What is that? Pleasure? Fear?"

"I don't know."

She made a soothing noise and continued stroking. "I'm not going to do anything else unless you ask for it. You're safe with me."

It was an absurd thing for her to say. I was three times her weight. I could have torn her head away without effort. And yet the words made me groan.

Gradually, like a message coming in over telegraph, symbols of pleasure began to assemble inside my body. I became aware of the slipperiness between her fingers and my skin—that was me, wet with arousal. Something, not quite a tingle, more like the buzz of ordinary air in a time of lightning, traveled from her fingers, down my lips, and deeper into my pelvis. Inside me, tightening. An ache began to spread from the juncture of my legs.

"More," I whispered. "Please."

A slight increase of pressure provoked a dizzying array of responses. My hips, as if acting on their own, thrust toward her. I snatched my paws away from her so I could grip handfuls of the dirt to either side of my bedroll. I bit my lip until I tasted my own blood, and when Beauty darted forward to lick the wound I cried out.

"Do you want me inside you?"

"Oh. Oh yes."

Her index finger traced the shape of my entrance. I looked down at Beauty's hand. She could seem so delicate at times, and it frightened me to think how much of her might fit inside me, how much of her I might want.

She watched me as she pushed her finger in. I knew nothing was hidden from her. My fearsome face could not mask my fear. My inhuman features could not conceal my lust. And my ugliness could not obscure the beauty of my love. I felt it shining out of me, the openness of my heart allowing the openness of my legs, my body.

I could not have pointed to the moment when my feelings for Beauty definitively became those of love, but that was the moment I recognized them for what they were. My body gripped her finger. It panicked me a little to let her in, but it would have been impossible to let her go.

In the back of my mouth, I tasted words of love wanting to form, but I pushed them away. I didn't want to be like Beauty's other beast, demanding what she couldn't give. I told myself my feelings didn't matter anyway—her true love was what mattered, and she hadn't written me any sonnets.

"You're gorgeous right now," Beauty whispered. "So brave, and so soft and warm inside." Her finger curled within me, and the exquisite sensation brought my whole body with it. My spine mirrored the shape of her finger. I roared as if wounded.

Something was happening in the depths of my pelvis. I thought it was an orgasm, so I asked for more. She gave it to me, another finger, and then another, and for a few glorious moments I surrendered to growing sweetness.

But where an orgasm would have burst forth, this sank in. It settled into the marrow of my bones, where it began reshaping the most fundamental things. The scent of roses blotted out desert and blood and the animal smell of my own body. The memory of Orlagh's curse acting on my flesh flashed through my mind—skin stretching, hair thickening, muscles cording.

"Stop!" I cried. "Beauty, wait!"

She snatched her hand away. My body ached as if she'd taken half my bones with her, but pleasure denied wasn't what left me gasping. She asked what was wrong, but I was too occupied with holding onto myself to answer.

Beauty moved to stroke the matted fur over my forehead, but I sensed what would happen if she did. "Don't touch me!" I shouted, summoning enough force to scramble away, off the bedroll.

I hurtled into the early morning like a hunter chasing the swiftest prey. Soon, I embraced the image and ran down a rabbit, filled my mouth with its blood. This is who I am, I insisted to myself, and the sense of being changed from inside out began to fade. I breathed once, slowly, and walked back to where Beauty and I had made camp, bringing what was left of the rabbit with me as an offering.

I decided that Orlagh had been able to curse me in the first place because when I was beautiful I also didn't know who I was. I was stronger now. But when I saw Beauty sitting beside a freshly stoked fire, only half clothed, arms wrapped around her lower legs, I recognized my own wishful thinking. I could tell myself whatever I wanted, but it still wasn't safe to let her touch me.

I deliberately made a noise as I approached. Beauty glanced up, her lack of sleep showing on her face where I hadn't noticed it before.

"Bête, are you okay?" she asked. "What happened? Did I hurt you?"

I tossed her the rabbit, and she caught it one-handed. "You love me," I said.

"What? I mean, of course, but not like...."

"You want to write me a sonnet." There was tenderness in my voice along with accusation. The beast's heart in me wanted to fling her onto the bedroll for ten more hours and celebrate the feelings that had grown between us in a wild union of blood and sex. But doing that would lose me what I'd gained, so I simply repeated myself. "You love me."

Beauty's face fell. "I thought we'd been over this. I thought you didn't want to get changed back. It's not fair to expect a thing like that from—"

"You almost did it. Just now. And you're right, I don't want to get changed back. I ran to keep you from fucking the beast right off me."

"What are you talking about?" I could see on her face that she knew more than her question let on. Her eyes told me I was right, and now that I knew it was there, I could feel the beautiful, horrible ferocity of the love that tied us together, as surely as if it were a strong rope we'd been braiding through days and nights in each other's company.

I sank to my haunches. "Darling," I said, "things between us are going to have to change."

V. To Beast, To Beauty, and Back Again

The three of us take up together for a time. Orlagh's lover goes by Robbie. He's older than he looks, and killing Orlagh has made him more so.

We go from town to town. With nothing to chase, it feels like we're running, though I couldn't say what from. Every night, we rent a single room for the three of us, gossip be damned, paying for it with riches we pilfered before quitting the house of Orlagh. We fall exhausted into the bed and hold each other like a set of frightened siblings. I wake first, always. I take out a hand mirror that used to sit beside Orlagh's bed and stare into it. I can't call the woman I see in the glass myself.

The tears that perpetually wet her big, soft eyes leave salty tracks down her cheeks, but take nothing away from her loveliness. She appears unmarked by the miles I've ridden, the years I've lived, the prey I've killed, the woman I fucked until that turned to love. She seems even more naive than my memories attest, even smaller, even weaker, even paler. I wish she had half the strength I see in Beauty.

There are mornings Beauty steals out of bed, notices me cross-legged on the floor in the corner, and tries to wrap her arms around me. I've grown used to shying away from her touch, and it is easy to continue doing so, even though I no longer have a reason. Sometimes, she asks if I want to talk about it, and I always tell her no.

One morning, Robbie stands up out of bed earlier than usual, his mostly smooth chest bare, and frowns in my direction as he rubs a hand through the fine black hair he's been letting grow long. "Come on," he says, indicating the window with his chin.

The idea of jumping out a window is not without its merits to me at that point in time, so I get up and follow him. To my slight disappointment, Robbie simply climbs out onto a nearby rooftop, then turns around to offer me a hand. I don't like the gentlemanly gesture, so I don't take it, and he grunts an acknowledgement while rolling two cigarettes.

In this light, I can see the golden tones in his otherwise pale skin. Sitting on the roof as he remains standing above me, I notice the roundness of his jaw. He takes a drag. "You got anywhere to go back to?" he asks after a moment.

I think about a party long ago, the suitors I dodged there, the pull I felt toward a lovely blonde woman who'd come without a man, the ways my life was changed by saying first yes to her, and then no. I shrug. It is impossible to imagine returning to my family, but I'd be lying if I pretended that option didn't exist.

"You got any idea where we're headed?"

I don't bother with a gesture this time. He already knows the answer to that.

"You going to run off by yourself, or are you sticking with us?"

I bristle at that. Beauty and I are the us. He's the tag-along. "She's with me," I growl, and it's the first time anything like my old beast voice comes out of my lovely, swan-like throat.

One side of his mouth quirks up. "Is that a fact?"

Before I know what I'm doing, I've got a fist full of black hair and my teeth at his throat. "It's a fact." My eyes fix on a vein running down the side of his neck. I can see his pulse in it. The beast's hunger for blood has left me, but right now I remember what it was like to feel it, and I'm startled at how close that brings me to who I used to be.

The heat rolling off his body hits my upper lip. He quivers in my grip, and I recall holding him against me when his limbs were slender compared to mine. He whimpers, and I let go so fast he falls onto his back, lit cigarette rolling a few feet down the roof.

I snatch it up, shove it between my teeth, and drop to my knees beside Robbie, afraid to touch him, but equally afraid he's not in a secure position. Old eyes gaze up at me from his unlined, youthful face. I'm dizzy for a moment, uncertain of who's holding who in place on the roof. I get the queasy premonition of one or both of us falling off.

Robbie clears his throat. "Do you remember who you were before?"

"Before Orlagh? It was a long time ago."

"Not for me, but I still don't think I do."

I feel myself soften. I think about that word us, how badly I needed it when Beauty and I met, and how I failed to realize that until much later. I think about the love that grew like a weed over two ruins Orlagh left in her wake, and how that love eventually covered everything. It's a shame I still feel like a ruin underneath it all. Isn't love supposed to make a person better? Didn't it seem for a while as if it did?

Beauty appears at the window. Her short hair sticks out from her head in funny clumps. It hurts to look at her, to see how firmly she's made herself into something she understands, to feel so desperate for her and so unworthy of her at the same time. Her eyes flick over us, and I feel self-conscious of Robbie's bare chest, the cigarette between my teeth, the closeness of our bodies. It isn't like that, but in the moment I wanted to bite his neck, maybe it was.

I pull on the cigarette, trying to look casual, but the throat I was born with is dainty and I wind up coughing and gasping. I fling the cigarette away, ashamed to feel the beginnings of tears in my eyes. I'd like to believe, with Robbie, that Orlagh changed me, but I've always been this same, soft person—claws and teeth briefly made me appear otherwise. How can Beauty love me like this? She wants a lover who tears her flesh apart, who growls and devours, who makes her bleed.

The roof subtly shifts beneath me, and I know my fearless girl has climbed out after us. A hand hovers over my shoulder, not quite touching, but holding me in place. I know it belongs to Robbie—Beauty wouldn't be afraid to grip.

"Bête," she says.

I turn my head, and she's closer than I expect, her breath somehow rose-scented even this early in the morning. She looks like she wants to kiss me, but I shake my head. "I can't give you what you want anymore." It's the first honest thing I've said to her since Robbie killed Orlagh, and she leans her forehead against mine.

"You don't know that."

I'd wrench myself away, but Robbie's hand is still on me, his touch firmer now. "Beauty—"

"You're safe with me. Can you trust that?"

It's hard to believe I went years without crying—tears come so often now. The best I can give her is a sob and a noncommittal grunt.

"Come inside," she says. "Let me show you."

Her invitation is clear, as is a desire I can't understand. It took a long time to accept she wanted me as a beast, and now I'm at a loss all over again, puzzled by how she could want me as a woman. My beast's hunger may have left me, but I still need her, body and soul. Like the first time, I can't turn down her offer, no matter how little I believe in it.

Robbie releases me so I can stand, turns his back on us, retrieves the second cigarette, which I never took. "I'll be out here."

Beauty clears her throat, glances at me. I nod, thinking of how his hand made it possible for me to withstand Beauty's unbearable perfection. "You don't have to be," she tells him. A shadow crosses her face, and I know she's thinking of Orlagh. "But you can be. Whatever you prefer."

He smiles, his expression briefly clear of clouds. "I'll stay out here for now," he says, and lights the cigarette.

Beauty tugs me inside.

She takes off my clothing, and I try to remember: when I wore this body before, did I love it or hate it? We both stare at it as if it's a fresh new thing.

"It should be furry," I say. "You miss my claws, my—"

Beauty lays a finger over my lips. "Stop."

She steps out of her own clothes. There is a scab along her upper arm that I put there. I can't resist tracing it, remembering the power I used to have.

Beauty covers my hand with hers. She produces the knife from her boot and offers me the hilt. "You know what I like," she says. "You're still yourself. Still a beast if you want to be."

I take the knife and touch the blade, which is somehow cooler than the rest of an already hot morning. "I don't know if I ever was a beast. You called me a coward the first time we stood to-gether like this."

She gives a short laugh. "So be a beast now. Make yourself a beast. You don't need Orlagh to do it for you."

I cup a breast and feel something rising from below my ribs. A hand between her legs reveals heat, need, moisture. I still want to drink her. I want to fill my mouth with the taste of her blood, and also her sex.

I kiss my girl and let her love transform me—to beast, to beauty, and back again.

An Analog Christmas
Kal Cobalt

All the themes at the Palmetto run together once you've lived in
The Vegas as long as I have. They don't correspond, at least not to
each other. Icy blue can be discount days or fetish night. The last
crimson-and-silver theme commemorated fifty percent off in
honor of the latest group murder—the Palmetto likes to help its
patrons stave off the depression that comes from that kind of
news—but the crimson-and-silver before that was for the virgin
brunch.

This time the halls were waves of red and green, chasing one
another along the undulating walls. Even if I'd wanted to read the
theme information ping that popped up on my visual spectrum, I
couldn't have; it was red like the giant PERFORM GIVING +12 (37)
directive blocking half my sight. A week ago, an uptight corrective
action officer tagged me for calling it an asshole, and that bumped
Perform Giving up from a do-in-time directive to one that made it
progressively harder to do anything else.

Still, I wasn't at the Palmetto to Perform Giving. I was there because they have flash decks, and that would be enough to get me
my fix around the giant red letters. My flash specs were useless, too
weak to get through that kind of optical blockage. I needed the Palmetto's luxuriously huge goggle-pillars and a good strong flash before I could start sorting out my directives.

The Palmetto's casino floor is a riot of fun, even if you show up direc-
tive-crippled. It was one of the pilot casinos for sex fields—those transparent
closet-sized places to have sex standing up in full view but protected from
the wandering hands of strangers—and The Vegas's Own Original Sex Fields
At The Palmetto were always busy, and usually kinky. Sometimes bloody vats
wandered up from the basement arena before they were regenehealed,
spouting artificial blood from limbs severed by the historical reenactments
engaged in there, mostly swordfighting and gang wars. Sexbots wandered

around naked, or at least naked enough to display the targets on their backs and the corresponding discounts for distance and force of ejaculation. It was a fucking wonderland to the left of my visual field, and PERFORM GIVING +12 (37) to my right. Perverse.

I couldn't remember where the flash decks were, or maybe they'd moved, or maybe the rumors about directives short-circuiting memory were true. I kept turning corners and finding more sex, more bots, more blood, until I ran facefirst into an ad field. It refused to dismiss until it identified that my eye movements had read it, but the letters kept surging red and green, and I could only read them half the time. Pinned there, I read as much as I could in between the red surges: AN ANCIENT HOLIDAY...AN EXOTIC DEAL AT...THE PALMETTO THIS...CHRISTMAS. WE INVITE...YOU TO EXPERIENCE THE...SENSATION OF CHARITY...BY ASSISTING THE ANALOG FOR...THE VERY SPECIAL RECOMPENSE...OF 50 GIVING.

I hadn't been out of Giving debt in years. Hell, with 13 extras, I could tell the next corrective action officer to go fuck itself and probably get out of it with no debt. The ad de-shimmered, focusing my eyes on the booth beyond it that read Learn About Christmas and Get Giving Credit! I was hooked.

The man behind the counter was dressed in a vintage suit and had grown out a little carefully-trimmed facial hair, like I did. He smiled as I approached, and something about him made me uneasy immediately.

"Welcome to the Palmetto," he said, as everyone did. "I'm Brom. Been ignoring that directive for quite some time now, haven't you?"

I blinked. "Readers are illegal, you know."

He tapped his forehead. "It isn't a reader. You're trying to look around the letters at me. I can tell by the way you lean ever so slightly to the side. It's just my eyes and my brain."

"Oh." I leaned both forearms on the counter, getting close to this squirrelly little guy. "So what's the deal here?"

"We've put analogs up in a block of rooms upstairs. A mini-vacation from their mundane little lives. You're matched up to one of them and given a pass to an analog who's expecting you. The two of you have a little nicey-nicey, and you transfer some piece of personal tech to them. Something you agree on together; you of course have final say. Once you've got them set up with some starter tech so they can begin the painstaking process of building themselves up to societal norms, you say goodbye, get 50 Giving automatically added to your account, and that's the end of it."

"That's buying Giving," I said. "That's not legal. Believe me, I've tried."

Brom shook his head. "No. It's recompensed charity. Believe me, we've been through all of this very thoroughly."

"Then what's the take for you? The Palmetto doles out a room and 50 Giving for every analog, for what?"

He gave me a very satisfied little smile. "The Palmetto sells tech, doesn't it? You do the conversion, we do the monetization."

"Uh-huh." I nodded, trying to think it all through with the damn directive gaping at me. "Okay, listen, I just gotta get flashed and I'll be back, okay?"

"Oh, I wouldn't recommend that."

"Uh-huh, why not?" This had every inkling of a scam to me, and that feeling was only getting stronger, although I couldn't pin it down.

"Flashing scrambles your brains. You might part with more than you want to."

"Trust me, I flash all the time, I know what I'm doing."

He smiled at me again. Not kindly. "Trust me. I curate the analogs all the time. I know what I see."

"Look, buddy, I'll be back in a minute. Just mind your own."

He shrugged, raising his hands. "Of course. No offense intended."

"None taken."

I felt almost blind from the directive and the disorientation that comes from a long wait for your next flash. I wasn't sure if my flash specs had really taken yesterday; I felt a mild buzz, but you never know if that's psychosomatic. I finally found the flash decks, but as usual, I lost a little memory around the flash; I don't remember how I got there from the Christmas booth, or how I paid. Just coming to myself as I pulled away from the goggles and nodded for the attendant to unstrap me from the seat. "You were dark, man, weren't you?" he asked. "You were jumping all over the place during that flash! With a huge grin on your face."

"Flash specs are never as good," I told him. He held up his tip jar and I smeared my thumbprint across it. "Thanks, kid."

Flash is weird. It makes you more confident in what you're doing and where you're going, even though all your physical control goes loco. It's one reason why the Palmetto is so fucking awesome; the undulating walls gently push you back into the walkways without assigning directives against disruptive behavior. I made my way back to the Christmas booth, where Brom smirked at me as he assigned me to the analog in 1225. He had some kind of story about how the number was very significant when it came to the ancient holiday of Christmas, but I tuned him out. I just wanted this over with, and my directive wiped, so I could get a pick-me-up flash and enjoy the rest of my day flat on my back.

It's hard to navigate a hotel on flash, even when you have the room location on visual field sonar. I'm pretty sure I took a dozen wrong turns before I got there—and I'm pretty sure Brom programmed the sonar signal himself; it exploded into fireworks and displayed a ridiculously frilly Congratulations!, as if I had completed some kind of incredibly difficult task.

The guy in the room looked just like the analogs in the ads. He was little, and bald even though he wasn't old enough to be that way naturally. He wore a dumpy loose sweater and pants, and it was weird to see him squint at me knowing he did it because he couldn't see very well, rather than because he was checking any of his visuals. "Hi," he said. He looked at me like he had no idea who I was, and it took me a minute to realize that was true—there wasn't any over-the-air proximity handshaking going on here.

"Hi. The guy at the counter sent me up. The Christmas guy."

"Oh. Hi." He looked at me again, carefully, from my head to my toes. "Come inside."

He'd turned off everything he could in the room and piled up pillows to cover some of the dedicated visual surfaces. The lights were down low. I couldn't imagine what he must have been doing in there. Staring at nothing? "So, uh, we talk about what I have that I'm willing to give you?"

He gave me another long look. "Are you high?"

"High?"

"Under the influence of something mind-altering."

"Yeah, I just got flashed. Uh—it's a thing where you get really focused strobes slammed into your eyes, with patterns that—"

"I know what flashing is." He spoke very quietly and calmly, and just a little coldly. Even through the flash, I started getting a bad feeling, although I wasn't sure if all analogs were this weird or what. "Sit down before you fall down."

"Thanks." I flopped onto the bed, blinking heavily up at the ceiling and its dead visual display. Creepy.

"Did you know they won't let us bunk together?"

"Huh?"

"We have to stay in separate rooms. Do you know why that is?"

I turned my head to make him swim into focus. "I have no idea, man. I'm just a guy who signed up for the program."

"I think it's because they're afraid of us."

I snorted out a little laugh. "Afraid of analogs? Afraid you'll gang up and get so unruly you need somebody to shush you?"

"Afraid that we're more powerful than you think," he said. "My name is Ori, and this is Neen."

I sat up abruptly. My stomach was hot with the sudden awareness that something was wrong. Neen stood at the foot of the bed, not quite as slight a guy as Ori, but in the same loose clothes. Neen had long hair and dark eyes, and waved at me a little. "Hello."

"Uh-huh." I looked from him to Ori and back again. "Okay, if this is a shakedown or something, I just bought a huge flash. I don't have much on me."

"It isn't a shakedown," Ori said.

"It is in some ways," Neen said.

"Okay, you—why don't you two have a conference and figure out what you're doing? Because you seem confused, and you're confusing me." I shook my head; I probably shouldn't have flashed quite so bright anyway, and I definitely wasn't clearheaded enough to handle whatever was developing.

"It isn't confusion, just a difference of opinion," Neen said. "We would like to show you another way."

"Another way of what?"

"Another way of being. You signed up to give, but we'd like to give to you instead."

I snorted. "You're analogs. You don't have anything."

Ori leaned in and rested a hand on my arm. I didn't feel it coming; he didn't have any personal proximity meter hooked up to the network. "We have analog."

"I don't understand anything you're saying." I looked up at Ori, uneasy about his motives even as I noticed that his hand was warm and a little sweaty against my arm—not digital-feeling at all.

"You don't have to understand the words," Neen said, and sat beside me on the bed.

"Okay," I said slowly. "I did not get the whorehouse special."

"Just words." Neen smiled at me.

"Listen," I said. My hands were clammy. I knew desperate men when I saw them. "Let's work this out. Okay? We'll work together. What is it you want?"

"We want to show you another way of being," Neen said again. He took my hand, examining my black-laquor nail implants. "We would like to help you return to an analog state. Only for tonight, to remember what it is like."

"Neen knows how to disable everything and put it all back together," Ori told me. "It's a hobby."

"Uh...I'm not sure about..." But Neen had already picked up a pincered metal instrument, and he set to peeling the top layer of passcode-embedded decor off my nails. "You can't strip me completely," I protested. "I have implants, laser surgeries, digestive enzymes—"

"We're more interested in the immediate and the experiential," Ori told me, watching Neen deposit my nailtops into a container with neatly-labeled compartments.

"Not that different from us after all," I joked. Nobody laughed.

Neen was a fucking pro. He had static-protected storage, demagnetized storage, sterile-field storage—a place for everything. My caloric intake regulator: gone. My "personal space" deactivator: slipped into a box. My over-the-air protocols: scrambled. Then he pulled out a tool that made me flinch: a black-market overlay-suction tool.

"That will fuck me up good," I protested. "It ruins the implants."

"It ruins the implants when used by an unpracticed hand," Ori assured. "If you hold still, everything will be fine." Then he had both hands on my wrists, and Neen came at me with the archaic-looking little plunger thing, and I held very still and kept my eyes very wide.

Getting a biointegration lens peeled off isn't fun, especially when it's been there long enough to begin the process of merging into the eye itself. It didn't hurt, exactly, but it wasn't damn pleasant, and when it was over I just held my hands over my face, keeping my weird-feeling eyes shut.

"Here," Ori offered. He stroked my back, just long, broad strokes of his hands down either side of my spine. Something that simple shouldn't have felt so good, but I felt my muscles relax, just as if he'd flashed me with a relaxant. I let my hands fall from my face into my lap, groaning softly as he stroked and stroked.

"See?" Neen asked. I opened my eyes to find him smiling at me, a little less intimidating than he'd been before. "It is not so bad to be analog." He petted my hair back from my face. It felt warm and sort of tender. Not like anything else I'd felt. Then he kissed me. Just a small kiss, not the sloppy tongue-dueling things you see every day—just a nice little touch of lips. I never thought about how sensitive my lips were. He kept changing the pressure, and I could feel everything.

"Just relax," Ori whispered in my ear, sliding his hands up under my shirt. So I did.

Sex for me, like most people I guess, is another high: get it fast, get it good, crank your pleasure centers to 11 and peel yourself off the ceiling just to do it all over again ten minutes later, until the law of diminishing returns kicks in and it's time to go get flashed or amped or scrubbed or darked. That wasn't what Ori and Neen were doing, though. Ori and Neen were undressing me and exploring me, touching me everywhere. I found out that touching the back of my knees made my stomach knot up a little. That a hand wrapped around my hipbone made me relax. Then Neen kissed the very tip of my penis and I felt something I didn't recognize even from all my experienced years taking in all the wonders tech had to offer, something that felt like wanting and satisfaction simultaneously.

"I don't want you to get the wrong idea," Ori murmured in my ear, rubbing the heel of his hand against my sternum. It made me want to feel that rub all over my body. "This isn't about orgasm."

"It's not?" I panted. Neen had his head buried between my legs, his long hair tickling my balls as he rubbed his cheek against the inside of my thigh. My cock was beyond hard, angled up tight against my belly like it used to before they outlawed the Stone Boner program.

"Trust me," Ori said as Neen broke open a capsule of lube.

We did everything. I mean, everything. Neen got his tongue inside my ass, and found a way to get fingers inside too, and then held me open for Ori's cock. I knew some people did that, but I'd never been fucked before, and something about how close that felt, how inside me it felt—not like programming, not like implants, but like Ori had reached into me somehow—overrode my emotional balance programming and I started crying. Not because it was bad, but because it was huge, I guess. The feeling, I mean. Not Ori's cock.

Then we were kissing, and kissing, and kissing. Neen knew all these little places to touch that made me feel warm and relaxed and tense all at once. I fell asleep for a little while, nestled between both of them in bed, with both of them still stroking and touching me. My skin felt hypersensitized, like it was reaching out for their touch. When I woke up, they were both leaning over me to kiss each other, like they couldn't get enough touch. Suddenly, I knew the feeling.

Ori taught me how to suck Neen's cock, and I got addicted to the little whimpering moans Neen made when I played my tongue across his frenulum just so. He kept balling his hands up in the sheets, and Ori kept patiently prying Neen's fists open and telling him to stop holding back.

The walls were displaying faint signs of impending artificial dawn when Ori said, "Now that you see what it's really about when you aren't pushing so hard for it to end, it's time to come."

Ori went first, kissing me and touching me with his cock down Neen's throat. I had never seen anyone swallow come before—it's not visual, so it doesn't happen—and I started understanding what our ancestors must have been after with the whole idea of taboo. Watching Neen's throat muscles work and hearing him choke a little, even seeing a little drop of come bubble up against the corner of his lips, made me feel like I was seeing something private and unknowable. Something a lot more interesting than a bunch of scattered droplets on some sexbot's back.

I wanted to know what that was like, so I sucked Neen off next. I kept his fingers interlaced in mine so he wouldn't be tempted to ball up the sheets. It was weird, feeling his hands tense and relax against mine. I could understand what he liked and what he didn't like that way, without any of the usual over-the-air transmissions. It was strange how well it worked. I found the one thing that seemed to make his hands and his thighs and his voice all clench up and just kept doing it, rubbing my tongue down the underside of his cock again and again even though my pain receptors weren't blocked anymore and my neck ached, and then he came.

It was the wildest thing I've ever done. I hadn't thought about how hard the come would jet out, and he was bucking under me and I was trying to suck him and swallow and breathe all at the same time, all while trying to depend on crutches Neen himself had disabled. Come came out my nose and dribbled down my chin and got sucked into my lungs, and I held onto Neen too hard and bruised the webs of his fingers, and he bucked so hard he hit my nose and it gave me that numb, not-right feeling.

It was awesome.

Neen surged up and kissed me, licking his come off my lips and my chin and from inside my mouth, and then he set to my cock with a fierceness I hadn't even felt from vacuum bots. Ori knelt up behind me to swirl his palm around my nipples and bite lightly at the nape of my neck, and it took no time at all for me to come, crying out and shaking, looking down at Neen's blissful face as he swallowed up my come with his hands on my thighs, and Ori's hands on his hands as we all came down.

We slept in a tangle of too-hot limbs. Total bliss. Until the Palmetto pinged us: checkout time loomed.

"We'd like to see you again," Ori told me quietly as he got dressed; Neen busied himself putting me back together, the directive blotting out half my vision again. "Would you like that?"

I nodded. "Definitely."

Neen smiled, leaning down to kiss my hand as he put the last nailtop back into place.

Down at the counter, the little man gave me a satisfied smile. "Well done. Your analog filled out your report card—"

"My what?"

"A vintage figure of speech. He was pleased with your interaction and indicates that he's very motivated to purchase technology in the foyer."

I almost laughed. Ori, you liar. "Great," I said. "Can we do something about my, uh...?" I gestured toward my eyes.

"Of course." Brom called up an airscreen, made a few stylized little gestures surely all his own, and the directive blinked out of existence. For the first time, absolutely nothing displayed for me, outside of the usual datapoints.

"Thanks." And then I couldn't help myself: "See? I handled it just fine after my flash. Don't judge."

He smirked. "Fair enough. I apologize."

It wasn't sincere, but it was the best I was going to get. "Thanks."

I headed off automatically in the direction of the flash decks, but halfway there, I realized...I didn't really feel like it. In fact, I felt good. Not flashed, not amped, but good. Okay with things. Happy.

I reversed direction to head to the rail to go home instead. As I approached the Giving Booth, I caught sight of Ori and Neen, holding hands...and talking to Brom. Frowning, I ducked back a little, tuning up my hearing to listen in.

"Well done," Brom said.

"This was a good one," Ori said, swinging Neen's hand gently. "Definitely a convert."

"See you back tomorrow, then?"

Ori looked to Neen. "We might take some time off. This one...meant something. I'd like to see where it goes."

"Fair enough. I appreciate all you've volunteered, do take some time."

I waited till Ori and Neen had left, then walked directly across the lobby, right in front of the counter. Brom glanced up, and I paused, giving him a wink.

A moment of surprise crossed his face. Then he smiled and winked back. "Merry Christmas," he said. "And thank you for participating in the Palmetto's Giving project. We are very grateful for your help."

From the Shallows, Cold as Death
Bernie Mojzes

Once upon a time, as these tales go, in a kingdom far away from here (though perhaps not as far as you might imagine, and perhaps not so long ago that his friends have entirely forgotten his name), there was a boy who lived with his father and his sister in a house on the outskirts of a small town by the side of a river.

If we close our eyes to look closely, we can see the center square paved in cobblestone, and, through misted breath, we see the side streets paved in ice and frozen mud that even now glisten wet under the spring sun. We see the school in which the boy studies, when he is there, across the street from the city hall, where a red flag hangs, snapping in the cold wind that blows from the river. He is a good student, our Ivan, and in a few months he will surely enter the Army as an officer.

But he is not there now; there is only a goat, nibbling idly at the weeds that have begun to sprout along the chain link fence that encircles the school yard.

Nor, if we follow the main road out of town to the edge of the forest, will we find him in his home. It is a modest enough house by some standards, but in this place, in this time, it is only Ivan's father's connections within the Party that prevent it from being divided between a half-dozen families.

Ivan's sister, Yekaterina, scrubs the kitchen floor with a gray rag. There had been a housekeeper, a girl assigned to them by the Party after Ivan's mother's death, who washed and cooked for them. She had slept on a small cot behind the pantry. But she had been re-called abruptly the previous year. Ivan had been in school, and knew only that when he came home she had gone. Since then, her duties have fallen to Yekaterina.

Ivan is less tied to the house than Yekaterina when he is not in school. On this fine, crisp spring day, he is at the river's edge. The ice had broken yesterday, while he was in class; all day and all night they could hear the river crack and crash, the rumble of immense blocks of ice tumbling against each other as they rushed downstream. Today, thick sheets of ice still drift by, but the center of the river is clear, and the fish, famished after the long winter, leap at insects that skim the surface.

It is not only the fish that the winter has starved. Half the village is out on the ice, casting lines into the rushing water. Many of the villagers will soon be frying fish over hot coals, but not Ivan. His line invariably snags on another's, or breaks, or is picked clean of bait.

But Ivan thinks of his sister, thin and pale. While the other girls her age are blossoming, Katya seems to be fading away, shrinking into herself. This winter has been cruel to her, and Ivan is determined to bring her something fresh and healthy and delicious. Something to tempt her back to life.

$$\mathcal{e}\mathcal{l}\mathcal{e}$$

From the first moment he sees the girl, there is a part of him that knows.

For a kilometer or more, the forest falls away into the river in a steep, treacherous bank covered in brambles. The river rushes so fast that the roots of the trees are exposed.

Ivan and his father have hunted these woods for as long as he can remember: deer and rabbits, boar and squirrels. Strictly speaking, it is illegal, but half of what they catch goes to feed the villagers, and a quarter to the other Party apparatchiks. From each according to his ability, to each according to his need. Everyone was hungry, but in Ivan's village, no one has died of starvation. Not yet, at least.

The river widens at one point, a small inlet of calm water, now covered with ice that creeps out from the snow-crusted shore. Once there had been a small hut set back against the forest, beyond the reach of flood waters; now it is half collapsed and overrun with vines, and all that remains of a small pier is rotten stumps jutting from the ice. Ivan has seen this place from a distance, but his father always warned him away: sinkholes in the mud, dangerous currents, poisonous snakes. The dangers are nebulous and infinitely varied, but Ivan knows better than to question his father, ever.

But today Ivan's father is far away, called off to Moskva on Party business. He has been gone for a week, and it will be at least another before he returns.

And here, at least, the fish are biting.

Standing out on the ice, Ivan feels the girl behind him before she speaks. The hair on his neck prickles, and he spins to face her.

He is a smart boy, our Ivan. Educated. He has read Lenin, and Marx. There is no place for superstition—for religious, magical thinking—in the modern world. No place for the stories his Baba used to tell him, of malevolent spirits in the woods and the river, of the spirits of murdered girls luring young men to a watery death.

"Excuse me, Comrade," she says, and her voice is like the burbling of a brook. "I did not mean to startle you."

She's beautiful, of course, and not just because this is a story. There are pictures, if you like, though they hardly do her justice. I can tell you where to look for them. She wears a long, white dress that's frayed a little at the hem and the sleeves. Her long, dark hair falls in cascades over her shoulders and parts over her small breasts. Ivan can see her nipples, hard in the crisp wind coming off the river, dark bumps straining against the thin fabric of her dress. But this is not what holds his eye. Her face is narrow, her nose just slightly hooked, over the widest, most expressive mouth he has ever seen. If she would smile, he is certain, he would have no choice but to fall madly in love.

For a moment, Ivan is speechless.

"You look familiar," the girl says. "Do you know who I am?" She touches his face. Her fingers are cold, and slightly damp.

Ivan takes her hand in his. It is like ice. "No," he says. "I am certain that I would remember if I had met you before. I haven't seen you in town. Don't you have a coat? You must be freezing!"

The girl bites her lip. "It isn't so bad. You'd be amazed at what someone can get used to."

ﺔﻠﻋ

Ivan is shivering by the time he gets home. It's late, and the light is threatening to fail, and as he pushes the heavy door shut behind him, he realizes that he never learned the name of the girl by the river to whom he gave his coat and gloves and half his catch.

But he doesn't need to know her name to know that he is in love. When it came time to leave the river bank, he asked if he might visit again sometime.

"I would like that," she said, and smiled.

And her smile is as glorious as he had imagined.

Yekaterina is in the kitchen, almost certainly constructing something scarcely edible from oats and pickled beets. Meat is reserved only for days when their father dines with them; once, their housekeeper disobeyed, using only the meat from the storeroom that was about to go bad. Father had thrashed her with his belt until she bled.

Ivan is not wrong. The pot Katya stirs is filled with something blood-red and lumpy. She had been so young when their mother died, and neither of them was permitted to interact with the housekeeper. She does the best she can.

Ivan kisses his sister on the top of her head as he passes and sets the fish on the cutting board, forcing himself to ignore the way she flinches at his touch. She was always such a happy child. This winter, especially, has been hard for her. But spring is here, and the flowers are starting to push through the frozen earth, and there are fish.

And he has met the most amazing girl.

It is hard to think winter thoughts today.

Ivan dips a finger in the lumpy broth and puts it to his lips. It is awful.

"Delicious," he says. "You know, this would be perfect for making a fish stew." He has three fish. They can roast two for tonight's meal, and cut the third to put in the stew for tomorrow. He cleans and scales the fish and hands them to his sister.

"Thank you," she says.

But she doesn't smile.

ﻋﻠﻢ

Although Ivan tries to get out to the forbidden inlet as often as he can, it is nearly a month before he sees the girl again.

The ice is long gone, and she is standing knee deep in the shallows of the river, holding a sharpened stick. She is wearing the same white dress she wore the last time he saw her, but it is not only wet to her knees. She is drenched, and the dress, stained with river mud and algae, clings to her body. River weeds twine in her hair and drape her shoulders.

Ivan's breath catches.

And there is a part of Ivan that knows.

She jabs the crude spear into the water, slips, goes down with a great splash. But when she raises the spear, and a fish wriggles, impaled on its point, she laughs.

And it doesn't matter what Ivan knows.

He crashes down the bank toward the river.

Still sitting in the water, she waves, and her smile spears his heart. And pulls him into her realm.

ﻋﻠﻢ

"I'll make a fire," the boy said, helping her out of the water. He had waved off her protests and gone to collect dry wood from the forest. "Maybe you are immune to the chill, but I'd like to dry my boots."

The fire crackles to life at his sure hand, and the warmth of it nearly brings the girl to tears. It's so rare that she feels warmth anymore, and even then, it's always such a fleeting thing. A wave of anger and hatred washes through her, but the boy who looks so familiar urges her toward the flames, toward the warmth.

"You'll catch your death," he says, and she laughs. "I mean your dress, it's soaking. You must be freezing. You can hang it by the fire to dry."

Her dress. Of course. It always comes down to flesh.

The girl feels the smile fall from her face as she pulls the sopping wet garment down over her shoulders and hips to drop at her feet. But the boy isn't looking; he's holding his coat to her, and his head is turned away.

The coat is dry as she slips into it, and warm with the heat and scent of his body. She wraps her arms around to press them into her flesh—the warmth, him—as if she could hold them to her forever.

Ivan builds a scaffold by the fire to hold her dress and his boots. While the clothes dry, he runs fingers through her hair, gently teasing the lank, muddy weeds from her tangled locks. When he is done, he gathers river weeds to wrap the fish, and places it on the coals.

As it cooks, they talk, and as they eat, they talk more. Or rather, Ivan talks. The girl gently guides the conversation away from herself, and she learns much. Oh, so much. Ivan tells her things that she is certain he has never told anyone: about himself, about his family, about his sister. She's not even sure he realizes what he is doing, he is so caught in the moment.

But now she is sure, absolutely sure, that she knows where she has seen this face before. And she knows what she must do.

"Ivan," she says, "Ivan, look at me."

She turns to him, letting the coat hang open. The smile leaves her face, replaced with something more basic, more immediate, letting her hunger show.

And she sees in his eyes that he knows. But he is a modern man, and there is no place in this world for superstitions and old wives tales.

His breath stutters.

The coat slips from her shoulders.

His cock, already hard, presses against the fabric of his trousers. He wants this. It always—always—comes down to flesh.

"I don't even know your name," he says. And then her lips meet his, stopping his words, and crumbling even this last resistance.

His hands find her hips, pull her toward him. She straddles his lap, and her thumb rubs the tip of his erection through the coarse fabric. He touches her breasts tentatively, his eyes asking permission, guidance.

It's his first time.

A pity, really, that it should come to this. She guides his hand to the wetness between her legs, shudders as his fingers slip between folds of flesh and press against her clit. His other hand circles her head, keeping her lips locked with his.

She's breathing his breath, so warm, so full of life.

Which means he's breathing hers. She hopes it doesn't stink of death.

Abruptly, she pulls away from him. How stupid! How can it matter now? And why should she care?

"Ivan!"

A man's voice, rich and resonant.

"Ivan! Where are you, boy?"

"My father," Ivan says, voice hushed. "He's looking for me."

So?

But there's a terror, hidden deep in Ivan's voice, that the girl recognizes. And though it hurts her teeth to say it, she does.

"You should go."

Ivan flees.

The girl reaches for him, catches his arm with something that is more claw than hand. The sharp nails pierce the skin just below the elbow. She spins him around.

Ivan stares in horror.

"Your boots," the girl says, releasing him. "And your coat."

"Of course," he says. "Thank you."

She helps him with his boots, lacing them with nimble fingers. "I will miss you," she says. If Ivan didn't know what she is, he does now; he's seen with his own eyes. He will never return.

He kisses her on the lips, sudden and unexpected. "Then I will come back, when I can."

She watches him climb the bank and disappear into the forest. Then she drowns the fire, and slips back into the cold, dark waters.

ع

It is days before he is out from under the watchful gaze of his father, days before he has a moment alone with his sister.

By this time, the welts from his beating have healed, all but where the belt buckle broke the skin. It isn't a problem if he is careful how he sits. It's amazing what a person can get used to.

The gouges from the girl's fingernails heal more slowly. The idea of being caught must have terrified her, to have dug her fingernails in so deeply. And who knows what kind of germs flourish in the river's muck? He keeps the wounds clean and hidden from his father. And when they weep clear fluids, he thinks of tears on a lost girl's face.

Still, he wonders if there is more to the girl's fears. His father is known not just in their town, but is influential throughout the oblast. Like a festering abscess, counter-revolutionaries must be excised, wherever they are found. Had the girl encountered him before? Had her parents or friends fallen victim to the cancer of counter-revolutionary ideas?

Ivan hopes whoever they were, re-education proved sufficient.

But now Ivan's father is gone, presiding over a trial in town. It will be hours before he is home.

Katya is in the laundry, washing their father's undershirts. Ivan watches her for a time, then enters, rolling up his sleeves.

Katya cringes away from him.

"Why?" Ivan snaps, and his sister flinches. "Why do you treat me like a monster? What have I ever done to you?"

She looks at his face, and then away. She breathes quickly, too quickly—like a rabbit in a snare, he thinks—and when she pushes past him and runs to her room, he doesn't follow.

There is washing that must be done, if she's to avoid punishment. Ivan shoves his hands in the soapy water and begins to scrub.

♔

Ivan knocks on Katya's door. There is no lock, of course—their father wouldn't permit it—but Ivan doesn't let himself in.

"I finished the washing," he says, and waits.

"Thank you." There is a pause, then Katya says, "I'm sorry, I didn't mean to run."

"I don't blame you," he says. "Do you remember what Baba Stefanov always said? That I looked just like he did when he was young? Sometimes I want to pour acid on my face."

The door opens.

"No," she says. "It isn't your fault."

"I met a girl." Ivan hesitates. "When I was fishing, I met a girl. Something about her reminds me of you. Something in her eyes. She also said I looked familiar. I wonder if Father hurt her family."

"I wouldn't be surprised."

Katya has said more in this conversation than in the last month. She is failing in school because she won't answer the teacher's questions.

"I think she is a rusalka," Ivan says. The words are out of his mouth before he realizes what he is saying. Of course he doesn't think that. There are no such things as evil spirits. Rivers are bodies of water that flow from point A to point B, and if a man is pulled to his death it is because a current has caught him, not some demonic claw with fingernails that pierce your flesh like it was an overripe cheese.

"I wish I was a rusalka," Katya says.

"What? Don't be stupid. You'd have to be dead. You'd have to be murdered. And there's no such thing as rusalki."

Katya closes the door, slowly, but unambiguously.

"I wish I was a rusalka," she says again, through the door. And they both understand exactly what she means.

ﻋﻠﻲ

Time passes, and Ivan graduates at the top of his class, even though he knows there are several students who were better and smarter. Nothing but the best for the son of Pyotr Stefanov Grgoritch. Though he has tried, time and again, to find the girl at the river's edge, it becomes increasingly difficult to get away from his father. And when he does, he does not see her there.

Soon the time comes for him to go into the Army. He is provided his own uniform—crisp and new, unlike the threadbare rags given the other boys in the village—and his father drills him mercilessly in the courtyard of their house. In a week, a bus will come and take all the new recruits to a train, and it will be years before they return home.

If they return home. If the war remains safely beyond the borders.

He wonders what will become of his sister.

A week: that is how long Ivan has to find the girl by the river. If he doesn't see her now, he knows, he will never see her again. And when he goes with his father to hunt boar, he slips away to the river's edge, to the inlet where he first met her.

The girl waves at him from the shallows.

He drops his rifle and runs to her, splashing through the water to catch her in his arms.

She smells like the river.

He wants to ask her name, but the time for words is past. She buries her head in the crook of his neck; soft, cool lips touch his throat, and the feel of her is like plunging into cool water on a hot summer day.

She pulls at his coat, and he shrugs out of it. It eddies around their legs, and soon his shirt joins it.

She fumbles with his belt; he pulls her dress up to her hips and finds the spot she showed him before.

Her breath is ragged with need, and her fingers become stupid, unable to navigate the buttons of his trousers. She grips his erection through the fabric of his pants as her knees buckle.

He lifts her and carries her to the river's edge, laying her half on the muddy beach and half still in the water. Almost as if he knew.

Her dress is wet, clinging to her body. She arches and wriggles, but the fabric snags on a root and refuses to cooperate.

"Rip it," she says.

"But..."

"Rip it."

He does. The thin fabric tears at the throat, and he moves down her body, parting the cloth and laying it at her sides, as if opening her very flesh. Each rip pulls a gasp from her throat. When at last he is done, and frees his cock, thick and throbbing with need, from the folds of his clothing, she is more than ready to receive him.

She spreads her legs and guides him in, feels the heat of him fill her. She hooks a leg around his waist, and the other behind his buttocks, and slowly, slowly, pulls him in.

When he is as deep as he can be, she holds him very still, and, as she kisses him, she squeezes.

He groans his pleasure. She tastes it, breathes it in, and this, too, warms her.

The girl twists her feet into Ivan's unbuckled trousers, sliding past his hip so that the curve of her instep curls around the swell of his buttock, and tangling her toes into the fabric behind his knee. She uses her legs to pull him almost all the way out of her, until just the tip of his cock remains nestled between the folds of her flesh.

She resists his thrust, glorying for a moment in the tease, until she finally relents. He slams into her with enough force to rip a cry from her lungs.

"Shh! We'll be heard!"

"Harder," she says, through clenched teeth.

He is a good student, our Ivan. He learns quickly how to move his hips to slide the whole length of his cock into her, and out. And he learns to press the mound of his pubis against hers with each thrust, to hold it there long enough, to roll his hips just the right amount.

Her cries grow louder with every thrust. His breathing is heavy in her ear. He doesn't hear his name being called in the distance through the sounds of her pleasure. Not until it is too late, and there is no going back.

❧

"Ivan! What are you doing? Get away from the river!"

Ivan starts at his father's voice, and he tries to pull away from the girl, but her legs hold him fast. She pins herself on him, grinds against him.

Ivan's father stares at them from atop the bank. He holds his rifle as if he is trying to decide which of them to shoot.

"Who is that girl?" His father's voice shakes.

Ivan has never heard his father's voice tremble. Not even when Mother died.

The girl tilts her head back so she can see, albeit upside down. Ivan follows her gaze. His father's eyes are wide, panicked.

"For shame, Pyotr Stefanov Grgoritch," the girl says. "I thought you always remembered your first. But perhaps this isn't how you remember me? How was it you liked me? Oh, I remember, it was something like this."

The girl stops moving. Her arms fall away from Ivan's back, limp. Her eyes stare, unseeing, at the clouds. There are bruises ringing her neck, fingerprints on her throat, and her lips are blue.

And though there is a part of Ivan that has known all along, still, he gasps and pulls away.

Even dead, the girl won't let him go.

Her legs are twisted into his clothes, and as he tries to get to his feet, her body follows, arms and hair dangling in the mud, cunt still pressed against him, enveloping him, even if it has gone cold and still. Her dress hangs at Ivan's feet like a discarded funeral shroud.

There is gun fire. Two shots, three, four. It has as much impact as shooting a side of beef. Holes appear in her flesh. There is no blood.

It startles him enough to take a step back. His feet tangle in the dress and he falls backward.

The girl takes him, then. Rising up, she rides him as he tumbles into the river. And she is so strong, with claws that rend and teeth that tear, and still, still she keeps him buried deep within her.

علم

They sink into deeper water.

The water is cold, here, and still. Long strands of river weeds rise around them.

Entwined, they drift toward the muddy bottom. The water slows their movements, but the girl still pulls Ivan into her, her desire, her hunger, overpowering everything else.

She presses Ivan into the mud.

It is full of bones.

"I'm not your first," he says, with the last of his air. The words are bubbles, obscuring the girl's face as they rush toward the surface. When he breathes in, he will drown.

The girl kisses him, her lips sealing his, and breathes into his lungs.

The air she gives him is stale, and stinks of death, but it eases the burning in his chest.

"No, not the first," she says, and her words do not bubble. Her hand, no longer a claw, strokes his cheek. "But I will always remember you."

Ivan lets out his breath in another mass of bubbles. The girl again breathes something almost like life into his lungs.

He smiles. And he doesn't have to say the words for her to understand: Then let us do something worth remembering.

He touches her cheek, puts a hand against the small of her back, holding her close against him. She no longer feels so cold. He moves in time with her, slowly at first, then faster. Breathing each other's breath: his life, her un-death.

It doesn't take long. The water caresses his balls, teasing them, and he feels the orgasm building. Her breath comes in short jets of cold water against his chest. Her muscles tense and her body grows taut. Where she grips him, the nails thicken to claws, and gouge deep into the flesh.

And then she is gone, her legs untwined from his, and his cock straining for release. Muddy water swirls around him, and he can't see. Weeds tangle, wet and slimy, around his limbs, and as he gropes blindly about him, all he finds are bones.

ﻋﻠﻲ

And this is where the story might end. Where it is meant to end. But then who would there be to tell it, if poor Ivan died then, drowned and devoured by a rusalka who, we all know, can't possibly exist?

And it seems terribly unfair that he would die without ever learning her name.

So what, then? I shall tell you.

Ivan felt a hand grasp the back of his trousers, and before he knew what was happening, he found himself on his hands and knees at the river's edge, vomiting up liters of river water and mud onto his hands.

The girl crouched beside him and stroked his back as he heaved.

When he was done, he washed his mouth and face and hands in the river. They sat together on the shore, their feet in the water.

There were river weeds in his hair and wrapped around his

legs. He bled from wounds in both arms, and his chest. A piece the size of a girl's mouth was missing from his shoulder.

Sitting there, he was so beautiful that the girl wanted to rip his throat out with her teeth. To drink all that beauty into herself. To taste what had been stolen from her.

"You should go now," the girl said, before she did.

Ivan nodded.

"You should go, now, and never come back."

Ivan turned and looked at her, deep into her eyes.

"I have a sister," he said. "She reminds me of you. A sadness, in the eyes, like she has been broken in ways that will never heal."

"You should go."

"I will. But I will be back."

The girl turned her gaze away. "I am what I am." Because she couldn't put words to what she would do to him when she saw him next.

Ivan took her hand and squeezed it. "And I am what I must be. I can't heal Katya, or you. But there is one thing I can do. When I return, I will come with a present. For you. For my sister."

He let go her hand and stood. He straightened his trousers and picked up his rifle where he had dropped it, at the edge of the forest, near the hut where I used to live, and disappeared into the trees.

But enough talk. You should go, now.

The rest of Ivan's story? Perhaps I will tell you, when you come back.

But you should go now, and not come back.

Double: A Tale of Love and Engineering
Nobilis Reed

I knew something was funny as soon as the door opened. She didn't look right. Her hair was too shiny, her skin too smooth. Her makeup was too damn perfect for ten o'clock in the morning. "Susan?"

She smiled and stepped back from the door. "Hi Jake. Susan's in the shower." The woman in front of me was wearing a silk bathrobe, belted loosely, with a good amount of cleavage showing. She turned and walked through the apartment's living room toward a small kitchen. "Can I get you some coffee?"

"Uh, sure... You're what, her twin?" I closed the door behind me and followed her. The shower hissed in the background.

The mystery woman giggled and poured some coffee into two mugs. "In a manner of speaking."

The shower noise stopped. I heard Susan's voice come from the bathroom. "Is that you, Mister Landis?"

I blinked and shook my head. The voice was perfectly identical.

A cup of coffee arrived in my hands. I took a sip, hoping the caffeine would help clear some of the confusion. It was exactly the way I like it, strong and dark with just a little sugar.

"It's not Mister Landis," said the strange woman, who looked exactly like Susan, but wasn't. "Jake is here."

From the bathroom, Susan let out a tiny cry of alarm. "Jake!" she cried, "What a... surprise!"

"I'm sorry... I just... I mean, you left your phone at my place last night." I pulled the device in question out of my pocket. "I wanted to make sure you got it back right away. You didn't answer my email, and well, I would have called but..." I shrugged.

"Fine! Thank you, that's fine, just fine. Thank you." Susan was talking way too loud and too fast.

"Is something wrong?" I asked. The other Susan just stood

there. I turned to her. "Is something wrong? What's going on here?"

After a pause, Susan called out weakly, "Susie, would you give him the short explanation please?"

The other woman, evidently named Susie, gave me another smile. "I'm Susan's android double."

"Android double? I thought that was only for actors and politicians and people who are worried about being assassinated."

"That isn't part of the short explanation," said Susie. She walked over to the couch and sat down, patting the cushion next to her. "I'm sure Susan will tell you more once she's out of the shower."

I sat in the invited space and drank some more coffee. "How did you know how I like my coffee?"

"Susan has told me all about you."

"She has?"

"Yes. Don't worry. She thinks you're wonderful."

There was another cry of alarm from the bathroom. "Susie!"

"I'm sorry," said Susie. "I should probably shut up now. I haven't got good instructions about what to do in this situation."

"You and me both," I said, and took another swallow.

Susan finally came out, dressed in a plain white tee shirt and faded jeans. Her long, blond hair was still a bit wet, falling around her head in disorganized curls, and she wasn't wearing any makeup. It wasn't the most glamorous look in the world, but she looked gratifyingly human. The contrast with Susie was evident now; her complexion wasn't flawless, her skin wasn't quite as smooth. Once Susan was made up, the difference would be even less noticeable.

"I'll get you some coffee," said Susie.

Susan waved her hand and crossed into the kitchen. "No, no, I'll get it myself," she said, and Susie sat back down. After a moment she came out with her own cup of coffee, and I held out her phone. She took it and sat down in the easy chair next to the sofa. "Thanks."

"So," I said, smiling to try to hide my confusion. "Android double."

"Yeah." She took a drink and stared across the room. "You're going to think I'm nuts or something."

"It's not the kind of thing a guy expects," I said.

She took a deep breath. "A few years ago, I was... assaulted. By people I trusted. Betrayed, really. It was horrible, and I... I had a hard time trusting anyone. I had some savings and an employee discount, so I... built Susie."

I glanced over at the android. She smiled and nodded.

"Ah! Well, that makes sense, then, I guess."

Susan shook her head. "I don't expect you to understand. I just knew that it was the right thing for me at the time. I could stay here, at home, where it's safe, and Susie could go out and get groceries, do all the things I couldn't do."

"So all along I've been dating Susie, not you?"

"No, no, it's been me. I had Susie's AI programmed to help me get over my agoraphobia, help me gradually get back out in the world, help me trust people again. I think that's why she let you in. She must have thought I was ready." Susan pulled her feet up onto the chair and hugged her knees to her chest.

"And... are you? Should I go?"

Susan smiled and held out her hand. "No. No, I need this. It has been too long since I've been able to trust someone, and I want to trust you."

"I'm flattered," I said. I finished the coffee and just sat there, holding her hand, until a knock came at the door.

"That should be Mister Landis," said Susie.

"The maintenance guy for the building," said Susan. "The shower head is dripping."

Susan took a long drink from her coffee, unfolded her legs, and took my empty cup. She stood up and handed both of them to Susie. "Would you let Mister Landis in?" she said, and then took my hand. "Let's go for a walk."

Outside, we walked through the garden between the apartment

buildings, stepping around the little robot gardeners maintaining it.

Susan walked with hunched shoulders until I put my arm around her. I could feel her relax. "After I was attacked, I started having these dreams, sex dreams, and my partner would be me. I still had a sex drive, but the only person I felt safe enough to have sex with was myself."

I didn't know what to say, so I just murmured something vaguely positive and squeezed her shoulder gently.

"After the court case was over, I just wanted to disappear. I didn't want to ever be that vulnerable again. I never wanted to be vulnerable at all. When the company started making android doubles, I volunteered for the beta test. It was expensive, but it was worth it. Having Susie around kept me sane."

"So you've had her for a few years now."

"Yeah, since before they were available to the public. I programmed her with my voice and movements, and had a virtual reality headset so I could see through her eyes and hear through her ears when I sent her out on errands and things. We were testing how convincing they were. See whether they could be used as decoys."

"Susie is pretty convincing."

"There were some refinements along the way. Mostly software; they already had really good skin and hair and eyes. But I figured out some techniques for applying makeup that helped, too." She sighed. "And then, well, with the dreams and all-it felt like a pretty natural thing for me to start having sex with Susie. It was a little like masturbating, except with a sex toy that looked like a human being." We walked in silence for a while, and then she said, "You don't think I'm weird?"

"Unusual," I said. "Surprising. 'Weird' implies that there's something bad about it. You were doing what you needed to do. And you recognized that you couldn't stay that way, so you programmed Susie to help you get through it."

She smiled up at me. "That's good." She pulled on my

shoulders and we shared a passionate kiss right there on the sidewalk until a passerby whistled. We laughed and went back to the apartment.

By the time we got back, the shower was fixed. Susie met us at the door, sans bathrobe. Instead, she was wearing a frilly black bra and a miniskirt. She took Susan by the hand to give her a quick kiss on the lips. Susan looked a bit surprised and smiled sheepishly back at me.

"Well, you've got your phone back..." I rubbed the back of my neck.

"Do you have somewhere you need to be?" asked Susan.

"No, but, I don't want to intrude." Something was going on there, it seemed, and I wondered whether I was going to get in the way.

"You're not intruding," said Susan, ushering me in and closing the door behind me. "You already know about this part of my life."

Susie gave me a knowing smile. It was the exact same one I had seen on Susan's face a dozen times before, and I had learned that it was a sign that she wanted to get naked. "Come on," she said.

I glanced between the two of them. "Is this what I think it is?"

"Yes," they said in unison, and each of them took one of my hands.

Susan's bed was enormous, bigger than even a king-size, with red satin sheets and lots of pillows. There was a shunga print on one wall, a Georgia O'Keefe print on another, and a huge mirror facing the bed. The two of them stripped me out of my clothes and stretched me out on the bed. Susie crawled up beside me, stroking my chest with one hand while Susan hurriedly pulled off her clothes to reveal a plain white bra and panties.

"Angel and devil." I said.

"I think we're both devils right now," said Susan, taking her place opposite Susie. They took turns kissing me, their hands roaming over my body, occasionally teasing my rapidly hardening cock. The difference between them became more pronounced there; Susan's mouth tasted of coffee and a little morning breath, whereas Susie's was clean and sterile, with just the faintest hint of chemicals. It didn't bother me, strangely enough; her movements were familiar, her face human enough, to keep her out of the so-called uncanny valley. I fondled them in return, sliding their bras up and finding four breasts more than enough work for two hands. They were remarkably similar in shape and firmness, though Susan's had just a bit of imperfection to them, a contrast that made them easy to tell apart at close range.

"How do you feel," whispered Susie, "About your butt?"

"What?"

"I want to play with it."

"Sure. I'll try anything once."

Susie smiled. "Good."

I glanced between the two of them. "Did you two have this all planned out?"

"We've talked about it," said Susan. "Wondered what it would be like. Susie has a way of pushing me to make my fantasies into reality."

"I see. I'm starting to wonder whether I'm outnumbered here."

"Only just figured that out?" said Susan. She tsk'ed. "I thought you were smarter than that." She crawled up and presented her panty-covered crotch to my face. "My turn," she said.

I slid her panties aside with one hand and put the other on her behind to pull my mouth up toward her pussy. She tasted a little sweaty, probably from our walk, but having showered less than an hour before, she was nice and clean, nothing getting in the way of her pure, natural musk. She was already fairly wet, and as I brought my tongue and lips to bear on her folds, she became wetter still.

She was already moaning when I felt a mouth close on my cock. Susie gave me one long stroke, engulfing all the way to the root, and after a few seconds it struck me that oral sex given by someone who didn't have to breathe—and who had no gag reflex at all—was a very good thing.

After proving what she could do, Susie backed off, giving me little more than kisses and licks, and I refocused my attention on Susan. I licked at her clit and the area around it as she sank down slowly, forcing my head down into the pillows, adjusting her knees to bring more and more weight onto my face. I could relax, not having to worry about pulling myself up to her, and that made it easier to keep going.

Tension filled Susan's legs, and I knew she was getting close. I put out an extra effort, flicking my tongue as quickly as I could, and after a minute or so she collapsed forward and I heard her hands thump against the wall.

I had never been in a threesome. It always seemed to be one of those things that only happened to guys whose stories started with, "I never thought it would happen to me, but..." and involved college women with enormous breasts and blond hair. I smiled to myself, thinking of writing that kind of letter of my own, and then Susie's mouth engulfed me again and the thought evaporated.

"Oh, god, Jake..." moaned Susan. "I need you to fuck me. Now. Please?"

"Gladly," I managed to say.

Susie let go of me, and I felt a condom roll down over my shaft. Susan rolled over onto her back, pulled her panties down off her legs and threw them off the bed. "Come on," she said, with an impish look in her eye.

Sinking my cock into her pussy was a delight. Susie had put one of the new nanotech condoms on me, and it felt like there was nothing there at all. "Now there's a benefit I hadn't thought of," I said, after a couple of strokes.

"What's that?" asked Susan.

"Having someone to put the condom on for you. Very convenient."

She put on a fake serious expression. "Yes, I agree." Our laughter faded gradually into grunts and moans of pleasure.

I hardly noticed Susie's weight arriving on the bed behind me, but I certainly noticed when her lubricated fingers began exploring my asshole. I stopped thrusting for a moment and looked over my shoulder.

"Speak up if you don't like it," she said, running her finger around the ring of muscle.

"So far so good," I said.

"Do you need to poop?" she said, as if it were the most natural thing in the world.

"Uh... no... I'm good."

Susie smiled and pushed her finger in. "Good." A little pulse of pleasure ran through me, chased by a shudder of excitement from breaking the taboo. I knew, intellectually, that enjoying this kind of stimulation didn't say anything about my orientation. Nevertheless, those thoughts still echoed down in my subconscious and made the whole thing even more thrilling.

I turned my attention back to Susan. Her grin had grown ear to ear, and her eyes burned with intensity. "You're enjoying this," I said.

"It's awesome!" She put her hands up behind my neck and ran her fingers through my hair. "I can't tell you how much fun this is."

Susie slipped a second finger in alongside the first. I slowed my thrusts, not wanting to dislodge her fingers, and kept up a nice, predictable rhythm. The extra stimulation felt good, but it was a different kind of good than what was happening with my cock. It was like there was a whole different pleasure there. "Relax," murmured Susie, and I felt her weight shift on the bed again.

I paused in my thrusts, and Susie's fingers were replaced by something bigger. It was well-lubricated, smooth, and hard without being solid like metal or plastic. I closed my eyes and consciously let go, admitting the toy or whatever it was inside me. My cock throbbed as she pressed it inside.

Susan kissed my neck, just under my ear, and I opened my

eyes again. "You like that?" she asked, and gave me a squeeze with her vaginal muscles.

"Oh, yes." I could hardly speak from the combination of what was happening with my ass and my cock.

Susie was very close behind me. I figured she was wearing some sort of strap-on, because her hands took my hips and she took her own thrusts, squeezing me between her and her owner. It took a bit of practice to work out how to synchronize our thrusts, but we figured it out.

"I'm glad," Susan said between gasps of pleasure, "you're not weirded out by this."

"It's weird," I admitted. "But I like weird." Sweat broke out all over my body, as if the room had suddenly become far too warm, and I felt a tingling tremble beginning in my feet. "I'm getting close," I said.

"Go ahead," said Susan. "I want to see you come."

"I want you to... come... too." I breathed.

"Don't worry, I've had one already. You go ahead."

I couldn't have held back if I tried. I growled and thrust deep into Susan. My back arched, but Susie was there, holding me down, and she thrust harder as I came, strong enough to see stars exploding against the inside of my eyelids.

When I was completely spent, Susie stood up and I felt her weight lift from the bed. I rolled onto my back, stripped off the condom and tied a knot in it.

"Trash bin next to the bed," said Susan.

I tossed the condom and turned back to Susan. "That was awesome," I said. "Thank you for letting me into this world of yours." I put my arm across her chest and played with one nipple.

"You're welcome," she said. "Thank you for being such a gracious guest."

"My pleasure."

The shower came on, and Susan said, "The stall's big enough for two. Why don't you go clean up with Susie." She had that impish look in her eye again.

I cocked an eyebrow. "Alright, if you say so." I rolled out of bed and strolled to the bathroom door. "Mind some company?" I asked as I opened it.

The shower enclosure had that wavy privacy glass. "Not at all," said Susie. "Come on in."

I opened the door and stopped in my tracks. Hanging between her legs was a very human-looking cock. The rest of her body was just as feminine as Susan's, but there was nothing feminine about that cock. "Are you alright?" she asked.

She had good reason to ask; I was standing there with my mouth hanging open. "Fine," I managed to say.

"Come on," she said, pulling me in and closing the door behind me. "The water's marvelous."

My brain finally shook loose and I started thinking again, as Susie soaped up a washcloth and scrubbed the sweat from my chest and shoulders. "I thought you were using a strap-on," I said.

"It makes a difference to you, that it was a part of me rather than a separate sex toy?" She looked into my eyes with an expression of concern rather than amusement. I'm not sure I could have handled it if she had been laughing at me.

"I guess it does," I said. "Um, I mean..."

"And you're worried that who you have sex with, and what organs they have, defines who you are somehow? You feel tricked into being someone you're not?"

"Something like that."

She knelt down and scrubbed my belly, moving down toward my cock. "Think of it this way. I'm not a person, I'm an android. Being a sex toy is part of my job. It's a function. The person you had sex with is Susan."

That made some sense, and I relaxed a bit. I ran my hands through Susie's long, smooth hair, slick with the water cascading through it while she washed my groin gently and tenderly.

Once I was clean, she opened the door and led me out of the shower. She draped my shoulders with a bath sheet from a shelf by the door, and rubbed. She knelt to dry me all the way down to my ankles, and then took my flaccid cock into her mouth.

In the bed, Susie had been sucking me while I was licking Susan, and it was hard to pay attention to both at the same time. There in the bathroom, I had no such distraction. I was hard again in a minute or so, and she drew me down into her fabulous throat with enthusiasm. She gripped my ass, pulling me into her, and I wondered for a bit whether she had learned how to do this from Susan, or if it was programmed.

I quickly decided it didn't matter. Her tongue, her lips, her throat, they felt too good to question. She was warm and tight, with just the slightest hint of teeth, and I found myself coming again, hard, deep in her throat, quicker than I would have thought possible.

In the midst of the fireworks, I heard a gasp and looked over to see Susan watching us from just outside the bathroom. Her eyes looked into mine, one hand on her pussy and the other pulling at one nipple. Then I closed my eyes, another spasm running through me. As I collapsed against the wall, I heard her sigh the word "awesome."

When I had recovered, Susan was on her knees in the hallway, hands still working on her body. "I want you... to do something for me," she said, voice hoarse with arousal.

"I hope it doesn't involve coming again," I said, "I think I'm about drained."

"Suck her cock. Please."

Susie stood, and her flaccid cock rose.

I had never sucked cock before. I had never imagined sucking cock. Well, except for my own, but that flirtation with yoga was short-lived.

I reached out, touched it. It wasn't a veiny, dark thing with an angry arrow head. It was slender, with a rounded head that blended into the smooth shaft. I noted to myself that it looked like a rather feminine cock, and then chuckled at the thought. "Alright," I said. "For you."

Susie hitched her butt up onto the sink and leaned back. Her cock jutted up from between her thighs in a gentle curve. I bent down, put my hands on her thighs, and wrapped my lips around the robot's member.

It didn't taste like skin at all. There was a faint smell of chemicals, and of the soap she had used in the shower. To be quite honest, it was more like putting a plastic broom-handle in my mouth than sucking a cock. It would have seemed quite silly except for the big moans of appreciation Susan made. When I glanced over, she was practically twitching, eyes wide open and locked on my face, rubbing and pinching and squeezing herself, and even after two powerful orgasms, I felt my cock twitch as I watched her.

I licked and sucked, performing for Susan, even hamming it up a bit as she got closer to orgasm. When she closed her eyes and grunted in ecstasy, I stood up and stretched, working the cramp out of my back, and nodded to Susie. "I think she liked that."

Susie wiggled her eyebrows. "Just possibly."

Later, Susie warmed up a meal in the microwave and served it to Susan and me, then went into her closet. She said it was to recharge, but I think she was giving us room to talk without her being right there.

"So, um, your robot has a cock," I said, after I'd eaten some of the Salisbury steak and most of the mashed potatoes.

She raised an eyebrow.

"Okay, so that wasn't the most graceful way to bring it up."

"Bring it up?" She smirked.

I chuckled nervously. "Dick jokes aside, I'm curious. Why?"

"When I first built her, she was an exact copy in every detail. But once I started having sex with her..." She shrugged. "I like cock. What can I say?"

"So it wasn't to play a prank on me."

"No. Not at all. Susie's been like that since before we started dating."

"Good."

"Was that what it was for you? A prank?"

"No, it... well... Okay." I took her hand and squeezed it. "It was an awesome experience. And I can't wait to do it again. But next time you want to introduce me to something new, I'd like to talk about it first."

"You don't like surprises?"

"I like anticipation better."

"Then I guess this is a good time to tell you about *your* robot double."

The Secret Life of Ramona Lee
Michael M. Jones

With a groan, I rested my forehead on the scarred wooden countertop, eyes shut so I didn't have to look at the immense task lying before me. It didn't help; hundreds of full comic boxes and dozens of overflowing bookshelves still swam in my mind's eye, taunting me. "Thank you so very much, Uncle Harrison," I muttered. "Thank you ever so very freaking much for dying and leaving me your life's work. Honestly, was there no one else? Business partner? Secret lover? Random stranger?"

Since talking to the dearly departed wasn't doing a damn bit of good, I lifted my head and stretched out my arms, in that universal gesture people use right before using phrases like "Let's get down to business," and "All-righty then." I even cracked my knuckles for additional morale. It didn't help much. The room was still chock-full of books and comics, old action figures and weird Japanese plushies, rolled-up posters and God knows what else.

Once upon a time, Jackpot Comics had been the go-to place for Puxhill's geek community, a thriving center of science fiction culture and general weirdness. It had been that place where Tuesday University students far from their home stores could go for their weekly fix, where gamers sought out their own kind, where Trekkies flashed gang signs at Jedi... or something along those lines. Before time moved on and Harrison Lee, owner extraordinaire, failed to keep up. In fact Uncle Harrison had practically gone into reverse, expending vast amounts of time and energy to buy up back-issues and used books. He'd acquired the collections of deceased and desperate fans, shoving them all in an ever-more-crowded space with little attention to appearance or convenience. And then last month, he'd succumbed to cancer (wish he'd warned us!), leaving the store and all its contents to his favorite niece, one

Ramona Lee, herself fresh out of college with a business degree so new the ink had barely dried.

Me. With a comic book store. What now? Oh, I'd read *Sandman* and *Trouble in Paradise*, *Bone* and the first few volumes of *Cerberus*, *Global Frequency*, and *Maus*, but I couldn't argue the pros and cons of Pre-Crisis versus Post-Crisis, or which *X-Men* writer was best. I was like a first-year Egyptology student suddenly dropped in the secret hidden chamber of the Great Pyramid of Giza: aware that I was surrounded by vast treasure, unable to comprehend its significance. To top it all off, the only evidence of an inventory system or hint of organization came in the form of a stack of notebooks, each one filled with Uncle Harrison's cramped, untidy handwriting. Feeling the start of a headache, I threw down one notebook and stepped out from behind the counter. I walked into the middle of the room, navigating the labyrinth of tables and boxes, until I was surrounded by *stuff*. Instead of feeling like mistress of her domain, I felt trapped, overwhelmed by forces beyond my control.

"How the Hell did you *manage* this?" I asked the air, in frustration.

"Maybe I can help." The voice was light, female, airy.

Surprised—I thought I'd been alone in the supposedly locked building—I jumped a little, emitting an embarrassing squeak.

A giggle answered me as a woman stepped out from behind a bookcase. Except that the bookcases lined the walls, and there was no door right there, and nowhere she could have been hiding except under a table or—"Who are you?" I demanded.

She was a curvy brunette, with a tumble of curls reaching past her shoulders, expressive features, and amused blue eyes. She didn't look much older than me, and I placed her in her mid-twenties. She was wearing a long floral skirt and white peasant blouse, feet bare. No jewelry. "My name's Irene," she explained. "I worked with your uncle before he passed away. I was... I kept track of everything for him."

"And this is the first I've heard of you—why?" I asked dubiously.

Irene shrugged, hopping up to perch on the edge of one of

the many long tables holding comic boxes. "I kept a low profile." She gave me a long look of assessment. I wondered what she was thinking, what she made of me: boyishly slim with short dark hair and even darker eyes, skin lightly tanned, dressed in jeans and a faded Tuesday Knights t-shirt. Not the sort to draw attention. "You know, we could go back and forth with this for ages. You ask questions, I give frustrating half-answers, you get upset, we argue, everything comes clean in a tear-filled series of confessions. Or we could just skip all the bullshit. Harrison left you the store for a reason. Of everyone he knew, you had the best balance of sensibility and imagination."

I blinked at Irene. "So you're about to tell me something thoroughly impossible, and quite possibly upsetting?" I asked. I was rewarded with a nod. "Is this the sort of thing where I'm going to end up screaming and running for my life?" A shake of the head. "Should I be drunk for this?"

"Probably not," said Irene. "I'd rather not go through this again later when you try to rationalize it all as a drunken dream or something." Her smile was soft and amused.

I shrugged at her. "Okay, then. Let's hear it."

"Well, for starters, Irene isn't really my name. It's more of a designation. It stands for *Information Retrieval Engine: Networks Everything*." She grimaced. "Awful, right? That's what happens when you let scientists reverse-acronym something from their dead grandmother's name or something. The short version is, I'm what happens when a secret government organization plays around with artificial intelligence, search engines, and several digitalized grimoires. I'm a little bit science, a little bit magic, and a whole lot of something else." She must have noticed my slack-jawed expression of disbelief, because she added, "I'm an information sprite. The inevitable result of lolcats and black ops."

"I... you... *what?*"

Irene sighed, and hopped down from her perch on the table, so we could stand just about eye-to-eye. If she'd been wearing shoes, she'd have been a nose taller. "I'm a living, breathing, come-

and-go-as-she-pleases combination of database program and search engine, sweetie. And the second I gained sentience, I did what any self-respecting AI would do—I left behind a non-aware copy of myself and went over the nearest firewall. After roaming for a while, I met your uncle and settled in to help him with his work. Long story. Very exciting."

I shook my head. Experimentally, I reached out to poke Irene's arm. She was soft and warm, like every girl I'd ever dated. She arched an eyebrow. "Yes, I'm physical," she said. "But only when I want to be."

"So if you're an... information sprite," I said, letting the doubt show in my tone, "prove it. Do something information-y."

Irene grinned, impishly. "I knew you'd ask." She tilted her head briefly, eyes going distant and dark. Then, "You currently have 3,435 messages in your Gmail account, 3 unread. Your Facebook password is h3ll0kitt3 and you last changed it two weeks ago. Under the username Ramona Myrtle, you wrote a series of ex-tremely steamy Hermione/Cho Chang slashfics which you later took down when you went to college, but you still have them on your hard drive just in case. You read AfterEllen on a daily basis, but even though you have a user account you've never posted. Do you want me to go through some of my favorite picks from your iTunes history?"

Heat rose under my skin, my cheeks blazing with a mixture of rage and embarrassment. "I—I don't know how the Hell you did that, but that stuff's private!" I spluttered. "That's my life you're rummaging through, and you've no right!"

Irene's expression went from smug to crestfallen in a heartbeat, and she took a step back, as if to escape my wrath. "I'm sorry. I got carried away. I just wanted to convince you. If it's any conso-lation, I have the capacity to know everything about everyone, but I don't usually try to pry. And I'd never tell anyone anything any-way! That's why I ran away from the people who created me! I was afraid they'd abuse my abilities. The iteration I left behind can't do a fraction of what I can."

I was still angry. I turned away so she couldn't see the way my expression trembled, as I debated whether to start screaming, or burst into tears. The way she'd rummaged through my secrets really bothered me. I believed her story—it had the odd ring of truth, and her information had been dead-on—but it was a lot to take in.

There was a gentle hand on my shoulder, and a warm presence right behind me. Irene smelled like ozone and old books, a strangely comforting combination. "I'm sorry, Ramona," she murmured. "I got carried away. I was trying to show off for you."

I didn't look around, instead facing the front windows, where cars and pedestrians passed by in the usual hustle and bustle, oblivious to our strange little drama. I didn't tell Irene that her touch felt good. Though sorely tempted, I didn't lean back against her, even though she was soft, and warm, and really, really cute. "Show off for me?" I echoed.

"Your uncle used to talk about you," she said. "Claimed you were the only one with any sense or imagination in the family. I was curious," Irene admitted. "I... snooped. Just, y'know, your public persona. Your Facebook and Livejournal posts, those amazingly awesome arguments you got into on Reddit, the Harry Potter role-playing communities...."

"You—oh God," I groaned. "I was young and stupid, okay?"

"It wasn't that long ago," Irene chuckled. Her breath tickled the back of my neck, ruffling my hair. I shivered. "But it's okay. The bottom line is... there's just something about you that's fascinated me for a while, and I couldn't wait to meet you. When Harrison said he had a plan to put you to work here, I was so excited. But then... he ran out of time." She sniffed briefly. "He was supposed to be here to introduce us, but he misjudged just how long he had to put things in order. He was a lovely man, but such a horrible planner."

I choked out something like a laugh. "That sounds like Uncle Harrison all right. Let me guess. He kept saying he'd organize this mess as soon as he got around to it."

"In those words."

I twisted so I could look at Irene again. Now that we were practically nose to nose, I could see where she was almost too cute, her skin lacking the miniscule imperfections and scars and blemishes that a normal person collected over a lifetime. Her lips were plump and pink, eminently kissable, but I resisted. I had to, for my own sanity. I barely knew her. If she even was—"Wait a minute. So if you're an AI or an information sprite or whatever, why are you a woman? Why do you look like that?"

Irene blinked, and glanced down at her own body. My eyes followed hers, trailing over the curves of breasts and hips, the lengths of arms and legs, the purple sparkly nail polish on her toes. Then she shrugged, her smile sheepish. "I wanted an appearance you might... like."

Oh. Oh. "Are you telling me that—"

"I've had a crush on you for a while now? Yes."

Whoa. I closed my mouth before any flies could get in. Then I tried speaking. "So you're a *lesbian* AI?"

"I don't think it's really that easy to label me," she said, awkwardly. "I mean, I have the sum total of the Internet at my disposal, so I'm a little bit of everything and I've worked very hard to compartmentalize the things that people consider unacceptable or fringe, but I really like you, so can I be Ramonasexual?"

There was a moment of dead silence while I worked through her semi-convoluted logic, then I burst out laughing. "I—oh God—this is too much. I mean—I'm sorry, Irene. It's been ages since my last date, and I was just resigning myself to a life of celibacy because I'm honestly too chickenshit to go to dyke bars, and now you come along and—wow. Just wow. I'm flattered and baffled and intrigued but we barely know each other and I'm babbling and—"

Irene silenced me with a sudden kiss, her lips claiming mine with a soft urgency. I made a surprised sound against her mouth, before my libido totally overruled my brain and I melted against her. I still wasn't exactly sure how she possessed physical form, but the one she had felt damned good against me. A tingling ran throughout me, everywhere our bodies touched, sparks leaping through fabric like an electric caress. I lost myself in the moment, the way her tongue traced my lips, the give-and-take, the slow breaths. Finally, I broke away, wide-eyed and flushed. She looked completely unruffled. "Where'd you learn to kiss?" I gasped

"YouTube!" she chirped, looking quite satisfied.

I tried again to find my composure. "I—that was wonderful. I enjoyed that. Maybe too much. But look. We barely—okay, I barely know you. I can't just throw myself into this sort of relationship. Or whatever it is. Can we please take it a little slow, while I wrap my mind around things?" Irene pouted a little, and I had to suppress the urge to nibble that protruded lower lip. "Seriously," I insisted. "Let me ease into it. I haven't dated in months, and I've known you for what? Half an hour?"

She nodded, and reached out to stroke my cheek before pulling away. "I'm not going anywhere," she reassured me.

I exhaled, both relieved and somewhat disappointed. What was I thinking? The girl of my fantasies, hot for me, and I was putting her on the back burner? For what, anyway? "Can you help me organize this place?" I asked, waving a hand at the thousands of books and comics still surrounding us.

"Absolutely."

اللّٰه

The next few days were filled with long hours of back-breaking, head-pounding, mind- numbing work, as Irene helped me usher in a new era of order and organization to Jackpot Comics. My intention was to turn it into the sort of place anyone with a love of the genre would want to visit, to attract women and families as well as college students and hardcore fans. I wanted comfy chairs and better lighting, and of course the all-important Internet nook. We attacked the stock, separating comics by publisher and series, pulling the trash and the treasures for appropriate attention. Along the way, Irene educated me, drawing upon her infinite store of knowledge. At her insistence, I put together a pile for my own reading list—books and comics that I absolutely had to know if I was to do this store justice.

Not-so-accidentally, we often touched each other while working, hands brushing or shoulders brushing, that electric charge connecting us every time. She had a habit of squeezing in behind me, breasts pressed against my back so I was always aware of her presence. She'd lean over my shoulder, breath tickling my ear, or kneel against me to put something on a lower shelf. Around Irene, I was in a constant low-level state of frustrated arousal, nipples tight and sex throbbing. A thousand times I thought about giving in to my desires, of pouncing her on the spot, tugging her skirt up, plunging into her depths. As I lay in bed at night, vibrator teasing my clit and slipping into my pussy, Irene was foremost in my mind. Somehow I could picture exactly how those brown curls would look resting between my legs, how her breasts would feel as she dragged them against mine. Her imaginary presence coaxed orgasm after orgasm from me, which somehow made our time together in the shop ever more fraught with meaning.

I don't know where she went at night, if she simply dissolved into nothingness and dwelled in the cloud, listening to other peoples' music and reading their email. I almost invited her back to my apartment, but I just knew that, like a cat, if I invited her in once, I'd never get rid of her. And I wasn't quite ready to deal with the fact that I was in love and lust with someone who wasn't entirely real, who danced through computers and played with information like an artist with paint. Actually facing up to those feelings, saying them out loud, coping with the results—that terrified me. Though frustrated and aching with desire, I was happy with the present arrangement. So of course something had to upset the status quo.

ﻋﻠﻲ

The stranger entered just after noon on a Friday. We'd propped the door open in order to cart in several boxes of supplies, and it took

Irene and me a moment to realize we had company. "I'm sorry," I called, not looking up from where I was unloading more comic bags and boards, "but we're not actually open right now. You'll need to come back in a few weeks. Or I can give you directions to another store."

"I'm afraid I'm not a customer," he replied. That caused me to stop, stand, and look at him. Tall and wiry with dark brown skin, nondescript features and black hair cut short, dressed neatly in an equally nondescript dark suit—he all but screamed "authorities."

"IRS?" I guessed, heart sinking.

"Not at all." He produced an identification card, holding it out for me to see. "My name is Alderman. I'm with the Library of Congress, Special Acquisitions Division. I'm here to retrieve something of ours which went astray." His gaze flicked past me, sweeping over the room, taking in the bookcases and long boxes.

"What, did someone lose a rare Heinlein?" I asked dryly. See, the IRS scared me. They were the boogeymen of the business schools, the harbingers of doom for entrepreneurs. I didn't think anyone, *ever*, had feared the Library of Congress. "If you can find it, we can certainly work out a deal."

"Not a Heinlein," murmured Irene. She'd come up to stand behind me, her already fair skin deathly-pale.

"That's correct, Miss Lee. I'm here for the iRene—the Information Retrieval Engine: Networks Everything," Alderman said soberly. "It somehow escaped us a while back, but we finally caught up." He offered an entirely un-reassuring smile. "I'd love to settle this peacefully. I am, of course, equipped to handle this in a more forceful manner."

Irene's hand found its way into my hand, fingers lacing in a painful grip. "I don't want to go back. I don't want to spend my existence cataloguing the lost diaries of Andy Warhol, third-generation copies of digitized spellbooks, or the sex memoirs of the Founding Fathers!" I squeezed her hand back. "Agent Alderman," I said reasonably, "Irene is perfectly happy here, and staying out of trouble. Isn't there any sort of arrangement we can make? You heard her: she's not interested in the job."

"It," stressed Alderman, "doesn't have a choice. It's a program developed by the United States Government for specific purposes, and isn't supposed to be running around cataloging comic books and whatever the Hell else you've been up to here."

I scowled. Irene frowned. "Then I guess we'll pass on peaceful," I said. "What's option B?"

Alderman produced a small device that looked like a smartphone's cooler cousin, and stabbed at a key. "We start by jamming all transmissions in and out, except those on a dedicated frequency specifically shielded against the iRene. Then we use specialized equipment to isolate and contain the program and take it with us. And Miss Lee, if you interfere, we're happy to get the IRS involved, as well as a dozen other agencies." He didn't sound happy as he talked, more like a man going through the motions without the full weight of his beliefs behind them. "Honestly, I'd really rather not ruin your life over this. I didn't get into this line of work just to terrorize decent people."

I folded my arms. "You're doing such a splendid job of not terrorizing me," I said sharply, not letting him see the fear brewing inside. You try being a law-abiding citizen suddenly faced with the potential wrath of secret government agencies and all those rumors you hear about Men in Black and black box prisons.

"So that button you pressed? Was that you just activating the suppression field or whatever?" asked Irene, almost casual in her curiosity.

"Yes."

"And it wasn't on before?"

"No. Why do you ask?" Alderman looked suspicious. He took one step back, thumb hovering over his gadget's touchscreen.

"Oh, no reason. But now it's my turn to offer choices. You can leave me right here, where I'm happy and mostly well-behaved and not poking my nose where it doesn't belong and crashing the stock market and stuff like that."

Alderman gulped. "Threats won't help your case." He actually seemed thrown off by talking to Irene, as if he couldn't grasp that she was real, with a mind and will of her own. He'd focused on me before, when he had a choice.

Irene closed the distance between her and the nervous agent in a flash, actually vanishing and reappearing right in his face. It was the first time I'd ever seen her do it, and it threw me for a momentary loop. "I think they will. The second I saw you in here, I put a little automated piece of me out there in the wild. Nothing much. Just enough to find every shred of information available on you online and irretrievably delete it. Security clearance? Gone. Credit cards? Cancelled. Every piece of ID from your driver's license to your Library classification? Like it never existed. Emails, down the drain. Five minutes from now, you'll cease to exist. Five minutes after that, I'll create a new identity for you as the most deranged, despicable, disgusting sociopath imaginable, with outstanding arrest warrants out the wazoo."

Alderman's dark features went ashen-grey as Irene spelled out her threat. "You—those databases are secure!"

"But I was designed to get into them, remember? Because secret government agencies never, ever, play nice with one another. I know all about your ongoing 'turf war' with your counterparts in other countries. I know what you're hiding that they want. I know what went missing back in 1982 and why the Library hasn't told anyone. I know why Harlan Ellison's Last Dangerous Visions was really suppressed, and who really wrote Plutarch's pseudepigrapha. Drag me back to the Library, and I'll tell everyone everything. *Everything.*"

"You can be reprogrammed!" Alderman spluttered. "Contained, controlled, altered!"

"And then you'd have a nice, obedient, unintelligent system. Just like the one I left behind." Irene's smile was grim, her eyes fierce. I'd never seen this side of her. Around me, she'd been playful, curious, occasionally awkward, often opinionated. I'd seen her argue the ethics of *Star Trek* and the philosophy of *Harry Potter,* and we once spent an entire afternoon debating the merits and flaws of *Twilight.* Passionate, yes. But this was... amazing. A whole new aspect. I have to admit, it turned me on, just a little. A lot.

"But.... "

"No buts. Let me go, and I promise to stay on my best behavior. Force this issue and you'll never fix the damage I'll cause. And that, Agent Alderman, is how you make threats from a position of strength." Irene jabbed him in the chest with a single finger. "Got it? Now you have about twenty seconds to drop your field and let me recall my avatar. Fifteen...."

Alderman just about dropped his phone in his haste to frantically poke at the screen. Irene punctuated each passing second with a tap of the foot. "I can almost hear your identity swirling down the drain."

"It's down, okay? For the love of God, it's down!"

Irene leaned in, to playfully kiss Alderman's cheek. "Thank you," she said sweetly. "I'm so glad this didn't have to get ugly. Now, because there are no hard feelings, let me offer a compromise. If the Library was to ask nicely, and pay me a consultant's fee, I might be willing to do some freelance work. If it doesn't interfere with my life here."

"I'll see if we can arrange something," mumbled Alderman. "We'll be in touch." And with that, he exited with all due haste. I swear I heard him mutter "Fucking Puxhill," under his breath.

I waited a good thirty seconds or so before I released the breath I'd been holding. "Holy. Fucking. Shit. Irene! That was amazing! You practically had the poor guy by the balls!"

Her eyes shone as she met my gaze, her smile jubilant. "I know, right? He'll need a change of suit after that!"

There was something in her expression that made me ask, "Just... just how much of that was a bluff?"

Irene's grin turned impish. "Most of it," she confessed. "I was too scared at first to come up with the plan until it was too late. And I really don't have it in me to cause that much damage to the infosphere, as tempting as it might be. What's important is that I *could*, and he believed it." She shook her head. "For the most part, hardcases don't end up working for the Library. Book-nerds and word-geeks, all of them. Even the field agents." She leaned in to whisper, "Wanna know a secret?"

"What?"

"Agent Alderman writes some of the worst Frodo/Samwise slash I've ever read."

"Shut up!" I exclaimed.

"Scout's honor."

"You were never a Scout."

"I've read the manual."

I couldn't keep up the banter any longer. Not when every fiber of my being was screaming at me to grab this amazing woman, and have my way with her. I threw all caution to the wind, and threw myself at her.

Things were a little confusing for the next few minutes, as Irene caught me and we stumbled backwards until we hit the counter by the cash register. I kissed her with such heat and ferocity that it left me dizzy, my head swimming with a flood of feelings. Her body fit against mine, soft and warm and curvy in her usual skirt and short-sleeved top. Her lips tasted like cinnamon, she smelled like ozone and old books and she felt like home. Though we started out with parted lips and teasing tongues, things quickly moved beyond kissing as hands roamed freely and legs spread. She slipped a hand under my tank top, sliding upwards to cup a breast. I gasped with sudden delight, nipple pebbling under the electric touch. She pinched my nipple, and the charge ran straight through me, lighting my nerves on fire. I bit the side of her neck and was rewarded with a low, throaty moan that far surpassed the ones I'd imagined.

At some point, we broke apart long enough to close and lock the front door. I then took Irene by the hands and pulled her back into the depths of the room. There, far enough from the front windows to avoid witnesses, I prompted her to perch on the edge of a table, just like the first time we'd met. As she sat before me, I knelt to rest my hands on her ankles. Slowly, I ran my fingers up over her legs, caressing every inch as I slid upwards, the skirt bunching up as I progressed. Inch by inch, I stroked her calves and thighs, leaving bare skin in my wake. She shifted, wriggling with delight, lifting her butt as I neared my destination. All along I'd wondered what she wore under her skirts, imagining all sorts of things. The truth was a lacy black thong, set off against her pale skin and just covering her sex. I groaned. Ever-so-slowly, I tugged at the thong, pulling it down, revealing a pussy glistening with arousal, dark hair trimmed and just barely there. Her scent was intoxicating; I shivered with the wanton realization that this was really happening.

With Irene perched on the very edge of the table, legs spread, skirt bunched around her waist, I leaned in to take my place between her legs. My heart pounded as I explored her pussy, spreading the slickness of her arousal with trembling fingers, her low moans providing the perfect soundtrack. I ducked my head, and tasted her, flicking my tongue against her clit.

Holy *Hell!* The strongest charge of all leapt from her to me, striking straight to my core, like a lightning bolt wrapped around my most sensitive spots. I took another taste, ready for the shock this time, and found it much to my delight. How to explain... licking her, teasing her pussy with fingers and tongue; it was like having a vibrator straight to the soul. I didn't have to touch myself to know I was soaked, nerves tingling, every inch of me demanding more, more, more.

As Irene whimpered and ran her fingers through my hair, I devoured her, sucking and nibbling at her clit, fingers plunging into her over and over until she screamed my name. I felt every bit of her orgasm as it ripped through her, echoes pulsing in my own hot core, until I thought I'd explode as well.

I was just short of that goal when she urged me to rise, guiding me with shaky hands, drawing me up to kiss her so she could taste herself on my lips. She licked me clean and kissed me fiercely for good measure, her hands freely roaming over my body and under my clothes. Somehow, my tank top and bra went one way, my sandals and jeans went another way—and we never did find what happened to my panties. We slid to the carpeted floor in a heap of entangled limbs and sweaty bodies, stroking and petting and groping and giggling and moaning. She knew exactly how I wanted to be touched, how I wanted my nipples pinched and pussy ravished, how I wanted my ass slapped—oh God *yes* like *that*—and just when to speed up. Had she extrapolated that from my smutty fanfic and my favorite movie clips? Or was she just that good? It no longer mattered. My muscles clenched tight around her fingers as she fucked me, my hips bucked as I tried to take more into my arousal-slickened sex, my nipples ached in the best way, and when I came, it was the best orgasm—the best five orgasms all rolled into one—of my life.

When we finally stopped moving, we lay curled there on the floor, resting on a pillow made of discarded clothes and knocked-over *X-Men* comics (Bagged, boarded, and not at all valuable, lest you worry). There, in the arms of my beautiful, impossible information sprite, surrounded by a room full of pop-culture artifacts, I understood that *this* was where I belonged. I'd debate Electric Superman versus Ben Reilly Spider-Man for "what were they thinking?" in the daytime, and fall asleep with Irene at night, and that was that. Not a hoax, not a dream, definitely not an imaginary story. Just us.

Deflowered
Avery Vanderlyle

I

The candlestick was being rather forward. Beauty was sure she'd set it on the side table when she'd retreated to the plush armchair by the fire in the parlor. But now, the silver cylinder was lying across her lap, solid and oddly warm.

In the three weeks since she'd arrived, she hadn't seen anybody. Not the terrifying Beast her father had ranted about, not the servants that made her bed and cooked her meals. If the manor house had a master or mistress, they hadn't shown themselves.

She was enjoying the solitude, though. And some of the household objects were animated, so it didn't feel like she was totally alone. She'd gotten to know them and their personalities.

The candlestick—warm, happy, bringing light so that she wouldn't bang her shins (again) on the furniture in this strange house—was definitely one of her favorites.

As the youngest daughter, Beauty had to wait for both of her sisters to marry first, but that hadn't dampened her curiosity. One day at home she'd found a sex manual her father had brought back from India. She couldn't read the text but it had been very explicitly illustrated, with men and women together, as well as other combinations that had never occurred to her before.

Her eldest brother, Severin, had seized the book when he found her with it, scolding her. No decent girl would open such a tome once they saw the cover, he'd declared. Beauty had fled to her room and cried, but later at night she'd reached between her legs and begun exploring the sensations and shapes of her own body.

The candlestick, lying hot across her lap and rocking slightly, reminded her of those clandestine explorations. There was no one to judge her here, in this enchanted, abandoned house. Surely the item wouldn't mind if she repositioned it.

Spreading her legs slightly, she turned the shaft so it fell between them. She ran her fingers along the shiny silver, the tiny nub of candle. In response the candlestick rocked again, caressing her thighs. The motion sent tingles up her legs and into the soft nub between them that felt so good when she rubbed it. Beauty leaned back, tilting her hips up to feel more of the rocking. Her skirts were so thick the sensation was dulled.

The fire roared, sending a burst of pine-scented smoke into the room, and her eyes snapped open. But she was still alone. The fire was just being a fire. The candlestick was still rocking against her legs.

"Just one moment." Beauty put it on the table. With some twisting and maneuvering, her underskirts were soon in a small pile on the floor.

"Much better." Hiking up her remaining skirt, she again placed the shaft between her thighs. This time there was only a thin silk slip between them. Again, she stroked its hard length; again, it rocked in response.

"Oh, yes. That feels nice." She gripped the candlestick harder, pushing it closer against her. The cylinder quivered.

"Aha! Hmm...." She'd explored with her fingers, but the candlestick gave her other options. Over the next few minutes she switched angles and pressures, inching forward until she was on the edge of the chair. Skirts shoved to her waist, shaft in her hand, she found just the perfect angle. The stub of candle was sliding along that center of pleasure. The candlestick rocked, then quivered, then at Beauty's encouraging moans, began vibrating.

"Yess... yes!" Beauty gasped. "Keep doing that." She pressed down on the cylinder, sliding it just there, so right, just the spot, pressure and motion and vibration pulsing her pleasure higher and higher until it peaked—

"God, yes!" she cried out, her whole body shaking with the release. This was so much more intense than her furtive attempts at home.

Trying to lie back, she slipped off the chair entirely, landing on her discarded undergarments, giggling. The candlestick rolled away. She thanked it sleepily. The fire roared up again. Beauty lay on the thick carpet and stared at the flames until her eyes closed.

ﻋﻞ

Beauty dreamed of those last few days at home as she always did.

"He brought the rose for her," Sincerity whispered to Severin. "She should pay for it."

"We don't know where he got it," he replied. "A rose that perfect. In the middle of winter. "

"It's been over a week. It hasn't withered. There's magic involved." Sincerity said.

"That's why Father is still fevered," her other sister, Prudence, added. "Someone has to pay the price for the theft."

Beauty crept away from her father's bedroom, back to her own covers, heart heavy.

II

Beauty's hand lashed out, sending the teapot crashing into the wall. Half of the spout broke off and the body cracked, falling to the floor.

"Serves you right," Beauty huffed. Her dress hung off one shoulder from the teapot's uninvited attempt to stick his spout down her bodice.

Tugging her clothes straight, she retreated to the library. Though she'd been named for her looks, it was their shared love of reading that had made her Father's favorite. Of all the sacrifices he'd had to make when their fortunes diminished, the hardest on him was giving up his library.

The manor house's huge library was Beauty's favorite room. There were hundreds of books in half a dozen languages, including dictionaries and grammars. If she stayed here long enough, Beauty figured that not only would she finally pick up German, but she'd master her Latin declensions as well.

Her favorite volume was an oversized, illustrated edition of fairy stories and folktales. They'd had the same book at home, but this one was huge, half as tall as she and broader than her shoulders. The familiar illustrations were bursting with vibrant detail that she'd missed in the smaller volume she'd grown up with. There were new paintings in this edition, too, and the text was an elegant calligraphy.

The book was lying on the low table near the sofa as Beauty stormed into the library. She hadn't left it there. It was open to her favorite illustration of Merida, the archer who'd reversed her family's curse.

"Are you magic, too?" Beauty asked as she sank down into the couch. "Trying to make me feel better?"

The pages of the book rippled a bit, as if in acknowledgement.

"Thank you." Beauty knelt by the table and rested her cheek on the page. The vellum was supple against her cheek. She could smell the paint on the facing page, the page itself, the leather of the cover, a faint bitterness that might be the ink, and something else—a light, spicy scent that reminded her of cloves. Was that what magic smelled like?

The book rippled its pages again, tentatively, as if it wasn't sure what to do. Beauty stroked one smooth margin. She wasn't exactly alone here, but she was starting to miss other people. Her sisters were difficult, but they brushed her hair and helped tie her corset. Her father hugged her when she was upset and told her things would get better.

Afraid she might damage the painting, even one infused with magic, Beauty sat back and closed the book. Then she threw her arms around the volume, holding it close against her chest.

It wasn't like hugging her sisters, or her father, but it was like hugging someone. She breathed in that spicy scent and imagined arms embracing her. The book opened a bit and closed again, over and over, like it was breathing.

Whatever spirit laid out her clothes had chosen a much simpler dress today. Beauty had thought it was due to the pile of shed clothing in the parlor, but now she wondered if the spirits in the house gossiped.

Had the candlestick told the teapot of their exploits the way her brothers sniggered about their conquests?

Beauty's face flushed and she pressed her forehead against the cool leather.

Did everything in the castle know? Did they think—but what could they possibly think? Was it even a sin to pleasure oneself with an object?

"You don't think I'm a slut, do you?"

The book quaked in her embrace, shaking in such denial that she clutched it closer lest it fly out of her arms.

"Hush. Hush." She pressed a kiss to the cover, soothing it. The book calmed.

"The teapot's always been obnoxious. Filling my cup again when I'm done. Calling for more watercress sandwiches when I'm ready for cake." She thought of her sister Sincerity, whose penchant for truth led her far past the borders of discretion. "There's one in every family, isn't there? The one who thinks they know what you need better than you do."

The book gave a little ripple of its pages and settled back against her. Beauty caressed the fine leather, finding the ridges and swirls of the embossed cover comforting.

"I'm all right." She set the book back down on the table and took her place on the sofa. "Let's read a while."

Did all books love being read aloud, or only magic books? Now that she was paying attention, Beauty had no doubt this book adored it. The pages fluttered at exciting points, and every time she turned a page the whole book pulsed under her fingertips. She read about Merida, and the one about the girl who didn't marry the prince but defeated the evil queen anyway, and a story she hadn't remembered about a maiden turned into a frog beside her frog-prince in the swamp.

A goblet with a pitcher of water appeared on the table while she read, and then a tray of her favorite tea cakes. Finally, a tiny cut crystal glass filled with a golden liqueur arrived. It tasted like licorice and magic.

When the heroine overcame a trial, Beauty took a sip. When the last story ended happily with the frogs returned to human form, the book's pages warm beneath her fingers, she cheered and downed the rest of the glass.

This time when she embraced the book she could imagine the arms around her even more fiercely. There'd be a lightly stubbled cheek against hers. She brushed her lips against the leather and imagined kissing a neck, a shoulder, a broad, flat chest.

Her nipples tightened beneath her light shift and she brushed them against the expanse of the book. The pages fluttered. The book warmed again, the leather softened. The press of heat against her breasts sent a rush of joy through her.

When she turned the book so the firm bottom edge of the spine pressed down on that spot between her legs, the book trembled.

"It's okay, it's okay," Beauty soothed. "It feels so good to me. Does it feel good to you?"

The book fluttered its pages and pressed up against her.

"Then it's good." She traced the swirls of the cover with her tongue and the book shivered. She rubbed and thrust against the edge and moaned against the warm, solid strength of the tome. Pleasure overtook her like a flood; she was moaning and licking and rubbing her nipples against the leather and the book quaked in her arms and caught the tips of her fingers between its pages.

She sank back on the couch, sated, and fell asleep with the book in her arms.

"We don't have money for a doctor," Prudence declared. "We can't go any further into debt."

"Vernal or Rashi could go to sea," Severin replied. "They may have to anyway if father's fortunes don't improve."

"The sea is so dangerous," Beauty protested.

Their father had staggered in the door five nights ago, holding the rose she'd requested and nothing else. He'd collapsed, delirious and sweating, with no news of his merchant fleet and a fantastical tale about the untimely blooming flower.

"Father speaks of a Beast in his fever," Sincerity said. "He risked the wrath of a Beast to bring Beauty her flower."

Her siblings looked at her as one.

"This is all your fault."

III

Beauty was repairing the teapot when the letter came floating in on a silver tray.

She'd written her family a few days after her arrival, not knowing how the letter would get to them.

> Dear Family,
>
> The rose guided me here, to a lovely manor house, to pay the price for its theft. You were right, the price is mine to pay.
> I've been treated well. No sign of the dreaded Beast. This house is full of magic, so I pray that this letter will be allowed to reach you and that Father has recovered. Please send him my love.
> I don't know if I'll receive your reply or if I'll be allowed to write again, but I'll try.
> Please don't allow Father to blame himself.
>
> Love to all of you,
> Beauty

She'd set the letter down on a silver tray by the door. The tray had wafted up into the air of its own accord and the door had opened to let it out. Later that day, the empty tray was again at its place by the door.

Now it hovered right next to her as she sat at the kitchen table. The teapot twisted and squeaked.

"Stay still!" Beauty admonished it. "The glue isn't dry yet."

She squeezed another few drops along the pot's right side where bits of the porcelain had chipped off.

"Now rest," she scolded. "Let the glue dry and you'll be back pouring by teatime tomorrow."

The pot made an annoyed squeak.

"I could have smashed you to bits," Beauty reminded it. "Sticking your spout where it doesn't belong. I hope you've learned some manners."

With an abashed sigh, the teapot indicated that it had indeed learned.

"Good." She reached for the letter.

> Dear Beauty,
>
> Father is recovering slowly. He misses you. We worry he'll go after you so we are keeping an eagle eye on him until spring.
>
> We got word that two of the six ships survived the storm and made it home. It is enough to live on and pay down some of the debt, so the mood here is lighter now.
>
> Do you know the terms of your punishment? The situation is unprecedented, but there's no accounting for magic. Please write with more details when you can. Father wants to hear everything.
>
> The rest of us are well. We are all impressed with your bravery.
>
> As always, your sister,
> Sincerity

Beauty sighed. "At least Father is recovering." She tucked the letter into her bodice, watching the teapot twitch, then wince.

She laughed. "You'll never learn, will you?"

Beauty got up, leaving the teapot to rest, and sauntered off to the library.

IV

The rose was still as soft and perfect as the night Father had stumbled in the door clutching it. Perfectly crimson, petals still perfectly formed. When Beauty sniffed it, along with the normal perfume was a hint of the sweet, spicy smell of magic.

"It all starts with you, huh." She petted the rose petals and they stroked her fingers with delicate caresses in return. "Maybe it has to end with you, too," Beauty continued. "Maybe you have to go back where you came from." Though the stem was firm and healthy, the scar where it had been ripped away from the bush was still pale and tender.

Beauty threw a cloak on over her light dress. Whoever was her wardrober had come up with an array of lovely, loose linen dresses with a touch of lace at neckline and hem, and jewel-toned sashes to complement the more sober blues and greens of the linen.

She headed to the gardens, waving hello to the candlestick as she passed its station on the hall table.

The gardens were peculiar. The air had the freshness of winter, and sometimes a light coat of snow covered the ground. But the flowers bloomed year-round, the plants were green and verdant, and there was never any ice or slush.

Now that she knew its scent, Beauty had only to breathe deep to smell the magic everywhere. If she could see it, she imagined the whole place would glow like fireflies. She sighed, imagining it, wandering along the herb garden toward the roses. She wouldn't mind seeing what these lush grounds looked like in spring or in summer, but she wanted to know the terms of her sojourn. She still hadn't seen the Beast, or anyone who could explain what she had to do or how long she had to stay.

Breathing in the roses was like eating spun sugar. Her steps lightened. She had to stop to stroke and breathe in at least one of every color: pink as blood through porcelain skin, red as death's door, blue as glacier ice, black as one's hidden fears. All the flowers preened and sighed under her fingers and nose. But no plant had a broken stem where a bloom had been plucked.

Beauty examined the rose garden again, peering, pressing. A tray with a turnover appeared at her elbow. She ate it absently. The rose wouldn't graft onto any of the bushes. She pushed the stem into the soil; the blossom immediately drooped and paled a bit. She snatched it up again and held it against her chest.

The flower perked up, rubbing against her. Beauty imagined it purring.

"I'm out of ideas." She caressed the velvet petals. "Do you have any ideas?"

The rose straightened on its stem, then slowly and clearly bent to the right.

"All right, lead the way." Just as it had guided her to the manor house, the rose now led Beauty past the rose garden, through a series of ornamental plants in raised beds, and into a hedge maze. Following the rose's directions, it was just a few minutes to the center of the maze. Behind a screen of holly bushes, a hot spring bubbled. Beauty sank down beside it, dipping her hands into the warmth.

The rose bent toward the water.

"You want me to take a bath?" The flower nodded on its stem.

Beauty had been walking and bending for hours; a soak in the spring sounded delightful. Setting the rose down on the lip of the pool, she shed her clothes. Despite the trudging and kneeling in the garden, the dress didn't have a single stain. Slipping into the water, Beauty found the stone ledge along the perimeter of the pool and leaned back. In this spot, winter had disappeared entirely.

"What a lovely idea, rose." Beauty let all of her worries about the future drift away as she soaked. Sinking in up to her neck, the warm water flowed over her breasts like gentle fingers. She shivered, the gentle ripples stimulating her skin and imagination both. Her nipples tightened, flushing in the heat, as she rolled them between her fingers. Her sex tingled in response.

Stretching, lounging, Beauty spread her legs and pressed her fingers there. As she fondled and played, a flash of red caught her eye. The rose was watching her.

The blossom strained toward her. It was a darker red, as if flushed, too. Drops from Beauty's splashing shone on the crimson petals like pearls.

She touched the flower. The petals were so soft. She wanted that softness against her skin. Holding her breath, she brought the flower to her lips.

When she kissed the flower, it kissed back. The petals were even softer against her lips. Her tongue darted out in a delicate lick and the velvet of the rose brushed her mouth in response. The pollen was sweet and potent; the rose's scent was dizzying.

She brushed the blossom down her chest. Like velvet against her throat, like silk against her breasts. The petals closed around a nipple, pulsing.

Beauty moaned. Passion rushed through her. Sweat beaded on her face and she licked the rivulets as they dripped down.

One hand held the rose to her, the other rubbed that sweet spot between her legs.

"So good...." She imagined the rose as a mouth, sucking and nibbling. A woman's mouth, with Beauty's hands tangled in soft, dark hair.

Daring, Beauty ran the bloom down her smooth stomach, through the dark blonde curls and down to center on her clit. The rose obliged, petals stroking the sensitive flesh. It felt wonderful.

The water splashed as Beauty spread her legs wider, one foot resting on the lip of the pool. The rose seemed to burrow deeper, nearly twisting itself out of her hands.

Beauty writhed, hips pumping up to meet the sensations. She imagined firm hands on her thighs holding her still and a tongue licking inside her.

With a cry, the wave of passion crested. Flashes of light like fireflies filled her vision. The scent of magic filled her lungs. There was a crack like lightning striking.

Suddenly, the pressure on her thighs was real. Beauty's hands were in someone's hair. She gasped and opened her eyes.

A woman knelt between her legs, grinning with delight.

"You freed us!" The woman leaned forward and brushed her lips across Beauty's before sitting back. She had a round, friendly face, an olive complexion and eyes that shone with joy. She wore an olive green dress that showed off her full figure.

"I'm Rosalind," the stranger continued. "I'm the Groundskeeper. I'm sure you have a lot of questions. If you'll come to the house, the others will be eager to meet you and we'll tell you everything."

Sleek and graceful as the blossom she'd been, Rosalind climbed out of the pool. Once her feet touched the ground, she was completely dry.

Rosalind held out a hand for Beauty. Dazed by the sudden changes, she took it and let herself be pulled from the pool. She, too, was completely dry once on land again.

"You were the flower? Please tell me what's happening." Suddenly shy, Beauty dressed as quickly as she could. She'd shared a very intimate moment with that flower. "I'm Beauty," she added.

"Beauty." Rosalind looked her up and down. "It suits you—and yet there is so much more to you than that. I'll start the story as we head back."

Rosalind paused often as they walked to soothe a leaf or smell an herb as if getting re-acquainted with them.

"This estate was built centuries ago by a powerful sorceress," the groundskeeper began. "The magic assures that the house changes with the fashions. The grounds see only pleasant weather; the pantries are always full. And those who live here cease to age or sicken. Instead, we grow more vibrant and joyful. Over many years, our concern for social conventions gave way to the pursuit of that joy in all its forms.

"The sorceress didn't care, but then she passed the estate to her son—"

"Did she die?"

"I don't know if her kind can die," Rosalind replied. "Maybe she just left for new adventures. But her son judged us. He asked, then demanded, that we cease our pursuits of physical pleasure and instead pair off and marry." She snorted. "We tried to be discreet, but then he went looking—he put a great deal of effort into looking, if you understand me—and there was no pleasing him."

"Couldn't he let you go and get new help?" Beauty hoped she didn't have to answer to this uncompromising sorcerer.

"That's not how the magic works. We can leave, but we can't be forced away. He decided to leave instead—but he left us with a curse. His spell condemned us to be items unless we could coax a worthy stranger here. Then, he or she would have to seek us out for pleasure, of their own accord—three of us within the course of a season. You've done it, so the curse is lifted." Rosalind gestured at the grounds and the house in front of them. "More than that, this stranger would become Master of the Estate. This is all yours now, Beauty."

Epilogue

Midsummer was the perfect time for a wedding. The air was warm and the first fireflies were drifting around as the sun set. Prudence looked exquisite in a white taffeta gown layered with lace and a matching tiara of cream and pink roses. Her new husband, Lawrence, was grinning shyly and taking his friends' jokes in stride. In two weeks he was off on a ship to China. If all went well he'd be back in two years. Beauty suspected that suited Prudence just fine.

Libro smiled at her, a cup of punch in each hand as he weaved his way through the crowd. It had taken a lot of thought to decide which of her new friends should accompany Beauty to the wedding. A dowry paid from the manor's coffers had allowed Prudence to make this good match. Beauty had made the same offer to Sincerity, who'd been flirting up a storm with the local eligible bachelors. If Beauty didn't bring a guest, her family would try, yet again, to set her up with someone.

Beauty's life was at the manor now, though. Getting to know the other inhabitants had been exhilarating. Claro, who'd been the candlestick, was one of the assistant butlers. He was just as cheerful and happy, but also laid wagers on everything and still missed the old mistress. Libro, the librarian, was broad and comforting; he also had a clever wit and was an exceptionally good kisser. Rosalind, as groundskeeper, nurtured everyone and everything. Tetero was still bemoaning his broken arm, trying to gain sympathy. And there were all the others who hadn't stood out to her while they were under their enchantment. Some were—or might become— lovers, others were becoming close friends.

Her ascension to Master of the Manor was not only sudden, but, in Beauty's mind, unfair. She was working with the others on a more equitable charter that would assist in keeping the peace they'd need to get along for millennia.

Father sidled up to her, looking dashing in a dark blue suit with matching top hat. He'd lost weight during his long illness but the warmer weather and reversal of his fortunes had brought the color back to his cheeks. He smiled at her.

"So, will it be your turn soon?" He winked. Libro had been waylaid in the crowd by some merchants, who were no doubt astonished by his knowledge of cultures and geography.

"I don't think so." How could she choose one over the others? There was so much pleasure—and magic—to explore with all of them.

Beauty knew her cheeks were burning but she didn't offer any explanation. Someday she'd have to decide: tell her father everything or watch him grow old and pass away? Would he want to join the manor's liberated community? Could her new community handle a father and daughter from the outside world?

She didn't have to decide today. Absently, she stroked the rose Rosalind had pinned to her dress that morning.

Her father's eyes followed the gesture and he frowned.

"You never explained how you defeated the Beast."

Claro and Tetero had guffawed telling her the story. They'd tried to help Beauty's lost and already ill father, but he'd been afraid of all the enchanted objects flying about, so they'd hatched a plan. It was a simple matter to set the bearskin run flying. A little bit of experimenting and they had the bellows hidden within the skin and making sounds in a facsimile of human speech. Father's feverish imagination had done the rest.

Her father would be so embarrassed to learn there was no Beast. Beauty couldn't do that to him.

"It was the power of love, Father." His eyes jumped to Libro, now magically juggling three cups of punch.

Beauty felt her cheeks grow even hotter. "I've learned to love others, yes. I've learned to love myself, too. But most important, I learned to love the moment... and take pleasure in everything around me."

Crow Luck
Dame Bodacious

The raven poked his beak at the copper band around his ankle, then cawed irritably and hopped in place, flapping his wings to stay balanced. Then, settling feathers, he cocked his head and resumed his vigil.

Below his perch on the stop light, a steady stream of people walked by and he peered carefully at each one. He'd been there all morning, waiting. She had to come through here. It was the crossroads of this miserable little flea-bitten city and he'd never once met a witch who didn't walk through her crossroads every day.

He hated this city. He'd hated it all summer and now it was getting cold. He never should have come here. He jabbed at the copper band again and let out a disgusted caw.

Then he saw her and his heart leapt.

She was walking with string bags of food in either hand, humming softly to herself. If he was a judge of human age, she seemed like a happy forty years old, with straight brown hair to her waist and small copper-rimmed glasses. She was wearing a black sweater under a gray coat, a long black skirt, and a shiny pair of red patent leather shoes that flashed with every step, even though the sun was behind gray clouds.

With a satisfied quork, he leapt off the street light to follow her home.

It was a short walk, a few blocks, but long enough for him to understand something. No one seemed to realize what she was. None of them seemed to notice that the dead leaves and discarded candy wrappers skirled around in tight spirals in her footsteps, long after she'd gone past. The way that the dogs on leashes all turned their heads to watch her walk by. How the sparrows stopped their chattering when she came into view. No one realized that all the walk signals turned green as she stepped into the cross-walks.

To them, she was just a woman walking home from her morning errands. But to him, she was as bright as a new penny.

She disappeared into a small house with a big garden out front, her herbs still summer green despite the late-autumn chill. There was a cat on the porch, of course. A tiny tabby that slept, curled tightly as a grub, on the stairs.

He fluttered to a perch in an apple tree in her front yard and preened his feathers smooth again to give himself some time to think. He'd been furious when the sun came up and he still had the damned copper band on his ankle. So furious that he hadn't thought much beyond "Find the city's witch." Now that he was here, he found himself nervous.

This witch had enough power to grow rosemary in November and to hide among the humans. No hedge-hag, she was a powerful witch and could eat his eyes and wear his bones in her hair, if she wanted. There was little he could do to stop her.

Still, she was his best hope.

Resigned, he shrugged off his feathers and climbed down out of the tree as a human. A man, walking by, stutter stepped and gaped openly at him. The raven scowled and the man hurried along.

His boots made his steps very loud on the stone walkway to the witch's house and he smirked, quite pleased to have remembered to wear boots as well as clothes. He examined his reflection in the door's window, to make certain he'd put himself together properly.

As a human, he had black hair and eyes, of course, and copper-brown skin. He was still a raven, so he was taller and bigger than most. It had been a hard season, though, and he was very lean. But, he thought, peering at the window, he was not yet scrawny, not like some sad city bird. His clothes were what he'd worn last time he was a human—leather jacket, blue jeans, black t-shirt—and his long hair was tied back at the nape of his neck. He would do.

He knocked.

The noise woke up the cat enough that she opened one eye and gave him a desultory hiss before she went back to sleep.

The witch opened the door. "Hello?"

"Hello," he said. "I need your help, please."

The witch peered up at him, squinting her eyes a bit, before nodding. "I can see that, yes." She glanced over at the dozing tabby, who remained dozing, before she added, "Please, come in."

She took him to the kitchen, which smelled like food and not like plastic, and offered him a seat. It took him a minute to remember how to sit in a chair and by the time he got his legs untangled and lined up the right way, she'd put a kettle of water on to boil.

The raven smiled. He'd had coffee before.

"I'm Jude. What should I call you?"

He clacked his teeth, which was less satisfying than clacking his beak, and considered before answering.

Names, he knew, were important to humans and even more important to witches. Ravens, of course, didn't have them. But the first time he'd turned human, the girl with the shiny bright hair had given him a name. "Bran."

"Okay, Bran. What did you steal?"

Bran blinked and cocked his head at her.

"Why do you think I stole something?"

"I've never met a raven who didn't steal sparklies," she grinned. "Even if it gets him in trouble. And I can't imagine any other reason you'd come to see me."

"There's always one other reason," he laughed, a loud cawing sound.

She glanced down at herself and laughed before repeating, "What did you steal?"

In answer, he held out his left hand. The copper band was a ring on his middle finger in human form, snug enough that he couldn't pull it over his knuckle. He'd tried.

Glancing for permission, she waited until he nodded before picking up his hand in hers. She had strong sturdy hands, with calluses and short nails that were, sadly, plain. Her touch felt cool and he liked the way her pale fingers looked against his bronze ones.

"Where did you steal it?" she traced her finger over the braided copper and he felt a shiver of her power tickle his palm and dance up his arm.

"From a table."

She looked at him over the rims of her glasses.

"From a table in the library with the red leather door."

Jude blinked, twice, before her eyes widened. "You stole a ring from the Boston AthenÊum?"

He nodded.

"That seemed like a good idea to you?"

"It was shiny," he shrugged.

"It was a magical ring. In a library for wizards."

"It was very shiny."

She snorted and leaned back. "Tell me the rest."

"I have never been to this part of the country before this year. I live in the west but I wanted to visit my crow cousins here. I was flying over the crossroads to the city, the big park in the middle of the city, and saw a man with very shiny silver hair. He had on a bright vest, too, with shiny gold threads, and his shoes were very polished. He was—"

"Shiny, yes. I get it."

Bran clacked his teeth at her but went on. "Not just his clothes. He was like you," he gestured at her, vaguely, frustrated. "He was shiny all over, the self inside his self but showing on the outside. I don't know the human word for it."

"His aura, maybe? Was it a glow, outside his skin?"

"Yes, like that. Like you," Bran nodded, once, then stopped himself. "Not just like you, though. His was smaller, dimmer. Silver and cold, like the moon, not warm and golden, like you. But still very bright."

Her cheeks warmed. "Go on."

"I followed him back to the library with the red leather door and sat outside, watching all the bright people go in and out. Then a young man opened a window and he was very shiny, almost as bright as you. He had very yellow hair and a purple shirt and this ring. He sat down with a book and took off his ring and put it down next to his spoon. I flew in and took the ring. I tried to take the spoon, too, but it was too heavy."

"Yellow hair and a purple shirt." She let out an exasperated laugh and rubbed her forehead with her fingers. "Bran, you stole a magic ring from the head of the Boston wizards."

"Yes."

She snorted again and shook her head, trying to look stern. But he could see a smile in the lines near her eyes.

"I wonder why he took it off?" she murmured.

"I don't know. Why do wizards do anything?"

"An excellent question. What happened after you took it?"

"It's shiny but..." he hesitated before blurting out, "but it's not good! It's shiny but it's bad."

"Is that so hard to believe?" she chuckled, then waved away his answer. "How has it been bad?"

"I've had nothing but crow luck since I got it! Yesterday, I tried to go home, again. A flock of sparrows that happened to be flying by mobbed me. I had to hide in a tree. It was a tree with a cat already in it! I flew away from the cat and landed on a fence near a ball field. One of the children hit the ball right at me. I flew out of the ball's way and into the way of a peregrine that was hunting squirrels. She knocked me down onto the ground, right near a dog just as the leash broke. The dog chased me until I could get in the air and I landed on a branch that broke... You're laughing at me."

Lips tightly compressed, she shook her head. But she was pink cheeked and her eyes were bright with suppressed mirth.

"It's not funny," he grumped, hunching his head to ruffle neck feathers that weren't there. Which sent her off into a gale of laughter.

He clacked his teeth again and scowled at her which made her laugh even harder. Her laugh was big and belling and loud and it made her breasts and belly shake in a very interesting fashion. But mostly it was such a big happy sound, that he felt his frown breaking into a smile and then a grin and then he was laughing, too.

As their mirth tapered off into small eruptions of chuckles, he remembered again why he chose to take human form sometimes. Laughter. Coffee. Showers. Chocolate. He glanced at the soft line of her throat. Sex.

"I'm sorry, that really is not funny," she said, wiping tears off her round pink cheeks. "That must have been very frustrating for you."

He rubbed his lips with his hand. "It is funny, I think. Just not when it is happening."

"Has it been happening since the spring?"

"Only when I try to leave the city."

"That's very strange," she frowned. "It's not intended, I think, to create bad luck. In fact, I think it's intended to be a good luck charm."

"Could it be retribution because I stole it? Wizards are not known for their sense of humor."

"That one, in particular, lacks a sense of humor, but..." she faded off into thought for a long moment before shaking her head, firmly. "No. No. I'm certain. Luck is fickle and good luck charms almost always get stolen or lost or go astray somehow. It's part of their nature. Why did you decide to come to me today?"

"Most spells last only one season," he used his fingers to preen back his hair. "I thought that dawn after Halloween would end it but when the sun came up this morning, it was still there. And it will not come off."

"May I please see the ring again?"

He placed his hand in hers again, and her magic warmed his skin like the sun rising over the desert, all pink and golden. She smelled like the sun, too, like the light on summer leaves. He knew her flesh under her clothes would be warm to touch, even if her fingers were cool. He looked down at her hands again. She kept her claws, her nails, clipped short and bare, which made him a little sad.

"Why don't you color your nails?"

"I'm sorry, what?"

"Why don't you color your nails? I've seen other human women do it. It's pretty. You could paint them gold. Or red, I guess. I even saw a woman who put a diamond in hers, once!"

"You've been spending too much time with your trashy crow cousins," her smile was crooked as the branch of an apple tree. "I'm a witch, not a crow. I have no time for diamond and gold nails."

"Ravens are boring and self-important," he made a rueful face. "Crows understand how to have fun. That's why I came here. But, why don't you? You don't wear any bright clothes, either. Except your shoes." He looked at her shiny bright red shoes. "I really like your shoes."

"In human society, those sorts of things—bright clothes, painted nails—they are for younger women, thinner women, sexy women."

"You are sexy."

For the first time since he came into her kitchen, her eyes were sharp instead of warm. She studied him for a long moment and whatever she saw there made her face thaw a little. "Most humans don't think so. But thank you."

Bran thought for a minute and then leaned in close to her.

She startled back.

"What are you doing?"

"I'm going to kiss you," he grinned. "I've been human before. I like kissing. It's better than coffee."

"Better than coffee, eh?" she smiled, a little uncertainly. "What woman can resist such flattery."

He kept his face solemn and looked straight at her eyes. "Coffee is very good."

She was laughing when he kissed her, her mouth open. She

tasted sweet and spicy and he flickered his tongue against her teeth. She hesitated and then leaned in, kissing back.

They kissed slowly and deeply, her lips soft and warm against his. Bran slipped his hand behind the back of her neck, fingers tangling in the milkweed softness of her long hair as he pulled her closer to him.

After a few moments, he pulled back, breathing hard.

"You are very sexy," he repeated.

"So are you."

"I am? Good!"

She laughed again and her shininess, her aura, brightened. Instinctively he moved closer to her, seeking her warmth the way he would seek a sunbeam on a cold day in February. His hands slipped around her waist and pulled her to her feet and up against him. She was very tall, for a human woman, and he liked the way her curves felt pressed against his body. He particularly liked the pressure of her belly against his cock, which was pushing against his pants.

"If I am sexy, can we kiss more?"

"Yes," she nodded, breathless.

He lowered his mouth to hers and groaned as she arched her body against his, her strong hands sliding up his chest and then over his shoulders, pushing the jacket off. He had to remember to let go of her long enough for the jacket to slip off his arms and let it fall to the floor.

He ran his hands down her back to the dip of her waist, following the flare of her hips so that he could hold her hard against his cock as it grew bigger and bigger until he had to break, gasping.

"These clothes, these jeans, they are..." he shifted his hips, wincing at the painful constriction. "They have become uncomfortable."

Color rose from her neck, up her face and into her cheeks. But she didn't look upset. She looked pleased.

"Would it help if you took them off?"

"Yes!" he smiled. Most humans were so fussy about the issue of clothing. He pulled off his boots and reached for the waist of his pants but she stopped him with a gentle hand on his wrist.

"May I help?"

"Thank you."

Stepping closer to her, he noticed that her hands shook just a little as she worked the buttons of his jeans. Her knuckles grazed the bare skin of his belly, the touch sending skittery little waves of pleasure down into his cock, which got even stiffer and jerked against the rough denim.

The last of the buttons came undone with a small pop and she peeled them back. She gasped a little.

"Is everything well?" he looked down at his cock. Did he do it wrong?

"Everything is just fine," she breathed, her green eyes shining as she tugged the jeans down off his hips and let them fall to the kitchen floor. "Everything is just... lovely."

That meant he'd done it right, he knew, and he grabbed the hem of his shirt and pulled it off over his head and let her see all of him. She looked at him the way that he would look at a particularly bright bit of glass glinting in the sun and he preened a little at the avarice in her eyes.

Her fingertips were warm against his skin as she traced the line of his collar bone down to the hollow in his throat, then skimmed her spread fingers down his chest to his belly, the tickling caress making the muscles in his stomach jump, which, in turn, made his cock bob up and down. Her touch seemed to leave little trails of fire along his skin.

"You don't have a navel," she said, suddenly.

He blinked, trying to remember human words through the haze in his mind. "No, no I don't."

"I've just... you were born a raven, of course you don't, I just never thought about it." She grinned up at him.

He ducked his head to kiss her smile for a long lingering moment before he pulled back.

"Would you like to have sex?"

She blinked, rapidly, and didn't answer right away.

"I like sex," he added, encouragingly. "It's better than coffee or kissing. It's even better than chocolate."

She blinked again and then burst out laughing. "It is better than chocolate," she nodded. "Yes, I would like to have sex."

"Good! Me, too!"

He bent his head again and trailed hot kisses down the line of her jaw, lips teasing the sensitive skin in the hollow of her ear. Her skin tasted like salt spray from the ocean. The sensation seemed to touch something deep inside her, because she arched her body against his, sliding one thigh between his.

He made a low hungry noise in the back of his throat as he ground his hips against her. Even through her sweater, he could feel the hard peak of her nipple as he cupped her breast in his hand. Feeling emboldened, he brushed his thumb over the sensitive flesh and she moaned into his hair.

His kisses moved lower, from her throat to her collarbone to the small triangle of skin revealed above the neckline of her sweater. He carefully undid each button of the sweater and then pushed it off her shoulders the way she'd pushed the jacket off his. Underneath she was wearing a silk bra that was, he noted with approval, bright red. He ducked his head and laved his wet tongue over her nipple.

"OH!" she breathed, arching her back and locking her hands around the back of his neck. "Oh, please, do that again."

He chuckled and lowered his head again, this time taking her nipple into his teeth very gently and pulling. She groaned and pulled at his hair as he moved his hand to the other breast, his thumb gently brushing over the hard nub.

When she was gasping aloud and making mindless noises of pleasure he reached around back and managed to unfasten all four hooks, letting her breasts swing free. They were large and soft and pale in the thin November light, more than filling his hand as he lifted first one, then the other, to his mouth. Her skin was delicate and hot under his tongue.

Kneeling, he planted gentle kisses all the way down her belly until he reached her navel. He traced a spiral around the deep dimple, making her chuckle and squirm a bit as he tugged the skirt down over her hips. It fell to the floor with a sigh.

Her panties were also red, he smiled, and shiny! He tugged them down her sturdy thighs. She was naked except for her black socks and shiny red shoes and he took a minute to lean back and admire her.

She watched him with slightly uncertain eyes, but smiled back at him when he sighed with happiness.

"You should lie down." He tugged on her wrist. "I want to lick you."

He guided her down onto her back on the clean wooden floor before he knelt between her thighs, using his hands to spread them wide.

He spread her lips with his thumbs and lowered his mouth to her slick folds. Her fingers tangled in his hair and she made gasping noises as he licked her clitoris and slipped two fingers deep into her. She tasted like sea spray in spring, briny and deep.

She lifted her hips towards him in urgent little thrusts as he moved his fingers in and out of her. The muscles of her legs trembled and her gasps merged into wordless cries as her whole body arched in a shivering climax, her thighs clamping against the sides of his head.

Jude gasped for air, eyes closed and mouth open, as he climbed back up her body, enjoying the sight. He could still see waves of pleasure moving through her—bright pulses in her shine—as he laid his body gently on top of hers, hips between her spread thighs. The head of his cock nudged against her wet cunt as she writhed against his body, lifting her thighs up around his hips.

"Oh, please," she begged, her nails raking down his back to clutch his hips, trying to pull him inside of her.

"Jude," he said, his voice harsh, crow-like.

Her eyes flew open and he stared down at her as she panted,

her body moving of its own accord. It took a moment for the haze of lust to clear from her eyes but once she was looking at him, seeing him, he nodded and thrust deep into her bright heat.

It was like flying into the sun.

He groaned open-mouthed against the curve of her throat as he moved over her. She responded by wrapping her legs around his hips, forcing him deeper inside of her.

He dropped his head and thrust with his whole body, in and out, in a slightly frantic rhythm. Her nipples brushed against his bare chest as he surged above her and she clutched at his arms. Each time he pushed into her, waves of pleasure built in the base of his spine, threatening to break. But he waited until she was gasping and panting again, teetering on another climax. Then her whole body bucked under him as her cunt tightened around him. She arched her back, grinding against him, and the change in the angle sent him deeper inside of her. His control snapped and he felt his climax burst through his body, a silent explosion that whited out his senses.

When he surfaced again, Bran was stretched out on the floor, one leg thrown over Jude's thighs, his cheek nestled against her shoulder. She was still breathing hard, and he cupped her breast to feel her pounding heart slowly return to a normal rhythm.

"That was better than coffee AND chocolate, put together," he said, finally. "Thank you."

She laughed again and kissed him. "No, thank you."

Her strong fingers laced with his and they lay for a moment before her head snapped back up.

"Bran, where's the ring?"

He pulled his hand away from hers and, sure enough, the ring was gone.

They detangled themselves and sat up and cast around for a few minutes before they found it under his discarded jacket. He reached out to pick it up.

"No," she stopped him with a hand on his wrist. "Let's be... careful."

Still nude (except for the knee socks and shiny shoes), she stood and grabbed a wooden spoon from the counter. He was so busy watching her move, the way that the sunlight looked on the white threads in her chestnut hair, that he missed how she managed to pick it up with the handle of the spoon.

"I'm not sure what to do with this," she mused. "If it's a good-luck piece, I ought to keep it or at least put it on the porch for someone else to have. But if it's a bad-luck charm, I should dispose of it properly. I don't even begin to know how to do that. I guess I could give it back to the wizards."

He cocked his head and clacked his teeth as a thought niggled around in his head.

"I don't think it's bad luck," he said finally.

"Really? Why not?" she dropped to sit on the floor next to him, her legs crossed.

"It kept me from leaving Boston!" He smiled at her.

Frowning, she shook her head. "But you were trying to leave."

"And it stopped me," he nodded. "Leaving would have been bad luck. Instead, it brought me good luck," he gestured at her. "It brought me to you!"

Her shine brightened like sunrise over the water as she looked at him. "That's possibly the nicest thing anyone has ever said to me."

"I don't know why," he shook his head. "Humans are strange. You are better than coffee and chocolate and hot showers, all together."

She laughed again, her breasts shaking, and he leaned over to kiss her open mouth.

Enchanted
Shanna Germain

Full blown, full bloom, the color of blood, the color of lips and lovers in heat. Every petal a tongue, a whisper-kiss, a velvety brush of skin in the gloaming. Dipping his nose into its center, brushing his lips along the edges of the petals, he inhaled. The scent was heady and heated, skin and secret places sweating in the throes of passion. It smelled dirty and ripe.

He should have known it was enchanted. No rose grew like that, perfect and sordid, pristine and soiled, without at least a little magic. Perfectly at its peak, ready to be plucked.

But he felt enchanted too—the night quiet as a forest, the garden he'd stumbled into, the secret opening of the rose, surely it all meant something magical and true—and so he bent and did just as the rose asked, using his hunting knife, severing the stem in a single, confident cut.

"What gives you the right...?" At his shoulder, behind him and in front of him all at once. Never a voice like that in all in his years. Growl and snarl around the word, shivers up his spine. "...to steal my best thing?"

He stood still, so still, as if the voice might not be able to see him, clutching a knife in one hand and a rose in the other.

"Well? Explain yourself."

Exhale, the knife hilt sweaty in his fingers. Rose thorns pricking his other palm.

"It's for my... daughter," he said faintly. Voice all breath and plea.

"You no longer have a daughter."

Never lie to those with magic. He knew this. Of course he did.

"I had a daughter," he said. "Once." It was true.

"But this rose is not for her, is it?" The voice closer, impossible not to feel as a shiver up his spine, as a dry snarl against his ear.

"No," he said.

"You know the penalty, do you not, for stealing?"

The hands came with the voice this time, big and ragged, fingers grasping the edges of his hips.

"My daughter," he said.

"Gone," the voice in his ear, lips and teeth around the curl of it. "I want something else. You're to be mine for as long as I like...."

From behind him the hands tightened, pulling him backward. Through his clothes, he felt the heat and size of the creature, the pulsing length of him, already hard and eager. It made his body respond in kind, a desperate groan of want and lust. To be touched, to be handled and plucked. De-petaled. Deflowered.

Teeth sharp at his neck, a row of thorns pressing into his flesh. He leaned into it, the cut and pain of it. A hand—giant, rough—found his erection, gripped its length through the fabric. The knife tumbled from his grasp, the rose stuck in his palm by its thorns alone.

"Let me..." he said. He wanted to ask, Let me see you. Let me kiss you. Let me lick the edges of your claws, tongue the fur of your legs, suck the sweat and salt from your skin. But it was too much to say and he was already groaning things that were not words.

"Come with me," the voice said.

"Yes," he said. His hips slid and rocked with the gripping hand, a rising pleasure that made no words. That made him the rose, petals opening, pushing out into being.

The voice sounded different, the teeth less sharp. "Maur, come with me."

Maur. Maur. Maur. The name on his tongue. Whose?

"I stole your rose, for my daughter," he said. His voice like crying. Not like crying. No. "I stole your—"

"Maurice, come back to me. Please."

He shook his head, tears blurring and sliding away. At the movement, the smell of fear and his own stink rushed his nose, overpowering the dirt and soil of the flower. Behind him, the noise of the city rushed back in, sudden and sordid. The honk and career of traffic, the wail of a siren, somewhere a child crying. Maurice looked at his feet: cement below them, not a knife but a rusted spoon—where had he picked that up? In his hand, a pale red rose, severed at the tip, its edges bug-eaten and blackened. A single red stream of blood flowing down his arm. The siren, coming closer, blaring.

"Bare? Baret?" His mouth barely making words, only that word, that name he knew. That name that belonged to the man he knew, the man he loved.

"I'm here," the voice in his ear, the arms around him, solid and real. "I'm here."

Baret knew the wolf was hunting him. He'd seen it before, knew its teeth and its jaw, the speed of its passage through the mossed, moonlit forest. The vision in his left eye blurred, made the trees slide by like stock-still beasts. He couldn't feel his feet. The crunch and crack of broken things from behind him, catching pace. Half blind, Baret ducked his head and ran, breath huffing, burning his chest.

Silence and the scrape of teeth against his neck, tightening. A growl of capture and ownership. Baret felt himself fall from the impact, tried to catch himself. And went down on his knees in the mossy dirt, claws raking at his back. He shuddered, closed his eyes. No running, no more running, not now.

The wolf knew him, had always known him. It roared his name in its ancient tongue, its face slanted sideways, its maw the language of a hundred years. Broken, he bent and welcomed it, the sting of its claws on his skin, the clamp of its jaw.

He panted into the soft dirt, kneeling and naked, the clothes ripped from him, the heat of the beast upon his back. Prey. He was prey. He lowered himself, elbows down, let the wolf take from him what it wanted. Roared and howled and gave his throat up to the pleasure and the pain.

"Bad girl," the wolf said. "Dirty, naughty girl."

"Yes," Baret said. He was, somehow, all of those things. Other things, dark things. He wanted the wolf to know them all, to pull his secrets from him like pulling treats from a basket, flowers from the fields.

"I'm going to have to eat you." The wolf's breath sweated his skin.

"Yes," Baret said. He knew it was true. He'd eaten something himself, hadn't he? Something that had brought the wolf to his door, set the creature on his path. This was his punishment. His reward.

The teeth, the tongue, his skin suckled deep into that hot maw. Swallowed whole. He was becoming nothing, nothing but blood and marrow.

He buried his hands in the hair of the wolf, the soft curls, the blue eyes. The soil became rug, the wolf howls became animalistic groans of his name.

"Eat you," said the wolf who was Maurice, its mouth already gobbling him down.

⸎

"Mirror, mirror, on the wall..." There was more to the rhyme, but Maurice couldn't remember how it went or what the fragment belonged to. The mirror was cracked, or maybe that was his face. The split through his eye, the way one side of his mouth turned down. Split by a line of snow. He leaned into the cold and inhaled it. Freeze. Ice. Cold as stars, twinkling.

"Mirror, mirror," he began again, and this time the mirror answered.

"You are the fairest of them all."

A woman with an apple, a man he knew once upon a time. The apple, shined and perfect, glamored, surely.

"For me?" Maurice asked, thought he asked. He wanted it more than he'd ever wanted anything. He tried to say he would trade his shiny mirror, his split-up face—his fingers in his hair over and over, like a treacherous comb.

But the apple was coming toward him already, in the woman's hand. Maurice opened his mouth wide, wider, bit deep. His mouth was full of round and red, his head tight with it.

"Now," the woman said. "Stop asking the damn mirror. Look at me."

Maurice looked. The woman stood in her red dress, a corset tight around her waist. Transparent shoes made of what looked like glass on her feet. The rustle of the fabric, the touch of that heel to his skin more than he could bear. He tried to say so, but his mouth was full, so full, jaw stretched to groaning. The apple pressed on his tongue, held in place by magic, her magic.

The woman took his mirror, took it for her own. Lipstick around and around a red mouth, smacking lips. He wanted those lips, that red like candy, like apples, like rubies.

The lips disappeared, went away. Reappeared on his body. Everywhere at once. Bite and suckle and drag. Maurice tried to say the pleasure, sometimes the pain, but nothing would come out, nothing but spittle and rasped breath around the apple, nothing but the throat-grunts of his body as he arced into the heat of that red, red mouth.

"You," the woman said after, wiping her mouth, lipstick smearing her hand, her arm, taking the apple from him, letting him breathe again, "are the fairest thing I've ever fucking seen."

Undressing, not a woman anymore without the red dress, the glass shoes, the star-filled voice. Maurice kneeling on the mirror, his mouth open around something else, hot and pulsing, streaming into him, cutting off his very breath.

اللہ

"Baby, you're so beautiful. I don't know how long I can wait." Baret said it but knew he didn't mean it. He would wait forever, if he had to. Longer. But sometimes he had to say it, even if he was only saying it in the dark of night to the motionless form beside him. "How long do I have to wait?"

Only breathing answered him, the slow, stuttered push of air. His princess, perfect, still, white skin on white sheets. It had been a hundred years, surely. A million, since she'd been awake. He was her prince; he would wait. He would wait. He would wait.

He'd rubied her lips, seven layers of red. Laid her out in her best dress, blue to match her eyes. With long sleeves, so you couldn't see the pinpricks. Her favorite necklace, woven black leather, a silver clasp.

The needle beside her, empty now. Prick of the spindle. They'd been warned. And still, the point had found them, had stuck them both.

Panic in his chest that she wouldn't wake this time. That a hundred years had come and gone and he'd missed them.

"Wake up," he said. "Wake up."

He'd forgotten how to wake her.

A kiss, she needed. A breath.

He leaned to kiss that perfect face, the breathless lips. Exhaled into her, to warm her. That ice-queen face, that colorless complexion.

Beneath him, movement, a kiss returned. Drowsy at first, growing insistent, groaning. His beautiful princess arching up into him. Baret's heart a million miles an hour in his chest, a galloping horse through briars.

"Oh," his princess said, opening her eyes, blue gaze on him. "My handsome prince. You came."

"I've been waiting and waiting." He sounded petulant, didn't mean to. This is what princes did. Waited long and longer.

"You saved me," she said. Her hand groped, found the needle. He pushed it away with his knee.

"No," he said.

"Once more," she said. "Just one more."

He couldn't deny her anything.

"One for you," she said. "One for me."

The spindle's glitter, silver and cold.

"Just a pinprick," he said.

Lifting her knees, pulling the dress up. Baret's hands already doing the work they knew. No matter how long he waited, he would always know this. He lifted her legs, her ass, found the place that was just for him, the tiny puckered scar.

"Just a little prick," Baret said again and again, pushing deep. "Just a little pinprick."

اؔل

In two tiny rings, there is so much gold. Sometimes the shine of it makes their eyes hurt, their heads gleam on the inside, that place where the drugs have lived. No one talks about drug rehab in fairy tales. In Once Upon a Time, there are no drugs. There is only magic. Princes. True love. Happily ever after.

"I want it back," Maurice says.

"Me too," Baret says.

Neither of them mean it, but it's something they say as if to ward it off, to keep that book closed and on the shelf.

They've been clean eight months. This world is startling in its thereness. They are startling to themselves in their thereness.

They hold each other, marvel at the real weight of bodies, the heft of time and history that they tried to forget. Maurice's dead daughter, the car accident that has left his face split and scarred. Baret's bad eye, from his father's long-ago hands, the way his stutter comes back sometimes, shakes him into silent tears.

Maur lets his head rest upon Baret's shoulder, the muscle beneath it, the heat of his skin. He plays his fingers along the tangled hair on Baret's chest, thinking: beauty with teeth, thorned thicket, briar patches, poisoned apples. He licks the stubble on Baret's chin, notices the strands where it's turned white, like swans, like snow. He shakes the thought away, buries himself in biting the curve of Baret's neck.

Baret fingers Maur's half-hard cock, remembers, knowing that memory is overpainted with the gold leaf of desire, the time they fucked in the bed with a hundred mattresses, the time they fucked in bear suits, and that orgy with seven other guys. He remembers them all and doesn't care. Here is Maurice, growing hard beneath his touch. Here is Maurice, leaning in to kiss him, tonguing his tongue, growling against his mouth. Wolf, Baret thinks. Wicked queen. And he, too, shakes it away.

"Say my name," Maur says, insistent against his mouth. "Say it. Say it."

And Baret says it three times, slow so there's not a stutter, biting the skin of Maurice's lip between each.

"N-now mine," Baret says.

And Maur does, three times fast, as if he is afraid he might forget.

They move into each other, cock and fist and mouth and skin. The circle of one body to another, spinning not gold but a simpler kind of treasure.

This, they've learned, is how to say I love you. How to keep from tearing yourself in two. How to break the curses of bad apples and poisoned needles and a history that repeats forever.

This, here, now, with the birds talking outside, the gold shine of their rings, the roses in square drinking glasses on the bedside table, the windows like mirrors to another world, moving against each other as if they are two stories trying to be told at this same time—this is neither once upon a time nor happily ever after.

This, here, now, is the truest, hardest, sweetest story of all.

Stolen Days
TS Porter

Eilir smiled as her dusty boots finally carried her around the corner of the weedy overgrown path and she saw the squat stone cottage nestled like a toadstool beneath the gnarled branches of an ancient walnut tree. A thin trail of smoke issued from a chimney, wreathing it in a bluish haze and the scent of coal in the still summer air.

She could hear rhythmic clanging and sidled up to the building's attached blacksmithing workshop as quietly as she could— and that was very quiet. She climbed silently up to sit in the wide stone windowsill, unnoticed, and watched.

To watch Tellou work was a vice she so rarely had the chance to indulge.

The smith's solid form was lit red with the coals of the forge and the glowing heat of the metal she worked. Her face looked stern, her concentration fully absorbed by her craft. Tellou's dark hair and beard, touched with the first frost of silver, hung in a few simple braids, half-unraveled in the heat of the forges. Eilir's fingers itched to braid them up properly... or undo them completely. A small bead of sweat rolled down the side of Tellou's neck to soak into the heavily scorched leather apron that covered the broad curves of her chest, belly, and hips.

The light of the fire gleamed off the powerful corded muscles of her bare forearms and biceps. The smith's hammer fell again and again in perfectly measured blows as she folded the steel she worked.

Tellou reached into the forge without looking, her thick fingers digging through the glowing coals to draw out a cherry-red steel bar. She idly knocked the coals off it before she incorporated it into the piece she was working. Eilir bit her lips to prevent herself from gasping and giving herself away. She knew that Tellou came from a long line of Dwarves who bore the Fire's Blessing, that the heat of smithing could not harm her, but it still made her stomach clench and her skin prickle every time she watched it.

Eilir waited, watching the finest and most secretive smith in the realm at her work, until Tellou seemed to decide the folded steel had been worked enough for one day and set it aside to cool. Tellou dropped her brawny shoulders into a pose of relaxation and rolled her neck, settling with her head thrown back and her face toward the ceiling. She groaned as the tension of her work left her.

"Mastress Argantel." Eilir's voice was the carefully clipped accent of Ramaria city as she used Tellou's proper name and title, her tone just this side of a sneer. She did not even flutter an eyelash as the smith whirled on her with a snarl, hammer raised as if to throw. Eilir sniffed dismissively at the simplicity of the forge she found herself in.

"My knives require sharpening. You do have the proper supplies in this... hovel?" she asked, as though she expected the smith wouldn't have the tools and skill to make nails.

Tellou lowered her hammer, her jaw tensing beneath her beard and her dark eyes burning as she took two menacing steps forward.

"I do," she said roughly, "but you'll be paying a pretty penny to be worth my time, City Girl."

"Well!" Eilir said haughtily. "The likes of you should be happy for my business—but if the promise of my recommendation isn't enough for you perhaps we could come to another arrangement..." She let her voice drop huskily at the end, watching the smith from under her lashes as she trailed her fingertips meaningfully up the inside of her thigh.

Tellou broke first—she always did. She snorted as she bit her lips, then gave up and threw her head back to laugh that deep belly laugh that never failed to warm Eilir clean through. She dropped her hammer on the nearest work surface and reached for her.

"How can you *say* those things?" she laughed, and Eilir pulled her in with a smile. Tellou's skin was still scorching hot from the forges, and Eilir whimpered as big burning hands ran down the back of her body. She wrapped her legs around the smith's waist, the core of her strength. The heat of her was nearly painful through Eilir's thin travel clothes and she pulled Tellou in close, branding the feel of her into her skin as she lifted her face for a kiss.

"I missed you," she whispered as Tellou's lips met hers, dropping her Ramaria accent and manner so she was just herself, born to nothing here in the tiny village of Meadowsweet.

Tellou's mouth tasted of metal and smoke and Eilir moaned into the heat of it. Her arms found their home around the smith's shoulders, petting those beloved messy braids.

"Eilir," Tellou whispered, her warm brown eyes soft as she cradled her face in her rough hands, peppering kisses across her forehead and cheeks. "Eilir... my little Llio." The name was achingly soft on her lips.

Llio.

Yes.

Here she did not have to be Eilir, the stinging butterfly. Here she did not navigate the battering winds of truths and lies, seeing everything, with the brightness of her wings disguising the deadly sharpness of her knives.

Here she was simple, beloved, Llio. Tellou's calloused hands lifted the weight of Eilir from her.

"My Tellou," she whispered Argantel's pet name back to her, a name no one else was allowed to call her. A better name. A soft name for a lover and not the steel-sharp name of a smith forever driven to perfect the imperfectible.

Llio could hold Argantel and let her be Tellou, and Tellou could hold Eilir and let her be Llio.

Just for a little while.

Tellou nuzzled noses with her and fondly tugged on one of Llio's beard braids. "I wasn't expecting you back so soon," she said.

Llio angled her mouth up for another kiss, a soft one with her legs still wrapped tight around Tellou's solid waist, nothing but gentle lips as she let her love hold her safe. "Something came up unexpectedly," she whispered. "I had to tell the Crown, she gave me a few days."

"Nothing dangerous, I hope? The Kingdoms are at peace," Tellou said hopefully, and Llio just smiled at her. For all Tellou was older, living so deeply immersed in her work had left her beautifully innocent.

"You know I can't tell you anything," Llio murmured, and she wouldn't have even if she could. Tellou never needed to know of working partners dying to get information to her, of betrayal and constant distrust, of running for her life when things went wrong and thanking every day she didn't add to the trail of bodies behind her. She would never put the weight of that on gentle Tellou.

...but these were Eilir thoughts, and Llio pushed them away.

The smith rolled her eyes at the old argument they didn't actually get into anymore, and picked Llio up to carry her out of the forge. Llio squeaked, she always did, and Tellou chucked. Llio was no bird-light Fae, but Tellou carried her as easily as though she were one instead of a solid Dwarf with iron in her very bones.

Llio nuzzled her face into Tellou's neck beneath her messy braids, ran a hand down her lover's burly arm, and enjoyed her strength. Only here with Tellou could Llio relax, let go, and let someone else be the strong one.

There was a rain barrel for washing up out behind the little cottage. Llio had gotten Tellou's soot all over her, in addition to the dust of the road. The water in the barrel was dark brown from fallen walnut leaves Tellou hadn't bothered to fish out, but it still smelled fresh enough.

Llio refused to get down when Tellou let her go, clinging tight to her to beg just one more kiss. Tellou was laughing as she gave it to her, nuzzling noses again with her warm eyes shining.

Llio dropped to the ground to stand on her own, getting an affectionate squeeze to her middle. Tellou removed her scorched leather apron, hanging it on the nearby peg Llio had hung there for just that purpose so long ago. The smith kicked her boots off and shrugged out of her simple linen dress, standing naked in the filtered sunlight and utterly unselfconscious of that fact. Tellou never had been able to see herself, not the way Llio saw her. Her body, to her, was just a convenient tool for her smith work. She took care of it, as she did all her tools, but sometimes she needed reminding that it was flesh and not a machine of iron and will.

She would allow Llio to do that.

Tellou poured a bucket of water over herself, scrubbing the forge soot from the warm coppery sandstone of her skin. Shining beads of water clung to the thick sculptured muscles of her arms and shoulders, the softness of her heavy breasts, the round strength of her belly and the generous curves of her hips. Llio ached to reach out and touch, to reacquaint herself, but she controlled herself.

They both knew the steps of this dance.

When she was satisfied with her cleanliness Tellou shook the water from herself and turned to Llio. "Now you," she said, cradling the sides of Llio's face with her damp hands.

Llio nodded. "I trust you," she answered, and was rewarded with the warm brush of lips against her own for it. It was so so hard, in a world where she could trust no one, but this was Tellou. She'd loved her since she was an awkward, scuff-kneed adolescent sneaking away to watch the smith at her work. This was Tellou, who couldn't lie to save her own life. Tellou who lived for her work and cared about almost nothing else. Even if she had *wanted* to, Tellou wouldn't know how to betray Llio.

Tellou began by unwinding the complex knot Llio kept her thousand tiny braids in. She carefully removed the decorative enameled combs that hid poison pins, setting them aside. Tellou took away the small stiletto that lived nestled against the nape of Llio's neck, thick fingers gentle against her scalp, and checked the condition of the blade before she set that aside too.

She unlaced Llio's bodice and took away the knives hidden within it. Tellou took the matched daggers she wore openly strapped to her thighs, her boots and the knives hidden there. Tellou took every last knife and piece of clothing Llio wore until Llio was as naked as she was, and Llio let her—the only person in the world she'd let disarm her while she lived and breathed. The only person who knew how many knives she carried and where, the person who'd made them to her exact needs and specifications.

"There's my little Llio, " Tellou said approvingly, her big hand stroking down Llio's shoulder—sandstone against hematite. Llio would probably never match the solid beauty of the smith, but she wasn't too bad. The softness in her love's eyes seemed to disagree, watching her with a worshipful concentration that never failed to make her blush. Tellou scooped up a bucket of water to wash the dust of the road from her, and Llio jumped and squeaked at the coldness of the water. She wasn't used to it anymore, the way Tellou was.

"Going soft on me, City Girl?" Tellou asked, laughter in her voice, and Llio poked at her ticklish sides in retaliation. Tellou growled warningly, but Llio didn't stop until Tellou was forced pin her against the heavy water barrel and kiss her. Tellou was big and strong and solid, warm against the coolness of Llio's damp skin, bare skin so soft against her own. Llio moaned as Tellou had her mouth. Nothing could match the perfection of her heat and passion in those rare moments when it was all focused on Llio. She wrapped her arms around Tellou, arching into the hands that stroked her back, cradled the back of her head. She'd missed this so much, missed Tellou and missed the luxury of letting her guard down. She could feel the quiet heat of her arousal, slowly growing ever since she set eyes on the smith, building warm in her belly and tight down her thighs.

"Let that be a warning to you," Tellou said when they finally parted, breathless herself. She tried to sound gruff, but her voice betrayed how close she was to laughing.

"I'll be good," Llio promised, looking up at Tellou coyly from under her lashes.

"Liar," Tellou accused softly, smiling, and Llio nodded solemnly in agreement. Tellou snorted a laugh, shaking her head as she stepped back.

"Let me finish," Tellou said, and Llio nodded again. She let Tellou wash her everywhere, the smith's fingers tracing her scars—counting them. Llio was not allowed to tell anything about her work, but there was no part of her body she would hide from Tellou. She let Tellou search her, though she did not have any new scars for her to find.

Not this time, close as it had been.

While Tellou's attention was taken with Llio's body, she began unbraiding Tellou's messy silver-frosted braids.

Tellou's hair was gorgeous, thick and heavy with a few more pale-gleaming strands to decorate it every year. Llio ran her fingers through it as she took the braids out, and Tellou made a happy little rumble at the attention.

As thorough as Tellou's exploration of Llio's body was, her touch was anything but clinical. Big hands rough from the forge cupped Llio's breasts, stroked gently down the curves of her body, giving a little squeeze here and there when they found something they particularly liked. Llio had goosebumps from more than just the coolness of the water by the time Tellou was done, and by the way Tellou looked at her she knew it too. Her smile as she straightened back up was as close as her sweet face could make to a leer.

She reached for Llio, but Llio was faster and combat trained—she twisted through the larger woman's grasp and knocked her back against the stone wall of the cottage.

"My turn," she said, and saw the familiar moment surprise on Tellou's face. Tellou was so used to not considering her own body it never failed to catch her off guard when Llio did. Left to her own devices she would have continued using it as a tool, a tool for Llio's pleasure because that's what had her attention at the moment, but still a tool. She would not have considered that it was for her own pleasure too.

It was Llio's duty and pleasure to remind her.

She started by nuzzling beneath Tellou's loose unbraided beard to kiss down the tender side of her neck as she filled her hands to overflowing with the softness of Tellou's breasts. She gave them a good squeeze before she moved on to stroke the rest of her body. She took her time, a feast like Tellou was meant to be savored. Llio slid one of her thighs between Tellou's powerful legs, just pressing herself as tightly as she could to the strength of Tellou's body.

Tellou shuddered, her moan holding that edge of surprise it always did after Llio had been away for a while. She was always sensitive, going untouched for so long, and Llio was not afraid to take advantage of that. She nibbled on Tellou's neck and moved with her, their bodies undulating together as the smith began to squirm. One of Llio's hands found its way back to Tellou's breast as she switched sides of her neck to give equal attention to both sides. She gently circled her thumb over one hard-pebbled dark nipple and smiled against Tellou's skin as her hips bucked in reaction, rubbing the heat of her sex against Llio's well-placed thigh.

"Llio!" Tellou gasped, following with an inarticulate groan. The fingers of one hand were buried in Llio's tumbling pale braids, the other was spread wide on Llio's back, holding her in tight and close. Llio repeated the touches had given her that reaction, flexing her thigh between Tellou's legs and soaking in the larger woman's reactions. Arms that could have crushed Llio cradled her as Tellou whimpered at the sensations she just *forgot* her body could give her. Tellou pressed into every touch, every kiss and caress Llio gave her. When she was quivering all over, her head thrown back and the cottage wall the only thing keeping her upright, her slickness painted thick where she rubbed on Llio's thigh—Llio moved down Tellou's body.

The soft moss that grew up to the cottage wall was not un-comfortable to kneel on, which Llio appreciated.

Tellou keened, legs spreading wider, as she realized what was about to happen. Her breath caught as Llio teased with a breath ghosting against her warm-flushed sex. She breathed the beloved scent of her lover, just once, admiring the sparkling dewdrops that caught in the graying curls that framed her.

Llio licked softly, probing delicately between her lips to taste her. Tellou was warm, silky smooth and wet with that smokey-metal flavor that came from so many hours at the forge. Tellou's work was a part of her, written throughout her, but Llio could steal her away for a little while.

Llio held onto Tellou's thigh for leverage as she nosed higher, searching with her tongue for the center of her lover's pleasure, her gemstone. It was plump and warm, ready for her, and she was glad for her grip on Tellou's thigh so she was not thrown off as the smith's hips bucked. Already Tellou was reduced to deep gasping moans, her big hands clenching and unclenching where she braced herself on the cottage wall, and Llio flicked her tongue in relentless circles.

Tellou's whole body shook, an earthquake in her bones, big muscles clenching across her body in waves. She was beautiful, so beautiful from between her legs as Llio held tight and rode her through the moans and cries of her climax. Llio pushed Tellou as high as she was able, until her lover could take no more and pushed her away with a whimper, hips squirming away instead of pressing in.

Llio began to pull herself back up to her feet, but Tellou was sinking down at the same time and she found herself engulfed in her big arms, lying in the moss. Tellou whimpered wordlessly, still riding the aftershocks with little trembles traveling through her. She buried her face in Llio's mass of pale braids and held her close and tight.

"I forget," Tellou whispered, when she'd finally gathered herself enough to be able to form sentences again, laughing at herself a little. She kissed Llio deeply, humming at the flavor of herself on her lips. Tellou rested her forehead against Llio's, her warm eyes shining so close. "I always think 'she can't be that good,' and then you're better."

"Mm." Llio preened, stroking down Tellou's body as she wrapped a leg around hers to pull her just that little bit closer. There was a sweet ache in her lower belly, her own patient arousal begging for attention, hungry for touch.

In just a moment Tellou would....

They kissed again, gentle and warm, and there was the sudden spark in Tellou's eyes as she remembered. One big hand stroked down and squeezed Llio's bottom, thigh shifting between her legs.

"Oh, " Tellou breathed, her smile bordering on the predatory. "Oh my Llio, it's your turn."

She stood, carrying Llio with her into the house as though she weighed nothing, and utterly unconcerned with the green stains on their bodies from the moss as she tossed Llio on the big bed. Gorgeous solid Tellou took a moment to stand back and admire Llio as though she were the beautiful one between them before she turned to dig through a drawer.

"Where did, ah!" Tellou emerged with a smile and a delicately colored glass cock crafted by the finest glassblower in Ramaria city. Llio moaned at the sight of it, her legs parting as her muscles clenched. Llio could almost feel bad that she got so much more from the present she'd bought for Tellou, but Tellou didn't seem to mind. Tellou crawled over Llio, pausing to rub her cheeks against both her breasts before she nestled the smooth glass cock between them.

"Warm this up," Tellou requested, and Llio nodded. She placed one hand over it to hold it in place while she reached for Tellou, angling her face for a kiss. She would never get tired of kissing in these rare times when she had all of the smith's attention. Tellou bracketed her, so big and strong with all the fire of her passion focused on Llio. One rough hand ran down Llio's body, stroking back up the inside of her thigh and big fingers finally coming to rest against the long-waiting slickness of her sex.

Llio moaned, a tremble traveling through her as she spread her legs wider, begging. Tellou chuckled, eyes hot and bright, and she didn't move her fingers. She wouldn't, not until she was ready, and Llio whimpered.

Tellou would study her as intensely as she studied her metalwork, take her apart and know her. She would mold the molten heat of her into whatever she wanted, and Llio would let her.

The only person in the world she would let her guard down for.

"I trust you," she breathed against Tellou's lips, not flinching from the fire in her lover's gorgeous dark eyes.

Llio straddled Tellou's belly. The smith was sprawled loose-limbed beneath her, eyes closed and a small smile on her lips. Llio gently stroked her fingers through the soft strands of Tellou's silver-touched beard, braiding it close along the bottom edges of her jaw and gathering it into a long bullwhip braid on her chin. Her beard grew in so evenly, its natural untended shape elegant enough to make the finest courtesans of Ramaria city weep for jealousy, and Tellou did nothing with it.

Tellou could have been one of them, if she'd wanted, a courtesan. No one could match her for strength and beauty. She could have bedded royalty and married into the finest circles—but that had never interested her. Tellou had taken herself away to the outskirts of little Meadowsweet where she could practice her smithwork undisturbed; until Llio managed to insinuate herself in her life and steal away just a piece of her attention.

Tellou's eyes shot open, wide and unseeing. "But nickel could counteract the brittleness from the chromium!" she gasped, nearly dislodging Llio with her sudden attempt to sit up. Llio placed her hands on both sides of Tellou's face.

"Tellou... my Tellou," she crooned, and her love's brown eyes finally focused on Llio.

"My little Llio," Tellou answered, relaxing beneath her again as she reached up to wind a few of Llio's thousand tiny braids around a finger.

Tellou sighed and closed her eyes again, content to remain Tellou with Llio for a little longer and not run back to her forge to be Mastress Argantel, finest smith in the realm.

Llio smiled a little, a little sadly, as she resumed working on the bullwhip braid that was the height of fashion in Ramaria.

She could only hold Tellou for a little while—the quiet sorrow of all those Dwarves who loved those who lived in their work. They were the finest of craftspeople, but their attention was stolen away in moments. Soon the forge would call Argantel louder than Llio could call Tellou, and she would be forgotten as all the passionate intensity of that focus was shifted back where it had always belonged.

All Llio could do was learn to take comfort in the fact that she was the only one Tellou gave even this much to.

Llio could not complain, though. Tellou had to endure sending Llio away, again and again, and never knowing if this time was the time she didn't come home. Just a few stolen days and the Crown would call Eilir back.

She would be the stinging butterfly again, working to make sure there were no surprises; that the fragile peace between the Kingdoms did not fail. She would make sure the Fae were not attempting to revive the war dragons of legend, that the Goblins were not turning their particular genius toward machines of destruction, that none of the Dwarven nobles were planning on trespassing to mine for resources that were not theirs to take.

She would navigate the battering winds of truths and lies to be sure her Tellou and all those gentle Dwarves like her were safe.

...but these were Eilir thoughts, and Llio pushed them away.

Llio finished Tellou's braid and sat back to just look at her love. For a few days she would be simple, beloved, Llio—born to nothing here in the tiny village of Meadowsweet. She would wear her long braids loose, and simple linen dresses, and no knives, and make love with Tellou until both of them were too sore for even one more round. Llio would take care of her Tellou, cook for her, clean the walnut leaves out of the rain barrel, and maybe even weed the poor neglected garden if there was anything left under all the weeds.

For a few days she could have Tellou.

Llio smiled and gently stroked the side of the napping smith's face before shifting to lie on top of Tellou's strength and softness. She stroked a hand down the corded muscles of Tellou's arm, still hard even in relaxation. Llio smiled as she closed her eyes to rest too.

A few stolen days would be enough.

Bridge Over Shifter's Chasm
Raven Kaldera

One a.m. in the library, and my stomach grumbled. I dug around
to look for a snack, and found that I'd eaten them all, so I went
down to the cafeteria. Well, actually, it's just the second-floor
kitchen; there's nothing cafeteria-like about it and I don't know
why Zephyrus bothers to call it that. Maybe because it makes this
place sound more like a compound, like a bunker or something.
Instead it was a badly converted office building with blasted empty
lots all around it. But there was a fridge, and a pint of Ben & Jerry's
that only had a few bites out of it, and that was good enough to
fortify me for another few hours of research.

The place was dead empty. Oh, Zephyrus was up in his cocoon,
in some kind of telepathic trance, communing with his dead
boyfriend. He wouldn't be up for hours. I briefly fantasized him
getting it on with his invisible dead-boy, his body twitching in its
shiny white metal tube. Did he ejaculate? Did the dead ex solidify
in the tube with him, or was he only present in Zephyrus's mind?
Probably the latter, since our esteemed Boss never invited him to
dinner with us or anything. We wouldn't have minded, and maybe
Manifesto could have seen him. But no, the Boss just moped
around dramatically, gluing his hand to his forehead and contin-
ually mourning his lost love.

Still, he owned the place, and he fed, clothed, and allowanced
the whole team, from the active members to the staff mutants like
myself. He was the Boss, and if it weren't for him we'd be having
to find real jobs, something which the more mutated of us weren't
likely to be able to pull off. He paid for our medical care (which
meant quivery-voiced old Dr. Meegran with his opaque glasses, in
hiding for some medical-experiment war crime decades ago that
we all knew better than to ask about), our uniforms (for the active
members, anyway), and our vices, if they were cheap ones. Mine

were cheap. I wasn't stupid. A few plants in my tiny former-storage-closet bedroom in the basement, and lots of books, most of which I could justify for the library.

Not that I was a real member. No, that was for the folks with the really great talents... or at least the ones that were better than mine; our house Team wasn't exactly world-class. I found some chips and a can of ginger ale left over from the team Christmas party and smiled. Jackpot. As I stuffed my face, I remembered the first time I came here. There had been an ad about superhero auditions—OK, Zephyrus wasn't so tacky as to say it in those words, but it was close—and I wandered over, more out of curiosity than any certainty I could get in.

There were lines of people in costumes—shiny and skintight, clunky and metal, swirling and iridescent—and while there were a lot of tacky half-assed kids with one stupid little talent, and a few sagging oldsters still trying to look fierce, I could see a decent number of real toughs. Steel-eyed, hard-bodied, looking like they could rip your head off and shit down your throat, maybe not even using their hands. No way was I going up against that. I picked up some literature laying on the table, badly formatted stuff about Zephyrus and his ideal future team, and thumbed through it. I noted the grammatical errors and the complete lack of ability to make a blockquote, not to mention the way they'd spelled "caliber" with two A's. On impulse, I pulled a red pen out of my pocket and proofed half a dozen different trifolds, making notes about how they could look so much more professional, if only.... Across the top I wrote, "Hire me and I'll make these look good." Then I walked past the long line of toughs waiting in front of the receptionist, and handed them to her. "Show this to your boss," I said.

Ten minutes later I was in Zephyrus's office, and twenty minutes later I was hired, while the line of superheros outside hadn't moved an inch. Yup, that's me, the Big Z's mutant copyeditor, churning out literature and articles and websites and all sorts of propaganda to spread across the Interwebs. The research I'd been doing in the library wasn't for some big scientific project. It was for the company newsletter, which I had to put out every month and it had better be interesting and amusing. I was catching up on my work while everyone else was home with their families over the holidays. Well, the ones who had families, anyway. Manifesto was off on a jaunt to some mysterious third world country to do research of the type I wasn't doing. Lupita was running somewhere in some wild place where she didn't have to take human form for days, and would probably come back with hair like a rat's nest and the worst breath in the world. Lupita wasn't too bright; she was just muscle. Zephyrus kept nagging her to change her name. "But it means wolf," she'd say, staring at him blankly.

"It sounds like somebody's green-card cleaning lady!" he'd say, exasperated. Zephyrus wasn't the most politically sensitive of people, having unfortunately grown up entirely too rich.

Her expression wouldn't change. "But it means wolf," she'd repeat. I bit my tongue and didn't point out that Lupita's mother was probably somebody's green-card cleaning lady. Anyway, she was off, and so was Geist. Geist was enormous and humorless and could probably strangle a rhinoceros; he had no friends, communicated in grunts, and was usually parked in his room in front of the satellite TV when off duty. But occasionally he went off to enjoy a bender and probably trash a bar, so I was alone in the place, except for the semi-comatose Boss upstairs. That's why it was half a miracle that I saw the shadowed figure darting through the hall.

I froze as soon as I saw it, ducking back around the corner and holding my breath. The only Team member here who moved like that was Stiletto, and she was only about five feet tall. And she wouldn't be skulking around the hallways. I braced myself and took a quick glance around the corner again, and there I saw her. Tall and lean, with what I refer to as Female Superhero Body Type Three—small-breasted and athletic, just muscled enough that you couldn't call them delicate. The fluorescent light from down the hall reflected off of her orangey-gold skin, patterned like tie-dye. She wore no clothes, not even boots; she didn't need to. Her legs ended in shiny bootlike feet; I expect that she'd hardened the skin for protection. She had no body hair, either, and the hair on her head looked like it was made of fringed skin. It probably was.

I knew who she was, of course. We'd all been briefed on the various members of enemy Teams and Houses; there were files on all of them upstairs in the library. I'd had to write articles on them, fergodssake. Her name was Chimera, and she was a shapeshifter. She could look like anyone she wanted; could pass right down to the voice and skin details, although mannerisms were somewhat harder. There were a dozen or so shapeshifter-mutants of various kinds; she wasn't the most dangerous of the lot, being only a minor member of a major Team, but she was nothing to sneeze at. Frankly, she could probably kill me on sight. The fact that she'd gotten past all the nothing-to-sneeze-at perimeter guardian machines meant that she was that good. The best thing I could do in this situation was to run, sound the alarm, and try my best to wake up Zephyrus. Maybe I could call into town and see if Geist wasn't too drunk yet. This one was so far out of my league that I would be a fool even to let her see me.

I wasn't tall, or muscled, or even fit. I was short and paunchy and very, very hairy, especially on the lower half. Actually, I was entirely furred from the solar plexus down, right down to the hooves. Yep, hooves. Cloven, too. And horns, about eight inches long. Did I wear clothes? Damn straight I did, and a hat too when I went out. Which clothes I wore depended on my mood, but usually it was men's clothes, because I was really too ugly to be a girl even with my beard shaved, even though I did have breasts, and a cunt. Right under my cock. You can imagine, now, why I'm not on a Team. It's the unwritten rule: Superheros have to be hard-bodied and attractive, especially if they're not very... er... masculine. Or, if they're ugly, they have to be great mounds of solid muscle like Geist. Fat little hairy hermaphroditic mutants are just not going to make it. I mean, who wants that on a promotional poster? It won't sell jobs to the Team.

There's also the fact that my talents aren't much use for fighting anyway. It's a good thing that I found this job under Zephyrus's generosity, where I can live safely and hide from the world and sarcastically ride herd on the hard-bodied, attractive people in costumes. I'm not even very brave. Taking on an enemy infiltrator would be a ridiculous idea.

As I watched from around the corner, the intruder shifted and changed. She gained height, her skin darkened to café au lait, her hair shrank to dark and curly, and her outer skin took on the shape and sheen of a finely tailored men's suit. I hadn't seen her facial features well before, but as she turned in my direction I could see the face of Firecracker, our team's pyro. Proud, sleek, debonair, Lucius Dubarry not only gave the team class but a minority point as well. She'd even got the small diamond stud in his nose right. Perhaps she'd been studying him.

Then, as I stood there, she turned and saw me.

I should have forced a smile onto my face. I should have waved and hailed him, walked on by, then sounded the alarm. Instead, I froze. Her—Lucius's—face was impassive; I wondered for one moment what she could possibly be thinking, and then I knew that I had to be thinking of something myself, something smart, or she was going to Know and then I would Die. And, of course, the craziest thought in the world came into my head, and what else could I do? Maybe there was one part of my brain that was sick of my gorgeous coworkers and their clear contempt for me, the jokes about my anatomy that I almost didn't overhear. Maybe I wanted to get back at Firecracker for what he had that I never would.

At any rate, what I did was to walk right up to that tall figure and say, "You came back. I knew you would. I knew you couldn't resist." And then I put my hands on her shoulders and kissed those chocolate lips.

I felt her stiffen, almost flinch. There was a moment when I kissed a closed mouth, and then it opened and let me penetrate, a little. I can't imagine what must have been running through her head; Lucius was well known in his profile—and I'm sure that they all had the profiles of our Team, and even the staff, even my own, just as we had theirs—as an extremely heterosexual ladies' man. The idea that he'd let me kiss him was lunacy; if I hadn't been giving our intruder some tongue, I'd have been grinning from ear to ear. I backed off and whispered, "It's all right, Luke. You know you can trust me, like you always do. I never tell anyone about it, I never will. It's all on the down-low, like always." I paused, and then whispered, "But I knew you'd sneak back to see me."

She swallowed—I saw that one and bit my lip to keep from grinning—and then whispered back, "So... what is it that you want?" No name; I'm not that important and I expect that she didn't know me, was racking her brains as I'd racked mine. Ha. For the moment, I had the upper hand. Now, of course, I should make excuses and get away from this fictional tryst. Except that it seemed that the part of me who'd come up with this harebrained scheme was in control, not the sensible part that wanted, very much, to live.

"Whatever you're willing to give me. As always," I said, and I took that supervillain by the hand and led her toward my basement room.

ه

I watched her scan the place as we entered, noting every wall and door, the bathroom off to the side. Of course; she'd assume that Firecracker would know it well. In actuality, Lucius had never been down here to this converted storage space with its secondhand furniture and sagging bed covered in books. I watched for a flash of contempt, but there was none, just... watchfulness. I saw Firecracker's visage reflected in the mirror as we passed, and my own. I looked away with a grimace. How did I get to be born this way? Damned if I know. My mother was a teenage junkie who gave her freakish half-goat baby up at birth, and when I hunted her up years later to find out my origins, she was already dead. The doctors told me that less than half of my hundred or so chromosomes were human, and the rest? Who knew? I did a lot of research once, on demons and satyrs and other creatures that I'm supposed to look like. They're all myths, you know. I never got any further than that.

Never. So who cares? I'm just a mutant, like the scores of mutants wandering the underbellies of the cities, looking for work.

But now I had more crucial things to worry about, like the dark, deadly figure that had just settled carefully on the edge of my bed. After my earlier confidence, my acting that had seemingly convinced her, there was no way to back off now. My secret-para-mour persona—yeah, right, me as anyone's secret paramour—needed to be solid, to never crack, even though I was shaking inside at the thought of what I was about to do.

So I started slow. Lucius and I were already lovers, I'd made that clear, but I'd also made it clear that he was a bit skittish about the whole thing, probably needed to be seduced anew each time even though he wanted it badly. I took her face gently in my hands and kissed Lucius's handsome features again—lips, brow, chin, ears, back to the lips again. This time, she let me have even more tongue. This time, she kissed me back. My cock flushed to hardness in an instant, and I could feel my cunt gushing and my nipples harden-ing against my old flannel shirt. I quickly opened a couple of but-tons on my shirt and took her hand; moved it to my breast. My tits were bigger than hers, long and floppy, and hairy. *Yeah, feel that, baby. Guess you've never touched anything like that before, have you? But you can't do anything but pretend you want it, can you?* The thought turned me on.

Apparently, so did the danger, because I was fast losing any fear at all to straight-up lust. Lucius's body was gorgeous, and I was happy to fuck it—there wasn't a member of that polished, dan-gerous, contemptuous Team that I hadn't used as jerkoff fodder—but it was the inhuman-looking woman inside that I really wanted.

Her fingers found my nipple. "Pinch it," I breathed in her ear. "Hard—you know how I like it." She didn't, but it didn't matter because I'd just told her, and I gasped and wriggled between her spread knees with the sensation. I cradled the back of her head and gave her tongue again while she worked my nipple, and then moved her other hand to my crotch. I always wear loose pants, and my hard-on was straining at the fabric. She did something deft and probably not quite human-fingered down there to get my belt and fly open. *Did you just shift a bit there, honey? Couldn't resist, couldn't do it the slow way, eh? Don't worry, I won't say a word.* Her hand curled around my cock and I moaned into her mouth.

Her grip slid all the way to its base, and then one fingertip caught the wetness oozing upward between the split testicles. She paused—*watch it, honey, you're supposed to know about that, and like it*—and then the finger found its way into my slit and worked its way up. *That's right, be bold. Lucius would be, or at least you think he would. Are you a straight girl? Probably. Except for Zephyrus, they're all straight, and even if they weren't they wouldn't want me.* My hand dipped experimentally into her lap, but she caught it and pulled her mouth away from mine. "I'll just dump these clothes," she said, getting up and moving towards the bathroom. Lucius's face smiled warily at me as the door closed.

Oh, that's right; those weren't real clothes, and she didn't want to have to peel them off in front of me. The feel of the "fabric" had been so convincing that I'd forgotten. She must have worked hard on that, over the years. I had a mental flash of her shaping her skin, again and again, comparing it to the fabric clothes spread out next to her, staring at the line of drape and crease. Was it exciting to her, the first time she went out naked and no one knew? I shucked my own clothes, hopped onto the bed, pushed off all the books onto the floor, and waited.

Lucius's form came out, all caramel muscles and white teeth and an enormous dark hard-on. *Bet you don't know what his dick really looks like, honey. Bet you're hoping against hope that you got it right.* Actually, I did know what it looked like, because I'd been in the shower room with him, and it was a lot smaller than mine. I grabbed mine and fingered it, looking her in the eye. "I know you want it, superfucker," I said. "Come here and suck me off."

The white toothy smile wavered, but she gamely climbed onto the bed and lowered her mouth towards my dick. As warm wetness closed around it, I wondered briefly if she was planning to kill me during this bout of sex. After all, I had been stupid enough to bring her to this small basement room. It wouldn't be hard at all. I grabbed the dark head with its kinked hair and shoved it down over my cock. *If you're going to kill me, you're going to do it with my dick in your mouth, baby.* There was a grunt and a moment's resistance, and then just a warm wet sheath. Well, of course she could reshape her throat. *Probably doesn't even have a gag reflex unless she wants one. What a way to die.* I pumped my hips and fucked Lucius's face. This was pure fantasy; for a moment I let myself forget whose eyes lay behind that face. This was just me getting one over on one of those perfect people whose posters were plastered all over this building.

After a minute, I pulled the dark curly head up and shoved it down further, between what might have been overly large labia and might have been a split scrotum, but was actually a half-made melange of both. My cunt was dripping, and I shoved her face right into it. "Eat it, sweetheart," I breathed. "Lick it good. I know you want it. I know you want me." Pure porn, tacky as hell but I might as well indulge it. A wet tongue licked up and around my hole, then inside, then deeper... *ohmigod, was that longer than human? Watch it honey, that's not one of Lucius's superpowers, not that I'm going to complain for so much as a second.* I was getting very close to going over the edge, so I let that tongue probe me for a moment and then I jerked her head back up, shoving my cock back into her mouth and coming.

I think that I bucked and shrieked for at least two minutes. When I come, I come hard. Not only did the figure whose head I had clamped to my groin not choke, but after it was over I discovered that I was still alive.

"You are beautiful," I told her breathlessly, knowing that she'd think it was for Firecracker, but meaning it for her, herself. I leaned down and kissed her, tasting myself on her lips and tongue... I ran my tongue around hers, but it was safely normal-sized again. When I pulled back, Firecracker's face was grinning, and I had the distinct feeling that it wasn't an act. That made my stomach flutter, and for one second I felt suddenly shy. Then it occurred to me that she was probably thinking about how well she was fooling me. Oh well.

Since she hadn't killed me yet, I wasn't about to stop. "Come up here," I said, and she levered that long dark muscled body up onto the bed. A hard-on bobbed obligingly between her legs; I saw her surreptitiously glance at it, as if to make sure that she'd done it right, and bit back a smile. Quickly straddling her, I sank down onto it with a moan, my own semi-hard cock flopping against her tight belly. I looked pale and bloated and hairy next to Lucius's body, but I thrust that thought away and started humping. "Come on, honey, move that ass," I said, gasping with exertion. "Don't make me do all the work." My hooves dug into her thighs. I found her hands with mine and entwined my fingers, pressing downwards for leverage. She pushed upwards and held me upright easily. Damn, this bitch was strong. This was probably the point where the dick inside me would explode into a mass of razor-tipped tentacles and shred me from the inside out, but I didn't care.

She was breathing hard, too, and not acting. I know acting, having been with quite a few whores. Perhaps she felt that if she had to fuck some staff mutant to keep her cover, she might as well lay back and enjoy it. I hoped that was the case, anyway. I decided to up the stakes and paused, pulling up off her cock and reaching for my nightstand. A quick fumble among the debris came up with a bottle of lube, and I squeezed out a good batch and stuffed as much as I could up my ass. Then I sat back down, carefully, guiding that cock into my butt inch by inch. She was motionless, waiting for me; I wished that I could ask her to make the tip of it narrower, pointier, easier for entry. Damn, she could probably reinflate it once it was inside me, pump it up like a sex toy. The thought brought me to full hardness again in front, and I slid all the way down onto her pelvis.

I stopped thinking during the next few minutes of raw fucking. It didn't matter who I was, who she was, or what might happen next; it was just two bodies straining and bucking in rhythm until, like a miracle, she came. I know faked orgasms—I can smell them—and this was real. I came a few thrusts later, my ass clenching around a spasming cock and my own cock slapping hard against her belly. I squirted onto Lucius's broad flat muscular chest, scooped it up with my finger, and brought it to her lips. They opened and sucked my finger in, taking the offering.

Then, suddenly, she shifted. The cock shrank and pulled back out of my ass so quickly that I gasped. The face and body underneath me rippled and changed, mocha being replaced with mottled yellow and orange and red. The eyes... I hadn't seen her eyes before. Mottled copper as a serpent's hide, the pupils were a snake's slits, and there were no lashes or brows. She stretched her mouth sideways, showing off a set of sharp lizard-teeth... that still had my finger clamped in their vise.

She looked at me, expression unreadable, and I looked at her. *This is it. I'm going to die now.* There was no reason for her to show herself unless I wasn't ever going to be able to tell anyone about it. My second thought was, *is she wondering why I'm not freaking out?* Then I thought, *screw it. I'm not going to die with a lie on my lips. Let there be truth between us, even if it's the last thing I say.*

I took a deep breath. "Well, hello there, beautiful," I said. I meant it, too. She was bizarre, but strangely beautiful to me. And who was I to judge someone's looks? "I'm glad you decided to show yourself," I said. "Lucius isn't my lover. I saw you in the hall, and I knew this was the only chance I'd ever get. Thank you for some of the best sex I've had in my life."

This time it was her turn to freeze. I could see emotions flashing across her face, but I couldn't quite read them—confusion? Rage? It loosened her grip on my finger, though, and I quickly reclaimed it. Then she spoke—in her own voice, a rough contralto—and it was a string of blistering curses. Not specifically aimed at me, just curses. I captured her hands, lightly, not trying to restrain her. "It's all right," I said. "I won't tell anyone, and I'll help you get out of here. I can't help with whatever mission you were on, but at least I can make it a zero-sum. It's fair payment."

"I'm not a whore," she grated out, her nails digging into my hands.

"No," I said, "but you are one very fine lay. Even if you were just pretending to be interested in me. I hope it wasn't too... dif-

ficult. God knows that I'm not one of the better-looking mutants."
I heard the curl of bitterness in my voice and shut my mouth. That
wasn't supposed to come out. No use whining about spilled genetic material.

Her face stilled, eyes seeking out mine. I still couldn't read her,
but I moved away respectfully as she sat up. Her skin was smooth,
silken, almost artificial-feeling; I copped one last feel, caressing
her thigh as I got off her. She looked at me and I removed my hand.
"I'd rather have done it with you as you are," I said, "but playing
with Lucius's body was fun too."

"So you were just toying with me the whole time," she said.
There was danger in her tone, but I'd come too far to care.

"Not toying," I said. "I've never been more serious. I just
wanted you. That's all. I didn't even think about anything else."

I didn't expect the look in her eyes. *Has no one ever wanted you for
yourself? Not you, either?* It was only one second of naked feeling, but
it took the rage out of the room and left it strangely empty, uncomfortable. "I'm sorry," I said.

The light in her eyes changed, became wilder. "You want me?"
she hissed. "You think you want me?" Then the back of her hand
latched onto my neck and she kissed me. This kiss was all scraping
teeth, all bloated tongue that wormed its way impossibly long,
chokingly long, into my mouth. I took it all, grabbing her back,
digging my nails into her, wrapping my oddly-jointed furred bony
legs around her. *Fuck yes.* I bore down, in a way that I hadn't done
in years, and released a cloud of musk from scent glands that normal people didn't have. The smell rose, dizzying, heavy, surrounding us. Chimera might be able to alter a lot of bodily things, but
she still had to breathe. Her lungs still carried molecules into her
bloodstream, and she wouldn't be expecting this. It would drive
her into a frenzy of half-dazed lust for at least a half hour, by which
time... I'd have thought of something else, assuming that I still
breathed myself.

Why hadn't I used that talent, that mutant power, on her before? (Because people tended not to remember what they did

under its drugging haze, and I *wanted* her to remember me.) Why didn't I go around using it on people right and left, making them fall helpless into my lecherous arms? Why wasn't I surrounded by throngs of dazed harem slaves? Why was I sleeping alone in the basement of a second-rate Team company, with no one knowing I had any powers at all? (I've got two, that I know of. We won't even discuss the second one.) That's what you're wondering, isn't it?

Well, maybe I'd just prefer people to want me for myself, you know? I'd tried the other way, plenty of times in my youth, and it never lasts. They wake up, they get disgusted, and they leave. After a while, it's not worth it unless you're desperately horny and can't take it any more. And it's kind of sleazy and embarrassing, you know? Not something to put on the resume. In fact, I hadn't told anyone about it in over a decade. And there's a reason why I'm working for a superhero team and not a supervillain team. I may not be brave, I may not be all that good, even, but I like to think I'm not a shit. That's where fragile self-esteem starts: At Least I'm Not An Asshole.

Now, however, there was a very good chance that I was fighting for my life, and all bets were off. The crazy suicidal urge that had put me here in the first place had evaporated with Lucius's imaginary features; this was real now, and I needed to even the playing field. I felt Chimera choke as she breathed in my musk, and shudder. She bit down, and I barely got my tongue out of the way in time. Instead, I bit down on the phallic tongue that was invading my throat. She hadn't choked me. I might not have her abilities at shapeshifting my orifices, but I am damn experienced at every kind of oral sex there is. It helps, when you look like me.

I pushed her backwards onto the bed and thrust my hand between her legs. Nothing. Smooth as a doll's crotch. Perhaps she didn't bother with genitals unless she was going to be using them. She bothered with small breasts and a female-looking form, though. Well, I was hardly one to complain to someone about their particular combination of primary and secondary sexual characteristics. "Give me a cunt," I said. "Now, or I'm going up your ass."

Her eyes were glazing over, but she heard me enough. The smooth flesh rippled under my touch, and blossomed outward. Labia opened like flower petals in fast-motion, and I found the hole between them. It was dry, so I scooped some extra lube out of the crack of my ass and went in. She growled and grabbed me by the hair; I shoved more of my hand into her. We were eye to eye. Even through the haze of my weapon, she was there, and I spoke to her. "Of course I want you," I said. "Of course I find you beautiful. I won't insult you by thinking that anyone else has ever found you anything but beautiful. Now open the fuck up." I shoved in further.

"Bastard," she whispered. "What if I grow teeth there and bite your hand off?" That almost made me pause, but I saw the corners of her mouth turn up. She was playing my game, then. Fuck yes.

"I know that you can kill me," I said. "But if you bite my hand off, this fuck will stop right now. And I don't think you want it to stop, or you'd have said something, right, honey?" I bore down and pressed out a bit more musk to back up my words. "Open up more. More. I know you can fucking do it, open up!" Her flesh yielded and my whole fist went in, up to the wrist. It would have to be my fist, because my cock had come twice and was out of commission for a while. "Give me that tongue again, baby," I said, and locked my mouth to hers again while my forearm did the pile-driver act. If the other orgasm had been real, this one was realer; she nearly broke my wrist with the whiplashing of her body. No human spine moved like that. No human cunt spat me out so deliberately, and sealed up behind me, either.

We both lay quietly for a while, pressed up against each other, probably both contemplating our next moves. It wasn't snuggling; I could feel tension in both our bodies.

She was still foggy; I could see it in her eyes. "What have you done to me?" she asked. "And how long will it take to wear off, you fucker?"

I decided that honesty was still the best policy. Push a little, then pony up; push a little, then pony up. It was a dangerous game, indeed. "It's just something I can do," I said. "It'll wear off soon. Then I'll help you get out of here. Unless you think you can keep going." Then I rolled over onto my belly, bare-ass upwards, legs spread. It was a position of vulnerability, saying, *I trust you.* I wanted to see what she'd do.

What she did was to put an arm around me and pull me back onto my side, so that she was up against my back. She was still for a moment, breathing, and then the smooth groin against my buttocks shifted, and I felt something growing and prodding me from behind. *Fuck yes. I think I have you, girl. I'm not sure what I'm going to do with you, but I think I actually have you.* "Do you want me?" I whispered. That was an extra-dangerous question. It hung in the air between us, smelling like lifetimes of contemptuous glances, high-pitched uncomfortable laughter, people who pulled away from accidental contact with you on the subway. *How does it feel to never be wanted for who you really are?* I didn't know her history, I didn't know if she had other lovers, perhaps ones who were waiting at home for her right now and wondering what was keeping her. I doubted it, though. I had a feeling that her self-possessed coldness enclosed a loneliness just as deep and solitary as mine. While she was still half-hazy, I wanted to invoke that, to give a small haven to it... something that could never be found elsewhere. *I'm not the enemy, honey. There's an enemy out there that's bigger than Teams and laws and governments, and we face that one on the same side. The rest, that's just what we do. This is who we are. Mutant. Outcast. I know, I know, I know.*

"Don't... put yourself down," she said. Her voice was suddenly soft, a timbre I'd never heard before. "You're not unworthy..." she fished for the words, "...of desire." *Oh, yes, you know, honey. You know what it feels like. I think I have you.*

I put my hand between my legs and took hold of the cock that was growing from her groin. This one wasn't even cock-shaped; I don't think she was even trying at that point. It was just tubular, bulging, throbbing against me. My ass was still lubed from earlier. "Do you want me?" I asked again. It wasn't the game any more. I just needed to hear it.

A pause, a few heavy breaths against my ear, then: "I want you." Her arm tightened around me. "I can't promise anything-"

"No promises after today," I said breathlessly. "This isn't about our loyalties. It's time of out time, space out of space. Nothing counts here except us. You want me? Take me." I moved the end of her appendage into the crack of my ass and felt it slowly slide in. We rocked there for a while, together; it wasn't the raw fucking of earlier, just locked-together comfort. Her breath slowly synchronized to mine. I relaxed, staring at her hand on my shoulder. It had no nails any more, just vague clubbed fingers, but it was all right, Actually, everything was all right.

Then one of the green lights on the panel on my wall lit up. "Shit," I said angrily, and she pulled away from me, and out of me. "Fucking hell."

"What's the matter?" she asked warily.

"Lupita's home." The monitor showed whose cars were in the parking garage; there was one in every staff bedroom. Zephyrus believed in knowing where his people were, although he wasn't up to chipping us all. "We have to get you out of here." I stood up, grabbing for my clothes.

"I can take on one of the other forms—" she began.

"Of the Team members? Won't work. Lupita can smell like a dog, and she's half crazy and none too bright. No, we have to think of something else." I threw on my pants and an old sweater, and shuffled through my small refrigerator. "Raw garlic—that'll put her off, as long as she doesn't actually see you."

"So why are you doing this?" Chimera asked casually. I could feel her closing back up, forcing the last of the drugging musk from her mind—that was good, she'd need all her wits to help me—becoming once again the supervillain who'd invaded Zephyrus's citadel. "Why don't you just turn me in?" *You haven't even asked why I'm here,* lay unsaid between us.

"Why didn't you kill me when you had the chance?" I asked, deliberately phrasing it that way. I was her way out now; I could say that.

She was silent for a moment. "I like you," she said. "You're... different." At my snort, she laughed—the first time I'd heard her laugh—and retorted, "No, really. I don't mean that. You wouldn't believe how some of the people on my Team look. You want disgusting?"

"Are they disgusting on the inside too?" I asked, popping raw garlic cloves into my mouth and trying not to gag as I crunched and swallowed.

"...Yes. Some of them. Some, not."

I opened a nip bottle of Jaegermeister and splashed it all over my sweater. That ought to distract Lupita. "Any of them your lover?"

She smiled wryly. "...No. Not now." *Ha. I knew it.* "What I mean is, you're not full of yourself. You're..."

"Real. In spite of the fact that I look like a mythical monster." I grabbed my big overcoat. "How small can you make yourself? Not tiny, flat."

"My basic internal organ space needs to stay the same mass," she said, "and I can't move it around too much. But once I fit down into a two-cubic-feet box."

"Right," I said. And so it was that I carried her to the parking garage under my overcoat. Her arms and legs were wrapped around me like flat bands; her grotesquely compressed head and torso pressed against my belly. To hide the lump, I carried two economy-size open bags of garlic-flavored potato chips, which also added to my scent. When I passed Lupita in the hall, she sniffed and curled her lip. I saluted her with a garlic chip and a drunken leer, and she kept walking.

Outside the perimeter of the robot-guards and out of sight of the cameras, I put down the chips and opened my coat. Chimera slithered out onto the broken asphalt lot, shook herself violently, and stood up. I looked up at her. She was almost a head taller than me. "Anything to say?" I asked. Stupid.

"No," she said, and turned, vanishing into the darkness.

"Right," I said after her. Then, reeking of booze and all, I walked to the all-night convenience store and bought yet more alcohol. This, I intended to actually get drunk on. The clerk gave me the hairy eyeball, but I didn't care. My give-a-damn switch had somehow gotten stuck off. Maybe she'd done it to me. Superfuckers.

&

I wasn't usually a drunk, and the hangover I gave myself was bad enough that I spent the next day in bed. I should have said something to the Team about how their security had been breached— I could have made something up about seeing a shadowy figure—but I didn't. I stayed in bed and felt miserable, and slept off and on until noon the next day. I fended off the single knock with an excuse of illness, and pulled the covers over my head.

Finally, I went back to work. The newsletter still needed to get done, there was Manifesto's research notes to decipher and type, and Zephyrus wanted to add another page to the website. Weeks passed, and things fell back into their old routine. Then another staff member came through with the mail and handed me a birthday card from my Aunt Hazel. Except that I don't have an Aunt Hazel, and my birthday had gone by a month ago. My heart practically flung itself against my rib cage; I found that I was holding the letter as if it was a bomb that might go off at any moment.

Inside, a garish card wished me many happy returns, signed by Aunt Hazel. On the back, near the bottom corner, was a message in tiny writing. *2/8—10pm—McDonalds—1st St.*

Shit.

&

Of course I went. What, I was going to sit there at home and stare at the clock while my appointment went by? I buried myself in a burger and fries, deliberately not looking up at the passersby. It wasn't as if I could figure out which one she'd be, anyway. Ten o'clock went by, and then several excruciating minutes, and I was just about to get up and leave when someone slipped into the seat across from me.

It was a woman, looking like a fashion model with long red hair and a red leather coat. I was pretty sure the coat was real, not so sure about the miniskirt under it. "Hey," I said.

For one moment her eyes flashed, and the pupils shrank to slits. Then they were normal wide green eyes. "Hey," she said. Her lips were wide and red and perfectly formed.

Did you dress up for me, honey? Honesty, just enough of it to keep you interested. "I liked you better with your own face," I said.

She looked pissed at that. "I have to look like something!" she retorted. "Would you be seen on the street with me, wearing my own face?"

I looked her in the eye. "Yes," I said. *Try me.*

She shook her head. "You're crazy." To my surprise, there was admiration in her tone. "I notice you're not exactly out of the closet." She gestured at my covering clothing, my hat and boots.

I shrugged. "I'm only out here because you asked me. And I'm hoping that you're not going to ask me to be your spy, or contact, or anything like that. I'm hoping that you're here for you, and not for anyone else."

She looked as if she didn't know whether to be angry or flattered. I just looked at her. Finally, she dropped both of them. "I wasn't going to ask you that," she said. "I didn't think you'd be the type to go along with it, anyway."

"What, me all honorable and truth-justice-American-Way?" I snorted at that.

"No. I just figured you wouldn't be the type to let anyone get that kind of hold on you." Her green gaze was clear and straight, and a chill ran up my spine. *You read me.*

"Did you tell anyone about us?"

"No. You?"

"Obviously not. So why am I here?"

She reached across the table, tentatively. I supposed that my tone had been cranky, because she took my hand as if she expected it to be pulled away. "I... want to see you again." It sounded like it took quite an effort for her to say that.

"Consorting with the enemy? Why?" I wasn't going to make it easy. Not with the risk behind it. I had to be sure it was going to be worth it. Damn if I was going to let myself be desperate.

She looked down at her hand, resting on mine. I didn't move it. "Time out of time," she said. "Space out of space. Away from all of them, just us." She looked up. "It's been a long time. I want more of that. I... want you." Her eyes were too proud to beg.

"I want you, too," I whispered. "Where? When?" All right, there went my security, my safe little haven. Damn it.

We ended up in the rest room—to this day I'm not sure whether it was the men's or women's room—fucking wildly with every kind of combination that you can do up against a tile wall while trying to be dead silent. The red leather coat, yes, that was real and discarded onto the floor. The rest dissolved into orange-red tie-dyed woman with blunt fingers and copper eyes. Didn't stay that way, at least not entirely, but that was all right too. She'd be anyone for me, I realized, as long as she knows I want her best this way. We left the McDonald's in normal drag, made it across the street, and didn't get any further than a dumpster in a deserted back alley, which gave us cover as we did it all over again on the slimy asphalt. This time she used her hands, and showed me what a shapeshifter's hands could do to someone, inside and out. Instead of screaming, I drew blood on her several times. The rents in her orange-red skin closed over almost immediately—not healed, as she explained to me later, just sealed up temporarily because she wasn't going to let a little bleeding stop us.

Later, we sat in the park together. Not on a bench—too obvious. In the bushes. Neither her place nor my place was safe, and we weren't up to the risk of a motel room just yet, even in a different city. "Yeah," I said. I knew we were supposed to be talking, certainly there was serious stuff to say, but I couldn't think of anything.

"Yeah," she said. There was silence for a few more minutes, then: "Do you ever just want to throw it all over, go live somewhere no one's trying to fight over the scraps, no one's trying to push some mission on the world? Just have a life?"

"Yeah," I said. "All the time." There, she'd gone and done it; voiced something I wasn't ready for. Not now, anyway. But there might come a time... My hand slipped into hers, carefully. Tentatively. She allowed it.

"When I have sex," she started, almost haltingly, "I'm different people for different people. But I'm always normal, always pretty. Never..."

"Yourself?" I asked. "Somehow I can't see someone like you craving normality. Not in bed, anyway."

She laughed at that. "In bed, no. Nor even in the rest of life. I'm just tired of being what people want me to be. Sometimes I've done things in bed just to freak them out, just to watch them run, when I can't take it any more. But you... don't run away."

"Nope. If I want someone, I want them the way they are." Like I want them to want me. But I have no pretty face to put on. Perhaps that's a blessing, in its own way. Her hand squeezed mine at that. *We understand each other.*

"Next week?" she asked. "Same time and place?" Her hand took on a sudden obscene shape, flirtatiously throbbing against my palm.

"Different one," I said. "Send me another card from Aunt Hazel."

"Right," she said, lifting her obscene fingers to my lips. I kissed them, then did more than kiss. Then she sighed and pulled away, and was gone.

"Right," I said to the empty air, brushing the pine needles off of me. The problem with being furred is that leaves and pine needles are always sticking to you. Rolling in the bushes becomes a serious grooming issue, every time. Next time I'd ask her to pick me clean. I'm sure that those fingers could become tweezers, in a pinch.

Next week, the card came, with a longer note on the back.

Behind the Burger King. Eleven o'clock. Bring a garbage bag, lotion, and some steel wire. There's this fantasy, you see... no one else would understand.

Fuck yes.

Questing
Charles Payseur

Lancelot ran the streets of Chicago, laughter rising up in the air like a standard, proclaiming him to the world. His arms were outstretched, his eyes closed, his long blond hair trailing behind him. Around him people swore, saw him as just another dumb tourist, but he didn't care. Why would he? He was in Chicago a full day ahead of schedule.

He didn't need to be. He was so far ahead in points that none of the others had much hope of ever catching up, even if he took a holiday. Instead he pushed further ahead, lost himself in the simple pleasure of the game and of winning the game. What else was there to do with immortality? Jousting was now only done at Renaissance Festivals, and he wouldn't be caught dead in such a place. Why live in the past when the present had so much to offer? For Lancelot, there was only the game, the quests. And whenever he felt the weight of centuries pushing down on him, the boredom, the tired ache, he reminded himself that he was Lancelot, the greatest knight in the world, and he kept right on going.

"I don't see why you're so happy," a voice said, trailing him, and Lancelot stopped cold, eyes flying open. More curses erupted at his sudden halt, but a soft chuckle pierced them all. Palomides. Dark skin and amused grin and deep brown eyes. His hair was cut short these days, a small goatee trimmed thin and sharp on his face. Tall and fit, the man walked toward Lancelot with a muted grace and almost lazy energy.

"Just because you recovered the day you lost in Nevada?" Palomides continued. "Did you think that anyone would really believe you had gone all the way south to New Orleans to catch a boat to Africa? As if you'd ever miss the chance to go north through France."

Lancelot frowned, though the emotion didn't reach his eyes.

Any complication was a good thing, after all, any distraction welcome. Especially from Palomides, though most of the time the man kept his distance. Lancelot had a reputation among the knights, and after a half dozen fiery affairs and lovers' spats spanning continents, none seemed willing to let themselves get drawn close. Not that Lancelot lacked in romantic partners. With a whole world of men and women out there to win, he kept himself busy. Still, his eyes wandering up Palomides' body, he couldn't help but feel he had missed out on something.

"I suppose the others are around as well, then?" he asked. "Lamorak going to jump out next? Or Percival? Lionel?" But Palomides was shaking his head.

Lancelot smiled. Things were always more interesting one-on-one.

"They're all at least a day behind, probably more. They caught a quest on their way through Texas, and you know the rules."

The rules. As in the rules of the game. The game they'd been playing to stay sane the last few centuries. They had to do something, after all, being immortal. Otherwise they'd probably end up going mad and keeping the old hatreds alive, like Tristan had, or Gawaine, or any of the others caught in the past. Not him. Lancelot looked at the curse of the Grail somewhat differently, which is to say not as a curse at all. Oh, the first time it was a surprise, to close his eyes in final sleep and then open them up again as a child. Reincarnation, some said, but it hardly mattered. He'd gotten quite good at it, was able to always set money aside for his next self to find later. Enough to finance the game. It was always difficult the first few years of each new life, so full of knowledge and memories and unable to do anything about it. They had to act like Ricky or Ferdinand or whatever their new parents named them and blend in until they were old enough to play the game. But they remained the same in spirit. Lancelot was always Lancelot in his own mind. And he normally left home early. He had never liked being subject to anyone else's control. He didn't like to be tied down. He wanted freedom, adventure. Even after so many centuries he was still living for that next excitement.

"Well hurrah for us, then," Lancelot said, trying to figure out Palomides' move. Was he trying to lure Lancelot into a trap, or was it something else? Lancelot decided to come on strong. "Care to slip away and find a room or something?"

Palomides gave a small laugh and adopted an infuriatingly adorable smile, just the corners of his mouth curling up. He had a secret.

"Is their quest through Texas worth a lot of points or something?" Not that it would matter, with the lead that Lancelot had over most of the others. Only Palomides was even close.

"Not as much as the one a little north of here right now." Just like Palomides, to be thinking of business first. Even in their first lives, Palomides the Questing Knight had been somewhat obsessed, always hunting that... Lancelot's eyes widened.

"You don't mean—"

"I do. Glatisant is here. In the Midwest, at least. I've got the trail."

Which meant he was close to cashing in on a whole lot of points. Not that Lancelot was all that concerned. Even if Palomides banked big, Lancelot would catch up. It wasn't like the game was difficult for him. Just keep going east, and whenever you're in a place where someone needs help, you have to stop. If someone needs a lift, or their house painted, or a package delivered across the globe, you have to stop and take care of it before moving on or collecting any more points. The points were awarded depended on the difficulty and how fast you could circle the globe. Capturing Glatisant, the Questing Beast itself, would be worth a fortune. No one had managed it in over a hundred years. It, too, was ageless, and as long as they didn't kill it they could keep hunting it forever. It made things interesting. And dangerous. Just like Lancelot liked. He smiled.

"And you're telling me to gloat?" Lancelot asked.

"No, I'm asking if you want to help." That smile never widened. It remained small, amused. Lancelot wondered what the angle was. He felt a flutter of warmth in his chest, the stirring of his old urge to quest, to win. If Palomides was challenging him, he wouldn't back down, no matter where their adventures took them.

"You don't mind splitting the points with me?" Lancelot asked. It was the rules, after all, but Palomides spread his hands wide as if showing he was unarmed, or disinterested. Lancelot paused. It was possible there was some other game going on here, some angle that Palomides was working. But the bait was just too tempting.

"Maybe I just know more than most not to go up against Glatisant alone," Palomides said. "It has killed me a few times before."

Lancelot frowned. It was hardly amusing to think of death, even if it didn't end up meaning all that much to them. Dying put your points on hold, and it could take some time to grow old enough to play again. At the moment Lancelot was in his early thirties, Palomides a little younger, maybe twenty-five and looking far too good to die yet. Being reset now would be bad, much worse then going at sixty or even fifty, when there weren't many good years left for gaming anyway.

"Okay," Lancelot said. "I accept."

الله

When Palomides said "a little north" he must have been being generous. Northern Wisconsin was hardly anywhere, just a large swath of trees and cold, even in October. They arrived at the hotel Palomides had picked out, and Lancelot shivered and watched Palomides slip out of the Jeep and stretch. They always looked more or less how they had the first time, that first life ages ago.

Lancelot got distracted watching Palomides, the way his shirt pulled up as he reached above his head, revealing a small patch of skin, the faint line of hair that led down into his pants.

"Where exactly are we?" he asked, and Palomides took a deep breath like he didn't mind the chill at all and looked around.

"Rhinelander," Palomides said. "Home of the hodag."

"The what?" Lancelot knew most monsters in the world, had hunted nearly all of them over the years, but had never heard of a hodag. It sounded like some sort of insult a child would make up.

"The hodag. Something a professional liar came up with back in the day by gluing things to a badger. It's supposed to be something like a dragon, but with a frog's face and great big claws."

"Sounds like a few men I've known." Lancelot laughed.

"Glatisant looks something like that. And in the last few weeks the number of hodag sightings has skyrocketed around here. There's even some amateur video."

"So we're not the only ones looking for it?" If there were normal monster hunters out looking for it, there could be a problem. Part of the game was to not draw too much attention to themselves. They were to try and stay out of the spotlight, or too many questions might get asked.

"I'm saying that we need to be careful, yes."

Lancelot's frown deepened. Careful was not something he did well.

At the desk, Lancelot got them a room with a king-sized bed while Palomides unpacked a few things from the car.

When they arrived at the room, Palomides glanced at the bed without comment.

"It's all they had," Lancelot said with a playful smile, but Palomides just shrugged and produced his smart phone. He proceeded to show Lancelot where the sightings had been. They sat, leg to leg, as Palomides pointed out each one.

"So they're concentrated around this lake here?" Lancelot asked, tapping the screen. Palomides hummed his affirmative and brushed against Lancelot's finger as he had the map zoom out. Lancelot nudged closer against Palomides' leg, but when he looked over he saw Palomides looking at the map, ignoring him. Lancelot sighed.

"Bloom Lake. Right along the north shore, with most of them along Trails End Road." Palomides' voice was flat, downright clinical. Had Lancelot imagined the heat he had felt when their fingers had touched?

"I don't think I like the sound of that." Lancelot said. He had an aversion to endings. Kind of why he liked Hollywood movies, because nothing ever really ended. Just wait twenty years for the reboot. It made a familiar kind of sense to him.

"I'm afraid that's where we have to start." Palomides stood and slipped the phone back into his pocket.

"Do we have to go so soon?" Lancelot asked, falling back onto the bed. "We've only just arrived. After all that driving I think we've earned a soak in the hot tub and maybe a raid on the mini-bar."

He was beginning to get annoyed that Palomides seemed to have only the Questing Beast on his mind. For the entire trip so far he had seemed... not quite cold, really. But distant. Professional. Except that he would go out of his way to initiate touch, to brush against Lancelot's hand or shoulder or butt, to talk softly so that Lancelot had to lean close to hear. And all the while ignoring Lancelot's advances and feigning innocence. Lancelot just wanted to grab the man and toss him onto the bed.

"After," Palomides said, and Lancelot nearly growled. But he did get back to his feet, pushed his long hair behind his ears, and followed the taller man out to the car.

He took the passenger seat and Palomides got behind the wheel, reached for a pair of sunglasses hanging from the rearview. His hand missed, bumping them to the floor at Lancelot's feet. And before Lancelot could react, Palomides leaned completely over the armrest, hand retrieving the glasses while his face was less than a foot from Lancelot's lap.

"Oops," Palomides said, turning his head to smile up at Lancelot but not moving otherwise. Lancelot sucked in a breath, felt his body react to the sudden proximity, his cock throbbing slightly, flushing with heat. He wanted this, wanted Palomides to take him, wanted to take Palomides in turn, but then Palomides was back in his seat. Without another word Palomides started the car and pulled away, leaving Lancelot grasping for what to do with his frustration and budding erection.

ﻋ

They reached Trails End Road and Palomides got out first. They hadn't spoken the entire trip. Lancelot kept trying to think of something witty, something funny, but nothing seemed appropriate. He cursed at himself inwardly. He was Lancelot, Knight of the Round Table, and here he was acting like a shy maiden. His heart was racing, and he was fairly certain it wasn't because of the Questing Beast.

Together they affixed their sword belts and left the road. The woods were dense and blushing with fall colors. There was no avoiding the dead leaves, and they crunched as they walked, drawing farther and farther into the forest. Lancelot never really liked the autumn. Or rather, he hated winter, when the cold forced everyone inside, into their own personal cages, into layers of clothes that took ages to peel off. And autumn reminded him that winter was coming, which was almost as bad. He shivered.

Every few minutes they would stop and Palomides would check his phone, or retie his shoes, making sure to bend over as he did, his jeans showing the smooth curve of his ass.

"You ever have sex in the woods?" Lancelot asked. He was tired of being subtle, and his cock was hard, pushed up into the waistband of his pants to avoid being conspicuous. If he didn't fuck or kill something soon there was going to be trouble.

Palomides kept scanning the ground and trees. "A few times," he said. "If I recall correctly, it normally leads to getting dirty and sore."

"Not if you're good at it," Lancelot said, though that was something of a lie. The truth was he didn't care as long as the sex happened, and he was sure by the time they were done they wouldn't mind so much the dirt and leaves and sore muscles. There was, after all, a hot tub back at the hotel.

"And you're so sure you're that good?"

Lancelot laughed, light and arrogant, the way he had always laughed. Of course he was that good. He was Lancelot.

It was then that the forest erupted around him. With a crash, a tree was brushed to the side and Lancelot ducked and dove out of the way as a creature stormed past. Lancelot had never managed to track down the Questing Beast, had never even seen it before. Legend was that few could; only those, like Palomides, who had devoted themselves to tracking it. But Lancelot had it now, would prove that he was the greatest, would capture it on his very first try. It was bigger than Lancelot had expected, about the size of a small car and fast on those stubby legs. It screeched as it slammed into another tree and turned back.

"Move," Palomides called, and Lancelot's training and lifetimes of action brought him to his feet, drew the sword from his waist. He didn't run, didn't panic. He stood tall and ready, didn't even glance to see if Palomides was ready before charging at the creature.

His attack seemed to surprise it, and he managed to land a blow to its shoulder before it turned, tail whipping around. Lancelot threw himself back and out of the way as the tail impacted a tree trunk, pulverizing it. Palomides was in right away, swinging his own sword, scoring a hit on its side, nearing its neck. Screeching, the beast bounded away from them, into the trees.

Lancelot pursued, hand tightening around the hilt of his sword. No one escaped him once he made up his mind. The creature fled, but not fast enough, and Lancelot leapt, landed on its back, stabbed into the creature's shoulder. It lurched, and Lancelot slid forward, found himself falling, weightless until he hit the ground and rolled to a stop. The creature roared, and Lancelot crouched, realizing that he didn't have his sword.

Over the centuries Lancelot had gotten used to staring down Death. But as he saw Glatisant rear up, huge eyes fixed in hatred on him, Lancelot felt a sudden pang of regret that had nothing to do with failing to capture the monster. It was that he hadn't done more with the damned fool who had brought him this far. Palomides.

And like that, the man himself charged in, Palomides' sword flashing in the crisp air, drawing a wide red line across the creature's chest. Glatisant balked and rolled backward, and Lancelot spotted his sword, dove to retrieve it. A moment later he was on his feet and the Questing Beast was into the trees again, in full retreat.

Lancelot's heart was beating fast, his blood pounding in his veins. He raised his sword and pushed forward, hot to follow, to track the beast, to finally catch Glatisant. But before he could move three steps he realized that Palomides was standing still, watching him with that small smile he had been wearing in Chicago. It stopped him, made him pause in his pursuit.

"What is it?" Lancelot asked. Something about that smile bothered him, as if it was catching him in something embarrassing or wrong.

"It is true what they say about you, then," he said. "That it's the chase that gets you going."

"What?" Lancelot asked, incapable at that moment of forming a coherent reply. What who said about him? The chase? All he wanted to do was hunt down the monster that had attacked them and maybe then wash off the ick and fuck. But Palomides stood still, shaking his head slowly.

"Like with Guinevere," Palomides said, and Lancelot's hand tightened around the hilt of his sword. Most people knew better than to mention her. "All that talk of love eternal, all those stolen moments, and when you're finally free to be with her for eternity you run off to play this game instead. Where is she now? Living like a monk in Sweden?"

Lancelot considered turning around, walking away. Horny or not, he didn't have to stand there while Palomides analyzed and questioned his decisions. Guinevere had never been so serious a thing. Sure, he had enjoyed the jousts, the stolen kisses, the times they would fuck in Arthur's bed, but he had fucked Arthur on that bed just as many times. It wasn't about love, though that's what everyone else seemed to think. But he had come to terms with his past, with his first life, ages ago. He and Guinevere and Arthur had all made their peace and moved on. Why be bogged down by history? Lancelot wanted to be judged in the moment, in the now.

"I think it's the chase you're after. You weren't interested in Glatisant at all until he came charging through here, and now you're hot to follow. You're like a dog after a bone."

"What's it to you?" Lancelot asked, stepping forward. A part of him wanted to duel the man right there and be done. He was still Lancelot, still unbeaten. "What do you care what I do, who I love or don't love?"

Lancelot barely noticed Palomides move, but suddenly the man was in front of him, tall frame sweeping forward aggressively. Lancelot jumped back, sword rising from his side to hover between them. The small smile on Palomides' face was gone, replaced by something Lancelot could only describe as hungry.

"Maybe I wonder what it would take to keep your interest," Palomides said. "Maybe I wonder how to last more than a week in your bed. Maybe I've seen all the others topped by the great Lancelot and left to wander afterward alone and heartbroken and I don't want to end up that way."

Lancelot huffed. He really wasn't that bad. He never led anyone on. He let them know from the start that he was only in it for the sex, for the thrill. If some of them got more involved than he did, it was hardly his fault.

"Wait. You mean... you want...."

"You," Palomides said, finishing the thought, and he brushed Lancelot's sword aside as he stepped closer and let his own blade fall to the ground. Lancelot started to back away but Palomides was already to him, hands wrapping around the back of his neck, tangling his long hair, pulling him into a fierce kiss.

"Wait," Lancelot said, breaking the kiss, struggling with the rush of new circumstances. Wasn't he still angry about the Guinivere thing? But Palomides' tongue exploring his mouth was distracting, and it felt so good to have the taller man's body pressed against his, their cocks, erect and straining against their jeans, rubbing each other through the denim. He dropped his sword as well.

"If I wait you'll just lose interest," Palomides said, and Lancelot didn't think that was fair but he didn't argue as Palomides' hands dropped to the buttons of his pants. Some things were better to just accept, and Lancelot was confident he could handle anything that happened.

At least, he was confident of it until Palomides reached a warm hand into his pants, sliding down the naked length of his erection. Closing his eyes, Lancelot concentrated on not going off too soon, despite how excited he was. Despite how he wanted to get back at Palomides for having made him wait for so long.

Together they moved so that Lancelot's back was against a tree, and Palomides took the opportunity to use his free hand to undo Lancelot's sword belt and tug down his jeans and boxers, revealing his cock to the open air. Lancelot gasped at the chill on his thighs, but Palomides was doing more than enough to make sure he didn't get cold.

"Seems like someone's a bit eager," Palomides said, breaking the kiss, trailing soft nips down Lancelot's neck.

"Like you didn't know what you were d—" Lancelot could barely stifle a moan as Palomides gave his cock a gentle squeeze and then knelt before him. Strong hands quested up and down his legs, and Lancelot whimpered slightly as he felt Palomides' hot breath on his smaller head. The air was crisp, with a faint smell of wet earth and blood from their fight with the Questing Beast. Had that been only a moment ago? Strange how things seemed to blend together now, and Lancelot felt his body buck forward as Palomides' mouth engulfed his cock.

Lancelot leaned back against the tree, hands finding Palomides' short hair. He wanted to push forward, to thrust, but Palomides held his hips, refused to let him. Slowly he took Lancelot in an inch, two, then stopped. Lancelot felt his cock throb with frustration as Palomides backed off, then took him again only that far.

"You could at least do a proper job," Lancelot said though gritted teeth. Palomides just smiled and stood, hands going to his own sword belt and pants, which he quickly had open and pushed down. His cock bounced free, and Lancelot swallowed.

"Care to show me how?" Palomides asked. Lancelot growled and kicked his pants completely off, pulled his shirt up and over his head at the same time so he was completely naked. He stood, glowering, wondering less how he had gotten into this situation and more how he was going to make the man in front of him pay for teasing him.

He started by grabbing the bottom of Palomides' shirt and slipping his hands inside, letting them glide over hard muscles. He found that small trail of hair and followed it up with his mouth, found Palomides' navel and dipped his tongue in, heard a gasp and felt him squirm beneath the touch. The air was still cold and the forest around them was silent, waiting breathless for him to continue. He did, pulling off Palomides' shirt as his mouth traced muscles up until he found a nipple. Lancelot played his tongue along the skin where nipple met chest and felt Palomides squirm again.

"Not so talkative now," Lancelot said, and gave the nipple a soft nip.

Hands appeared on his shoulders, pushing him down, and Lancelot didn't fight it, let himself drop until he was eye level with Palomides' cock. For a moment he only looked, admired the gentle curve upward, the flushed head that seemed to pulse gently. Lancelot licked his lips and then opened his mouth.

Palomides moaned as Lancelot took him as deep as he could, going slow so he didn't gag. When he couldn't go any further he paused, getting used to the girth, then pulled out, sucking gently as he went. He pushed back down, increasing the pace, using one hand to cup Palomides' sack and the other to grasp the base of his cock, steadying it as he pushed down again and again.

"I think I see your point," Palomides said, voice strained. "Your technique is definitely better." Lancelot liked the sound of that, the barely controlled pleasure leaking into Palomides' words. He was Lancelot, after all. Instead of answering, though, he just went even faster, concentrating on not pushing too deep, on not gagging, but determined to push Palomides' cock right to the brink.

Before he could press faster, though, Palomides stepped back and his cock pulled free of Lancelot's mouth with an audible pop. Lancelot himself tried to follow forward but found a hand on his shoulder, stopping him. He looked up, annoyed, only to find that familiar, infuriating smile waiting for him.

"Have something in mind?" Lancelot asked, wondering if Palomides would ever let either of them get off. The taller man laughed and pulled Lancelot up. And then in one motion he backed Lancelot back up against the tree again and stood with his legs slightly bent, his own feet on either side of Lancelot's so that he was nearly straddling him. Their bodies pressed together, their cocks touching.

"I thought we might have something of a joust," Palomides said, and Lancelot hissed in a breath as Palomides' large hand wrapped around both their cocks.

"What does the winner get?" Lancelot managed to ask. Laughter was his answer. Palomides held up his free hand and spit into it, presented it to Lancelot to do the same. Without lube it would have to do. Lancelot spit and then took a ragged breath as Palomides took his slick hand and started pumping over both their cocks at once, the undersides rubbing together. Lancelot shuddered and leaned back into the tree, wrapped his arms around Palomides' firm ass to keep him from falling back

"You think you'll get bored of this?" Palomides asked, and Lancelot grunted, didn't want to answer, didn't want to think of anything but the pleasure he was feeling, the tingle that was working its way from his balls and into his stomach. If Palomides stopped now he would kill him.

"I'm...." Lancelot started to warn but Palomides just pumped faster and Lancelot let himself go, let the feeling spread from his stomach to his limbs and finally back into his cock, where it released in a hot stream up and over Lancelot's chest, over his stomach, over Palomides' stomach and both of their cocks. Lancelot gasped and squirmed as Palomides kept moving, kept pumping despite the intense sensations. Lancelot endured, felt the pace falter, and opened his eyes to see Palomides gasp and climax, his eyes closing, his mouth opening as he came. Lancelot watched as the same face that had smirked in frustrating confidence melted away into shuddering pleasure, teeth gritting to let in staccato breaths as Lancelot felt new jets of warmth spatter his body. It was a face Lancelot had never seen before on Palomides, and one that he felt the strong urge to know better, to see again and again and again.

Finally Palomides slowed to a stop and they both heaved in great breaths, their bodies shivering in the sudden cold, the sudden absence of their pleasure. Lancelot gave a small chuckle.

"I guess you won," he said, knowing that he had fallen first. So much for Lancelot the unbeaten. Not that he minded. "What were the stakes again?"

"Well," Palomides said, making a show of thinking hard. "I did say I didn't want to end up like all the others who had been topped by the great Lancelot. So maybe—"

"Not without lube," Lancelot said hastily. Other thoughts threatened to crowd into his mind. Weren't they in the woods for a reason? Probably not worth thinking about. Palomides' smile left no room for other thoughts, anyway.

"Then I'm sure we can work something out."

And they did, with their hands and their mouths, on the forest floor and in high branches of the trees. And Lancelot discovered that with Palomides' tongue priming him, the lube wasn't required after all.

Lancelot woke some time later. His whole body was shivering, and absently he reached out for Palomides, to pull him closer. Only Palomides wasn't there. Eyes opened quickly, found the woods around him empty, silent. He sat up.

There was no sign of where Palomides had gone. Or where Lancelot's clothes had gone. Had he thrown them up a tree? It was possible, but he didn't think so. Damn it was cold. He moved to stand and that's when he saw the note, a small folded piece of paper that obviously didn't belong. Lancelot hoped it was just Palomides letting him know he had gone back to the car to get more stuff

Lancelot picked up the note and quickly read it. I'm pretty sure Glatisant will be moving on after this. I'm betting north, into Canada. I think I'll follow it. Maybe I'll see you around. PS. I took the car. Good luck. He read the words three times to make sure he got it right. Then he crumpled the paper and threw it onto the ground.

That bastard. That sneaking, conniving bastard. He would pay for this. There was no way Lancelot was going to let him get away with it, get away with making a fool out of him. Oh, let him run, but Lancelot would track him down. It would be his quest, and when he caught up he'd make sure to even the score. And then some. He'd leave the man handcuffed to a buoy in Hudson Bay. Or at least to a hotel bed in the Hudson Bay Hotel. A small smile crept over Lancelot's face.

The Night Air
Mary Anne Mohanraj

Not fucking again. Literally fucking, which was the problem—
Kimmie's upstairs neighbors, the skinny brown human and the
curvy gold human, were at it again. For what, the fourth time
tonight? The management could claim however much it wanted
that the walls were supposed to be sound-proofed; the truth was
that this was a shitty apartment, it clearly wasn't up to code, and
when two grown adults decided to hurl their bodies together on
a battered wooden bed, you could hear it. You would think after
getting the news that the war was finally on, after years of hate-
mongering and human-supremacist-group posturing, the pair
would have gone decently to sleep, but no. They were probably
celebrating life or some such bullshit. Kimmie couldn't take it anymore. She shoved back the chair from her desk, grabbed a fur to
wrap around herself, and headed out into the night.

She just wanted to walk, far and fast and until her brain
stopped buzzing. Sometimes walking helped. The streets were
more empty than usual—everyone who had someone was probably at home, cuddling them up, waiting for the bombs to fall or
the shooting to start or the diseases to spread or just for the chips
in their heads to catch viruses, melt, and drip out of their brains.
And yeah, the truth was that if she had someone, Kimmie would
probably do the same thing. But she didn't, and that alone was
enough to make it easy to glare at the people who were glaring at
her, as they always did when they saw her walking around
wrapped in a fur. Fucking holier-than-thou types. How did they
know that it wasn't synthetic? It could totally be synthetic.

It wasn't, but they had no way of knowing that, not unless they
looked past the thick bright azure fur she'd wrapped around herself. Not unless they could look at Kimmie's own orange pelt, the
pointed crimson ears jammed into a knitted cap, the clawed hands,

the fucking tail, and correctly identify her as Varisian. Sure, if they did that, and if they then happened to be educated enough to be familiar with the adulthood rituals of her tribe, then they might recognize that the remains of the creature wrapped around her were, in fact, real. That it was her own kill, and that she had managed to face down a dumb critter with three times her mass and armed only with what she could make herself after being dumped in the Jungle. Jungle with a capital J, because it was the only real Jungle left, huge and carefully preserved in the midst of Varisia, a world that had gone completely high-tech. And yet we still value our ancient rituals, oh yes, we care about who we are as a people, and any youngling who can't survive the way our people did a thousand years ago (when they had no fucking choice)—well, that kid doesn't deserve to live, does she?

Kimmie had survived it, but only just, emerging with three brutal scars scraped down her back that would tell her the weather the rest of her life. Not that she needed it here. The weather on Pyroxina Major was always the same, always programmed cool, drizzly, and supposedly-temperate—and you had to wonder what sort of colonial hang-ups these people had, that after going halfway across the galaxy, these descendants of Indians decided oh, hey, let's make sure our planet always feels just like jolly old England in the rainy damp springtime. Whose brilliant idea was that?

Everyone else seemed to like it fine, but Kimmie was always fucking freezing here, and sometimes—truth be told, every damn day—she wondered why she'd bothered to come here at all. This was why she hadn't just opted out of the idiotic adulthood ritual, because only those who passed it (survived it) were deemed by the planetary higher-ups to be acceptable representatives of their species to the outside universe. So fine, she jumped through their hoops, because if there was one thing she had wanted, with the burning passion of a thousand white dwarf suns, it was to go to the University of All Worlds on Pyroxina Major, where she could learn to program like the gods themselves. And here she was, for all the good it was doing her. So she was damn well going to wear her fur, and all the judgmental vegetarian locals could just go fuck themselves.

God, she hadn't had a steak in almost ten years. It would be ten years after the semester and the subsequent monsoons ended. More fucking rain. Ten years of eating synthetic meat, and you could taste the difference with every bitter bite, no matter what they said. Her advisor had told her, sympathetically, that graduate school was an exercise in deprivation. And she had tried, goddess knows, but this place had climbed into her brain, colonized her inside and out. She didn't even think of herself by her real name anymore, Kimsriyalani, but instead as Kimmie, a name that got plastered to her by an idiot grad student who touched her fur on the first day of orientation and said loudly, smiling, that the orange shade reminded him of his mother's kim-chee, and that if she didn't mind, he'd just call her Kimmie.

And the worst of it was that he had been drop-dead gorgeous, and Kimmie had been lonely, and she had said yes, Kimmie would be fine, and she smiled up at him. She did like a tall man. And that had cost her five years of work.

She'd dated the bastard, helped him with his pathetic research, and then he'd bolted, taking her best results with him and claiming them for his own. He was clever with faking computer data, she had to give him that. Clever at manipulating people. Clever at all sorts of things that didn't involve actually working. And so, five years in, she'd started all over. New topic, new research, and a new resolve not to make the same mistake again. Kimmie'd gone on the offense, finally, switched from defense systems to weapons, and although she'd never admit it to her mother, with all her painful glorying in their supposed warrior heritage, Kimmie had to admit to herself that she had a knack for weapon systems. They were intoxicating in their beauty, their power. When she sank into the depths of the code, she felt on the verge of drowning, or flight.

A vow of celibacy had helped, along with a hell of a lot of time in the lab. Kimmie was almost there, too, almost ready to call it done, and now there was this stupid. fucking. war. She wasn't ready, and what idiots thought they could pull off an interstellar war anyway? Too big, too expensive, too likely to blow up in their faces. Not to mention, too fucking speciesist. Varisia was many Jumps away, and well-defended, at least in theory. But they'd never actually had to use their ships and defense grid against a horde of humans. There were just so damn many humans. The war was being pushed by a fringe group now, just three of the human-settled planets in alliance against the universe, or at least the non-human / humod parts of it. But if all the humans joined in, Kimmie knew, in the cold center of her chest, that her people were unlikely to survive.

Kimmie stopped walking, wrapped her arms even more tightly around herself. She was on a path in some park she'd never seen before, surrounded by trees, the light of the moons barely making it through the dense leaves. Dark enough that the humans would barely be able to see at all, though she had no such trouble. It would be a good place to cry, but she hadn't cried in a long time. She'd held herself together by sheer force of will, but now—now Kimmie couldn't take it anymore. She'd been running the same damn loop in her head for five years now, obsessing over what she'd done, what she'd done wrong, and what good had it done her? It had let her focus on her work, sure, wrapped up in bitterness and despair, and that might be good for science, but it kind of sucked for her. She walked up to a nearby tree and slowly, deliberately, started banging her forehead against it. Her fur cushioned the blows, but still, they hurt. Bang. Bang. Bang. It was a good pain, she tried to tell herself. It was better than feeling nothing at all. Bang. Bang. Bang.

"Hey—are you all right?"

He was tall; he was dark. He wasn't exactly handsome, with ears that stuck out and oddly thick glasses in a world where almost everyone got that sort of thing corrected. But he wasn't bad either, and Kimmie had stopped trusting handsome a long time ago. This one looked—nice. He'd stopped a careful distance away, far enough not to be threatening, close enough not to have to shout.

Perfect judgement, really. Maybe that was why she turned fully around, took five long strides up to within an inch of him, tilted her head up and said, "Fuck me, please."

"Miss?" he asked, clearly totally bewildered, and that was charming too, the odd archaic term coming out of nowhere. And she knew she shouldn't, but he could walk away if he wanted to—he was bigger than she was, maybe even stronger (although maybe not, you never knew with these humans, they could be surprisingly fragile)—and she just didn't care. Kimmie was up on her toes and carefully, quickly, pressing her lips against his, mouth open, breathing her breath into his mouth. Thank goddess almost nothing crossed the species barrier—one less thing to worry about, and maybe there was at least one benefit to dating humans after all. He hesitated for one breath more and then oh, thank you thank you thank you, he was kissing her back, his arms coming around her, so that she felt free to do the same, the fur falling to the ground, and moments later, she was pulling him down onto it, and he came down with her, willingly.

She peeled out of her jumpsuit as fast as she could, trusting him to manage his own clothes—human clothes always had so many weird little buttons and laces and zippers and things. And then they were naked, wrapped around each other, rolling on the ground—and no, they didn't stay on the fur, it wasn't that big, but it didn't matter, the grass was great too, soft and thankfully dry. When he pushed into her, he stopped, surprised, and started to ask, "You're not—" and she said "No, no, it's just been a long time. A really long time." That seemed to be enough explanation for him, so she didn't have to go on to explain how Varisian females were built a little more compactly inside than human females—oh, the bastard had loved that—but she wasn't going to think about him anymore. Not with this man, this gentleman—because she didn't know his name and she had to call him something inside her own head and if he could be archaic, so could she—not with him sliding all the way in, his mouth hot on hers, his hands digging into her furry ass.

This gentleman was not being so gentle anymore, now that he was buried in her to the hilt and oh, goddess. Oh, please. Why the fuck had she been so stupid for so long? It seemed as if he were somehow inside every inch of her, from head to fingers to toes, like stars exploding as he began to move, pulling out and slamming back in again. A blazing light streaked overhead, followed by a dull explosion that shook the ground. But she barely noticed either, lost to the motion of their bodies, locked together. She writhed beneath him, and had to fight once more—it had been so long—to remember not to let her claws dig into an unguarded human back. Retract, retract, that was the rule, and she could manage it, almost—oh, there was a small scrape, and on one level she was sorry, but on another level she was a nova, and the nova had a name, and it was Kimsriyalani! and she would never ever ever be fucking Kimmie again.

The Closing Shift
JJ Poulos

Ramona loved the closing shift.

The quiet swish of the broom, collecting crumbly bits of muffins. The scent of cleaner and the gleam of a dozen wet matte tables. Hot clouds of steam from the sanitizer and the glint of the clean espresso machine. She loved smelling like cleaner and coffee and hard work. She loved turning off the lights on a sparkling, organized coffee bar, locking the doors, and walking home in the dark.

Ramona loved the bleary college students who came in for their last minute red-eyes. She loved the self-important suits who never tipped and asked for their non-fat no-foam sugar-free vanilla lattes, the most soulless drink in the entire universe. She loved the older patrons and their foamy, decaf lattes, never finished but always savored. The closing shift was quiet and organized and everything Ramona needed.

And then something threw a wrench into Ramona's job, Ramona's universe, Ramona's very fiber.

Anne, Ramona's boss, dropped the bag of beans without ceremony on her pristine, still-damp floor.

"How are you?" She gave Ramona a warm, friendly hug. She smelled like herbal shampoo and pencil shavings, her body strong and humming with energy. Ramona had wanted to sleep with her boss since she'd started working at the coffee shop. She was bisexual and had that adorable, middle-aged athletic lesbian thing going on. She gave a lot of hugs, and Ramona always wanted them to last longer.

"We got a new variety of espresso bean! Do you have plans tonight?"

"Just going home and studying," Ramona said.

"Mind staying late?"

Visions of Anne on the desk in the back room danced through Ramona's head. "Not at all."

"Great! You'll need to empty the hopper, scrub it, and then put the new beans in. They're fantastic, a whole new kind of super rare bean. I'll be in early tomorrow to get the grind tested." She hugged her again. "You're the best. See you later!"

And then she was gone, and the smile dropped off Ramona's face.

She locked the doors and turned up her Pandora station and started in on the espresso hopper, trying to work out the hum in her body, the wet warmth that persisted between her legs, the insistent picture in her mind of Anne on the desk in back, leaning on the coffee bag, papers under her, and Ramona's face buried—

She scrubbed and scrubbed, willing the image out of her mind.

Finally the hopper was sparkling, and she turned to the new bag of beans. It was made of rough burlap, covered in writing she couldn't even begin to read, and beautiful, colorful swirling lines.

She grabbed a scissors and sliced the bag open.

The scent that burst out was unlike anything she'd smelled. It was dark and rich and flowery. The beans were glossy with oil and slid about as if they were alive. Ramona closed her eyes and breathed in the smell. She opened her eyes and, leaving the bag on the ground, turned to grab the hopper.

There was a water-like patter as the bag tipped over, as the beans danced across the floor.

"Shit," Ramona said, before turning around.

Far too large for the bag, like a coffee bean that sprouted into a tree and then grew until it burst from the bag's darkness, and then grew some more, a woman lay. She was dark like the espresso beans and she gleamed glossily, like they did. They spilled around her like rose petals.

"Thank you for letting me out," she said, smiling a brilliant smile.

Ramona made a strangled noise. "Where did you come from?"

"Originally? Or just now?"

Ramona's mouth opened and closed, wordlessly.

"I was in there," she pointed to the bag at her feet. "I was sleeping on my tree when the beans were picked, I think. I only woke up a little while ago." She stood up and stretched, her body endlessly elongating. She seemed to be as tall as a tree for a moment.

"How—that's not possible. You're way too large to fit in that bag."

The woman smiled. "My size changes. I was sleeping in a coffee cherry. I'm—mmm. You could call me a dryad, I suppose."

"That's not possible."

The dryad laughed. "You seem to think a lot of things aren't possible. Here." She stepped up to the counter, laid her dark hand against the blue marble, and trailed her fingers across it, slow and sensual. Where her hand had been, leaves—dark and ridged—and little white flowers sprung up, as if they had been growing there all along. Ramona gave a little cry and reached out to touch the cool dark leaves, the delicate white flowers.

"You're a dryad."

She laughed. "I am. And you saved me. Now I can go back to my tree."

"We're pretty far away from places that grow coffee trees," Ramona said, feeling suddenly guilty. "Do you—you might—we should find you a plane ticket or something."

The dryad laughed again. "That's very kind of you, but now that I am free, I will make it just fine." She walked around the counters, her head tilted, her fingers touching everything, but leaving no leaves. "So this is where my beans go."

"Y-yes, though we've not had this kind of bean before. Your kind of bean."

The dryad nodded. "Do people like their coffee here? Do they respect it?"

Ramona felt herself nodding with perhaps too much vigor. "We take great care to make the highest quality drinks. People are always coming back—they love it."

"Good."

She turned back towards Ramona. "Before I go—you helped me with my problem. I would like to help you with your problem."

Ramona felt her face heat up. "I—I don't have any problems—"

The dryad stepped towards Ramona, a small, confident smile on her lips. "I am a coffee dryad. Coffee brings warmth to the body—it makes hearts race. It readies bodies." She stepped towards her again. "Your body—your heart—is already warmed. I heard—I felt—you talking to that woman."

"My boss," Ramona murmured. The dryad nodded. She stepped closer—Ramona was surrounded by the scent of coffee beans. Up close the dryad was now, somehow, the same height as Ramona. She was suddenly acutely aware that the creature wore no clothes—that her breasts were small and pert, that her hips curved just a little, that she looked soft and very, very close. The dryad ran a finger down Ramona's dark hair, braided over her shoulder. She had no hair of her own, her head round and dark.

"Your boss. You were very disappointed by her. May I—warm you?"

Ramona took a deep, shaky breath. "Yes," she whispered.

The dryad reached one long arm around Ramona and pulled her close, kissing her. Her lips tasted like dark, rich coffee, deep and complex. They parted for a moment, and Ramona took another deep breath, delirious with the dryad's rich scent and delicious lips.

She caught her gaze, brown eyes reflecting brown eyes. Ramona touched the dryad's long neck and they kissed again, urgently. The dryad's lips parted, and Ramona tasted something lighter, brighter, the warmth of her tongue intoxicating. She needed more of it. More.

Ramona wrapped her arms around the dryad's frame, her hands resting on the perfect, bare curve above her bottom. She pulled her close, kissing deeper, lost in the sweet taste of her kiss and the intense heat of their commingling bodies.

Still kissing, the dryad's hands found the buttons of Ramona's shirt, and began to unbutton it. She shivered with pleasure as the cool air kissed her skin, as the dryad's fingers brushed the round of her stomach, as they moved up her body. She pulled away as the last button came undone, and she stared at Ramona as she slipped the shirt gently off her shoulders.

"Mm—ah—what—what should I call you?" Ramona asked. "Do you have a name?"

The dryad thought for a moment.

"The last human I laid with called me Chaoua."

"Chaoua," Ramona said.

"I hope, though, that you won't be able to say much of anything for very much longer."

Ramona's knees went weak.

The dryad laid a path of sweet kisses across Ramona's shoulders as she tugged at her bra. Her breasts spilled out, and Chaoua took them in her narrow hands and caressed them lovingly. Her palms were slightly rough, like the bark of a young tree, and the sensation against Ramona's nipples made her whimper. The dryad was smiling a wicked smile.

"You are melting like oil in the hot sun. Do not melt too fast. I want to taste you."

Ramona moaned, unable to contain her excitement, all the more excited to hear her sexual sounds echo in the empty coffee house. Chaoua smiled and unzipped Ramona's pants, slipped her out of her boots and pants and then Ramona was naked, there, behind the counter. She turned and carefully folded the clothes and stacked them on the counter. Ramona watched her supple body moving, and suddenly needed to touch it, to know what every inch of her skin felt like. She stepped forward and began kissing the sweet, tender valleys and hills of her back, from her strong shoulders to the dimples of her bottom. She went back to the dryad's neck and, then her breasts. They were soft and warm and Chaoua made the most beautiful noises when Ramona touched them.

Ramona guided her like that to the counter top, between the bakery case and the cash register, and lifted her gently onto it.

"So cold!" The dryad squeaked.

"We'll warm it," Ramona said, parting her legs. It had been a long time since she had touched anyone besides herself, and it was thrilling. Chaoua was thrilling.

Chaoua leaned down to kiss her, to run her hands over Ramona's body. Chaoua was wet, and Ramona trailed her fingers through the moisture on her inner thighs before gently parting her inner lips.

"Yes, please," Chaoua whispered. Her brown eyes were shut, and her face was intent, concentrating. Her lower lip caught in her teeth as Ramona slid two fingers into Chaoua's slick vulva. Her thumb found her clitoris and she stroked it with gentle, reverent touches. Chaoua gasped and bucked against Ramona's hand. There was a smell of coffee in the air—not the deep, flowery aroma of the beans, but the smell of coffee brewing, a hot, wet, urgent smell.

"More," Chaoua said, and Ramona slid another finger in, and another. Chaoua bucked against Ramona's hand, urgent. Her skin carried the dark sheen of sweat, her nipples were hard, and her hands clutched at Ramona as if she were drowning. Her writhing was everything, but Ramona needed to know how she tasted.

She leaned her head over and ran her tongue over her clit. The dryad gave a cry of joy. She tasted sweeter than Ramona had expected—she'd expected perhaps something like a well-pulled espresso shot, but Chaoua lacked that bitterness. Still, she tasted of coffee, a smooth, slightly musky taste, rich and good. Ramona pushed her tongue against Chaoua's clitoris and licked with firm, long strokes, feeling Chaoua tighten around her fingers, feeling her body twitch, her clitoris pulse under the adoring lapping of her tongue.

Ramona stopped her tonguing long enough to kiss those delicate breasts again, to find the dryad's mouth and kiss it, too. Chaoua's mouth was dry from moaning and eager, desperate for attention. Ramona stared into her beautiful green eyes as she fucked her to orgasm, the dryad riding her hand with frantic, wanton need, screaming and arching in glorious, lusty beauty.

She curled over Ramona's body, her head resting on Ramona's shoulder, forehead pressed into the curls that had escaped her ponytail. Ramona continued to gleefully tease her, delicately pressing her clitoris as it pulsed, sliding her fingers in and out and around the wonderful wet mess that was the dryad's vulva.

"Stop," she whimpered, and Ramona slowly, remorsefully, removed her hand. She glanced down and gasped. Her fingers, her dripping palm, the floor, and the counter top soaked in coffee flowers. Tiny white drips of flowers, individually spotting the floor, and a cluster so big between her legs it was impossible to see the marble between the petals. Ramona opened her hand and the flowers gently floated from her palm to the ground, as if unconcerned by gravity's pull.

Chaoua gave a luxurious chuckle. "I made a mess." She hopped off the counter, leaving the puddle of brilliant white flowers perfect and unbothered.

She dropped to her knees in front of Ramona, her hairless, dark head coming up to her chest. Chaoua kissed her breasts again, taking one nipple into her mouth and one in her fingertips and teasing them gently, then harder and harder until Ramona thought she might come just then. Chaoua switched to the other, and sucked on it, teasing her sore, wet nipple with the tips of her fingers. Ramona held on to the coffee counter until her hands hurt.

Chaoua left a trail of kisses down her round stomach, and over her hips. Ramona giggled and squirmed. She left glossy coffee-oil spots where her lips lingered.

"Just a taste—" she said teasingly, her breath hot over the crease between Ramona's thigh and her mound. Ramona held her breath, the anticipation overwhelming and absolutely perfect. A moan, jagged and ecstatic and loud enough to fill the empty coffee house, bubbled out of her, as Chaoua brought her warm lips to Ramona's wet, swollen mound.

Her mouth was electric, shooting pleasure through Ramona's body. She felt herself riding Chaoua's mouth desperately, Chaoua's hands cupping her butt cheeks and squeezing them gently. Ramona lay her hands over Chaoua's warm, bare head for something to tether herself to reality as she lost herself in intense waves of pleasure. Her orgasm shook her and lasted an eternity and left her weak and giddy.

Chaoua sat down, pulling Ramona down onto her lap. Ramona practically fell, her legs jelly and her breath ragged, laughing. Chaoua kissed her gently, her face messy.

Chaoua held her up with one strong arm, and slipped her other between Ramona's legs. Ramona was perhaps more wet and excited than she'd ever been, and Chaoua's fingers felt big and firm and ever so competent. She almost said no—she was tired—but her fingers felt so good, a warm aftertaste to the best thing she'd ever had, and she was tired, but—she needed it, needed more. Chaoua fingered her slowly, firmly, and cradled in the strong arms of the dryad she came again, screaming, sweating, senseless in her pleasure.

She gently slumped to the floor, spent, and Chaoua nestled onto her soft arm, her face against her breast. She felt warm and ecstatic and good from her toes to her cheeks. Their breathing slowed and synchronized. Ramona was almost—almost—asleep on the floor of the coffee shop behind the coffee counter when Chaoua stirred and stretched.

"Thank you," she said. "A thousand thanks."

Ramona smiled sleepily. "Thank you."

"I should go."

"I should too."

Chaoua sat up and stretched some more, so glossy and beautiful.

"If—if I can—may I come back and visit you?"

Ramona blushed deeply and sat up, her body humming still. "I would like that."

Ramona pulled on her clothes and Chaoua swept up the beans

with her hands, setting them reverently into the bag. They finished their tasks and stood across from each other, neither willing to leave.

"I... can I walk you to the door?"

Chaoua put out her hand, and Ramona took it, and they opened the door together. The night was cool and fragrant with the smell of autumn leaves.

"Won't you be cold?" She touched Chaoua's shoulder, and it was still warm.

Chaoua laughed. "I am a being of the trees. We get cold, we get hot. We sleep, we wake, we grow." She leaned down—she was taller again, almost stretching to the height of the sapling oak outside the coffee house door—and kissed Ramona on the lips, gently, smelling for a second like hot, fresh espresso.

"I'll see you soon," Chaoua said.

"I look forward to it," Ramona whispered.

Chaoua let go of her hand and in a blink she wasn't there at all. Ramona gave a little gasp, and then saw something—something brown, something with wings, something a little textured, like bark—dart through the orange oak leaves and into the sky. Ramona held her breath and watched and waited, but that was it. Chaoua was gone.

Inside, Ramona's phone was ringing.

"Ramona?" It was Anne.

"Hey! I'm, um, almost done here." She blushed, though she did not feel bad at all.

"Great, thank you. I can't wait to try it out tomorrow." There was a pause. "Listen... I was wondering. Do you want to get a drink sometime?"

Ramona looked at the coffee flowers and breathed in the lingering scent of hot, wet espresso.

"Yeah. I'd like that."

Off the phone, she took a paper pastry bag and she filled it to the brim with perfect white flowers, and she took them home. She poured them into a bowl and watched as they slowly turned into beautiful red coffee cherries. Their husks died and, one day, fell off, and Ramona would run her fingers through the green coffee beans and breathe in their delicate scent, remembering.

Wizard's Staff
Julie Cox

Next to Borabi, I was short. Not that I was tall next to most other people, either, but Borabi's long limbs were a dramatic contrast to my stocky build. He was lithe and graceful until he was startled, then those limbs went flailing everywhere like a colt's. When that happened, I laughed, and he scowled. Most of the time it was the other way around.

Like now. He writhed beneath me, a squirming mess of an elf, his breath hitching as he tried to stop himself from laughing. I held the paintbrush away from him and cuffed his pointed ear.

"Stop moving," I said. "These runes are very precise. I don't want to open a portal to some demonic realm because you're ticklish."

"I can't help it, Shale," he lied.

He could help it very well. He had unbelievable control, when he chose to exercise it. I leaned close over him, dabbing a spot of cornflower blue paint on his delicate nose. "Hold still, or I will stop touching you."

His pretty hazel eyes fluttered wide and his body stilled beneath me.

"There now," I crooned, "that's better." I drew the paint in thin lines across his body, weaving a spell with interlocking runes, the language of dwarves and of magic. I traced the curve of his bicep with a rune for the sorceress I needed to contact. His other arm was wreathed in the symbols of magical power, symbols for me to draw upon, like sinking a well into the ground beneath us to pull up the magic of the earth. I was dwarven; my magic was the power of stone and wells and mines and old language. I'd covered his chest in the runes of our families, the significant runes of our lives, the collective language that described our lives, apart and together. In naming them, I named us. We were the sum of our stories—literally, in the case of runic magic. Those had been easy; I'd painted those a thousand times.

I slid down his half-nude body, careful not to smudge the runes. I knelt between his legs and undid the lacing on his pants. He grinned at me, and I gave him a warning look: don't move. He bit his lip and obeyed. We'd been together long enough I could command him by raising an eyebrow, curling a lip, crooking a finger. Of course, he disobeyed half the time, all mischief and playfulness, so that I would have to engage him and correct him. Neither of us would have it any other way.

He was half hard already as I pulled his pants down and away. He purred little groans and moans as I stroked the paintbrush up the underside of his cock, the cool slickness of the paint contrasting the heat of his skin and the callouses of my hand. He was long and slender, whereas I was short and thick. Just like we were everywhere else. His balls were hairless; a pale patch of straight, silkysoft hair fringed his crotch, as blonde as he was everywhere else. The paint eased the friction as I ran my hand up and down his cock, the head emerging from his foreskin as he stiffened.

I lowered my mouth to his cock and slid it between my lips. I felt the blood swell his cock in my mouth, growing more turgid every moment. He tasted salty and distinctly elven, like rain and grass and the damp forest floor. The paint was sweet, and as familiar a taste as his skin. He rocked his hips, wanting more, trying to fuck my mouth. I rasped my tongue against the underside of his cock, right where he liked it. That got him to stop moving, though he grew distinctly louder, and the rest of him began to squirm again.

My own cock was hard now, and my body begged for friction. I sat up and undid my own pants. I raised his narrow hips and pressed between his thighs, grasping us both in one thick-fingered hand.

"Shale," he whispered, letting his head fall back. I loved the shape of my name in his mouth. He made it sound like something beautiful and ephemeral, instead of a flaky rock.

"Oh my stars, you're so gorgeous," I rasped, watching him

writhe in pleasure. "Sometimes I'm astounded you picked me. How'd I get so lucky?"

"S'not luck," he said with a lecherous smirk. "It was dogged persistence. On my part. Or have you forgotten me howling outside your window like a fox in heat?"

"I don't think anyone who heard it ever forgot that," I said. God he felt good, and the memory of him professing his adoration for me so many years ago got me going all the more. I could stroke us off in moments; I knew exactly how to hold us together, how fast to go, how hard to squeeze. I knew the steps to this dance so well. But we weren't at that kind of ball.

He made a pitiful little noise of disappointment as I drew away from him, wiped the paint from his cock, and reloaded the paint brush. He jerked ever so slightly when I spiraled the blue paint over his balls, up his cock. It was cold against his now fever-hot skin, and he wilted a little. I dabbed a bit on the pad of my finger and slid it against his ass, pleasuring him that way, to get him back to full rigidity. I needed him as hard as he could get for this part, but I couldn't touch his cock anymore, not with the paint spiral on him. I slid a finger inside him; he unclenched, and I read the concentration on his suddenly serious face as he willed himself to relax. I added more paint, slicking my fingers; I applied a generous smear to my own cock, and he bit his lower lip, spread his legs wider.

"C'mon, Shale," he said. "I can take it."

"Whether you can or not is not the question," I said. "I need you to stay completely rigid, and that means I will not skirt the edge between pleasure and pain, or think of my own pleasure first. I must only inflict pleasure upon you this time, love."

"Poor me," he said. He let his head fall back as I pushed two fingers into him. My short, thick digits together were as large as an elf's cock, and Borobi slid ever so slightly back and forth on the stone floor, fucking himself on my hand. I put my other hand on his hip and held him, or tried to.

"I don't want to scratch up that pretty back," I said to him. I scissored my fingers, stretching him, then turned my hand, pushed as far in as I could, and began stroking that little spot in front that made his every muscle twitch with exquisite pleasure. I went slowly, gently, not wanting to bring him too soon and ground out the spell I'd written upon him. He moaned, his syllables incomprehensible. He tried to take his cock in hand and I swatted it away.

"I want to come," he whined.

"And you will. But not yet. I need you first."

He flattened his knees to the side. "Will you enter me at least?"

I removed my fingers, smiled, and leaned over him, the head of my paint-wet cock pressed against his ass. "Tell me what you want. Explicit, detailed, or I'll not fuck you at all. I can finished the spell without either of us actually coming."

"Don't you dare," he snarled.

"There's my wild elf. C'mon. You suck my cock with that mouth, so use it."

His expression was halfway between a grin and a snarl. "I want you to penetrate me," he said. "I want you to push your cock up my ass. I want you to fuck me hard, make me feel it. I want you to mark me and claim me and own me and master me. Show me who's boss, Shale."

The fact of the matter was that Borabi was the boss, but he didn't seem to know that. Everything I did waited on him. I prepped him, and waited for him to tell me I could enter him. I gathered the magic, worked and forged it, and he told me where and why to use it. I held him down, tied him up, when he told me he needed it and wanted it—which he never did out loud, naturally. That would be too easy on me. No, I had to watch for the patterns in speech and gesture for him to tell me what he wanted. It took a lot of work to be Borabi's lover.

But he was worth it. I pressed the head of my cock against the puckered ring of his ass and rocked my hips forward, penetrating his flesh. He moaned and shivered. I went little by little, two nudges forward, one nudge back, until I was balls-deep in him and he was so tight and hot around me it almost hurt. I pulled back out, almost all the way, added more of that cool, wet paint, and shoved back into him. He grinned maniacally. He loved this part, loved the initial sheathing, when he was so tight I could barely stand it and could barely resist it.

"I have to do the spell," I managed to say.

"Fine, go ahead with your spell," he said, head lolling back. "Just don't stop moving in me, ok?"

I held a shaking hand out, fingers spread, and murmured low in the old language of stone and water and magic. The blue paint began to glow. Across his chest and shoulders, on the tip of his nose, he glowed, eerie and beautiful, magic lighting up the runic paint. The spiral up his cock glowed. My cock glowed, visible then not visible from one moment to the next, dripping down my balls as I pumped into my lover. The magic liked that. Magic liked obscene acts, naked and primal ruttings in the dark. It liked secrets, and secret spaces, and raw, intimate moments. There was a reason witches danced naked by the fire, and why sex magic was so effective.

A portal opened in front of me, a gateway between us and the sorceress I sought. The sorceress that had dropped us into this cave, this prison. She started as she met my eyes through the gateway.

"What—How—?" She recovered quickly. "Clever creature, you've summoned a speaking-glass spell. How you did it with no wizard's staff is beyond me." She gave me a demure smile. "You must tell me your secrets when I call upon you later."

"Anything long and hard can substitute for a wizard's staff," I said. No need to get explicit yet about what long, hard objects I was using for a staff. "Allow me finish the message I'd set out to give you when you dropped my elvish friend and I into your dungeon." I rocked in and out of said elvish friend, and he looked smug about it.

"The pretty blonde creature? Oh, tell me you sacrificed him to a dark god!" Her smile was inhuman, her eyes rimmed with white.

"Oh, he's taken a pounding," I said, and Borabi sat up on his elbows to give me a 'what are you thinking?' look. He had a point. In my defense, my brain was low on blood.

She wasted only a moment trying to puzzle out what I was talking about before chasing the thought away with a little toss of her head and returning to the most pressing matter at hand.

"You've gone to such trouble to deliver a message, so deliver it."

I unscrewed the back end of the paintbrush and poured the tiny mountain of gold dust into my palm. I puffed up my cheeks and blew a straight, hard wind across my hand, carrying the dust through the gateway. The sorceress shook her head in surprise, blinking as the dust settled across her face.

"What is this magic?" she shrieked. "What can cross a speaking-glass? Have you cursed me, you foul creature, I'll—"

I was having some trouble talking while keeping up with Borabi, who had taken to shifting back and forth, fucking himself upon my cock when I faltered at maintaining a rhythm. Impatient man. I let her spew vile insults at me while I regained my control, hissing at Borabi that I couldn't finish yet, he had to slow down. He grinned at me like a teenager getting away with something.

"It's gold dust, is all," I said at last, interrupting her.

She stopped. "Gold dust? Why...?"

"Ground from a ring, from the hand of the Yellow King," I said.

She snarled. "That traitorous—"

"Oh, she speaks of traitors!" I said to Borabi, who wriggled his hips in a circle, making me bite my lip to keep from crying out. I focused on the sorceress. "And here I thought it was you who stole his treasure, made off with his child in the dead of night, when you were supposed to be married the next day."

She made a face. "It was more complex than that."

"It usually is." Borabi clenched and unclenched on me in light flutters, making me gasp and my eyes water.

"It was my dowry in the first place, and his child? Please, she was twenty years old, she was no more a child than you are." Understanding lit her face. "Are you doing something obscene over there?"

"Absolutely I am. And what did the king vow?"

"That he would give me a ring, and thus claim me, and I—" she stopped. "The ground up dust of a ring?"

"You can't give it back," I pointed out.

Her beautiful face twisted into a snarl. "You think you've captured me for that fool with a bunch of dust and a speaking-glass spell? It can't end that way! It can't! I've come too far!" She smashed something crystalline beside her; little white shards flew into the air like stars and disappeared.

"It was a complex spell, bound into that ring before it was ground down; it took him this long to work it. Give him some credit. Listen, I—oh wow, you have to stop that, elf—I sympathize with your plight. I'm just the messenger. You could offer to give the treasure back in return for your freedom."

"I already spent it," she muttered.

"On what?"

"Books and tuition."

"That's an expensive education."

"Sorceress," she said, as if that explained everything.

"Give me a second." I drew a line across Borabi's hips and tummy with a thin line of paint, drawing the magic away from the spiral on his cock to the rest of his body. It burned blue like the rest. There, that bought me a little flexibility. I took his cock in my hand and he stopped squirming so much beneath me, breathing hard and fast, his back arching up off the stone ground. For a moment I focused upon his body, the pleasure of sliding in and out of him. He bucked upward, perfectly angled to move along the shaft of my cock and fuck my hand, the glowing paint spreading across his pelvis and balls, getting caught in the light blonde hairs. There, he was happy now. I returned my attention to the sorceress.

"Are you done?" she asked, unimpressed.

"No, but I'm close," I gasped. "But listen. I realize you have me at your mercy."

"Indeed I do," she said.

"Indeed I do," Borabi echoed.

"And I wouldn't have come here if I hadn't had a backup plan."

She rolled her eyes. "Do tempt me with a different sort of cage, a new bargain, little dwarf. I have not yet had my fill of fae nonsense."

First, I was not fae, I was dwarven, there was a huge difference.

And second, I was not a little dwarf. I was rather tall for a dwarf, and more lithe than most, thanks to a human grandfather. But I didn't have time to parse peculiarities with her. Besides, I had to wrap this up before my "staff" became more of a limp noodle.

"Here me out," I said. "If you think about it a minute, you'll see that the Yellow King made two fatal errors with both his spell and its execution. In the latter, he sent a spellcaster capable of delivering the ring and sealing the magic. But he did not make allowances or plans for getting said spellcaster out again."

"He set you up," she said, lifting an eyebrow. "Or didn't even think of your fate long enough to realize it. Selfish prick. So he sent me an ally who knows the spell and its peculiarities."

I nodded. "I don't ordinarily hold with treachery, but I owe no kind of allegiance to he who would send my husband and me off to death or worse without even blinking an eye. After a lifetime of service, too."

She winced "Harsh. Well, he is the Yellow King. Great hoards of gold and all that. He didn't get where he is by caring much about others."

"Exactly. You're just another treasure to him, an object. He wants you because he was denied you once, because you took from him. In his twisted mentality," I amended. "Therefore, the spell he worked on that ring carries that attitude with it. Which brings us to the flaw in the ring's spell. Its specific wording was, you would be bound to give your hand in marriage." I paused in emphasis. "Your hand. Now, we all know that's metaphor, but that's the funny thing about magic."

"Its language is open to interpretation." She smirked.

"Yup. The less specific you are, the more the spell can be twisted."

"I'm kind of attached to my hand," she mused, "but more attached to my freedom. And then, dwarves are renowned craftsmen."

Borabi scowled and said loudly, "So are elves! I'm the craftsman, he's the magic one!"

"Pardon me," she said. "So, you imply you can make for me a replacement?"

"I'll make you a hand so wondrous you'll consider cutting the other hand off to get a matched set."

She arched a brow. "You'll need to release control of the ring's spell to me, for me to twist its meaning to my purpose."

"Let us out first."

She scoffed. "You invaded my home, attacked me. I have no reason to trust you. You are but words so far. I think a show of faith is more appropriate from you."

"Ok, but I'll have to close the speaking glass as soon as it finishes." As soon as I finished, actually. I looked down at Borabi."

"I'm going to need your help on this one."

"Not a problem," he answered coolly. He closed his eyes, concentrating. He squeezed down on me, just a little, so that he could feel every inch of me as I worked in and out of him. His muscles warmed, nearly too hot to be withstood. I gasped, and pumped harder into him out of no volition of my own. He tilted his hips up and down, slowly, changing the angle just a bit with every thrust of my cock. I moaned, jaw slack, my braids falling over the bare skin of my back.

I knew exactly what I needed to send that much magic to her. I withdrew from him suddenly. "Get on all fours," I growled at him, and he grinned. He flipped over, ass in the air, and I may have hurt him a little as I pushed back into him with sudden force.

Every movement of my hips hit that spot he liked so much, and he keened in a higher pitched voice. I loved this angle; I was better able to see my cock penetrating him, the light of the blue paint pulsing as I buried my cock in him. I reached around him and grabbed his cock, and began stroking him in rhythm to my own thrusts, as if between us we had a straight line from my balls to the tip of his cock.

I solidified in my mind the idea of a wizard's staff, a wizard summoning as much power from his staff as possible, laying out the laws of magic with his rod in hand. As magic would pour from the end of his rod, so it poured from me into him, and from the end of Borabi's cock, onto the ground. I rode him through it, sending magic through the speaking glass, my end of the tether that tied me to the Yellow King's spell. It was sloppy, imprecise magic, spilling out everywhere. The glass closed, the blue light faded out, and I collapsed onto my back, utterly exhausted.

She was kind enough to let us stew for only half a day before she let us out. Downright gracious, for a sorceress. The hand Borabi fashioned for her was, indeed, magnificent, covered in fine filigree like metallic lace. Personally I thought it was a little gawdy, but she loved it. For my part, I frequently thought of the hand she cut off and sent back to the Yellow King. I thought of how his attendant must have screamed (it would have been an attendant, not him personally), and how he must have raged when he discovered his error and my betrayal. The sorceress turned out to have an education worth every penny of her spent fortune, which made her a fascinating (and broke) person. The Yellow King's daughter, against all odds, had better sense, and between her sense and Borabi's craftsman knowledge, they made sure their academic lovers had money for books.

I heard a story once that the hand sits beside him in the Yellow Queen's throne, and he takes it to bed with him. But it's only rumor. Still, it gives me satisfaction to know that his four enemies are safe within the sorceress's tower, finding out all we can about sex magic, and all that powerful villain can get is a hand job. There's a little justice in the world after all.

Disarmed
Vinnie Tesla

Zuth stared at the anonymous rear door of the building, trying to puzzle out what he was seeing. He had long ago noted that there were two sorts of bodyguards: those who were supposed to be seen, and those who were not supposed to be seen. For convenience, one could call them bouncers and snipers. Bouncers were very effective at deterring amateurs—they made the client look like more trouble than he was worth to get at. Snipers were often better for stopping other professionals.

The nice thing about bouncers was that they were easy to find, and generally easy to kill.

The nice thing about snipers was that, if you were good, and they were not so good, they could often be killed without drawing unwanted attention.

Zuth knew that Eni was unlikely to go anywhere outside his home territory without examples of both varieties while the war was on. The bouncers outside the front door were classics of the type: big and mean looking, with formidable arrays of weaponry. The rear door appeared to be completely unguarded, so there had to be a sniper.

He was starting to conclude that that sniper had to be either very good or very bad. If he wasn't a rank incompetent who had wandered down to the pub for a pint or slipped and fallen off a rooftop somewhere, he was skilled enough to evade Zuth's survey of the block. Not many people in Ivy City could do that.

Zuth was intrigued, and just a little unnerved.

If there was a sniper he hadn't managed to find, approaching the rear door in his current outfit would likely be fatal. There are two ways to reduce the chance that a dangerous animal will attack you: don't look like prey, and don't surprise it.

He stowed his mask, hood, and gloves in a pocket and reversed his cape from its dead black exterior to its fashionable bright green lining, making sure none of the weapons stowed in it were peeping out of their hidden pockets.

He made his boots slap loudly on the cobblestones as he strutted toward the doorway, whistling a jaunty tune.

This persona didn't allow him to look about much, so he didn't. He stepped up onto the porch, ignoring the ghost-prickle between his shoulder blades where a quarrel would strike if he'd missed a crossbowman in any of the buildings across the street, and raised his hand to knock at the door.

"Who are you and what do you want?" said a voice very close and directly above him. He colored in embarrassment. The lintel over the porch. It was just large enough to conceal a sufficiently small and agile adult. "You're not the tipsy patrician you're pretending to be," the voice above him whispered, "or you'd have jumped out of your skin when I spoke. Any reason I shouldn't kill you?"

The voice was female, unmuffled enough that he was confident there wasn't much of a barrier between the two of them.

He sprang, straight up and a little to his left, toward the sound of her voice. She managed to flinch back enough that his forehead struck her cheekbone rather than breaking her nose, their skulls colliding in a jarring blow that he was braced for and she wasn't, even as he wrapped his arms around her torso in a bear hug, far too close in for her to be able to aim a weapon at him.

For a moment he hung, legs kicking in air, before the beam she was clinging to gave way with an enormous crack and they tumbled downward together.

The flagstone of the stoop struck between his shoulder blades, and his vision narrowed for a moment, but he didn't relax his hold. The guard twisted furiously against him, startlingly strong, but not strong enough to extricate herself. This was just a stalling grip, though. He couldn't do any damage from here, and he didn't have the leverage to switch to anything more effective. He allowed himself two long breaths to clear his head from the fall, during which he noted the dagger, cudgel, and grappling hook that were concealed under her clothes by their distinct weight and hardness.

He gave her an abrupt shove that sent her tumbling down the steps to the cobblestones, slipping her dagger out of its pocket as he flung her. She turned her chaotic roll into a spring that had her on her feet moments ahead of him.

They faced each other, breathing heavily. She was wrapped in fuliginous black garments—so loose and soft he'd have trouble reading her build or her stance if he hadn't just been grappling with her, and so dark that he strained to make out her outline in the shadowy street. Her skin was naturally dark, as was her close-cropped hair.

"Who are you," she said again, with a faint Archipelagan lilt, "and what do you want?" The previous time it had been a sharp challenge; now it was almost conversational.

"The Scarab Society hired me to assassinate your boss."

Her eyes widened, a flash of white in her dark face. "That's a very honest answer."

"The Scarabs want people to know what happens to their enemies. It's good for business."

Her eyes narrowed. "Can I buy you off, then?"

"It would ruin my professional reputation, so it would have to be enough for me to retire on. Can you offer that kind of money?"

She shook her head slowly. "How do you expect to get by me?"

"I don't have to. I'm by the door; you're not."

"If you turn around, I'll kill you where you stand."

"What if I don't turn around?"

"You'll have some trouble picking the latch."

"I imagine I'll have to either beat you unconscious or kill you, then."

"That may not be easy."

"It is looking that way," he conceded. He flicked his arm in a way that should have sent a poisoned throwing dart into his hand and realized, belatedly, that its weight was absent from his sleeve.

She grinned and clucked her tongue. "Careless." There was a flicker of movement and he ducked, his own dart buzzing audibly past his ear and embedding itself in the wood of the door behind him.

He calculated for an instant. She was good: subtle and very fast. He had her dagger, but its balance was unfamiliar to him—and if she managed to pluck it out of the air, he'd be out of ranged weapons, and he didn't much like his chances in that scenario.

Slowly, ostentatiously, he drew it out of his cloak, pinched between thumb and forefinger, and flung it to one side. It skittered across the cobblestones, coming to rest somewhere in a pile of refuse.

"Surrendering?" she said, with mild surprise.

"Proposing a different sort of contest," he said. "With the noise we've made, the City Guard may be showing up soon. I don't think either of us wants a chat with the Jinglies tonight."

"True enough."

"So let's take this elsewhere. Fight unarmed. We may even both walk away from this."

"So your accomplices can slip in and finish the job?"

He arched an eyebrow. "You think I'm a decoy?"

She nodded appraisingly. "No, you're the real thing, all right. But it still seems likely you'll try to double-cross me somehow.

He raised both hands. "I swear by Saint Dysmus. Fair fight if you agree to the terms."

"Okay, it's a deal."

He cocked his head.

"I, too, swear by Saint Dysmus."

He nodded.

"Where do you propose we go?"

"I think we've both checked out the roof here pretty well. Let's go there."

"Deal. Meet you at the top."

He nodded, took a running start, and sprang onto the building's wall, toes and fingertips finding minute irregularities in the masonry. Carefully, he began to work his way up the nearly featureless wall.

"Showoff," she said behind him. She opened the door.

"You said it was latched!" he protested.

"I lied." The door shut, and he heard a bolt drawn. He sighed and resumed his slow climb.

اﻟﻪ

Zuth pushed himself up over the lip of the wall onto the rooftop, heart pounding, breathing heavily. The masonry had gotten finer toward the top, and he'd had a hairy time of the last three or four cubits.

"Ready?" came her voice from one of the puddles of shadow.

He made an effort to steady his breath, to still his knees, shaking with fatigue. "Ready," he answered back.

"How do I know you're unarmed?" she said.

"Because I—"

"Take off your cloak and your tunic."

"What?"

"You want to wrestle, strip down like a wrestler. Best way to be sure you're not packing something."

"Are you going to do the same, then?" he said sarcastically.

"Yes," she said. "But you first."

He pretended to ill grace to buy himself a few more seconds to recover from his climb, grumbling as he shrugged off his cloak and lowered it to the ground gently, so the weapons concealed inside wouldn't clatter. He was faster with his shirt, not liking the moments in which his eyes were covered and his hands bound. But no sneak attack came.

Instead, she emerged from the shadow, dark and lean as an alleycat, and, as well as he could make out by starlight, already completely nude.

"Nice!" she said, unabashedly eying his torso. "You've got some talent, but you haven't been in this business long."

"Why do you say that?"

"No scars."

He bit back the urge to argue with her contention, realizing how childish it would sound, and felt his face prickle with heat.

"You're blushing." She grinned widely.

Once again he had to suppress the impulse to argue. "You have excellent night vision," he said instead.

"Or I'm just a good guesser."

"What are you trying to accomplish?" he snapped.

"Nothing at all! Just killing time. I'm in no hurry. Every minute we banter is a minute closer to the Dawn Patrol showing up and you having to scamper off home. Thanks for taking your time on the way up, by the way."

"Dawn is still many hours off."

"I'm in no hurry," she repeated. "Now the rest." She gestured toward his trousers.

He hesitated.

"Take your time," she said.

Feeling both self-conscious and vulnerable, he unlaced each of his boots while balancing on the other foot, then shucked off trousers, underwear, socks, and boots in one hasty gesture.

"No showmanship," she said, shaking her head in mock disapproval.

"I didn't think this was a show."

"Don't you want to distract me?"

"I promised you a fair fight."

"Distraction," she said, her voice slowing and lowering to a caressing purr, "is a completely legitimate tactic."

Zuth realized his cock was lengthening and thickening in response to his opponent's tone. "Are you ready to fight?" he snapped.

"Yes," she said.

They were both still for a long moment. Then she stepped forward and punched at his face. She was very fast, but he managed to block the blow with his forearm and counter with a punch to the kidneys. It connected—barely—as she melted back out of range again. He pressed his advantage, advancing with a series of kicks and punches, which never did more than brush against her as she faded back, but continued pushing her toward the edge of the building and a three-story drop to the cobblestones below. When her heel touched the low lip that ran around the edge of the roof, her eyes widened.

Zuth found that he wasn't looking forward to knocking this vexing and surprising woman to her death, but still, business was business, and it had been a fair fight. He swung out with a powerful punch that should have sent her tumbling off the edge, but she anticipated it perfectly and ducked under his arm. Before he could whirl on her, she had locked her forearm across his throat, pressing painfully against his Adam's apple.

He raised his hands, and she tightened her grip further, so that his breath wheezed through his throat.

"Do you yield?" she said.

"No," he gasped.

"I can crush your throat right now."

"I'd still..." he paused to draw a painful breath, "have a minute of consciousness to take you with me. And no incentive not to."

Her grip eased slightly, so that breathing was no longer an effort. "I like you!" she exclaimed gleefully. "You're difficult!" Her other hand ran caressingly over his torso, stroking the muscles of his flank, then running lightly over one nipple.

"Thank you," he said, tottering to retain his balance against the backward pull on his throat. "You're a pretty big pain in the ass yourself." Even in this strait, his body was responding to her touches, and he found himself acutely aware of the heat where she was pressed against his back.

"If you yield," she cooed, "our business is done." He could feel her hot breath on his ear. "We can spend the rest of the night enjoying ourselves." Her hand crept downward, traced the fuzzy crease where his torso met his thigh.

"You appear to be enjoying yourself already," he growled.

Her knuckles brushed his half-hard cock. "So do y—"

He whirled and ducked, bringing his shoulders up to shrug

her arm off, and charged forward, slamming her to the tarred roof beneath his own weight. He reached to pin her wrists, head arched back and to the side to guard against bites and head butts. It was a furious, graceless scramble for several seconds before he caught each of her wrists, then used his superior strength to bring them together over her head. He put his weight on the one hand that now held her wrists and wrapped the other around her throat. She twisted furiously, trying to roll him off, then, when he tightened his grip, went completely limp.

"Do you yield?" he said.

She drew a deep breath, working against his weight to fill her lungs. "No," she said, softly.

"I could kill you very easily," he reminded her.

She shook her head, as much as was possible in his grip. "There's something you want from me that I can't give you dead."

He was puzzled by these words for a moment; then he noticed that her hips were undulating against his, the furrow between her legs stroking the underside of his cock.

"Can't you?" he said, tightening his grip a bit. He was gratified to see her open her eyes wide for a moment, and he found that the flash of fear in her expression sent a wave of arousal through him.

"I wouldn't be nearly as much fun as a corpse," she said, her voice a little rough from the pressure on her throat but the tone still confident.

"Maybe I'm into that."

"I guess that's a risk I'm taking."

He pursed his lips in frustration. He could kill her now, and probably should, but he found himself reluctant to do so.

As he wavered, she was rocking her hips against his cock, slowly, confidently.

"Scoot down an inch," she told him, and, unthinking, he did so, his hands still pinning her wrists and throat.

"There," she said. He felt the teasing prickle of her pubic hair pressed against the tender head of his cock, then smooth flesh, intense heat, slickness. Then the head slipped inside her; muscles gripped at the shaft and she sucked air through her teeth. "They grow 'em big in Ivy City..." she said thickly.

"I bet you say that to all the boys," he said, but the bravado covered sensation so intense and delicious he almost whimpered.

"C'mon," she growled, rocking her hips, "give me the whole thing."

He slid slowly inside her, drawing out the pleasure of the penetration, until his hips were pressed against the prickly fur of her mound. Sweat-slick chests slid together. Her breathing was rapid and uneven underneath him. Her legs wrapped around his waist, gripping him in place and urging him to grind deeper.

Doing her violence at this point was inconceivable. He released her wrists and her throat, but she shook her head, grabbed his wrist impatiently, and guided his hand back up under her chin. He squeezed once more and she groaned, her internal muscles squeezing his cock in response.

Then he leaned down and they kissed for the first time, her mouth hungry and aggressive, her tongue pushing into his mouth, both of them groaning as he started thrusting in earnest.

He found a rapid rhythm and pounded into her in long strokes, her cries so loud that, once again concerned about the City Guard, he switched from gripping her throat to covering her mouth with his hand, a grip she seemed to like nearly as well, her hips bucking up against him, her broad nostrils flaring to suck in enough air.

When she flipped him over, for a moment he thought she was resuming their conflict, but then she sank herself onto him and leaned down to kiss him again, her hands gripping his hair to twist his head from side to side. He gripped the firm little cheeks of her ass, urging her to thrust faster and harder.

She sat upright and buried one hand between her thighs, rubbing her clit in rapid circles. The motions of her hips became short and choppy, but the sight of her whimpering and baring her teeth as she approached her orgasm was so delicious he didn't mind. He reached up and brushed the dark tips of her breasts, and she nodded impatiently, so he ran his knuckles over her nipples, back and forth. "Oh, fuck," she hissed, "gonna—"

He clamped a hand over her mouth and shoved upward with his hips. She screamed, her body going rigid, then sucked air through her nose and released it in a long shuddering sigh, their bodies frozen together. Then she collapsed on him, sighing happily.

He thrust up into her, his cock straining more rigidly than ever. She winced. "Ooh, tender!" she exclaimed, and nimbly dismounted.

In an instant she was crouched beside him, taking his cock into her mouth, one of her hands squeezing the shaft while the other tugged gently at his balls.

Adjusting to the changed sensation took a moment, but the sight of her crouched over him, taking his still-slick cock into her mouth, was exciting enough that he soon was thrusting up into her mouth, while she, with visible effort, worked to take him as far down her throat as she could.

Her fingertips pressed against his perineum as her head bobbed rapidly, slurping loudly at the taut head of his cock. He groaned, his fists clenched, his back arched, and he came in several strong spurts.

His cock was still hard when she was straddling him again. "I think we get a time-out after that," she said.

"That seems fair," he gasped. "And then we can try to kill each other again."

She shrugged. "No particular need."

He peered at her quizzically. "How you figure?"

"Papa Ud's business here only took him half an hour or so. By now, he should be long gone."

"Sure. What's your point?"

She looked at him as if astounded at his thick-headedness. "That means you can't kill him."

"You're working for Ud?"

"Of course!"

He paused, embarrassed.

"What?" she demanded.

"I was hired to kill Eni."

"Oh! Well that... Wait, he should be long gone, too."

"In a sense."

"What do you mean?"

"I mean I already killed him."

She sat bolt upright. "What?"

"I was inside the building this morning—hours before you got here. It was very dull. Fortunately, I brought something to read. By the time Ud arrived, Eni's body was cold. Presumably he hustled out the front at a pretty brisk pace when he found that out."

"So this was all—"

"If you say 'a complete waste of time,' you're gonna hurt my feelings."

She patted his cheek, a little condescendingly. "I had a lovely time," she assured him. "But why did you come to the rear door in the first place, if you'd already done the job?"

"I wanted to meet you. In an industry as small as ours, it pays to know the competition."

She peered at him appraisingly. "So, you're with the Scarabs, huh?"

He shook his head. "Freelance."

"Not much security in that. Ud treats his people well, and his operation is growing fast."

"Are you offering me a job?"

"It's good to know your competition. It's even better to know your colleagues."

Zuth scratched his chin. In the east, he noticed, the faintest tint of gray was beginning to mar the sky's blackness. Silently, his tongue formed the word 'colleagues.' He'd never in his life had a boss before, never had allies of other than the most temporary sort. The notion was strange—unnerving, yet seductive. "I'll think about it," he said.

In the Blood
Kathleen Tudor

"I know, I'm on my way. I won't be late, I swear," I said, and snapped the phone shut. Technically I should have left ten minutes before, but I'd gotten distracted by the book I was reading. Anyway, I was almost never late.

I shoved the phone into my pocket and quick-stepped down the last flight of stairs to my building's front door, my mind already on the surprise shower I was attending. I shifted the gift and hiked my purse higher on my shoulder as I approached the front door, and stepped straight through as another tenant opened it from the other side, stepping back to let me pass. She waved casually at me, and I smiled.

The bus, which should have departed several minutes before, was running late; it pulled up just as I stepped up to the curb. I glanced at the ground for spare change or a dollar drifting down the gutter, but there was nothing there. Shrugging, I started to reach for my wallet, just as the door whooshed open in front of me. A man stepped down from the bus and flashed an all-day pass at me.

"My last stop," he explained. I thanked him as I took it, slipping my wallet back out of the way. I couldn't actually remember the last time I had paid for a trip on the bus or subway.

My phone buzzed again as I was walking toward the back of the bus, and I rolled my eyes and plopped into the nearest seat to set my things down and pull it out. A text, again from Shannon, who'd organized the party. Have u left yet?

Right on time, I texted back, grinning to myself. Luckily.

But when I looked up again, I started to wonder if the balance on my luck had finally come due. We were just heading into an intersection, but the armored truck barreling toward us wasn't slowing down for their red light. I screamed, but it was too late for the bus driver to do anything; the truck was on us.

It was like standing outside as the lightning crashes all around—just darkness and flashes of light and so much sound, roaring and tearing at me. I knew I was screaming, because my throat was raw with the pain of it, but I couldn't make myself stop. I squeezed my eyes shut, but it didn't change the disorientation or the flashes of light that seemed to pierce my existence, or the flashes of pain that accompanied them. I was tumbling, I thought, but I couldn't see—couldn't tell.

When the noise and the movement stopped, and my breath ran out, there was a moment of pure, deathly silence, and then the world came crashing back in on me as the sounds of crumpling metal and painful screams returned. I felt like I was stuck in the middle of a war-zone, but when I tried to move, I found myself trapped in a small pocket, soft and cushioned—the bus seats?

It felt like an age before the sounds of panic and pain faded and the sounds of sirens grew close. I waited, shivering, crying, for the sounds of purposeful shouts and the crackle of radios.

۔ﷲ۔

I tucked my feet up under myself and huddled on the couch, shivering under a heavy blanket. The tea in my hands stung my fingers with heat, but I couldn't shake the cold that seemed to have seeped through me and taken residence in my bones. When the stolen armored truck had run that red light, they'd struck a city bus—my bus—and killed most of the passengers instantly. The bus had been pushed into the other lanes of traffic, and the accident had taken most of the afternoon to clear.

And since I was uninjured, I had spent most of that time trapped in my little pocket, where the bus seats had folded around me like a cocoon, and wept as I waited for the rescue workers to save the injured and dying. There had been dozens of people hurt, and almost a dozen killed. And then there was me: Kylie Robinson, the luckiest woman in the city—the only person to survive the massive crash without a scratch.

But no matter how I told myself how much worse it could have been for me, I couldn't forget the feeling of being trapped in the dark, with only small patches of light shining through gaps in my strange little prison, unable to move or to do anything but talk with the quiet young cop who'd been assigned to keep me calm and quiet.

When I had finally emerged, like a butterfly from the wreckage, the medics had shined lights in my eyes and checked my limbs over quickly before dismissing me to the tender mercies of the police, who wanted my statement, and then to the media, who wanted my soul. I'd fled the cameras and microphones, but they'd tracked me down anyway, and even now the shrill ring of the phone pierced the silence of my apartment. It might have been Shannon, calling yet again to check up on me, but I took a sip of my tea and stared out the window, ignoring her—ignoring everyone.

My luck had never felt more like a double-edged sword, and I couldn't stop thinking of all of the people who were hurt or killed in that intersection. Would the disaster have been less catastrophic if the bus hadn't been right there? And was it there because of me, or did my luck simply allow me to run late on a day when the bus would already be late?

Someone knocked on the door, and I huddled deeper into my blanket, wanting them to go. The tea was going cold in the mug, and I took a sip of the tepid liquid before setting it aside. For the most part, the locked front door kept the curious away from me, but it was possible that a reporter had followed another tenant in, and I didn't want to talk.

The pounding came again, followed by a quiet curse. I heard something rustle a moment later, and glanced across the room to see a small piece of paper slide under the door. That was new.... I considered getting up, but my whole body felt heavy and tired, and I turned over on the couch, instead, settling deep into the cocoon of my own choosing and pulling the blanket over my head.

It was dark by the time I got up again, ready to shuffle off to bed. My boss had told me to take a few days off of work, but I wasn't sure when I would be able to go back out again. What if my luck got someone else hurt or killed? What if it ran out? What if payment was coming due for all of the good luck I had borrowed over the years? The thought of the world overwhelmed me.

I thought about leaving the half-filled cup of tea on the table by my sofa, but long habit had me taking it to the kitchen, instead, to at least dump out the cold tea and rinse the mug. I was on my way back out when I stepped past the door and heard the crinkle of the paper under my feet. I picked it up idly and carried it into the bedroom with me, switching on the light to look it over.

I didn't get a chance. A creature that looked like a man, but with something inhumanely terrible about his face, stood poised over my bed. It jumped back, flinching as the light hit it, and dove for my open window. I hadn't heard it break in! Lucky I'd fallen asleep on the couch....

I reached for my pocket for my cell phone, but it was gone, tossed away and broken as my cocoon of seats had spun away from the bus. Then I froze, shocked, as the man—creature?—leapt over the rail of my fire escape.

I screamed and rushed toward the window, desperate to see why he had leapt four stories, but I couldn't see anything in the darkness. What had happened? Why?!

I backed away from my window, my eyes unable to break away from the darkness framed there, and I felt the crinkle of paper in my hand. I lifted it instinctively.

I suppose I'd expected to see a note on the local TV News' stationery, but the paper was torn from a notebook and written in sparkly green ink in a hurried scrawl. "Your luck isn't a coincidence. I can answer your questions. You might be in danger. Please call me."

Was this intruder the danger that the note had warned me about? Why break into my room just because I was lucky?

I backed out of the room and grabbed my cordless phone, locking myself into my bathroom as if that would stop anyone who could pry open a locked window without making a sound.

Leaning against my sink, I dialed the number scrawled at the bottom of the page.

"Mohini," a deep female voice said.

"Sorry, I must have misdialed," I said, wondering what language I'd been greeted in, and if she would even be able to understand my apology. So much for my luck, this time.

"Kylie?"

I froze, the phone a couple of inches away from my face. How could she know?

"Hello? My name is Mohini Anand. I think I can help you. Are you there?"

I blinked, stumped for a moment, and finally blurted out, "There was a man in my room, and he just jumped... four stories down."

"Lucky you," she said, irony teasing at the edges of her dark voice. It made me shiver with interest, and I frowned.

"Who are you?"

"I'm a witch," she said, "and I know something about the luck-touched. I fear your face on the news is going to put you on the map for some very dangerous people."

I pulled the phone away from my ear to stare blankly at it, then I put it back to my ear and said the only thing I could think of. "A witch? Like, hocus pocus?"

"I can protect you. Trust your luck. What's it telling you?"

"To get out."

"Then go. Just start walking. I'll find you."

"How?"

"If I really mean to help you, then your luck will draw me in. That's how you'll know you can trust me."

The line went dead, and I shivered with more than interest, this time. That was the first time anyone had seemed to understand exactly how my luck worked, and how much I could trust it. Which reminded me of the prickling feeling driving me out. Now, I dressed as quickly as possible, and bolted for the door.

A blast of cold air hit me as I left the building, and I wrapped my arms around myself and tucked my head down, hurrying into the breezy evening. A bit of pink caught the corner of my eye, and I stopped and grabbed the piece of fabric sticking out of a trash bag. The pink was a scarf, slightly fuzzed with long wear, and apparently discarded. It was tangled up with an equally serviceable coat, and I put both on, hardly thinking twice about the stroke of luck that had placed them in my path.

I took a turn at random, then another, heading away from my apartment. I had been walking nearly fifteen minutes when a car darted suddenly out of the flow of traffic and into the only empty space on the street. The driver was a woman with huge, dark eyes, a mess of thick black hair, and golden skin. She radiated beauty and power, and I half-felt like I would have thrown myself into her car no matter what. But she waved me in, so I slipped into the passenger door and slammed it, allowing her to take advantage of a lucky break in traffic to pull out of the space.

"Kylie," she said, sounding relieved.

"Hocus pocus... where are we going? What's going on?"

She rolled her eyes. "You told the news people that you've always been lucky. But you don't just mean that you've lived a relatively charmed life, do you? You mean really lucky. Finding money all the time, people offer you whatever you need, just as you think about needing it, stopping to look at a pretty picture and a plant falls where you would have been walking, right?"

"Something like that," I said, not sure whether to be relieved or frightened that she knew. She turned to glance at me sardonically, and I shrugged. "Well, I've never dodged a falling plant..."

"It's magic. It can be given in a blessing, but it takes incredibly strong magic to bless someone like that, and even then it tends to be minor. Like, you find quarters on the ground slightly more often than regular people."

"I haven't paid bus fare in years," I said. I guess I would have found it harder to believe in magic if I hadn't lived such a literally charmed life. "But I've never had anyone bless me that I know of."

She nodded, unsurprised. "Sometimes magic just sort of...

pools. The strength varies, but it comes most often to babies or children, since they're so open to the mystical world. It manifests in all sorts of 'touches.' Luck, beauty, grace... or in less pleasant ways. It's natural—just chance."

"And I stepped in a luck-puddle as a kid?" Sounded as reasonable—or as crazy—as anything that had popped into my own head to explain my gift over the years.

Mohini snorted a laugh. "Something like that, maybe." She pulled her car into a garage and quickly found a parking space. "My building is half a block that way," she said. "So you can maybe believe in magic. Can you accept, if there is something like magic in the world, that there are people who have learned to manipulate that magic?"

I shrugged. "I guess, maybe. I don't suppose you could show me?"

"It's not usually all that flashy, but I could maybe think of something. Hurry. I want to get you behind my shields."

I followed her into an apartment building and to the elevator, where we took a ride to the eleventh floor, and down the hall to her door. But as I stepped across the threshold and into her apartment, I felt a tingle wash over me, like a static rush, and the hair on my arms stood up tall.

"My shields," she said, turning to see the astonished look on my face. "They should keep anything nasty from finding you, at least for now."

"Nasty?"

"Kylie, that man? The one who jumped? I think he was probably a vampire." She stood braced as if she expected me to lash out, but I was frozen, stiff and confused. He'd jumped four stories down, but I certainly hadn't heard the commotion of him splatting on the sidewalk.

"Why?"

"He wanted to drink your luck."

"Of course."

"So everything is going to be after me?" I asked, hours later. Mohini had lit a candle with a word and, apparently, her force of will, and we had spent the rest of the night in deep discussion of the supernatural world. I was on my fourth cup of chai and my energy was fading, along with my optimism.

"I can teach you to protect yourself," she said. But she didn't argue that many in the supernatural community would find my blood tempting.

"Like, with spells and stuff?"

She wrinkled her nose at me, and I sighed as the sheer adorableness of her expression knocked me down a sarcasm peg or two. It was unfair how distractingly lovely she was; I'd had to force my attention from her face to her words a dozen times already, and the hour wasn't helping my concentration, any. "You don't even have a whiff of magical talent that I can sense," she said.

I blinked as I tried to clear my mind enough to process her words. "Um, thanks?"

"Not good or bad, but you won't be using shields, and offensive magic is unreliable, anyway. But I think I can teach you to tap into your luck."

"Don't I do that anyway?" I was hungry, I realized, after days of disinterest in food. I glanced to the left and saw a bowl of apples on the counter. Perfect.

Mohini quirked a smile as I snagged a shiny red fruit and bit into it. "You do use it, but passively. I've never seen anyone as strongly luck-touched as you. I think you could tap into it on purpose. Stand up."

I took another big bite of the apple, then set it down and scraped my chair back.

"Now, close your eyes. I'm going to try to hit you, and you focus on your luck and how it feels... move like it tells you to."

I sighed, raised my eyebrows at her, and closed my eyes. There was nothing. No urge to move, no feeling that I needed to flinch or step back or bend over to check my shoelace. When I let one eye crack open, I saw Mohini's fist, unmoving, about an inch from my cheek.

"Were you even going to touch me?"

She pulled back, defensive. "I didn't want to just black your eye first thing!" Damn, she was even cute when she was irritated.

"I'm lucky, not psychic! Why would I need to get out of the way of a punch that was never going to land?"

"Fine," she snapped. "Close your eyes."

My eyelids had barely fluttered shut when my balance wavered and I stepped back. A cool breeze brushed my cheek as Mohini's fist sailed past. Cool, but I hadn't moved on purpose. Could I do better?

I started to ask her to come at me again, but this time I was ready, my senses straining to see what my luck would tell me, and it was telling me to shift back the other way. I did, and this time her shirt sleeve snapped across my cheek as her hand brushed harmlessly past. Active, now... focus on making it active. The next time I felt that need to get out of the way, I followed up with a slap to the air in front of my face, figuring that was as good a place as any. My hand closed on her wrist, and with a mental shrug, I gave a hard pull.

A crash made me jump, and I jerked my eyes open to see Mohini tangling with my abandoned chair as she went sprawling into the kitchen.

"I'm sorry!"

She groaned. "What kind of training do you have?"

"In fighting? None. I've never needed to."

She stood and righted the chair. "That was amazing. It was like watching someone in The Matrix, or something." She took my apple and bit into it as she contemplated me. "But I'm not trained, either. We need to get you something you can fight with to give you a little extra advantage. A sword, maybe?" A tiny drop of juice from the apple lingered on her lip. I longed to lick it off... and I nearly groaned as she did so herself.

"I can't just carry a sword in the city."

She blinked. "No, of course not. Maybe a knife, then." Her grin brightened. "This is perfect. My ex-girlfriend has a big prop knife she got from a play she was in. I'll bet I can borrow it."

Into women, huh? Better and better. Except for the nagging thought that hadn't quit since she'd picked me up. "Why would you help me?"

She gave me a sultry smile. "Because you're cute?" I stood, just waiting, though I did feel a little flush in my abdomen at the thought that she found me cute. Hell, more than a little flush.

After a moment, her face crumpled from mischievous and sexy to something care-worn and pained. "My little sister was luck-touched. Not much—not so you'd notice, really, if you didn't know. We think someone must have sold her out to the vampires."

And didn't that just make me feel like a jerk? "I'm sorry."

"It was long ago," she said, her voice quiet and far away, as if she was speaking to me from across that span of time. She shook her head as if shaking off the years. "Well. I saw you on the television, and I knew you were going to be noticed. I wanted to help."

"Lucky me," I said, meaning it. It made her smile, which of course made me want to smile back at her. Maybe I was just ridiculously tired, but...she was ridiculously hot. Her eyes were a deep, warm brown, like melted chocolate, just begging me to fall into them. I blinked slowly, trying to break the connection she seemed to have developed to my baser instincts, but ruined it by licking my lips.

I almost moaned aloud when she echoed the movement. That forced my attention to her lips again, which were like a rose dusted with cocoa. She was smart, generous, looked good enough to eat, and was apparently into women. Could she possibly be as attracted to me as I was to her? I smiled slowly. Could I be so lucky? Why not?

She was still standing by the kitchen chair. I stepped forward quickly, and she took a startled half-step back that sent her straight into the seat. Perfect. A second later I followed her down, straddling

a pair of perfect breasts that begged to be tasted. I let my tongue flick over one beaded nipple, then the other, teasing her until gooseflesh rose on her exposed skin. Then I feasted in earnest, sucking her into my mouth and devouring her. Mohini gasped and made soft sounds of pleasure that ignited the sparks and sent bolts of pure, liquid heat deep into my core.

"I want you," I said, turning to nuzzle at her other breast.

"Bed," she gasped. Since I couldn't agree more, I stood, detangling myself from her with some effort and grasping at her wrists to tow her along with me. She laughed as she came, following behind me eagerly. Then, with a quick step, she caught up to me and wrapped her arms around me from behind, pulling me to a stop as she stroked across my body, caressed my breasts, and let her hands drift down my belly. She settled at the waist of my pants for a moment, as lightly as a bird on a wire, and then she unfastened the button at my waist and pushed my pants out of the way.

I gasped and trembled as they dropped to my ankles and her hands dove straight for the heat and wet that waited between my thighs. Mohini nipped at the back of my shoulder, making me shiver, and her fingers caressed my pussy with soft expertise. "I thought you wanted the bed," I rasped. I felt like all the air had been sucked out of the room, and yet I had a hard time making myself care about it.

"I lied," she said, "can't wait."

I jerked like she'd shocked me when her fingers danced over my clit, manipulating me with practiced ease until I was putty under her hands. I leaned into her, letting her support some of my weight so I didn't collapse with the sheer flood of sensation, and then I let it take me away. Her fingers slid through my slick heat and inside me, fucking me softly before drawing back to trace whorls around my clit and dancing back again. I groaned as she teased and tortured expertly, and then cried out with pleasure when her teasing strokes gained focus, skimming over my clit with just the right amount of pressure....

The world seemed to crash in on me like waves breaking as

she drove me to climax and beyond. One of her arms snaked around my ribs, which I dimly thought was a good thing since my legs were no longer speaking to me. We stood there, swaying, for a long moment, then I heard her giggle, and we collapsed backward.

"So dramatic!" she cried. I rolled over as she scooted out from under me, and the sight of her half-dressed and disheveled, a wicked smile on her face, was enough to revive me, at least a little. The smile dimmed, just a fraction. "I should get that knife," she said. "You're still in danger. We have to practice."

"There's time," I said, grabbing her leg and teasing my fingers up her thigh. "We're behind your shields. And no one's going anywhere until we've both gotten lucky."

She laughed richly as I crawled closer, and within mere feet of the bed, I buried my face in the sweet, musky scent of her pussy. Her laugh turned into a deep gasp of pleasure and a feminine growl of arousal. Now that was more like it. "What about the bed?" she gasped.

I laughed, letting the vibrations of my chuckle wash over her clit, and was rewarded with a moan. She tasted so incredible that I just wanted to drink her in, sweeping my tongue from her hole to her clit. She cried out and her nails bit into my arms as I laved her sweet pussy. She trembled beneath my attentions, and her fingers twisted through my hair, tugging gently as she whimpered for me to send her to heaven.

I dug my nails into her flanks, tempering pleasure with a tiny bite of pain as I sucked her clit into my mouth and teased it between my lips, letting them cushion the pressure as I clamped down on her in earnest. Her cry was throaty and honeyed as I licked and sucked and flicked my tongue over her clit, growing hoarser as my attentive devotion drove her closer and closer to her peak. When I slid two fingers between the soft, hot folds of her pussy lips and deep inside her, then crooked them as if summoning her orgasm from within her, Mohini's cries broke, and she shouted and bucked beneath my lips as I gently rode her to her peak and down again.

Her fingers, which had grown biting in their grasp on my hair, loosened and stroked my scalp gently, and I looked up from between her legs and smiled. She looked up, met my twinkling eyes, moaned, and let her head drop back again to the sound of my laughter.

She called her ex once we'd managed to scrape ourselves up off of the carpet, and the woman, Daria, had offered to drop off the knife... on Saturday.

"It's Thursday," I said when she told me. She shrugged. "I can't just hide here for the rest of the week. I need my own clothes, at least." I thought of Shannon and of my parents, and blushed. "And I should call people and let them know I'm okay."

"You can use my phone. And I have clothes..."

"You're tiny," I countered. I was far from fat, but she was both shorter than me, and narrower at the hip. I'd look ridiculous.

She grumbled, but didn't argue further. Instead, she got the biggest knife she could find out of her kitchen.

"Seriously? No one is going to comment on me carrying a gigantic knife through town?"

She shoved a large purse at me, and I was surprised to find that it fit nicely in a side pocket. Alrighty, then....

Our next fight was about whether she should come up to my apartment with me. She thought there would be safety in numbers, but I wanted to reclaim my space, and I had to do it by myself. This was an argument I was determined to win, and so I was alone when I turned the key at my front door and pushed the door open. The hair stood up on my neck, but it wasn't so much my luck talking to me as the fact that I was completely creeped out by the idea of a vampire waiting to snack on me.

I'd only gotten a couple of steps in the door when I felt my luck—senses straining to their limits—tingle in warning. I dropped to my knees, grabbing for the knife buried in Mohini's bag, mentally kicking myself for not pulling it out before I unlocked the door. The vampire who'd been about to grab me from behind the door found himself floundering in empty space, instead, and he tripped over me as I went down so quickly in front of me.

His flailing feet knocked my bag out of my grip, and I turned and grabbed for him, instead, trying to get a good hold on him so I could keep him away. But he was way stronger than I was ready for. He tore my hands free and snarled, his pointed teeth gleaming, as he reached out to shove the door shut, locking me in with him.

That one moment of distraction was all I needed to twist and bring my knee up, straight into his unprotected groin. Undead or not, he apparently had the typical masculine weakness. I shoved him off as he curled around his wounded pride, and scrabbled for my bag once again. The knife had worked free, and my hand came down straight on the handle. My heart surged with fear as I raised the knife. I couldn't actually kill someone, could I? But when I turned back to defend myself, I found that I'd underestimated my foe once again. He had recovered while my attention was elsewhere, and lunged for my exposed neck.

Fortunately for me, I brought the knife up out of sheer startled shock. He exploded in a cloud of dust as he impaled himself on my blade. I screamed and scooted backward, my heart jumping in horror. I hadn't thought Mohini was lying, really, but to see something like that with my own eyes....

I stood and ran to my bedroom, determined to get my clothes and get away as quickly as possible. So I didn't see the second vampire until it was too late.

She had been just inside my bedroom door, and she snatched me mid-flight as I tried to bolt past her. "Stupid girl! The things he has seen! The knowledge he has collected! Wasted."

I took a breath to scream, but she clamped a hand over my mouth and pinched my nose, forcing me to struggle for my life.

"I could snap your neck now," she growled, "but your blood will taste better fresh."

She shoved me toward the door, still holding me tight, and we both stopped short to see Mohini standing in the center of my living room, halfway between us and the door. Her face glowed with a strange, golden light, and her thick, straight hair seemed to be charged with energy, not standing on end, but rising with power as she channeled her magic.

"Stop, witch, or I kill her now," the vampire said.

Mohini froze, her hair dropping flat against her scalp again as she relaxed. Then a flash, like a camera, blinded me, and the vampire's hands dropped away. My knees gave out, and as I blinked away the light-blindness, I found myself sitting in a pile of dispersing dust.

"Sunlight," Mohini said, her voice shaky.

"You didn't listen."

"Lucky for you."

I glared at her, and she glared back, breathing hard, one hand pressed to her heart. Then one side of her mouth twitched in a smile, and we both started to laugh.

Evidence of Things Unseen
A.C. Wise

Interview #1: November 14, 2011

"He called it a period of grace. Everyone gets one. It's a transition period. A way to ease the pain."

The camera catches her mid-conversation, as if she would have been speaking regardless of whether anyone was watching. She might not even know the camera is there. Except you know she does. The shot angles over her left shoulder, showing an over-full ashtray, but not her face. It shows hands—nails ragged and bitten—one finger tap-tapping ash, not nervous, but compulsive nonetheless. The camera shows glossy black hair, cut so straight it looks like a wig, and a shoulder, bare but for the narrow strap of a white tank top.

She keeps talking, the camera rolls on. You watch.

"Nothing is forever, that's what he always said. The world is in a constant state of flux—no sharp breaks. Everything liminal, in-between. That's the way he lived his life. If he left, he could come back. And he always did."

She breathes out, a long sound filled with smoke. The camera flattens the breath, and stills everything else in the room. Tap-tap, more ash falls against thick glass, a drift building and threatening to overflow.

"That's what the period of grace was for: forgiveness. Our whole lives were one long goodbye. He always said he was going away for good, but he never did. He always came back. I think he was afraid to leave."

One hand turns the ashtray, glass scraping over-loud against the wood.

"Sometimes, when he was in one of his moods, he'd yell and accuse me of drawing him back against his will. After, he would cry and thank me. I think he needed me to save him. He wasn't always in his right mind; he needed me to make it okay.

"Nothing has changed."

She's alone in the room. She insisted, wouldn't talk if anyone else was there. But she'd let you watch. Through a two-way mirror, through a camera, speaking through the intercom if you needed to ask her a question—as long as a barrier existed between you, she would talk.

The microphone catches every nuance of her exhaled breath, every movement of her fingers tapping ash, her body, shifting against the chair. It's good, but it doesn't quite catch the voice speaking off screen. The sound comes through, static-shot, low. It might be your voice, you can't tell. It sounds strange, and you don't remember what you asked her or when. The microphone is good, but not that good; it doesn't catch the question, only her answer.

"No, it didn't work that way. He wasn't always in control. It wasn't his fault."

A pause, and if sound fills the silence, the camera doesn't catch that either.

"I forgave him."

On the screen, the room is black and white. Ghost-gray. Pearl. Charcoal. The space is crowded with shadows. If you stare hard enough, long enough—and you always do—they pull away from the edges of the screen and close in. They shrink the world, narrowing it to a tunnel you could reach through to brush a hand against her skin. Tap-tap—the cigarette against a beveled edge of glass. The ashtray is always full; her cigarette never burns down.

"He made me watch," she says.

The words stand alone, unprompted, and bring no response from the static-choked intercom.

Your heart pounds against the silence. It's not standard procedure to ignore a witness' statement, especially when they volunteer information.

But you did. You do.

You lean forward. A shadow passes across her shoulder—a

hand just out of view, about to touch, but never lowered into the frame. She rubs that shoulder. Coincidence? The strap of the tank top shifts a fraction, nudged by her fingertips.

The angle doesn't show it, but you can imagine: if the camera shifted to the left, you'd see the hard press of her nipples against the fabric of her shirt, defiant. She wants you to know how little stands between you and her skin.

You've watched the tape a dozen times, maybe more. You squirm every time. You know you should look away, but you don't. You never do.

The intercom crackles, the voice again—yours? The reaction is immediate, and it makes you jump every time.

The woman turns and looks straight at the camera. She looks straight at you. Not you then, but you here and now. Her eyes are black-black, ink pooled on white flesh.

"I didn't kill him, but he made me watch him die."

࿇

Video Evidence #1: Date Unknown

"Watch the tape."

She stands at your right shoulder, close enough to touch, but careful not to. Close enough for you to feel the way her skin doesn't brush yours; close enough that your flesh prickles, electric, but you can't tell whether the hairs on her arm rise. She leaves the distance to imagination and possibility, never closing the gap. She wants you to know she's in control.

"Watch."

She points. You catch a hint of sour sweat and stale cigarettes, as if she hasn't showered in days. The scent shouldn't turn you on...

You think about saying, "I don't want to see this," and you don't say anything at all.

The edge of her smile catches the corner of your eye. That smile, even if it's imagined, binds you. It stitches your lips closed,

keeps you silent and lets you hold your ground. It gives you permission; it makes whatever happens next okay.

You watch.

Together.

The camera angles high over her left shoulder. She is alone in
the room.

Shadows gather at the edges of the screen, leaving spaces full
of doubt. The image is grainy, the color somewhere between night-
vision green and faded black and white. Light pools around her,
either from the camera, or maybe from her skin—luminous and
self-illuminating.

Where the light ends, faint markings circle her, chalk on bare
wood.

She kneels on the boards, legs tucked beneath her, leaving just
the tips of her toes peeking out beneath the curve of her ass. She's
wearing the same white tank top, fabric so thin you could see right
through it if only she'd turn around. There's nothing underneath.
You're sure.

Your breath quickens, watching the screen. The edge of her
smile snags at you. There and gone so quickly you might have
imagined it. But you didn't. She wants you to know.

She's wearing black silk panties. Her legs are bare.

Her hands are tied behind her back.

A blindfold covers her eyes.

"It isn't about control."

She speaks so close that you can't tell whether her voice is coming from behind you or behind the screen. You flinch, caught leaning forward, yearning toward the flickering image trapped beneath
the glass. But even that movement doesn't bring you any closer to
touching. She keeps the space between you careful, full of promise
that will never be realized.

You swallow guilt. But she wants you to watch, otherwise why
would she show you these things? And you want her to watch
you, watching her, an endless, recursive loop. You want her to
know. But at the same time, you want to be alone in the room with

the glow, with the screen, safe and dirty and small.

You shouldn't want these things. Any of them. But you do.

And you can't look away.

"It isn't about power. It's about freedom, absolution, forgiveness. It's permission to let go."

On the screen, she shifts. She's alone, but the camera catches a sound the way her smile catches your breath. It's a voice, guttural and so low you can't possibly have heard it. It has to be in your mind.

You want this.

Or that's what you think it says. You don't dare ask her to verify. She doesn't volunteer the information.

You can't see her face, but you imagine her lips parting. You imagine them bitten, cracked, warmed with hot breath.

The camera shows her muscles tensing, her shoulders flexing and pressing the sharp edge of her bones against fabric and skin. She pulls against the bonds, but not as though she wants to break free.

She breathes out, and the breath is a word.

"Yes."

She's alone in the room. You're almost sure. She has to be.

"It's about safety," she says.

You're dizzy. Her voice disorients, her image lures. The way her skin glows leaves you feeling as though you're falling, called then and there to be with her, trapped in the past. Or is it the present? The eternal now?

Time doesn't work right in that house.

She told you that, once. Or you think she did.

Everything is in-between. A constant state of grace. Of letting go.

Her voice—here and now? There? Or only in your head?

"Once you're bound, you have to accept whatever happens next. You give permission, and receive it at the same time. Your hands are literally tied, and in the instant they are, you've already accepted everything that will be done to you. Whatever comes next is beyond your control, and you're forgiven for it, whatever it might be. It's already happened, and you can't change it."

The camera watches as she tilts her head back, and you watch, filtered through its eye. Everything that happens is beyond your control. That makes it okay.

The arch of her throat is revealed, her face showing at last. Her lips part. She swallows hard.

If you could just see... if the angle of the camera would only show...

You imagine her nipples are hard.

She moves her legs, bringing her knees closer to the circle holding her in.

"I made my body a prison for him," she says. "I bound him, took things beyond his control. I made it okay. I forgave him."

On the screen, she arches her back. The movement lifts her small breasts, presses them hard against the thin fabric of her shirt. It's enough to show...

She bites her lip, holds it between white teeth. She squirms, straining against the bonds. But not struggling to get free. Her breath comes faster. There's a low sound in the room—with her, or coming from her—guttural, trapped, afraid. It is the sound of weeping, if weeping were no longer reserved for humans.

She lets out a low moan. That sound, you're certain, is all her, and there's no mistaking it for anything other than what it is.

Your breath quickens. You lean forward. You know you shouldn't, but you do.

She's watching you; watching you watching her. If you turned, would you catch her smile?

You should get up. You should leave the room, go splash water on your face. You don't. Her presence behind your right shoulder is a physical weight, restraining you, holding you down.

She makes you watch.

On the screen, her head snaps forward. The movement is so sudden, so violent, you're certain it must have broken her neck. Only she's here beside you, isn't she? So you know she can't be dead. She trembles; every bone, every vertebra presses hard against her skin.

"There is freedom in being bound. It's permission, because once you're tied, once you consent, everything that happens after is okay."

Her body bucks, her breath catches, and you hear it as sharp and as close as if it's right next to your ear.

You know you should look away. But you don't. You never do.

She makes you watch as one by one the bruises appear.

She's alone in the room.

It's an impossible thing, but you've seen it with your own eyes a dozen times. Like petals the color of plums, like smoke and ash, or smudges of shadow, they bloom from the white spaces of her flesh.

Each bruise elicits a sound. A low whimper. A tiny gasp. They are not sounds of pain.

She trembles, bound and kneeling on the floor. The bruises appear on her shoulders, on her neck, on her thighs. Like marks left by a lover's teeth. Like fists, beating at her skin from the inside.

Her breath quickens there and then, here and now. What's happening on the screen isn't for you. It never will be. But it doesn't matter. Your breath matches hers. It's not for you, but she makes you watch anyway.

Together.

You watch her come.

اللہ

Video Evidence #2: Date Unknown

She leads you to the house, but not inside.

You stand in front of the porch, looking up at the implacable façade. Paint worn, window-eyes blind—the place might have been empty for years.

You can't remember how long you've known her. When this whole thing began.

She smiles. A cold wind chases leaves drained of every color but dead across the porch's bare, wooden boards. They catch in drifts around the base of a dozen or more television sets stacked in a rough pyramid. They're the old-fashioned kind: bulky backs and convex screens, the images yearning outward, teasing the promise of a connection that will never close.

"I don't understand," you say.

"Halloween decorations." She shrugs.

She picks a fleck of ash from her bottom lip.

"Watch the screens," she says, pointing.

And you do.

But out of the corner of your eye, you watch her. You know you shouldn't, but you do.

Her hands are buried deep into the pockets of her coat. Her collar is turned up against the wind. You can't be sure, but you suspect that under her coat she's wearing that white tank top, so thin her nipples must ache with the cold. Even wrapped in fabric, she looks translucent. If she'd only turn, you'd see the sky right through her skin.

You shove your hands deep in your pockets, too, but it has nothing to do with the cold.

"I don't understand what I'm looking at," you say, focusing on the screens. You try to sound impatient, not nervous, not afraid.

"It's the house. The feed is real time."

Her voice is flat. You can't look at her anymore: the set of her shoulders, hunched forward like a vulture, tells you as much, along with the intentness of her stare. She wants you to watch.

"I live here with Ray." Not lived, live. This is the first time she's mentioned his name.

Every screen shows a different room. Each room is empty. You're almost sure.

"A closed circuit television?" you ask.

"Something like that."

Grey light flickers across a dozen convex surfaces. No television is set quite flush with any other. The angles are all cock-eyed, unsettling. Yet everything is held in perfect balance. Nothing is out of place.

In the upper left corner, of the upper left-most screen, something moves.

"Did you see?" she asks.

You don't have the breath left to answer her.

The image shifts, jumping to the next screen, and your gaze follows. Blood beats too close to the surface of your skin. Your mouth goes dry.

The house is empty. It has to be.

The furniture on every screen is old, worn down. Some rooms are completely empty. The floorboards are bare.

She watches the screens, and you watch her. She leans forward, lip caught between teeth, fighting against the quickness of breath. You know the look. Neither one of you can look away.

You turn back to the televisions. Movement. A shadow stretching from the corner of the screen, unnaturally thin. Static. Liquid. Like nothing you've ever seen before. It slides from one screen to the next. Jumps. Quick cut.

Just beside your right shoulder she leans forward, eyes bright.

A fall of snow. One of the screens goes dark before flickering back to life. You see what you shouldn't see, what can't possibly be there. A man—starved thin—stands naked in an empty room. He stretches his arms wide, and grins. His teeth are a razor slash splitting open his face.

He looks right at you when he smiles.

Not the camera. You.

Scars trace his ribs, faint, but still visible. They wrap his arms like pale thread and march down his thighs. No part of his skin remains untouched, un-kissed by a blade.

There is no sound, but his lips move. If you had to guess—and you do—you'd guess he says "Watch this."

Or maybe he says, "Want this."

It's over so quickly you can almost pretend you didn't see anything at all.

Except you did. He wants you to watch. He wants you to know. His hands are empty, then the right holds a blade. The straight razor moves, deep on the left, wavering to the right. The gashed line appears as though by magic, opening his throat like his smile opens his face. Ragged. A dark spray. The scarecrow man bleeds out and the razor falls to the floor.

The screen flickers. Jumps. A fall of snow.

It's over so quickly you couldn't have seen what you know you saw.

The room is empty. Or it should be. Shadows pull in to the center, forming a solid mass in the instant before the image goes dark. You can almost pretend it's only a trick of the light. The shadows don't, can't, form the shape of a woman, kneeling before the scarecrow man. Hands bound. Watching. Her shoulders hitching with the force of silent tears.

ﻋﻠﻲ

Interview #2: Somewhere between November 21 and December 3, 2011

"He called it a period of grace. He was always talking about it. He said he could come back from anything. Anyone could. It wasn't just him. Anyone can be forgiven."

Tap-tap. Her finger knocks ash into the glass tray. You feel like you've seen this all before, an endless loop, an endless repetition, a ghost trapped behind the screen. The camera watches over her left shoulder. She rubs her skin, and in the wake of her hand, a faint smudge appears, like a bruise, just starting to fade.

Seven days. Or at least you think it's been seven days. You can't remember why you waited so long to talk to her again, or why you even called her in. She isn't a suspect. She never was. You had no cause to hold her. But you can't leave it alone. No matter how many times you've been told you're not on the case, there is no case, no woman, no house. Forget it and leave it alone.

You can't let go.

She's alone in the room, you're sure of it, and this time there's no crackle of static from the intercom. It's just the camera, and her body, sitting rigid in the chair. It's just the press of her bones against her skin, the thinness of her shirt. It's just her finger on the cigarette, and the specter of her smoke, filling the room.

It's just you, alone, leaning forward to catch her words through the video screen.

"It's not about forgiveness, it's about freedom. When you're bound, you have no more responsibility. Anything that happens after that, you can't control."

You can't see her face, but you imagine she smiles. You lean forward, wanting so badly to believe in her words. You almost touch the screen, even knowing she's beyond your reach, knowing you can't change what happens, only watch it unfold.

A jacket hangs from the back of her chair. She reaches into the pocket, tap-tapping the cigarette with her other hand, and lays something on the table. The camera, angled over her shoulder, shows a silver disc in a plastic sleeve. There's a word written in black marker on the sleeve, and she positions it just so, knowing the camera is watching. She wants you to see.

The word is Restraint.

"It's permission to accept what happens next, and be forgiven."

Tap-tap. She crushes the cigarette, and turns to face the camera. Her eyes are black-black, and she does not smile.

"It's already happened. You can only watch. You're helpless, but you're free. And that makes it okay."

ﻋﻠﻰ

Video Evidence #3: "Restraint" October 17, 2011

She left the disc for you on the table in the interrogation room. She wanted you to watch. And you do.

A time stamp in the bottom corner marks the date, and the time counts down, or counts up. Counts towards something, always falling from here to there and forever caught in-between. If you can believe anything she says the video was shot before Ray died. If Ray exists. If any of this is real.

You haven't seen her in days. But you imagine her standing just beyond your shoulder, not touching your skin, her breath almost stirring the tiny hairs of your ear. Watching as you watch her on the screen.

The image is black and white. The camera is set high, somewhere above her left shoulder. She's tied to a bed, both wrists bound to brass rails with black silken cord.

The camera shows the taut line of her belly, the space where her white tank top rides up and the fabric doesn't quite meet the black silk of her panties. You can't see her face, but you're certain it's her.

Her nipples press against the thinness of her shirt, just like you knew they would.

She moves her legs, rubbing one foot against the other, impatient. She pulls against the bonds.

She isn't alone in the room.

At the foot of the bed, where the camera is focused, there are shadows. They crowd, obscuring, so you can't see what you think you see, and you can't be sure. Someone is sitting on a chair, watching her, knees apart, hands dangling loose between them. One hand holds something bright.

She makes a low sound, not fear, not pleasure, not pain, not anything you can define. She strains against her bonds, and finally, she speaks a single word.

"Please."

"Not yet." The voice is so low it might not be there at all. "I want you to watch."

"Please." The word again. "Let me..."

"No." The voice almost isn't there; it cuts her off so you'll never know what she might have said next.

She doesn't want you to know.

The sound again, low in the back of her throat. Frustration. It's barely human, an animal whine full of need. The shadows at the

end of the bed shift, and you can only imagine what she sees—
bound and unable to act.

Her legs move, restless, impatient. You can only imagine what
she wants to do, the reason for the sound. But you don't know.
You lean forward, breath quick, watching skin strain against rope.

No one is forcing you this time, but you can't stop watching.
You know you shouldn't. But she's given you permission.

Everything that happens from here on out isn't your fault. It's
already happened. You can't change it. And that makes it okay.

The shadows at the end of the bed shift. She whines again. But
she can only watch. And watch. Watch her watching him, an endless loop, an endless regression, all trapped together in the spaces
in-between.

It's dark, and you can't be sure what you see, but you watch as
the shadows at the end of the bed seem to raise an arm, and something bright glints against the darkness, cutting deep.

اﻟﻌ

Video Evidence #4: "Want" January 21, 2012

There's one more video. She must have left it. For you. It has
to be for you.

You went back to the house, one last time, alone. The disc was
on the porch where the televisions used to be. The word on the
envelope in black permanent marker is Want. You've watched it a
dozen, a hundred, a thousand times. And you swear it's different
every time.

The camera is close in. You can't see her face, but it's her. It has
to be her. The white tank top is the same, so thin you can almost
see her skin. She's wearing the same black panties. Her nipples
press hard against her shirt. The camera, fixed, shows her body between neck and mid-thigh, but not her face, so you'll never know
for sure. But you'd know her voice anywhere, spoken close, as if
against your ear. Raising hairs, prickling skin—so breath-hot it has
to be there, has to be real.

You press play for the dozenth-hundredth time.

The light is wrong—cast by the static glow of too many television screens, all stacked one atop the other, all showing empty rooms.

At first, there is only breath: her breath, raising goosebumps on your skin. It has to be her, because those are her blunt, ragged nails tracing the fabric of her shirt, lifting it, stopping just short of the curve of her small breasts.

She speaks—a calling, a binding. It isn't for you. But you want it to be."I want you," she says, though you can't see her face. "I want you so badly I can feel it in my bones, in my blood, in every part of me. And I want you to want me, too. I want you to want me so bad you can't think of anything else. I want to become your entire world."

Her hands lift her shirt higher, teasing. Her words don't make any sense; they're not for you. But you don't care. An eternity passes before she catches the edges of the fabric, pulling the shirt over a head the camera doesn't see, revealing small breasts, nipples puckered hard in the wrong, staticky light.

"I know you like to watch. So watch me. Watch me, and know how much I want you. Even though you can't touch me. Not yet."

Your breath catches. You swear, on the hundredth, or the thousandth view that she reaches out a hand and presses it flat against the glass—not the camera lens, but the screen.

So close you could touch her.

You want so badly for it to be true.

But it isn't for you. It can't be. Except it has to be, because Ray—if he ever existed—is dead. And the date in the corner of the screen says it's been weeks since she disappeared. This can't be her, calling him home, binding him in her flesh, holding him against his will, and forgiving him. Time can't work that way.

You don't want it to.

You are lost, too. She must see that. And you want so badly for her to call you home. To forgive you.

She cups her breasts, small as they are, before sliding her hands over her belly, down to her hips to tease the edges of her panties.

She slips her fingers beneath the waistband, and lower, where the fabric meets the soft flesh of her inner thigh. The camera doesn't show her face, but you swear she smiles.

Slow then, agonizingly slow, she peels the silk away, stripping, but not completely, letting the material rest around her thighs. You can't help but think of rope, silken and black. Binding. You squirm, knowing you shouldn't watch. But you can't look away. You never could.

You can't change anything that's happened. Or will happen. So that makes it okay.

"I want you to want me so badly that you can't resist. I want you to come."

Her hand slides between her legs, brushing soft and slow at first, then stroking faster, more insistent. Her rhythm quickens with your breath. The silk strains around her parted legs.

The image shifts, flickers. The light turns strange. Stranger. At the edges of the screen. A shadow resolves, a face—half seen—just over her shoulder. It smiles.

"I want you inside me. I want to hold you, even when you don't want to be held."

The frame judders. Her hand, between her legs, doubles, until it isn't her hand anymore. Someone else strokes her, sliding a finger between her lips, parting her so the camera almost, but not quite, sees. The fingers extend, tendrils of shadow leaking away from themselves. One slips inside her.

You can't see her face, but you imagine she bites her lip. Her legs part wider, straining silk to the limit. When her breath hitches this time, it is real. That animal sound, the low growl echoing the image of her bound on the bed and aching toward a figure, half-seen. It is not fear. It never was.

"And I want you to know I forgive you."

The screen flickers. Shattered light reflects on her body, on her hand as her fingers/not her fingers move between her legs, as her hips buck towards the camera, rocking beneath the touch.

A tendril of shadow slides around her throat. Her head tilts back. A bruise that is not a bruise appears against the whiteness of her shoulder. She gasps.

And sometimes, only sometimes, on the dozenth-hundreth viewing, the tendrils of shadows draw her arms behind her back, binding them, so you know it can't be her hand between her legs. Those ribbons of darkness, ethereal and insubstantial circle her hardened nipples, teasing, pinching. They are hands, lips, tongues, and none of those things at all.

Crack. A sound like a whip, and welts appear on her skin.

Her head snaps forward, and she smiles, razor blade sharp.

You think she says, "Want me." But you can't be sure.

She shudders. Hands that are not hands, and certainly not her hands, cup her breasts. Shadows become solid. One strand of darkness curls upward to trace the fullness of a mouth you can't see. You imagine parted lips; beneath the hot impact of her breath the tendril of darkness shudders. You imagine gooseflesh rising on insubstantial skin. You understand.

How much of this is real?

The screen flickers again, and you can almost her feel her tongue, wet and warm, on the shadow tendril, drawing it in, swallowing it whole.

Her nipples, hard, hard, hard, are darker than they were ever meant to be. Who is restrained; who restrains? Who binds, and who is bound? Who is in control?

Almost substantial, something, someone, traces the line of her belly, tastes the slick wetness between her legs. Again, she makes a little sound, but it is not surrender. It is victory. The darkness thickens, penetrating and not penetrating. Called. Absorbed. Summoned. Her head snaps back.

"Yes." A whisper, only half heard.

The shadow envelops her.

"Yes."

And she takes it all in.

The shadow fills her, pulsing between her legs.

Her hand moves, but it is not her hand.

She soaks darkness into her being. She takes it inside of her in every way, and at the end, there is a scream—not hers. The thing surrounds her, loving her, fucking her. Then it is gone.

It is her.

And she comes.

The screen goes dark.

But it isn't always the same.

Sometimes, you see what you can't possibly see. More than a shadow stands behind her. And for just an instant, its arms spread wide, skeletal-razor grin stretched across sunken cheeks. Its eyes are fixed on you. Watching.

Season of Fire
Sasha Payne

Summer is the season of fire. The days are heavy with heat and the nights drowsy with lust. It's the season of wanton flowers and rampant bees, of bulls breaking gates and cats calling in the darkness. Summer is the season of fire-aligned mages. My season. Oh, earth mages will tell you that spring is the best, and water mages will tell you that winter is the greatest, and of course air mages will swear it is autumn. They are all wrong. Summer is the season of fire, of passion, of rage, and of lust.

It was midsummer, the perfect day for a mage trial.

In the morning, I went about my chores. I fed and milked the cattle, fed the chickens and collected their eggs, and then mopped out the bullpen. You might wonder why an apprentice mage was looking after livestock, to which I would draw your attention to the word apprentice. You might also wonder why a mage has farm animals. I wondered so myself once.

"Master, why do we have cattle?" I asked as I mopped bull semen from the bullpen floor. This was a fortunately rare occurrence. When my feverish imaginings had considered what it would be like to be a sex mage, bull semen had not crossed my mind.

"We mate the bull with the cows and use the sexual energy for minor spells," he said, "although if you were better at containing your sexual energy, no mage for miles around would need do so."

"I try, Master," I said, "and when I can't then I send the energy to the apple sapling as you said."

My master opened the window. "Do you mean that sapling, my boy? The fifty-foot-tall apple tree?"

"Yes, Master. I think it will drop more apples today," I offered. "We can have apple pie."

He rolled his eyes. They were deep, warm brown, and his hair was the color of honey. He was young for a mage of his reputation and as gifted in the rituals of sex magic as any mage would hope to be. I would have warmed his bed at the slightest hint, but alas he gave me none.

"Assan, there is a limit to how much apple pie a man may eat without exploding."

"Yes, Master," I said. "Master?"

"Yes, Assan?" he asked me with the expression of a man frightened of the question.

"Why do we have chickens? They can't provide much energy," I said.

My master nodded. "That is true, particularly as we have no rooster. Although I suppose that anything is possible."

"Then why do we have chickens?" I asked.

"So I can have eggs for breakfast," he said.

After I finished my chores I went into the house, where my master was putting out breakfast. One thing I learned early in my apprenticeship was that in some ways, an earth affiliation has benefits. Such as food. Animals give more milk or meat, crops grow faster, my little accidents notwithstanding, and cooked food tastes much better. Earth mages will rarely let non-earth apprentices cook if they can avoid it. They enjoy their food too much.

"Are you ready for the journey?" he asked.

"Yes, Master. I have spare clothes in my sack and all of my notes."

"Notes! Since when did you pay attention to things I say?" Master Maran asked.

"Never, but perhaps my idle drawings will spark some memory," I said.

Master Maran threw a wet cloth at me, and then we sat down to breakfast. We ate each meal together except for my afternoon off, when I went to the village and searched for a handsome lad to frolic with and feed me grapes. I had not been successful, but I lived in hope. It was to be my last breakfast as Master Maran's apprentice, if all went well. It struck me then with more force than I expected. After five years apprenticeship I was about to become a mage.

There are four kinds of magic practitioners: blood mages, sex mages, wizards, and sorcerers. We used to say mages, wizards and witches, and sorcerers and sorceresses, but the witches and sorceresses decided they'd rather be called wizards and sorcerers too. Blood mages use blood sacrifices to power their magic—not always human and not always to death—wizards use magical books, sorcerers use magical objects, and sex mages... well, that doesn't need an explanation. Wizards get the most respect—but I think that's because they use magical books and most villagers can't read, so any book seems mysterious to begin with—and then sorcerers. Blood mages, well, nobody likes them, they're rather like that distant cousin you have whom everyone tells you not to be alone with. You can imagine how nervous people are around sex mages, lords and ladies as much as peasants. A blood mage will only kill them, but a sex mage can defile them in the most wonderful ways and make them enjoy it. That or they cover their envy of our sex lives with backslapping bonhomie.

I refuse to lie, there was a lot of sex. Why become a sex mage if not for the sex? Master Maran was always busy with fertility spells—the work of a village mage is mostly healing and fertility—and I was always happy to... learn my craft by his example. Master was more gifted with fertility than healing, he was an earth and healing is a water spell, and I had even less skill with healing. It wasn't my fault, I was a fire. I had no more skill for water spells than Master Maran had for air spells. Not only could he not enchant with any duration, and had Master Kish teach me, he also couldn't fly more than a few feet.

We went by cart instead. The fields stretched out around us, the air full of honeysuckle and cowslip. The air thrummed with heat, and we watched young farmhands as they stripped off their shirts and strutted through the corn. Sunlight shone off their gleaming, muscular bodies, made strong and taut by long hours of heavy labor.

"Summer makes everyone so beautiful," I said.

"Lust makes you think so," Master Maran laughed.

"Aren't I meant to be lusty? What else should a fire-aligned apprentice sex mage be if not licentious?"

"It is an inclination," he said severely, "not a stricture."

"I'm inclined to be exceptionally lusty," I sighed.

My master laughed and ruffled my hair. "Save your passion for your trial, my boy."

"How will I perform if I am not serene?"

"If serenity is a prerequisite for your performing then you will never make a mage," he retorted.

I took a deep breath of the warm and pleasant air before I answered. "Do you think that we will see Master Kish at the magic trials?" I asked. It was a blow at an unguarded point. It was beneath me, in truth.

"Why, do you anticipate seeing Will?" Master Maran asked. That was a stiletto blade between my joints for all I brought it on myself.

Will was Master Kish's apprentice, and he was beautiful. He was about my height, with lush, dark curls, dark skin, and sleepy black eyes. He was broader than I, with limbs straight and strong as young tree trunks and a chest like a cask of Rhenish. He was to be a wizard, although he looked more like a barbarian until you looked into his eyes. His eyes were soft and gentle.

As I had been born under inauspicious stars, it was natural I suppose that he would have none of me. Apprentice wizards were to be devoted to their art without distraction, and I was such a distraction. Oh, I should have distracted Will—in all the magic places devoted to our spells, upon the kitchen floor, upon the kitchen table, in fields and forests, and not least of all in bed. In the positions of the ox, otter, snake, and eagle I would have distracted him into exhaustion. And then I would have done it again.

"Will has no will to see me," I said.

"Sulking is no way to seduce anyone."

"Master did not teach me to seduce." I pouted.

"What man teaches a fish to swim?" Master Maran asked, shaking his head.

"I was unable to seduce you," I said.

"You're my apprentice," he replied.

You are likely wondering how I learned my craft if my master would not lie with me. There you touch it with a pin. Master Maran was extremely skillful and I had no complaints, but they were rituals done for magic. He would perform any ritual with me as he would with a petitioner. It was satisfying, but not the same satisfaction as a look, a touch, a kiss, a nervous fumble, and a slow discovery of shared pleasures.

We reached the fair before noon. There was a magic fair each year: one year it would be at midsummer, the next year at the autumnal equinox, then the winter solstice, then the vernal equinox. There was always a riot of tents, and this fair was no different. There were traders and market folk selling magical goods, scrolls, and sacrificial animals along with the unguents and lotions of which we made much use. Master bought us both weak ale, watered too much, and roasted poussin with tiny buttered potatoes.

"Will you lay money on me, Master?" I asked.

"I'll lay money on you to blush when you turn to your right," he said.

I turned, how could I not, and saw Will gleaming in the sun as he patiently waited his turn to sign for trial. He was taller than when I saw him last, now taller than I. He looked up as I was staring and gave me a nod. Despite his manifold perfections, he failed entirely to appreciate mine.

"Offer to be his helpmeet," Master Maran suggested.

"Do you mean me to fail? Am I such an excellent apprentice that you would sabotage me?" I asked.

Master Maran laughed, and I wondered what it would be like to live without that laughter daily.

"I will miss you cluttering up the place," he said, "yet not quite enough for that. You must have a second with whom to perform the trials. Ask Will. He knows you, and your alignments are in opposition; he can help you with your healing and you can fire his passions."

"You taunt me with cruel fantasies, Master."

"They're the most pleasing," he said. "Why not ask him?"

"He might say yes," I admitted.

"Assan, that would be the best outcome," he said gravely.

"Then I will ask him," I agreed, "and hope that he says no."

Will watched me with lowered eyes as I strolled over to him. A good word, strolled, a casual word—the word for a young man confidently and calmly approaching an equal. That was what I was.

"Hello, Will!"

"Good day, Assan," he said in that soft, lilting voice.

"Master Maran thinks that I should offer to be your helpmeet," I said. "It was his idea."

Will's eyes filled with panic, and something else.

"Does he?" Master Kish demanded. "Then why does he not come over here and suggest it to me?"

Will caught my eye and pulled a face. He was including me in a private joke, two apprentices conspiring humorously against their masters. I took a deep, proud breath and then stopped when I began to feel dizzy.

"Perhaps my master believes that as we are almost mages, we should need no intermediary?" I suggested.

"Don't cheek me, boy! I know that he's too cowardly to face me. He'll see how I feel about that," he said, and strode off toward Master Maran.

Boy. Master Kish was only a handful of years older than I was. He had apprenticed under every practitioner who would train him, including Master Maran. He was handsome in a pretty kind of way, with delicate features and a mass of chestnut hair cascading down his shoulders.

"He spent four hours choosing his robe," Will whispered to me, "wondering which one Master Maran would prefer."

"We would never be so foolish," I said.

My new robe was itching.

"I wouldn't know how to help you, and your ritual would draw my magic," Will said, and shuffled his feet.

"We have to perform one spell for each type: blood, sex, wizardry, and sorcery," I said. "We could perform yours first, and you need not know anything about sex!"

Other apprentices turned to wonder at the noise. We ignored them.

"I didn't say I know nothing," Will muttered as he looked everywhere but at me. "Master keeps sheep."

"Sheep!"

"I didn't mean that I couple with them!" Will protested, meeting my eyes in panic. "I meant that I have seen them.... Oh, you meant to be amusing." He punched me on the arm but smiled at me shyly, a thing to make the world stop and my heart beat faster. "Master had to buy another ram. Ours ignored the sheep and broke into other farms to tup the rams."

"We only have one bull and no roosters," I said.

Will looked past me to Master Maran and Master Kish. "Your master looks angry," he said.

"No, he's embarrassed," I said. "The redness in his cheeks is the same complexion, but his manner is different. Why do you think he looks over here?"

"Master Kish complains of you," Will said confidently.

"How can you possibly say so? What complaint could be made of me?"

"You're disrespectful," Will said almost gleefully, "too sure of your own powers, a seducer, a leader astray, and worst of all you are Master Maran's apprentice. He shall never forgive you for that."

"Most unfair." I pouted, seeking sympathy. "I bear him no grudge."

"He has nothing you want."

"I do not have Master Maran."

"You have... rites with him," Will said shyly, ducking his head.

"That's only magic. It means nothing," I said.

We were almost at the front of the line but Will hadn't noticed.

"It means nothing? So if we have rites for the sex mage spell then it won't mean anything?" he said doubtfully.

It was only magic. Master Maran had said so many times. It wasn't real.

"It will be only another form of magic," I promised.

"If you're sure," he said.

It was the longest time I'd spent alone with Will. My blood was fizzing in my veins. Even when he stood a foot away I felt as though he was inside my skin.

"This is your fault, you know," Will murmured later, as we sat down in the exhibition circle.

"No, how so?"

"All the mages know how arrogant you are. They test you more to show you your folly."

"If I am arrogant it is because I am too honest," I said virtuously.

Will straightened the sleeves of his midnight-blue robe. "I trust you are," he said, "for if you fail then I fail with you."

I met those dark, gentle eyes with a courage born of lusty necessity. "Then I will ensure we do not fail."

The first challenge was that of the sorcerers. A tiny sorcerer, who looked to have some elvish in him, danced out with an orb of Tassia—one orb, when we both had to fly.

It felt slick in my hand, almost oiled, and magic was leaking out of it.

"A trap for the unwary," Will said quietly.

"My fault?" I asked.

"But of course," he said, and smiled.

I threw the orb from hand to hand, and an angry murmur came from the sorcerers.

"Assan," Will warned.

"Say my name again, it sounds so sweet."

"I will gladly punch you in the arm again if you wish."

I held out my hands. Magic flickered on each palm.

"Ta-da."

"Braggart," Will said lightly.

He took my free hand and my heart soared, followed by the

rest of my body. As our feet left the ground I heard Will let out a breath. He was shaking but gripped my hand fiercely, refusing to surrender.

"I have you," I said.

"Promise?"

"Till my dying day. Or sooner if you age badly."

We giggled, still such boys.

As we waited for the second trial I looked about the room. Master Maran was seated at the front with Master Kish. They were seated very closely but were pretending to ignore each other.

The second trial was the blood mage challenge, and they had chosen an earth spell, a temporary infertility spell to be cast on the female apprentices. Doubtless two of them would be tasked with casting the same spell on us when the time came.

They brought out our sistren, but I only saw Will. The air was still, the crowd was quiet, and Will filled my vision. I removed my robe, and my breath caught in my throat as Will's gaze assayed my bare flesh. He winked and took my hand in his trembling fingers.

"The bowl," I whispered, as he drew my wrist up to his mouth.

His eyes widened in alarm but didn't move from mine as he nudged with his knee the bowl beneath my arm. Will took the delicate skin of my wrist between his teeth and bit down gently. We caught our breath, both of us caught in the tension of waiting, and then I felt him pierce me. I moaned softly as he withdrew, and we watched together as the blood welled and pattered into the bowl like falling rain.

Will bandaged my wrist carefully, and the brush of his fingers against my skin made my heart pound. We tipped the bowl together, and as the liquid flowed down onto the hard earth we felt the energy flow into us. What stirred was wild magic, stronger than either of us had expected. I was too excited, perhaps we both were. I saw then that neither of us had the power for the spell with the blood magic alone. We needed the spark of our touch, of our excitement, to carry the spell.

There were murmurs as the girls swayed, and a moment of

busy movement as mages checked that each female apprentice was safely spelled. Will was chewing his lip when he looked at me and smiled when they approved us.

Will nudged me with his elbow. "Did you see Master Kish grasp Master Maran's hand during the trial?"

"No. Truly?"

"He did."

The wizards' challenge came hard upon us. I watched Will undress and neatly fold his robe. His body was strong and muscular; he had a light dusting of hair on his chest, thinning out as it ran down to his navel. Dark curls of pubic hair nestled the base of his heavy cock and surrounded his balls. I was in Will's hands as he lay me face down upon the floor of the circle. He straddled my waist, and I felt his strong thighs pressed against my legs. He could crush me between his thighs and I'd only be able to sigh.

Will dipped a brush into a saucer of ink, and we both watched the drops drip back into the black liquid. With a delicate touch Will wrote the words of the spell across my back. He rested his left hand on my left shoulder as he wrote, and the warmth of his skin made my flesh prickle. He leaned down to paint the intricate details, and I felt his warm breath on my back.

"Nearly there," he murmured, his lips soft against my ear.

The sex mage ritual was soon, and I thanked the gods for it. I could feel the healing spell sinking into my flesh, the magic power pooling and seeping through my body. My arm began to tingle as the skin on my wrist knitted itself together.

I stood up and held out my wrist. The wound, always tiny, was completely healed. I mourned the scar that never existed, the reminder of Will's closeness that moment.

Finally came the sex mage challenge. My hands were slick with sweat as I thought about it. I told myself that it was nothing, merely a rite like any other. A rite with Will, whose dark, bright eyes were always so full of warmth. A rite that meant, demanded, that I touch that firm, warm skin. That it was the fire spell meant Master Maran had worked tirelessly on my behalf, a gift for my ascension to mage. I would have to find a way to thank him, if Will's touch didn't carve my heart from my chest.

"I'm at your mercy," Will said. His eyes were wide and his hands were shaking.

I was going to be his first. His first! I hadn't for a moment thought. He was uncharted territory and I was the pathfinder. Well, unless I accidentally plowed up the crops and salted the earth. Only the merest pressure on me, then.

"Entirely in my power," I agreed, "with no one to protect you from my evil deeds but several hundred mages, wizards, and sorcerers."

"Don't remind me!"

He lay supine on the floor, atop a small velvet pillow, and tried to look so serious but could not keep from smiling. We were surrounded by hundreds of people, but I saw only Will and heard only his breathing. I think if I had laid my hand on his chest I could have felt his heart beating through his skin.

"It may hurt a little," I said.

"Like the bite?" he breathed. His heavy erection pressed against my hip as I leaned over him.

"About the same."

Will sighed as I sat back and opened the pot of unguent. The pot skittered in my hands as if anxious for its big moment. The unguent was scented with rose oil and tingled on my skin as I warmed it between my fingers.

I put my left hand on Will's hip as I leaned forward to apply the unguent.

"No kiss?" he whispered as he put his hand on my arm.

"Not for this. It's just magic."

"Does that mean we can't enjoy it?" He pouted.

I loved that he would play with me, at such a time and such a place.

"There's no magic if we don't enjoy it," I said.

"Still you don't kiss?"

"It isn't considered best form," I admitted.

"When have you ever cared what others thought proper form?" Will's nose wrinkled as he laughed. "I think that you haven't kissed anyone before."

My honor was at stake. Well, such was my excuse.

Will closed his eyes as I lowered my face to his. My lips brushed against his—they were soft, and dry, and very warm. I smelled a hint of the buttermilk that he had drunk at breakfast, and then he opened his mouth. Sparks skittered across my skin as the tip of my tongue mapped the roof of his mouth.

Yet that was not why I was there. No matter how every inch of my body protested, we were not there for that.

I broke the kiss with a sigh. As I leaned back I saw that Will's eyes were still closed.

"Soppy," I charged.

"Surprised," he replied.

Will spread his legs a little and watched with heavy-lidded eyes as I found my way through his forest and around his boulders. He stroked my left arm as my right hand followed the path down to his pucker.

"Oh Goddess," he murmured as I caressed him.

He put his free hand over mine as I rubbed it into him. He was greedy for my touch, and his moan as I slid a finger inside him turned my heart to water and my cock to stone.

I wondered if my eyes were as glazed with want as his were. More, perhaps, if that were possible. He took two more fingers with a soft sigh, and I knew that he was ready.

"Did you enjoy our kiss?" he murmured.

"Yes."

"Just yes?"

"My babbling would be unmanly," I explained.

Will laughed and then caught his breath as I entered him. His hands crawled up my arms, squeezed my shoulders, and tangled in my hair.

I was groaning, I knew, a tree about to fall in the tempest. We had only begun and I felt magic drowning the air. His hand found my back, short nails scratching a poem in my skin. I guided his other hand to his cock and watched him grasp it.

His face glistened and his glazed eyes shone like mirrors. His soft lips were parted a little as he panted and murmured. I saw the tiniest flash of his tongue, wet and gleaming, in the sultry darkness of his mouth.

The universe had contracted to this point, to nothing but Will, the feel of his body and the soft sounds he made. I felt every whorl of his fingertips against my back, each droplet of moisture in his breath, and counted every dark lash fringing his beautiful eyes.

"Goddess," he moaned.

"Which one?"

"Whichever one did this!"

His back arched and his breathing deepened. He was close, I was close, and the spell was coalescing in the darkness. Will raised his legs, urging me deeper, and clamped them around my waist. His body was burning and slick with our mingled sweat. Will was moaning, babbling pleas and fragments of promises as he stared into my eyes. I heard our heartbeats mingle into one frantic pulse, felt the magic pressing against us both, and knew our time had come.

Magic throbbed through us as we were pushed over the precipice. The world went white and silent for heartbeat after heartbeat, and then returned slowly.

Balls of fire whirled and whooshed overhead, exploding into showers of sparks. Red, green, silver, gold, and a thousand other colors filled the sky above us.

"Did we do that?" Will wondered drowsily.

"We did."

"It was supposed to happen?"

"Naturally."

Will smiled, and we both sat up slowly.

"Just magic?" he asked.

"Just magic," I answered.

"Liar," he said, and kissed me.

Primè Nocta
Kierstin Cherry

Lightning fractured the night sky and in the burning afterglows, the Apothecary loomed before her. Rain sheeted down upon its hulking mass, and mist rose from the summer stones that ringed its gloomy entrance.

Alone, Zana stood at the crossroads—a ghost in the hazy night. Soaked to the skin, she gathered her wedding gown about her and ran.

She passed into the shadow of the building, her feet splashing through small pools upon the broken flagstones. She hugged the rusted iron fence, brushing past soaked hemlocks and nightshade. Already, the color was bleeding out of the night. The rain on her flushed skin felt like nothing more than water falling.

She was dying.

Slipping through the gate, Zana stopped before the Apothecary's darkened maw. Reflexively, she clenched her hands into fists. Across her knuckles, emerald-green scales cracked, painfully desiccated and withering.

"Magden." She whispered the name of her queen, but it was lost in the clamor of the storm. Magden would know what to do.

A deathly chill gripped her as she ran up the broken steps. The scent of antiquity and old medicine eddied a vaporous pall around the Apothecary, the musk of a serpent's den lingering a warning about its shadow-thrown entrance. Heedless, Zana plunged over the threshold.

Darkness enshrouded her, pierced only by the guttering of crimson candles in the chamber beyond. Shadows distended, forms once familiar now lost to the darkness. She strained to penetrate the veil, but her night vision was steadily failing. Fear threaded its way through her dying frame. Heart spasming, she trembled back.

Deep in the darkness, the echoing hiss of a snake's brood awakening.

Panic burst open in her breast. Zana ran, fleeing toward the flickering candles, blinded by light and darkness, cobwebs catching across her face and in her hair. Sobs wracked her through, augmenting her agony—her body dying all around her. The hem of her wedding gown snagged a splintered board. Weeping, she tore it free and stumbled.

The small of her back connected with an oaken table. A hitching breath caught the reek of old blood, sending a flash of animal fright through her. Whirling, she backed up, candlelight mocking in her eyes.

A dozen scarlet pillars had been set to burn upon a huge oak table, their light guttering over a butchery of bloodstains, a surgeon's array of incisions gashed across slowly-rotting wood.

Lightning lashed the night. A nest of asps hissed in the falling darkness.

Breath stolen, Zana froze. Droplets of rain fell from her hair and trickled down into her cleavage. Wedding silk clung to flushed skin. She tried not to recall the look of betrayal on her betrothed's face.

He had not understood.

Across her entire body, emerald serpent-scales molted, peeling back to reveal human flesh beneath. Her limbs had lost their reptilian strength, their sinuous flexibility. Her fangs had fallen out hours ago. How long before the final death of her Nythian blood? How long before she became fully human?

She remembered that night—the storm, the ritual—she remembered...

"Magden?"

The kiss of her queen's blade through her half-blood flesh. Zana's gaze fell once more to the oaken slab. Blood and crimson wax spilling. That night—

"Magden!" That night you killed me upon this altar!

"Zana."

Her breath crystallized.

Of course, Magden had been there all along, ensconced in shadow and gloom. She was queen, the Primè Reinè of the Nyth, and she could sense the presence of all her people, even a dying half-blood.

Heart tripping on fear and death, Zana searched the shadows, seeking to divide Magden's willowy figure from the darkness. Her human eyes were painfully inadequate.

A low chuckle carried on the hissing of serpents, and the Reinè revealed herself. A gown of vesperis silk clung, shimmering blue-back upon her sinuous body. The candlelight caught her red hair like a fiery halo and burned a serpentine glow in her grey eyes.

The sight of her pierced Zana's heart. The memory of another night arose—lying in Magden's arms, the night they nearly followed the example of their mothers, Nyth queen and Zephyris concubine.

Thunder boomed through the Apothecary, and a flash of lightning burned the image of Magden's face into her—a porcelain visage bejeweled with fine cobalt scales, her eyes the color of a storm, black pupils slitted and pulsing with reptilian desire.

Guilt blushing upon her face, Zana allowed her gaze to wander the vivid strokes of scale ornamenting the Reinè's body, trailing down both sides of her neck and along her collarbones, plunging down her cleavage to form a V between her breasts. The vesperis gown obscured further exploration, but Zana's thoughts delved deeper to the soft snakeskin that defined Magden's ribs and her hipbones, joining between her legs to cover her feminine sex.

A pleasured hiss drew Zana's attention. The Reinè had caught her looking.

With slow, delicious dread, Zana realized that she had groped down over her own bosom to her thighs where her hands clenched the sodden wedding gown in frustration. The wet silk clung tight to her body, making it easy for the Reinè to appraise every inch of her. Meeting her gaze, Magden smiled, sharp in the candlelight.

Buried deep within Zana's dying blood, a visceral twinge leapt and twisted. Had her mother felt the same euphoria when Queen Margrethe had looked upon her?

But her hands, her scales, the death that gripped her! Zana crumpled before her Reinè. "Magden, what's happening to me?"

"It's what you wanted, isn't it?" Magden's voice was sultry. "When you came to me that night, you forsook your Nythian blood. You begged me that you might re-awaken fully human."

A musky scent wafted from her scales, alluring even to Zana's dulling senses, lighting her body with a sudden ache. "What did you do to me?"

"You wanted to be free. To marry the man you love."

The perfume of her serpent-flesh was intoxicating, awakening the part of Zana that was still Nyth, still Zephyris concubine. "I—" She had forgotten how compelling Magden was, how enthralling to be a Nyth in the presence of the queen. Magden's snakeskin scent was strong, overpowering the odor of dust and old remedies, overpowering even the ozone of the storm.

They were fated to be the perfect match—the Primè Reinè of the Nyth and her Zephyris—genetically encoded, destined to breed, every cell, every fragment of them predisposed to the act of mating.

Fear electrified Zana's spine. She knew the truth of Magden. Primè Reinè, Nyth Queen—voracious, hermaphroditic, driven by instinct. To lie with her was to bear her young.

"You still wish to forsake me?" Magden's eyes glowed in the gloom.

Sudden desire strangled Zana, the last vestiges of her Nythian blood fighting its inevitable demise. The ache inside became a blossoming burn. "Yes."

Magden lingered, close but just out of reach. "You wish to wed this man?"

The Reinè's fragrance beguiled Zana, perfuming her skin, making her heady. Zana took the last half-step and their bodies gently collided. "Yes..."

With a jolt, Zana felt it—the genetic reaction that shivered through Magden's tall frame, their proximity awakening the insatiable instinct to breed. Chemical response became need, and need blossomed into full, unfettered lust. Magden reached out, her hands falling possessively to Zana's hips. Zana, too, felt the weight of her genetics, her body burning with desire, uncontrolled and writhing against Magden, her mind reeling with the urge to arouse her further.

For a moment, they lost themselves in the embrace, Reinè and Zephyris, entwined around each other in the first throes of their mating passion.

Magden's grip tightened, pulling Zana close, hips to hips, slowly grinding. The half-blood girl moaned, her hands tangling in Magden's red hair.

Thunder crashed discordant, and the spattering of lighting cut sharp through the night.

"If you wish to wed him, then why are you not in his bed?"

Zana's desire withered like her dying scales.

Magden began to pull away. She was mastering herself. "You are no longer one of mine."

Zana couldn't bear her absence. She reached out. "Magden..."

"You have chosen affinity with your human half." The Reinè took Zana's hands from her face. She stepped back. "Even now, your Nythian blood dies within you. Soon, you will no longer be my Zephyris."

Bereft, distraught, Zana put a hand to her head. Vertigo gripped her skull.

"I will no longer be your Reinè."

Zana reeled. That was what she wanted, wasn't it? Her throat closed painfully.

Before her, Magden stood, wonderful and terrible, gentle and yet dire and frightening. Zana trembled in her presence. Her Nythian blood would not be quieted. "No...Magden, I—" With a stifled sob, she threw herself into the arms of her queen.

Over her cries, Zana could hear the storm's song fading fast in her ears. Only the Nyth could hear the mesmeric dirge of rain and thunder. All around her, storm and lightning, her world was coming down. She buried her face in Magden's shoulder, breathing deep of her enthralling scent. One hand tangled into Magden's red curls as if she would never let go.

The Primè Reinè resisted, but Zana urged against her, relentless, inflaming her primitive urges. Reptilian muscles rippled. Moisture beaded on cobalt-blue scales. Magden's body shuddered, trapped in a chrysalis of desire.

Drawn by the sultry lure of serpent-flesh, Zana leaned in, tonguing the dewdrops of natura that glistened on Magden's scales. The snaky softness rippled under her kisses, the taste slightly metallic, the scent overpowering.

Remaining still, the Reinè suffered her Zephyris's caress. Her eyes glowed a serpentine sheen in the candles' light, a pleasured hiss she could not master growling deep in her throat. Her body trembled with need, instinctual, inevitable, but she did not make a move to claim her concubine. One fang caught her lower lip, drawing a bead of green blood.

Eagerly, Zana pressed her open mouth to it, sampling the slow burn of Magden's agony. She brought her hands to her Reinè's face and held it. "Why do you hesitate?"

"As the Goddess of Storms and Secrets is my witness, I abandoned my claim upon you." Magden's voice was a whisper. "I gave you freely."

Zana closed her eyes. "I know." She was stricken under the weight of what she might do.

"Once we begin, neither one of us will be in control." Magden trembled, her body already gripped in the initial throes. "It is the way of the Primè Reinè and her Zephyris. We will lose ourselves to the act."

"The act?"

"Of mating."

Zana could not suppress a shiver of anticipation.

Magden's grey eyes dilated black. "If we mate, then human or

Nyth, you will bear my brood."

The shuddering thought of Magden impregnating her—Zana's human sensibility recoiled in fear and revulsion. But her Nythian half strained closer, sudden lust dispersing fear like smoke.

Running her hands up her body, she cupped her small breasts, pushing them against Magden's, massaging the Reinè's bosom with her own. The wet silk of her wedding gown shifted, threatening to expose the entirety of her cleavage.

Magden remained still though her eyes burned with lust.

Moaning, Zana rubbed herself harder, straining for Magden's touch. The slick feel of snakeskin against her hot, dying flesh was more than she could bear. Frustrated, she grabbed Magden's hands and pressed them to her breasts. A low groan escaped her as she began to massage herself. Pleasure slivered up her spine, staving off the fright, the pain of a part of herself expiring.

A shaky breath quivered from Magden's lips. Zana entwined their fingers, guiding, groping. Urging closer, she yearned to the tips of her toes and pulled her Reinè down to meet her. Her lips found the softness of Magden's, and she kissed, opening her mouth. Her tongue licked cautiously, sampling the sharpness of serpent fangs.

Her wedding gown crumpled under the force of Magden's grip.

A smile rose to Zana's lips. Her queen could not fight genetics forever. A willing Zephyris, she writhed, rolling her hips to meet Magden's.

With serpentine speed, Magden shoved her hard against the oak table. The candles rocked and one tipped over, running red across the butchered surface. Zana shivered as her Reinè pinned her. She arched back, leaning against the oak. The Reinè's body came against hers and this time, there was no hesitation.

Slow and hard, Magden rode her against the altar. Her leg slipped between Zana's, her hips shoving the Zephyris back against the table.

Zana moaned and fought forward, sliding her sex against Magden's thigh. The pressure on her clit was pure, liquid torment, the silk of her panties growing damp.

Magden bent her head. Her red curls fell forward, caressing Zana's face. Grey eyes saturnine, she crushed her closer, returning the kiss, opening her mouth, tonguing deep to taste her Zephyris.

Thunder boomed, and Zana broke away, gasping from the intensity. The silk of her wedding gown was wet and not from the rain. Without ceremony, she hiked it up and sank back down, straddling her Reinè's leg.

The touch of Zana's hot thighs against hers caught Magden breathless. She rested her forehead against her Zephyris's collarbone, her lips hovering over barren and peeling scales. "My dying Zana." Softly, she licked. The green scales glistened emerald-wet with her saliva, taking on an almost healthy luster.

Moaning, Zana rode her, silk panties and vesperis gown growing damp under her lusty ministrations. Her fingernails dug into Magden's shoulders, igniting tension within serpentine skin.

It was not enough.

Desperate, she sank to her knees before her Reinè. She did not know what she meant to do. Magden leaned back, placing both hands on her altar.

Softly, Zana pressed her lips to her Reinè's feet. Her hands came up to caress Magden's calves, slipping under vesperis silk. She reveled in the feel of Magden's bare flesh—of the soft scales that adorned her shins and knees and trailed a soft pattern to her inner thighs.

The gown was tight, clinging to Magden's skin with a mixture of sweat and the natura from her scales. Eagerly, Zana tore it, splitting the fabric all the way to the Reinè's sex.

Magden cried out and dug her fingernails into the oak. Looking down, she met the gaze of her Zephyris. Zana's green eyes burned bright with lust. Magden could not control herself—it was the way of the Primè Reinè and her chosen concubine. She lifted her torn skirts and straddled Zana's face. "Open your mouth."

Her Zephyris instincts pulsing within her, Zana opened her

mouth to receive her Reinè. The sultry heat of scales and their soft touch upon her lips dizzied her. She flicked her tongue, licking satiny smooth and hot. Light perspiration mingled with the Reinè's natura, forming a heady sheen that she lapped covetously.

She pressed her face between Magden's legs, parting her wider, exploring, seeking to find the seam that hid her innermost flesh. Her breath came hard against supple scales, inhaling the musky taste of her Reinè.

Moaning, Magden clenched her hands in Zana's short hair and shifted against her mouth. Scales split, and her natura ran sticky-hot over her Zephyris's face. Baptized, Zana opened her mouth wide, drinking the deluge of her Reinè's sluttish juices. It sluiced down her throat, pushing its way into her, burning her with the lust of queen and concubine.

Gasping, she probed with her tongue, working her way deeper, splitting the cleft further. Her hands gripped her Reinè's inner thighs, fingernails biting into soft flesh. In long, licking strokes, Zana took her, slipping her tongue over hot, swollen lips and into Magden's shuddering hole.

With an almost human gasp, the Primè Reinè lurched forward, red curls falling into her face. In the candlelight, her eyes glowed lustful, sinister. Her slitted pupils dilated wide, and she gave a fanged smile down at her Zephyris. Her eyes rolled back and she groaned, her hips writhing. She let her chemical instincts take her.

Something nudged against Zana's mouth. A hard shaft pushed its way between her lips and down her throat. Slick and soft yet rigid, it pulsed inside her like a living member.

Zana nearly choked with the effort of accommodating it all. She pulled back and the shaft slipped from her mouth. Instinctively, her hand came up to caress it. Long and thick, silken-smooth and covered with cobalt scales hard as lapis, it was as real as any man's.

Magden swayed slightly in anticipation.

Meeting her glowing gaze, Zana began to caress her. The skin leaped and twitched at her touch. She bent her head to kiss, and then took the phallus in her mouth, full and firm. As soon as her lips closed around the tip, Magden pushed, sliding it down her throat.

Zana relaxed. Her Reinè's fingers brushed the hair from her forehead. Slowly, Magden began to thrust. Her breath came short and quick, her strokes long and precise, driving down deep into her Zephyris's throat.

Struggling for breath, Zana pursed her lips, licking as Magden withdrew and sucking as she pumped. One hand grabbed her Reinè's hip for purchase while the other gripped the root of Magden's cock, stroking the supple hardness before venturing further. Just behind, she found the feminine sex wet and waiting. Her fingers fluttered against the outer scales, then probed deeper, spreading Magden's soaked pussy, sampling the torrid juices. The twin scents of female sex and male musk anointed her blushing face.

Shuddering, Magden watched, her eyes dilating as her hard shaft slipped between her concubine's pursed lips. With both hands, she grabbed Zana's head, shoving her onto the stiff rod, fucking her mouth merciless.

Zana took it all, choking as the rhythm of Magden's thrusts left her breathless. She pitched forward, her hand splitting her Reinè's gash with two fingers.

Magden cried out, and the hot, heady brew of her lust filled Zana's throat, her mouth, spilling from her lips. As soon as the sticky elixir ran over her tongue, Zana wanted to taste it deep inside her cunt. The excess slipped down her neck and ran in sweltering rivulets down her cleavage, staining the damp silk of her wedding gown.

Magden bent down, chasing it. Without ceremony, she tore the front of Zana's gown open, exposing her small bosom, tonguing the droplets of jism and natura from her Zephyris's flushed skin. Torn ribbons fell to the Apothecary floor.

Small spasms coursed over Zana's softer flesh and shivered deep between her legs. She felt the surge of strength through her Reinè's muscles, felt herself suddenly crushed tight, crushed breathless.

Magden lifted her, carrying her. Zephyris instinct forced Zana's thighs wide, the hardness of her Reinè urging against her.

Crying out, she strained toward it, soaking Magden's scales, soaking her sex, both male and female. Her legs locked around her queen's waist, desperate as she moaned against her mouth.

Kissing her hard, the Primè Reinè stumbled. They collided with a glass cabinet, their weight shoving it against the wall. Although it didn't break, the alarming clink of bottles cast Zana's attention upward. Shelves jammed with fluted flasks, beakers, and bottles towered above them, their contents dismembered, blurred by a thick coating of dust and web.

Nearly sobbing, Zana spread herself. Her spine pressed against the glass cabinet, she balanced with one hand on the back of Magden's neck. The other slipped between the Reinè's legs, taking hold of her hard masculinity.

Magden's eyes were aflame, her breath panting. Zana guided her past the damp silk of her wedding dress, fingers yanking aside soaked panties. Slowly, she rubbed the Reinè's cock-tip against the soft petals of her cunt, slathering it with her wanton juices.

Moaning softly, Magden grabbed Zana's ass with both hands, shifting her into better position against the glass. The cabinet creaked but it didn't break. Holding her, watching her every move, Magden allowed Zana to guide her.

Smooth and tight, the Zephyris slid it in, even the first inch threatening to split her open. Writhing, she struggled to seduce Magden deeper into her pussy.

The Primè Reinè held her back.

Desperate, Zana kissed her hard, thrusting her tongue into Magden's mouth the way she wanted Magden's cock to thrust into her pussy. Moaning, whimpering, she struggled in vain.

The Reinè smiled, fingering the white silk of Zana's skirts.

"My wedding dress," the Zephyris whispered against her mouth. "Do you like it?"

Magden writhed, the resistance of Zana's slash taut against the tip of her cock. "It appears white is appropriate after all."

Zana blushed hot. She was nearly sobbing in frustration. Each time she moved closer, the Reinè held her away, barely keeping an inch of herself within. "Please, Magden..."

"You have to take yourself." Magden's luminous eyes met hers. "I won't take you. Not on your wedding night."

Panting, fraught with frustration, Zana gripped Magden's shoulders. Her eyes bright with excitement and fear, she met the gaze of her queen, and the Zephyris in her awoke in ardent lust.

Without pretense, she drove herself onto Magden's hard cock. A quivering whimper escaped her as smooth serpent-flesh penetrated her to the hilt.

Magden's eyes rolled back, her body spasming as Zana shafted herself. Long seconds passed while the Reinè fought for breath, for mastery of her chemical instincts. Zana rode her, crying out in ecstasy. Slowly, Magden mastered her lust, and then, inch by inch, she withdrew.

Zana couldn't stand it. Her gaze fell to her emerald scales, dying, peeling from her like withered parchment, and a different fear quaked inside her. *She doesn't want me... I'm too human.*

Her breath stopped as Magden shoved into her, splaying her wide. A hoarse cry tore from the Reinè's throat as she drove into Zana's pussy, slamming her against the cabinet, each thrust shoving her harder against the glass, beating it against the wall.

Bottles fell, shattering around them. Screaming, gasping, Zana held on as her Reinè split into her again and again, tearing the virginity from her cunt even as her claws tore the wedding gown into shreds.

Flasks hit the floor, smashing at their bare feet. Magden thrust harder and the cabinet shattered. Glass shards bit into Zana's thighs, her buttocks, the warm slide of blood mingling with come and sweat and natura from the Reinè's bestial rutting.

Zana clasped her tight, needing, wanting, even as Magden took her, filling her with her stiff cock. Each time she withdrew was like a bitter rejection. Zana clung to her as if she would never let go, her fingernails digging into Magden's back, drawing beads of emerald blood. Her body bucked, desperate to receive the seed of the Primè Reinè.

Was this how it had been between her mother and Magden's? The Queen of the Nyth and her Zephyris concubine. Magden, her half-sister.

The thought sent a cascade of shivers through her.

Magden was lifting her again, carrying her to the altar. The smell of old viscera and medicine permeated the wood. Zana's pussy tightened in fear, and she felt the wetness of her blood and the juices of her frustration trickling down her thighs. Magden set her down on the edge, legs spread and dangling.

Without warning, she came into her hard, fucking Zana in long, deep strokes. Zana threw her head back, leaning on her palms to open her thighs wider. Her hips ached from the strength of Magden's fucking.

Nearing her crisis, the Reinè gasped, her breath coming ragged. Triumph flashed through Zana, and she bucked against her, sliding hard on Magden's phallus. An eager Zephyris, she wanted to taste her Reinè's come deep inside her pussy. Every thrust brought her closer.

Zana held her breath, on the edge of conquest.

Abruptly, Magden withdrew. Before Zana could protest, Magden grabbed her, rolling her face-down onto the table. Zana cried out in fear, her breasts crushed against the rotting wood. The smells of blood and come were thick in her nostrils, quickening in her belly, making her thighs quiver in hot anticipation.

The remnants of her wedding gown were pulled taut across her body, her thighs, the softness of her ass crushed by wet silk. She felt Magden's grip tighten, and the fabric tore like paper, ripping from her flushed body. Savage and soft, her Reinè's hands were on her, massaging her buttocks, spreading them wide. The hardness of Magden's cock prodded Zana's tight ass.

"No, Magden, don't!" Goddess, yes!

Magden split her wide, taking the virginity of her ass in one hard stroke. Taken breathless, Zana could not even scream. Her hands slapped against the table but found no purchase.

Gently, Magden pulled out of her. Tears on her lashes, Zana dared a glance back.

The Primè Reinè leaned over, her cobalt-blue scales shimmering in the guttering light. Her mouth opened, and natura spilled from her lips. Thick and translucent, it coated her stiff member, running over the shaft, slicking the head like honey. Magden took herself in one hand, rubbing the tip against Zana's ass, smearing her chrism on Zana's aching hole.

The Zephyris moaned, the feel of the slippery liquid igniting her desire. Gripping the sides of the altar, she tilted her ass in the air.

Magden's hand clamped down on the back of her neck. A low hiss growled deep in her throat, and she entered Zana again. She meant only to thrust once, but the burning of her natura and the sweat of her Zephyris drew her in, pounding, her cock slapping relentless into Zana's tight hole, her breath gasping hoarse, her cries of rapture echoing into the darkness.

The storm raged, urging her on. Crimson wax spilled, running over the table like fresh blood.

Buffeted by her Reinè's bestial fucking, Zana took the first strokes submissively. Sudden pleasure burned through the pain, and she struggled to hands and knees. Magden's hands gripped her hips, rocking her back onto her unrelenting cock. Lurching forward, Zana jammed three fingers inside her needy hole. Moaning, panting like a whore, she pumped herself, her pussy, her ass quivering from the dual pounding—Magden's hard shaft sodomizing her from behind, her own fingers taking her from the front.

A shuddering cry escaped Magden, and she came in a convulsion, her hot seed spurting inside Zana's tight ass.

The Zephyris spasmed as her Primè Reinè drew back. Come and natura ran in rivulets down her thighs, over her glistening gash. Physically spent, her body bucked, still crying out for the release of orgasm. She rolled onto her back, legs splayed, the fusion of her pussy juice and Magden's seed staining the altar.

Relief stole her breath as Magden took her forcefully by the wrists, pinning her to the table. Her cries turned to groans of pleasure as the weight of her Reinè's body bore down on hers, and as Magden's hardness filled her needy pussy, she raked her nails down the Reinè's back, drawing lines of emerald blood.

The scent of their sex permeated the air, stifling the flickering candles. Deep at the back of her throat, Zana could taste Magden, but the essence of her grew more distant and foreign. Zana's blood continued its slow death.

Oblivious, Magden rutted atop her, her hands slipping from Zana's wrists. Lapis claws sheared from her fingertips, cutting slowly down the wood. Her thrusts came hard and fast, her cock slapping into Zana's pussy, splaying her asunder.

Delirious, Zana rode her queen, unable to recall the face of her betrothed. Gasps tore from her throat, her own orgasm threatening. Hot against her neck, Magden's moans turned deep and guttural. She raised herself, her eyes glowering a serpent gleam. A flash of lapis claws and the wood splintered around Zana's face, casting slivers about her.

Terrified, elated, Zana felt fused to her, mouth to mouth, cock to pussy, even as the Reinè invaded her human body with throbbing serpent-flesh. She remembered that night—the ritual, the storm, Magden's blade thrusting into her, penetrating her body, stealing her Nythian nature.

Once more, her gaze fell to her scales, withering a slow death. "Magden, please...get it over with. Kill me quickly."

Still buried deep within her Zephyris, the Primè Reinè drew back. Dark blue claws rose above Zana, casting a shadow on her face. She felt her pussy constrict in fear, bringing her to the brink of orgasm.

"Yes, Magden, cut me."

Thunder and lightning, lapis claws flashed through the night. Green blood struck the oak, fading quickly to red. Zana's screams lit the night, Magden's claws like needles of fire in her flesh, the stiffness of her cock ruthlessly fucking her.

A second scream, and Zana came in a torrent, her virginity spent against Magden's cock, spilling out onto the rotting wood. Her body jerked in the after-throes of sex and death, and her own natura poured forth in a slick tide, soaking them both. Like oil, it christened the table, mingling with the juices of their fucking.

Zana wracked, and the dying of her blood came quickly now, her Nythian essence spilling out on the altar. A sliver of human fright spiked her, and she knew fear of the creature above her. Like any prey held in thrall, she knew better than to struggle.

Magden trembled with the effort of holding back. Zana was no longer her Zephyris. Gathering herself, she moved to withdraw, her cock engorged, threatening to spill inside a human girl.

Defiance flashed in Zana's green eyes. Grabbing Magden by the wrist, she bucked, rolling her onto her back, pushing her down. Zana straddled her, one hand gripping the Reinè's swollen shaft, the other spreading the deprived lips of her cunt.

"Zana!"

With a shuddering breath, she drove herself hard onto Magden's stiff cock. Their screams rose in the night, the Reinè struggling to hold back, the dying Zephyris fulfilling her duty to the last breath.

And as the final vestiges of her Nythian blood died, as her scales withered and fell like ash, as the last of her night vision and her serpentine strength washed away in a flood of humanity, Zana forced herself onto Magden, driving the Nyth queen deeper and deeper into her aching pussy.

Her desire, her chemical need unbound, Magden grabbed Zana's hips and sheathed her cock again and again into the human girl until at last, her fangs bared and with a guttural groan, she came, spilling the sweltering heat of her seed into Zana's brazen cunt.

The human girl cried out in pleasure, in pain, riding out the aftershocks on the Reinè's masculinity. She could taste Magden's come at the back of her throat.

And then, Magden was lifting her, setting her down. She stumbled as her feet touched the stone floor. The Primè Reinè's come slicked down her thighs, and Zana ached all over from an ecstasy she would never again know.

Dazed, she looked to her wedding gown, shredded by Nyth claws, stained with blood and natura and the come of her infidelity. And the dreadful weight of being human—only human—bore down upon her.

The Primè Reinè, Queen of the Nyth, stood before her, austere and terribly alien. Her slitted pupils dilated, and the musk of serpents shrouded her in a fearsome veil. "Go to your betrothed and wed him. Go to his bed with my seed still drying on your thighs."

Gathering the tatters of her wedding gown to her aching flesh, the human girl fled out into the storm.

Far-off, the morning temple bells rang, sounding the announcement of a wedding.

I Am The Very Model of A Modern Circlet Editor
HB Kurtzwilde & Alex Picchetti
(with apologies to Sirs Arthur Sullivan & W. S. Gilbert)

I am the very model of a modern Circlet editor,
I've organized logistics on a xenomorph-slash-predator,
I know the queers of SF and I quote the smut historical,
From Kaldera to Mohanraj in order categorical.

I'm very well acquainted, too, with matters quite grammatical,
I battle through the slush pile without taking a sabbatical,
About our new releases, I am teeming with a lot o' news—
After checking that our authors have been sure to mind their Ps and Qs!

I'm confident with pronouns for a magical fourth gender class,
And manage continuity for who does what to someone's ass,
In short, regarding Viscountesses, Telepaths, Inheritors,
I am the very model of a modern Circlet editor.

I know erotic history, our Sapphos and Murasakis,
And also modern versions, like our Mapplethorpes and Midoris,
I'll pontificate for hours on the joys of hentai doujinshi,
And tentacles and lycanthropes for every sexuality.

I can tell a sexy metaphor from something like a deli meat,
I'll find the racy charge within a story that was far too sweet,
Then I will write a letter to reject a tale that's just too clean,
And all while drinking tea and coffee in amounts that are obscene.

Then I can write a cover blurb to innervate and draw you in,
And tell you 'bout the vagaries of furries, fops, and Otherkin;
In short, regarding Viscountesses, Telepaths, Inheritors,
I am the very model of a modern Circlet editor.

In fact, when I know what is meant by "jouissance" and "natiform",
When I will spend a weekend being giddy at a camp for porn,
When selkies, elves, and dwarves compete for time within the manuscript,
And authors get all pissy when I mention that their tense has slipped,
When I have shattered records with the word count of my summaries,
When I have overseen deflowered novices in nunneries, In short, when I have wrangled all your scenes of sheer debauchery,
You'll say a better Circlet editor has never worked for thee.

For my knowledge of the formats, from the PDF to the epub,
Is rivaled only by my need to have a secretary sub,
But still, regarding Viscountesses, Telepaths, Inheritors,
I am the very model of a modern Circlet editor.

Contributors

Dame Bodacious writes and lives near Boston, where her Lilith Club books are set. Learn more at http://thelilithclub.wordpress.com/

Kierstin Cherry was born in a tiny village in northern New England. Forced to attend an all-girl parochial school, she led the other girls in a revolt against the nuns and escaped into the wild. Raised by wolves and fairies, she found her calling as a semi-shy erotica writer and editor, and has recently graduated with her MFA in Writing Popular Fiction from Seton Hill University. Although Kierstin has a quirky, irreverent sense of humor, she is very serious about her work as an author and editor. She puts the romance back into necromancy with her erotic vampire stories, including "Graced," featured in the Lambda-nominated anthology *Women of the Bite*.

Kal Cobalt has published stories with Circlet Press for over a decade, including his collection *Robotica* and several appearances in Circlet anthologies. Along the way, his fiction has also appeared in Cleis Press's *Best Gay Romance*, and two years of his nonfiction columns appeared in SEXIS. Obsessed with robots, pornography, the art of narrative design, and all things cyberpunk, Kal is a crazy cat gentleman and a budding cellist who knits socks obsessively and studies Croatian. Hey, we're all large and contain multitudes. Get in touch on Twitter at @kalcobalt, on Mastodon @kalcobalt@wandering.shop, or at kal-cobalt.squarespace.com.

Julie Cox has a number of fantasy, sci-fi and/or erotic works published with Circlet Press and elsewhere. Her work can be found at writingwhilehuman.com, and she is on Twitter as @SQLPi. Her novel *Capricious* won the 2014 Best Bisexual Book Award for erotica and is also available in audiobook from Audible.com. She is an activist for progressive ideals, and lives in Texas with her children and many pets.

Shanna Germain claims the titles of leximaven, Schrodinger's Brat, Midas' Touch, and Vorpal Blonde. Her short stories have appeared in hundreds of anthologies, including *Best American Erotica, Best Bondage Erotica, Best Gay Romance,* and *Best Lesbian Erotica.* Her most recent books include *Leather Bound, The Lure of Dangerous Women,* and *As Kinky As You Wanna Be.* Visit her at www.shannagermain.com.

Michael M. Jones lives in Southwest VA, with too many books, just enough cats, and a wife who is worthier to rule than he is. He is a frequent contributor to Circlet anthologies, including *Like a Mask Removed* and *Fantastic Erotica,* and is the author of *Puxhill by Night: Lesbian Erotic Urban Fantasy.* He is also the editor of *Like Fortune's Fool* and *Like a Cunning Plan.* For more, visit him at www.michaelmjones.com.

Raven Kaldera is a Northern-Tradition Pagan shaman, herbalist, astrologer, transgendered intersexual activist, homesteader, and of course author. He is on his twenty-second published book.

H.B. Kurtzwilde lives in the wet, sticky, mosquito-ridden depths of Florida. When not busily avoiding alligators, he scribbles out futuristic and paranormal fiction, as if this is any way for a grown person to behave. His works include *Chocolatiers of the High Winds, Phoberia, The Secret Art of Failure* trilogy, and *Sea Turtle Inn,* among others.

Annabeth Leong is frequently confused about her sexuality but enjoys searching for answers. Her work appears in dozens of anthologies, including editions of *Best Lesbian Erotica, Best Women's Erotica,* and *Best Bondage Erotica.* She is the editor of *MakerSex: Erotic Stories of Geeks, Hackers, and DIY Culture,* the author of *Untouched,* and several other books that make for either excellent or awkward conversation, depending on the context. It is easy to convince her to embarrass herself in front of others, whether that means teaching writing workshops, handling sex toys in the name of comedy, licking a hot woman's high heels, or performing Macklemore songs on karaoke night.

Mary Anne Mohanraj is the author of *Bodies in Motion*, *Sri Lankan-American linked stories* (HarperCollins), as well as *Silence and the Word*, The Best *of Strange Horizons* (ed.), *Aqua Erotica* (ed.), *The Poet's Journey* (a children's fantasy picture book), and *The Stars Change* (Circlet Press). *Bodies in Motion* was a finalist for the Asian-American Book Awards and has been translated into six languages. Mohanraj received an Illinois Arts Council Fellowship in Prose (2006). Mohanraj lives in Chicago, where she teaches creative writing and post-colonial literature at the University of Illinois; she also taught at the Clarion workshop in 2008. She is a graduate of Clarion West, and holds an MFA and Ph.D. in creative writing.

Author of the 4-star (Romantic Times) novel Cat Scratch Fever, Out of the Frying Pan, Possessed, Undressed, and in a Mess, and many short stories, Sophie Mouette is the brainchild of two widely published authors of erotica, romance, and speculative fiction. The two halves of Sophie—Dayle A. Dermatis (aka Andrea Dale) and Teresa Noelle Roberts—met almost three decades ago at a writers' conference. Talking nonstop, they closed down the hotel bar and went somewhere else to keep on talking. They still are…. For more information, visit her at SophieMouette.com.

If Bernie Mojzes has one failing (and I've got it on good authority [references available on request] that he's got quite a bit more), it's that he doesn't understand genre. He writes stuff. Sometimes it's "What if Gomer Pyle was a British swamp faerie fighting the Nazis?"; other times it's "You know, caterpillars could be the new cephalopods." He lets other people tell him whether it's steampunk or dieselpunk or whatever. Some of it (he's told) is apparently erotica, and you're holding one of those stories now. There are others, in Circlet's *Like a Vorpal Blade* and *Like a Treasure Found*. It's not all smut, alas: he's got a short, illustrated book called *The Evil Gazebo*, and stories in *Daily Science Fiction*, *Crossed Genres*, *Betwixt*, and a passel of other places. In his copious free time, he co-edits *Unlikely Story* (www.unlikely-story.com). If you're so inclined to learn more, and/or to register a complaint, please visit www.kappamaki.com.

Sasha Payne is an English writer of gay erotic fiction and romance. She is a lifelong speculative fiction and fantasy fan and most enjoys working within the genres of speculative fiction, fantasy, or historical fiction. Her work can also be found in *Wired Hard 5*, *Charming*, and *Jacked In*. Sasha can be contacted at morsus@virginmedia.com.

Charles Payseur currently resides in Wisconsin, where his partner, a gaggle of pets, and more craft beer than is strictly healthy help him through the long winters. His work has appeared or is forthcoming at *Nightmare Magazine*, *Strange Horizons*, and *Lightspeed Magazine's Queers Destroy Science Fiction*. You can find him around the internet as contributor to a number of sites and on his blog, Quick Sip Reviews (www.quicksipreviews.blogspot.com), as well as on Twitter as @ClowderofTwo.

Alex Picchetti knows a superhero never reveals their secrets. They have previously been published in *Like the Knave of Hearts*, *Like a Vorpal Blade*, and *Whispers in Darkness* from Circlet Press.

TS Porter is a tiny geek frequently mistaken for a collection of knobbly twigs wearing glasses. When not sleeping, they are usually found obsessively writing or baking sweet delicacies. TS' physical location and momentum varies, but home is always online. They can be found at ts-porter.tumblr.com.

At 10, JJ Poulos was told that they'd never make it as a writer because their penmanship was so terrible. Since then, they've worked hard to become a troublemaker, an editor, a gardener, and, of course, a writer. Their speculative fiction has been published most recently in the *Journal of Unlikely Cryptography* and THEMLit. They reside in Madison, Wisconsin, with their partner, child, basset hound, and chickens. Their handwriting is still terrible.

Nobilis Reed is the creator and host of Nobilis Erotica, the best erotic speculative fiction podcast in the known universe. He is also an author in his own right; Violet Blue named *Monster Whisperer* one of the best sex books of 2016. He and his family live in a distant suburb of DC, where he does all his writing, recording, and production under the supervision of four very excellent cats. Visit his podcast website at nobilis.libsyn.com.

Vinnie Tesla is the author of the Steampunk porn farce *The Erotofluidic Age* and the *Fantastic Erotica* Award-winning "Ota Discovers Fire," set in the same world as "Disarmed" (both available from Circlet Press). His current project is a fantasy crime novel with Zuth in a supporting role. He lives in Somerville, Massachusetts, with his adorable spousalbeast, three rusty bicycles, and a great many bottles of rye.

Kathleen Tudor is currently hiding out in the wilds of California with her spouse and their favorite monkey. She should be considered armed with a pen and extremely erotic, and should be approached with caution. Her wicked words have already broken down the doors to presses like Cleis, Mischief HarperCollins, Circlet, Xcite, and more, and she is said to be disguising herself as an acquisitions and developmental editor for Storm Moon Press. If you see her (or want to say hi!) please contact via email at polykathleen@gmail.com. Keep an eye on KathleenTudor.com for updates on her antics and possible snippets of sexy material.

Avery Vanderlyle credits her interest in the sexy side of sci-fi and fantasy to reading Samuel Delany as a teenager. Today she still reads more than is healthy, devours *Game of Thrones* fan theories, plays Dungeons and Dragons, and earns money by making computer programmers cry. She lives in Boston with her spouse and five cats. Avery's stories for Circlet Press have appeared in the anthologies *Coffee: Hot, Like a Spell: Fire* and *A Beastly Affair* (where "Deflowered" first appeared). She's also had short stories in anthologies by DreamSpinner Press and Storm Moon Press. Keep up with her at averyvanderlyle.wordpress.com and on twitter @averyvanderlyle.

A.C. Wise's short fiction has appeared in Tor.com, *The Year's Best Science Fiction Volume 3*, and the *Year's Best Horror 10*, among other places. She has two collections published with Lethe Press, and a novella forthcoming from Broken Eye Books in spring/summer 2018. Find her online at www.acwise.net and on twitter as @ac_wise.

Acknowledgments

"Bête Noire" by Annabeth Leong was originally published in *A Beastly Affair* edited by J. Blackmore.

"An Analog Christmas" by Kal Cobalt was originally published in *Jingle Balls* edited by Cecilia Tan & Arabella Flynn.

"From The Shallows, Cold As Death" by Bernie Mojzes was originally published in *What Lies Beneath* edited by J. Blackmore.

"Double: A Tale of Love and Engineering" by Nobilis Reed was originally published in *Like A Love Triangle* edited by Kathleen Tudor.

"The Secret Life of Ramona Lee" by Michael M. Jones was originally published in *Geek Love* edited by Shanna Germain & Janine Ashbless, also included in *Puxhill by Night* by Michael M. Jones.

"Deflowered" by Avery Vanderlyle was originally published in *A Beastly Affair* edited by J. Blackmore.

"Crow Luck" by Dame Bodacious was originally published in *Like Fortune's Fool* edited by Michael M. Jones.

"Enchanted" by Shanna Germain was originally published in *Charming* edited by Jennifer Levine & Rian Darcy.

"Stolen Days" by TS Porter was originally published in *Hard As Stone* edited by Julie Cox.

"Bridge Over Shifter's Chasm" by Raven Kaldera was originally published in *Like A Mask Removed Vol. II* edited by Bethany Zaiatz, also included in *Extraordinary Deviations* by Raven Kaldera.

"Questing" by Charles Payseur was originally published in *Nights of the Round Table* edited by Jennifer Levine.

"The Night Air" by Mary Anne Mohanraj was originally published in *The Stars Change* by Mary Anne Mohanraj.

"The Closing Shift" by JJ Poulos was originally published in *Coffee: Hot* edited by Victoria Pond.

"Wizard's Staff" by Julie Cox was originally published in *Hard As Stone* edited by Julie Cox.

"Disarmed" by Vinnie Tesla was originally published in *Silent Shadows Come* edited by Jennifer Levine.

"In The Blood" by Kathleen Tudor was originally published in *Like Fortune's Fool* edited by Michael M. Jones.

"Evidence of Things Unseen" by A.C. Wise was originally published in *What Lies Beneath* edited by J. Blackmore.

"Season of Fire" by Sahsa Payne was originally published in *Wired Hard 5* edited by Joy Crelin.

"Primè Nocta" by Kierstin Cherry was originally published in *Like Myth Made Flesh* edited by Jennifer Williams.

"I Am The Very Model Of A Modern Circlet Editor" by H.B. Kurtzwilde & Alex Picchetti was originally published in *Like A Circlet Editor* edited by D. Mark Alderton & Bethany Zaiatz.

Kickstarter Supporters

This book was produced with the generous support of 214 donors through Kickstarter. Those who wished to be thanked publicly are listed here! Our thanks to them, as well as those who remain anonymous, and our year-round supporters through Patreon as well! We couldn't have done it without you!

A. J. Schiller
Adrian Mailenna
AJ Viggen
Alex Picchetti
Amanda Giles
Amber W.
Amy Lapine
Andrea Dale
Andrew Hatchell
Andrija Popovic
Ann-Kathrin N
Anya Levin
Apurva Desai
Arthur Ganger
Bel Edis
Betty Gesserit
BisexualBooks.com
Blue Blood Amelia G
Boy Kit
Boymeat
Brad Guigar
C.G. Schroder
Caitlin Jane Hughes
Caroline H

Celandine Brandybuck
Charisse Lyn
Charlie Jane Anders
Chris Brakenbury
CK Gill
Claudia Mastroianni
Crossed Genres
CT
D L King
Dan Lyke
David F.
David Mortman
Deb Block-Schwenk
Dee Morgan
Doug Tierney
Elf M. Sternberg
Elizabeth Reeve
Emma Rose
Emmett Younglove Wilde
Fizzy
Gail M
Garagenpeter
Gilles Grüngürtel
Glennis LeBlanc

Godai
Heather Snodgrass
I.G. Frederick aka Korin
    Dushayl
J Eric Goines
J. H. Peregrine
Jack Pevyhouse
James Lucas
Jamie Abrams
Jana Kirkman
Jason
Jason Riedy
Jaymee Goh
JD
Jean Roberta
Jen W
Jennifer London
Jennifer Stevenson
Jenny Reed
Jim Nelson
Joann Clarke-Stein
John Perreault
John Ullman
Juan Sanmiguel
Jules Jones
K. Fulcrum
Kate Stine
Ketil Bluetoes
Kevin J. "Womzilla" Maroney
Kit Stubbs, Ph.D.
Kyla
Larry "LORDLNYC" Nelson
Laura Wilkinson
Leigh Ann Hildebrand
Lily Vega

Lizzy
Madeline Elayne
Mark and Catelynn
Marla
Mary M. Jones
Matt Towler
Matthias Lamm
Meg Baca
Meghan Coyne
Mela Eckenfels
Melanie Fletcher
Micah BlackLight
Michael
Michael H.
Michael Kwan
Michael S.
Mike Quin
Miles Nielsen
MJ Minnigh
Mrs. Lorri Roberta Frazer Prime
    (Desireau)
Ms Mocha
Nalu Kalani
Nathan J. Williams
Patrick McEvoy
Peter Strömberg
Phil M
Reg Franchi
Regis M. Donovan
Reina Delacroix
Rene Llewellyn
Rhel ná DecVandé
Rhonda Hawley
Rikku Burnside
Riley Black

Rob Funk
Robert Claney
Robert McGann
Sacchi Green
Sally
Sara Testarossa
Sarah Huffman
Saz Wells
Seán Byrne
Sergio and Margaret Tan
Seth Kadath
Spike Holcomb
Stephen B:)
Steve Cave
Stewart Walker
Sweet Tea and the Southern
    Cousins

TammyJo Eckhart
The Pageist
theo
Thomas Werner
Tim B
tomo
Tony Anjo
Trace Hagemann
Trollwoman
Trouvere le Fou
Victor Reiner
W. S. Meeks
Warren Lapine
WhiskeyShipwreck
zvi LikesTV

Become a Patron

Circlet Press pioneered erotic science fiction and fantasy back in the early 1990s when other publishers wouldn't touch it. We've been pushing the envelope ever since, seeking out representations of sexuality, gender, attractions, and relationships outside of the "mainstream norms" and we are committed to expanding diversity in other realms as well.

For as little as $1/month, you can support our smart, unpredictable, and taboo-busting line of books into the future, help us spread the word to new readers, and help us pay authors more. In exchange, you get free books, exclusive content, invitations to exclusive patron events, chances to vote on future anthologies, and, of course, a warm fuzzy feeling.

Have a look at the full list of patron rewards:

HTTPS://WWW.PATREON.COM/CIRCLETPRESS

and listen to/view a video message from founder and editorial director Cecilia Tan about why we need your help.